Praise for Anna Lee Huber's previous Verity Kent mysteries

Treacherous Is the Night

"A thrilling mystery that supplies its gutsy heroine with plenty of angst-ridden romance."
—*Kirkus Reviews*

"[A] splendid sequel . . . Huber combines intricate puzzles with affecting human drama."
—*Publishers Weekly*

"Masterful . . . Just when you think the plot will zig, it zags. Regardless of how well-versed you may be in the genre, you'll be hard-pressed to predict this climax. . . . Deeply enjoyable . . . just the thing if you're looking for relatable heroines, meatier drama, and smart characters with rich inner lives."
—*Criminal Element*

"Huber is an excellent historical mystery writer, and Verity is her best heroine. Sidney and Verity are a formidable couple when they work together, but they are also very real. They don't leap straight back into life before the war but instead face many obstacles and struggles as they readjust to married life and post-war life. Nonetheless, the love between Sidney and Verity is real and true, and the way that Huber creates their re-blossoming love is genuine. Topped off with a gripping mystery, this will not disappoint."
—*Historical Novel Society*

This Side of Murder

"Huber paints a compelling portrait of the aftermath of World War I, and shows the readers how devastating the war was for everyone in England. . . . I am looking forward to reading many more of Verity Kent's adventures."
—*Historical Novel Society*

"I loved *This Side of Murder,* a richly textured mystery filled with period detail and social mores, whose plot twists and character revelations kept me up way past my bedtime. Can't wait for the next Verity Kent adventure!"
—Shelley Noble, *New York Times* bestselling author of *The Beach at Painter's Cove* and *Ask Me No Questions*

"A smashing and engrossing tale of deceit, murder and betrayal set just after World War I. . . . Anna Lee Huber has crafted a truly captivating mystery here."
—*All About Romance*

"The new Verity Kent Mystery series is rich in detail without being overwhelming and is abundant with murder, mystery, and a bit of romance. The plot is fast-moving with twists and turns aplenty. Huber knows what it takes to write a great mystery."
—*RT Book Reviews*

"A captivating murder mystery told with flair and panache!"
—Fresh Fiction

"Sure to please fans of classic whodunits and lovers of historical fiction alike."
—Jessica Estevao, author of *Whispers Beyond the Veil*

PENNY
FOR YOUR
SECRETS

Novels by Anna Lee Huber

This Side of Murder

Treacherous Is the Night

Penny for Your Secrets

Published by Kensington Publishing Corporation

PENNY
FOR YOUR
SECRETS

A Verity Kent Mystery

Anna Lee Huber

KENSINGTON BOOKS
www.kensingtonbooks.com

KENSINGTON BOOKS are published by

Kensington Publishing Corp.
119 West 40th Street
New York, NY 10018

All Kensington titles, imprints, and distributed lines are available at special quantity discounts for bulk purchases for sales promotion, premiums, fund-raising, educational, or institutional use.

Special book excerpts or customized printings can also be created to fit specific needs. For details, write or phone the office of the Kensington Sales Manager: Kensington Publishing Corp., 119 West 40th Street, New York, NY 10018. Attn. Sales Department. Phone: 1-800-221-2647.

Kensington and the K logo Reg. U.S. Pat. & TM Off.

ISBN-13: 978-1-4967-1320-9 (ebook)
ISBN-10: 1-4967-1320-6 (ebook)
First Kensington Electronic Edition: November 2019

ISBN-13: 978-1-4967-1319-3
ISBN-10: 1-4967-1319-2
First Kensington Trade Paperback Printing: November 2019

10 9 8 7 6 5 4 3 2 1

Printed in the United States of America

For my Uncle Eldon and my sister-in-law Carmen Irma.
Heaven received two new glorious angels this past year,
but your love and kindness are still greatly missed here
on Earth. Thank you both for blessing my life
and the lives of so many others.

ACKNOWLEDGMENTS

Every book presents its own challenges, and for this one it proved to be time. Because of that, I'm deeply grateful to my mother and my husband for spending extra time with our girls so that I could squeeze in more writing. As always, their love and support bolster me, and I'm so blessed to have them. I'm also thankful to my daughters for all their extra hugs and ungrumbling acceptance of pizza, sandwiches, and plowman's dinners for suppers night after night during the last few weeks before my deadline.

Thank you to the team at Kensington, including Wendy Mc-Curdy, Norma Perez-Hernandez, Ann Pryor, Vida Engstrand, Lauren Jernigan, Alexandra Nicolajsen, Samantha McVeigh, Carly Sommerstein, and countless others for their stellar and tireless efforts on the Verity Kent series. Double thanks to Wendy for her patience and understanding, and allowing me the extra time I needed to wrangle this book into shape. My gratitude also goes to Kevan Lyon, my literary agent, for her ongoing encouragement and steady guidance.

The plot of this book is also indebted to several real-life historical figures from whom I garnered inspiration, including Gladys Spencer-Churchill, the 9th Duke of Marlborough, Consuelo Vanderbilt, and the still missing crew of the *Zebrina*.

As always, I am incredibly grateful to my friends and family, and all my readers for their love and support. Your kindness and excitement feed and nourish me as a writer, and I'm thrilled I get to continue to explore my fictional worlds with you.

CHAPTER 1

Three may keep a secret, if two of them are dead.
—Benjamin Franklin

September 1919
London, England

"Verity, darling." Ada grasped my hands and pulled me into her poppy-scented embrace, kissing the air next to my cheek. "I'm so glad you could make it."

"But, of course," I replied, searching her eyes for signs of strain. "Your letter was most persuasive."

If she still felt any of the frantic energy that had filled her missive, she didn't show it. In fact, she all but ignored my comment, allowing her gaze to sweep up and down my form. "And what is this? You look stunning." Her fingers brushed over the jade-green beaded bodice of my gown with its dropped waist. "This color is divine. It makes your eyes sparkle."

I laughed. "If anyone looks stunning, it's you."

Indeed, it was true. Swathed in a gown of crimson satin that left little to the imagination, her neck dripping with diamonds, there was no better word to describe the impact of Ada's appearance. Her dark hair and eyes, gently lined in kohl, were a striking contrast to the fluid red of her gown and the soft wash of color on her lips. A wash of color that the more staid guests of tonight's dinner party were certain to find too brash, not realizing their hostess had already made a concession to their feelings by not applying it as boldly as she normally would.

However, her husband didn't seem to appreciate the difference.

"Yes, subtlety has never been Ada's strong suit."

Her smile took on a sharp edge as she flicked a glance at him. "You know Rockham. Always so frightfully swank," she drawled sarcastically.

The marquess stiffened and I stepped sideways to offer him my hand in greeting, hoping to prevent him from responding in kind.

"Of course. Good evening, my lord."

He bowed. "Mrs. Kent."

"And this must be your long-lost husband," Ada declared, turning toward Sidney with an arch smile. "Well, you *are* a gorgeous one, aren't you? Now I understand why Verity was so broken up when she thought you were pushing up daisies over in France," she remarked in her usual irreverent manner, casting me a speculative glance. "And why she was willing to rusticate with you in some drafty cottage in Sussex for nearly four weeks."

The fact that our eight-bedroom cottage was far from drafty, and far from Spartan—boasting a staff of four and all the modern conveniences—mattered not. Anything outside of London was flippantly deemed rustic, and therefore bleak, by Ada's current standards.

She offered him her bejeweled hand. "I'm charmed to meet you."

Sidney smiled and bowed over her hand. "Likewise, Lady Rockham."

"Please, call me Ada. Lady Rockham is far too stuffy to use among friends." She flashed him a saucy smile. "As I'm sure we will be."

I was accustomed to Ada's flirtatious behavior. It was simply how she was. In any case, I knew I had nothing to fear from either her or Sidney, and so long as she didn't cling to him, and he kept his replies to light banter, I was content to ignore it.

However, I didn't think Rockham viewed the matter so affably, despite the five years she'd spent as his mistress before he'd been granted his divorce from his first wife. His eyes tightened at the corners, and his lips flattened into a thin line of disapproval.

Threading my arm through Sidney's, I pulled him forward to shake Rockham's hand so that we might move on before his temper got the better of him. But Ada grabbed my arm before we could make our escape.

"Verity, can you slip into the dining room and check the seating arrangements?" she whispered, a note of anxiety creeping into her voice. "I'm still not sure the order of precedence is correct, and I would hate to insult someone."

Not having been born into the upper class with all its rules and protocols, Ada had struggled to keep up with the duties and responsibilities of a grand lady. I had helped her manage as best I could since her marriage to Rockham two years prior, but there were so many minute matters of decorum, so many tiny strictures that had been ingrained in me since birth that it was impossible to impart them all.

"Of course," I began to say when Rockham interrupted me.

"You cannot ask such a thing of Mrs. Kent," he hissed. "As marchioness, it is *your* responsibility to manage such things."

"Do you think I don't know that?" she snapped. "I am doing my best."

He shrugged, running a hand over his gray hair slicked with pomade. "Calliope managed just fine."

My eyes widened at his mention of his first wife's name. It had the predictable effect of making Ada's face flush with rage. I pressed a hand to her arm. "I'll see to it," I murmured before hurrying away.

"Well, that was decidedly awkward," Sidney muttered as we passed into the opulent hall decorated with bronzed friezes and rococo flourishes. Before us a carved double staircase arched upward toward an intricately painted ceiling and walls draped with silk a shade of mignonette green.

"To say the least." I paused beneath a painting of one of Rockham's sullen seventeenth-century ancestors to glance back at the pair, their backs both stiff with suppressed anger.

"I would say she's deliberately provoking him, but he seems to require very little goading to behave like a self-righteous prig."

My gaze shifted to meet his, amused by his assessment of the marquess, of whom I was no great admirer. "She is quite coquettish."

"No more than a dozen other ladies I've been introduced to since my return," he countered. "And many of them were from gentler pedigrees." His deep blue eyes warmed as he realized I hadn't taken offense at my friend's behavior. "Young ladies have become downright brazen during my time in France."

"Well, what did you expect, leaving us all home alone to fend for ourselves?" I squeezed his arm, urging him across the patterned marble floor toward the Rockham's pretentious butler, Deacon.

As was all too common among butlers of the elite, Deacon was an utter snob, and it was evident he didn't approve of his employer's bourgeois-bred wife. I doubted he'd approved of his previous American-born wife, either.

I lifted my chin to direct a penetrating stare at him. "Are the seating arrangements correct?" I bit out in a voice that said I would tolerate nothing less. Ada might not yet have mastered the demeanor every aristocratic and gently bred lady knew she must keep tucked under her cap for instances like this, but I had learned at my mother's knee how to demand respect and compliance. And no one did it better.

"Yes, madam," he intoned.

I scrutinized his sharp features through narrowed eyes to ascertain his truthfulness and then dipped my head once, trusting that if the arrangements weren't correct, they would soon be set to rights.

Gliding away, I couldn't help but shake my head at what a sad state of affairs my friend had to contend with that she couldn't even rely on her staff to help her ensure the correct order of precedence was maintained. In my parents' household, the butler was one of my mother's chief allies. And as much as it had rankled when he'd tattled on me as a child, I could appreciate that matters were just as they should be.

Catching sight of my reflection in the mirror hanging above a floral-draped console table, I paused to adjust the diamond and pearl bejeweled pin that held back the auburn waves of bobbed hair framing my face. Sidney hovered beside me as I swiveled to the left and then the right, smoothing my hands over the shimmering material of my bodice as I inspected my appearance. My gown was a trifle more daring than I usually wore, but since I'd been certain Ada and her friends would be dressed even more audaciously, I'd decided it would be the perfect occasion to try this new style.

Sidney's warm hand pressed against the small of my back, his thumb brushing against the skin revealed by the deep vee there. He dipped his head to speak into my ear while his gaze held mine in the mirror. "Have I told you yet how much I like your hair like this?" His breath feathered over my skin, soft as a caress.

"No," I replied. I hadn't lopped it off until after the armistice, when it was no longer necessary for me to sneak through the electrified fence between neutral Holland and German-occupied Belgium in my capacity as an intelligence agent working with the Secret Service. Such a style would have made me much too conspicuous.

"It suits you." A roguish twinkle lit his eyes. "And it grazes the nape of your neck in such a delightful manner. I can't help but wish to press my lips to it."

My breath quickened as he turned his head as if to do just that, his thumb brushing across my spine. I stepped away, turning to face him, as I summoned the poise that had served me so well throughout the war. "But not here, I trust." I arched my eyebrows in gentle chastisement. "Or else you might send one of the more straitlaced matrons into a swoon."

His grin widened. "Not here, then." But after a pause, he added with mischievous delight, "Unless we require a distraction."

My lips quirked. "Let's hope not."

Not so long ago, such a playful exchange would have been beyond us, such a simple jest unthinkable. Four years of war and separation, followed by the fifteen cruel months when he'd allowed me to believe he was dead—despite the fact it had been for very good reason—had all but destroyed our relationship. But the time and effort we'd put into the past three months had gone a long way to salvaging a marriage I'd worried was hopelessly broken. There was still much work to be done to completely restore our trust in each other, but now that felt as if it was only a matter of time, rather than a stark uncertainty.

His gaze softened, as if entertaining a similar thought, and I reached for his hand as we crossed the threshold into the salon.

The immense room was far larger than most London drawing rooms, and far more extravagant, being iced in gold, white, and cream décor, like some baker's frothy confection. An Adam-designed ceiling with a small, coffered dome at the center even topped the walls of luminescent gold silk. Ada had told me that at one time the salon had also doubled as a music room, and it was said Mozart had played there on his visit to London in the 1760s.

Other guests congregated throughout the space, some sipping cocktails while others abstained. It wasn't difficult to differentiate between those who were friends with Ada and those who had been invited by the marquess. Though some of Ada's friends were also members of high society, they were the type who frequented the nightclubs in Soho and Leicester Square, and so were happy to imbibe and converse with the brightly dressed women whose tinkling laughter filled the room. None of the marquess's guests were society's greatest sticklers to the established rules of decorum, but they still sat stiffly throughout the room, pretending to ignore the frivolity and the colorful assemblage, though the pinched expressions on their faces told a different tale.

Before the war, the chances of my meeting a woman like Ada would have been decidedly slim, let alone my becoming friends with her. But times were changing, despite the protests of those who wished otherwise. The lines that had so strongly divided classes for centuries were now more blurred than ever, if not hopelessly muddled given the chaos and comradery of war. While some despaired of this jumbling of class distinctions and muddying of blue blood, I welcomed it. I had no desire to return to the prewar days of adherence to outdated protocols.

In any case, Ada wasn't precisely outré, but her upbringing had been rather unconventional. Her father had been a gentleman poet. Not a particularly noteworthy one, but he'd enjoyed some success with a book of romantic sonnets. While her mother had been an artist of great passion, but no acclaim. Or so Ada described her.

Having been raised in such bohemian circles, it was no wonder she had a flair for the dramatic, and that she'd chosen to reject many of society's norms. At least, until two years ago when she'd agreed to wed Rockham. It was a love match.

Or, at one time, it had been.

Pushing my worries over my friend's marriage from my mind, I advanced into the room to greet the other guests while Sidney went to fetch us drinks. Having strolled through both the drawing rooms of high society and theaters and nightclubs alike throughout the war and after, I was already acquainted with many of them. But only one of them was capable of making me break into a wide smile at just the sound of her voice.

"Verity Kent." She stood with her hands planted on her hips in a fabulous gown of gold silk lamé, a feathered stole drooping from her creamy mocha shoulders. "Where have you been, doll?"

I moved forward to embrace her, admiring her pearl grapevine earrings. "Hullo, Etta."

"I haven't seen you in months. Not since you told Goldy he was a fool for backing Paper Money over The Panther or Grand Parade at the Derby. I started to think you'd gone into seclusion or something." Her gaze shifted over my shoulder. "I'm sure *I* would have if my husband was such a tall drink of water and he'd suddenly come back from the dead."

I turned to find Sidney hovering at my elbow, a grin curling his lips. I accepted the gin rickey he held out to me, condensation already forming on the glass, and gestured toward my friend.

"Sidney, I want you to meet Etta Lorraine, the best jazz singer this side of the Atlantic. Perhaps both."

He bowed politely over her hand. "Lovely to meet you, Miss Lorraine."

"Oh, heavens. None of that Miss Lorraine stuff. It's Etta. Particularly if you keep making my friend Verity happy." Her eyebrows arched in both a question and promised retribution.

But far from being intimidated, Sidney's eyes glinted with mischief. "Every chance I get."

Etta threw her head back and laughed before tapping him with her ebony handled fan. "Hoo, boy, you *are* a scoundrel, aren't you?" She dimpled at me. "And just what *ma petite* needs."

I shook my head, lowering my glass after taking a cool drink. "Where's Goldy? This is what happens when he lets you out of his sight," I teased. "You're already causing trouble."

"I would say I'm more likely to get her into it."

I lifted my face to accept a swift buss on my cheek from Goldy as he joined us.

"Lovely as always, Ver. Ada told me you'd be here." He passed a drink to Etta before reaching out to shake Sidney's hand with his gloved one. Having suffered horrible burns to the right side of his torso, he rarely removed it. "Kent, it's good to see you, old chap. I was pickled as punch to hear you'd survived after all. *And* exposed a group of traitors to boot. Well done!"

"You're one to talk. Heard you took out an armament factory with only half a left wing on your plane."

"Well, there was a bit more involved than that," Goldy replied, suddenly chagrined.

Sidney nodded, his own good humor dimming. "There always was."

Etta and I exchanged glances, realizing we were crossing into territory where we couldn't follow them, and from whence they were likely to emerge with morose dispositions if we allowed them to dwell there much longer.

"You two were up at Oxford together, were you not?" I interjected, hoping to jar them from their reminiscences.

Goldy nodded. "Along with your brother Freddy." His lips curled into a grin. "Who, a little birdie told me, turned respectable. I couldn't believe it."

"It's true," Sidney confirmed. "Thriving medical practice. Wife and young daughter. Townsend is now an upright citizen." His gaze flicked to mine. "For the most part."

I smiled at his jest. It was impossible to believe my older brother had given up all of his shenanigans, but for my sister-in-law's and niece's sakes I hoped they were of the harmless, prankish variety.

"What of you? Does your family still own its aviation company?" Sidney asked him.

"Yes." He sipped from his glass before adding hesitantly, "Actually, I've been thinking of investing in some of these efforts to form passenger services. The first scheduled flight between Paris and London flew just a week ago, and with Alcock and Brown making the first successful flight across the Atlantic in June, it's only a matter of time before we're crisscrossing the globe through the air."

I had little knowledge or experience with aeroplanes beyond the dreaded sound of their approach as I scrambled for cover from the coming bombardment, along with the other citizens in the German-occupied towns just behind the front. But even being aware of the amazing advances made in aircraft production during the war, and some of the covert weapons Britain and Germany had been developing for them, I had a difficult time believing people would ever regularly fly across the ocean as passengers. Not when they could already cross the Atlantic on a ship in relative comfort in three days.

But if Sidney harbored any of the same doubts, he didn't show it. "Well, you always did have a head for business, and you certainly have the flight experience, so if you think it's worth pursuing, then I believe it."

Goldy's shoulders straightened under Sidney's regard. "You think so? Well, thanks, old chum."

He brushed it aside as if it was no consequence and turned to ask Etta about the latest club she was performing at, but I couldn't disregard it all so easily. Not when Goldy seemed to stand taller, his eyes alive with his plans.

Sidney had always been the type of man whom others seemed to want the good opinion of. They wanted to impress him, to call him their friend. So, when he offered his thoughts on something, they listened. And when he gave them his approval, it was like gold.

However, since his return, I'd noticed how cautious he'd been to offer his endorsement, or express his judgment of any kind. It was as if the war had stolen that ability, that confidence from him. So to see him do so now, and so casually, made my chest tighten and the back of my eyes burn.

I blinked, focusing my gaze on my drink as I rubbed my finger over the condensation on the glass. Sidney cast me a look of concern, but I shook my head and forced a brighter smile.

The number of guests gathered in the salon had grown, and while the room still wasn't precisely crowded, he used the opportunity afforded by someone nudging me from behind to drape an arm around my waist and pull me closer to his side. There it remained even after they'd passed.

There was a slight stir as Ada and Rockham entered the room arm in arm, though it appeared perfunctory. She certainly stepped away quickly enough, moving toward another gentleman whom she appeared to lavish attention on. Rockham's jaw hardened, and I felt my stomach dip at my friend's misstep. Flirtatious comments and daring gowns people might overlook, and expect her husband to do so also, but such blatant fawning over another man—and in front of Rockham, no less—was beyond the pale.

"She's been cozying up to Ardmore for months now," Etta leaned over to whisper. "Shows up at the club on his arm."

I wasn't precisely shocked by this news, but I was disappointed. I wasn't naïve. I understood that infidelity ran rampant among the upper classes. Many high-ranking gentlemen boasted a mistress, and their wives quietly indulged in affairs on the side as well. It was well-known that Rockham himself had claimed one mistress or another during the duration of his first marriage—

Ada being that woman the last five years of it. However, that didn't mean I approved of the matter.

When I'd met Ada, I'd initially overlooked the matter for the sake of expediency—having needed to cultivate her acquaintance—but I'd quickly deduced that she and Rockham were also in love. It had helped ease my conscience. It also helped that I was friendly with Rockham's first wife, and well knew she was perfectly happy for him to take his attentions elsewhere. Their divorce had seemed ever imminent. As for my opinion of Rockham, I was more inclined to side with Calliope, but Ada had seemed to genuinely care for him. So when they wed, I'd been happy for her.

But now, just two years later, the marriage seemed to be dissolving before my eyes.

I was not so unmindful that I didn't recognize that part of my unease stemmed from the fact that my own marriage had been on rocky ground until recently. And though relations between me and Sidney were much improved, here was evidence of how easily it could all fall apart again.

I watched Ada as she worked her way through the room, chatting with guests and gesturing broadly. This was all a choice bit of theater, for it was obvious she wasn't as cheerful and blithe as she wished to seem. Her voice was pitched just a shade too high, her movements a degree too forceful.

I wasn't the only one who noticed, for Etta shook her head, making a humming noise of sympathy.

"I take it all is not well in Eden?" I remarked softly.

Her cinnamon-brown eyes shifted to meet mine. "No, honey. It's not."

"Does Rockham have a new mistress?"

"Not a permanent one, but I've seen a progression of jeunes filles on his arm," she replied, peppering her sentences as she usually did with the French she'd learned from her mother, who had been born on Martinique. "Each one more stupid than the last," she added derisively.

I looked at her in question.

"They all think they'll be the next Lady Rockham."

I wasn't sure I would classify them precisely as stupid, but more foolishly hopeful. After all, the war had left my generation with a distinct shortage of young men. But I understood what she meant. Just as I grasped how precarious Ada's marriage truly was.

"How did it fall apart so quickly?" I murmured more to myself than anyone else, but Etta answered me nonetheless.

"It usually does, honey. And the cracks were beginning to show long ago." Her eyes scoured my features. "Maybe you just didn't want to see them."

I exhaled, conceding she was probably right. For all the horrible things I'd witnessed during the war, all the dark potential of human nature, I was still remarkably ingenuous when it came to my friends, preferring to view them through rose-colored glasses. Not for the first time, I wondered if that was a fault or an asset. Was I being indulgent or blind?

CHAPTER 2

Ada swooped over to join us. "Etta, dear, did I tell you how absolutely smashing this gown is." She ran her fingers lightly over the feathers. "You must tell me where you got it." But before Etta could even reply, she had turned toward me, arching her eyebrows in query. "Verity, darling, were you able to handle that little matter for me?"

"Yes, all is set."

"Marvelous," she gasped, squeezing my arm. "You are a lifesaver, my dear." Her gaze shifted to my husband. "Is she not a wonder, Mr. Kent?"

Sidney smiled at me warmly. "That she is."

Once again, before the person she was addressing could reply, she'd already whirled away to beckon to someone. "Verity, there is someone you simply must meet."

It was all a bit much, and I found myself searching her eyes, wondering if perhaps cocaine could be blamed for her near-frantic energy. I knew she indulged in drugs from time to time, and had even hosted opium parties in the past. But although her eyes were bright, her pupils were not dilated.

She pulled forward the man she had hastened toward earlier upon entering the salon. "This is Lord Ardmore. And this is my dearest friend, Verity Kent," she told him.

His mouth creased into a pleased smile and he dipped his head in a shallow bow. "Mrs. Kent, I'm utterly charmed. Your reputation precedes you."

"Does it?" I replied evenly, though I was confused as to which part of my reputation he was referring to.

"Your husband's exploits are not the only ones of which there has been great talk. On Umbersea and elsewhere."

By this last statement and the shrewd gleam in his eyes, I took it to mean he was aware of our part in foiling a rather nasty scheme in Belgium six weeks prior.

I'd heard of Ardmore. That he held some sort of position in Whitehall, though I couldn't tell you exactly what it was. I knew there was some connection to Naval Intelligence. One that even C, my former chief in the foreign division of the Secret Service, didn't seem to be privy to the details of. The fact that the government had chosen to explain away the incident in Belgium as a mere accident meant there were very few people who knew the extent of my and Sidney's involvement, and the discovery that he was one of those few told me a great deal about the influence this man had.

I judged him to be somewhere between the ages of forty-five and fifty, with pale-blond hair streaked with gray, and a small mole just above his left ear at his hairline. He was tall and trim, though probably a stone heavier than he had been in his youth. With his mossy-green eyes and a distinguished appearance, I could understand his appeal to Ada. Rockham wasn't often praised for his looks.

However, there was something about the man I didn't like. Something that immediately put me on guard. Perhaps it was the fact that he was encouraging Ada to stray from her marriage vows. Or maybe it was his shadowy connection to military intelligence, one I could tell C—whom I trusted implicitly—was wary of, even if he'd never stated so outright.

Whatever the case, I couldn't help but search Ardmore's facial features and those striking eyes for some greater explanation why he'd wished to meet me beyond the fact he was bedding my friend. Not that he gave anything away. A man of his position—whatever it was—would never divulge his intent so easily.

"Ardmore and I are going to the Embassy Club tomorrow

evening," Ada was saying. "You and Sidney should join us. And invite Daphne and George as well," she added, referring to my two closest friends, both of whom had also worked for military intelligence in different capacities. "We'll make a party of it!"

It did not escape my notice that her husband was not included on the guest list.

I glanced at Sidney, unsure how to answer, and uncertain I even wanted to. "Perhaps we will," I replied noncommittally.

I was saved from having to say more by the abrupt arrival of Rockham. His shoulders were rigid with attention, his head thrown back to thrust his chin upward at a haughty angle.

"Ada, your presence is needed elsewhere. Deacon is signaling that dinner is ready, and you are not paying the least bit of attention." His eyes flicked up and down her form, clearly finding it lacking, and then landed on Ardmore. "I would have thought you would at least try to be a little more circumspect," he snapped in a lower voice. "You are a marchioness now, after all. But I suppose I was wrong."

Her eyes narrowed into slits. "As circumspect as you, boring everyone with talk of your horses and your *glorious* exploits through the halls of Parliament during the war?"

I glanced about us, shocked by their spite and their willingness to air their dirty linen in front of everyone. Neither of them was making much of an effort to keep their comments from being overheard.

Rockham bristled. "I've never claimed my service was glorious."

She scoffed. "Really? You could have fooled me."

His gaze shifted toward Sidney. "Of course, our men who fought and died on the fields of France and farther abroad are to be lauded. But I do like to think I did my little bit to keep the Huns at bay. To right the cause of liberty and . . ."

"Blah, blah, blah," Ada interrupted, rolling her eyes. "*Some* gentlemen did make contributions. And the rest should quit beating their gums." She strode past him toward the entrance, where Deacon no doubt hovered.

If looks could burn, Rockham's glare would have incinerated Ardmore on the spot. His lip curled with derision. "And here I thought you were known for your circumspection, what with all the secrets you have to keep." Then he whirled around to storm after his wife.

My skin prickled at being in such close proximity to so much anger, as if the daggers aimed at others had been deflected on to me. However, Ardmore, for his part, didn't appear the least bit ruffled by what had sounded to me like a veiled threat. He turned away and went in search of the lady he would escort into dinner with a perfectly affable expression on his face. I couldn't decide whether he was that unfeeling or simply a brilliant actor. Either seemed as likely.

"Well, that was awkward," Sidney murmured again into the stilted silence that had descended over our quartet. A refrain that would echo through the night, it appeared.

"You can say that again, *chéri,*" Etta concurred. "I'm just glad I don't rank high enough to sit next to either our host or hostess."

I agreed. There were times when being a mere missus suited me to a T. Even though as things now stood, that wouldn't last forever. Sidney was currently the only son of his father and his father's two older brothers, which meant that unless either of Sidney's uncles fathered a legitimate son before he died, which was highly unlikely, Sidney would eventually inherit his oldest uncle's title.

I smiled in delight as Crispin Ballantyne approached to escort me into dinner. As one of Sidney's few friends from his Oxford days who had survived the war, I had seen rather a lot of him in the past few months. Not that I minded. Crispin was kind and levelheaded, though he possessed a rather morbid sense of humor, and unlike many soldiers who'd returned with such a twist in their personality, he'd come by his before the war.

Having served as an artillery officer, he'd suffered some hearing damage, so I tilted my head toward his copper-red pate so that he could hear me as we followed the other guests into the dining room, where the focal point of the room was a stunning chimneypiece of Verona marble. A carton pierre ceiling of monochrome medallions swirled above the table laid with glittering crystal and silver over crisp white linens. Vases of red roses and pink Carthusian were interspersed with shaded candles, while lush vines of ivy and clusters of golden pears were woven between them down the center of the table.

We found ourselves seated several chairs from Ada's left. Far enough we could choose to ignore whatever drama might unfold, or listen in as we chose. Truth be told, now that the quarreling couple was separated by the long expanse of the table, I didn't expect there to be any further unpleasantness, but I was swiftly proven wrong.

As the bowls of soup were whisked away by liveried footmen to be replaced by plates of delicate sole in lemon cream sauce, Ada wriggled in her chair, reaching down to extract something that had either been tucked behind her seat cushion or attached to her person. When she plunked it down on the table next to her plate, I began to suspect it was the latter, for she could never have concealed something so hefty beneath her sinuous dress. Seated to her right, Lord Paget startled, confirming my suspicions of what the object was.

"My lady, what are you going to do with that?" he asked warily, struggling to retain his composure at the sight of a revolver on the table.

Ada shrugged. "Oh, I don't know. I might just shoot Rockham." The words were droll, but the glint in her eyes when she glanced toward her husband at the opposite end of the table was pure malice.

A stunned silence fell over those at the table near enough to hear Ada's words, broken only by a nervous titter from one of the women. Fortunately, Crispin's wit did not desert him.

"Well, not before I've finished this scrumptious sole, I beg. For I suppose I should be obliged to set my fork aside if you choose to put a bullet through our host."

Ada's lips creased into a smile. "Very well, Mr. Ballantyne. I should hate to deprive you of your meal."

"Excellent," he declared, lifting his glass of white wine in a mocking toast to her benevolence.

As the others began to chatter softly again and Ada's attention was claimed by the lord on her left, I glanced down the table toward Sidney. His eyes met mine as he chattered to the woman beside him and from the shrewd look in their depths, I could tell he'd seen what had just happened.

"That was some quick thinking," I murmured to Crispin.

"Yes, well, I thought it best to turn whatever drama it is she's insisting on playing out into a comedy instead. That perhaps that would salve her vanity." His gaze darted to mine in chagrin. "My apologies. I've just recalled she's your friend."

"No, you're right. Parts of this evening do rather feel like some sort of tragedy written for the stage. The question is, why?"

I glanced surreptitiously at Ada, trying to understand her whims this evening. Her behavior had always tended toward the dramatic, and at times she could be temperamental, but tonight was different. Tonight she wasn't just capricious, she was almost volatile.

"Whatever the answer is, I think it might be best if the gun was safely removed from her vicinity, lest Rockham do something idiotic to set her off again."

"Leave it to me."

Fortunately, I'd had enough interactions with Deacon that the butler and I seemed to understand each other. Deacon's insolent treatment of Ada might anger me, but I was objective enough to recognize the fault for her troubles with the staff did not lie completely with the servants. He was an excellent butler, and as such he would not wish to see disaster, in any form, befall his employer. So when I caught his eye across the room, before casting a swift glance toward the revolver, he comprehended immediately.

Under the cover of filling our glasses with champagne for the next course, he swept the revolver from the table and into his pocket without Ada appearing to notice. I breathed a little easier without the gun ruining the ambience of the room, and made a note to myself to thank Deacon later for his quick fingers and discretion.

The remainder of the meal passed without incident. But when the ladies retired to the salon ahead of the gentlemen—a tire-

some tradition the marquess insisted on continuing to observe—
I hovered outside in the hall, waiting for our hostess.

"Ada, darling, what on earth were you thinking?" I asked as
I pulled her to the side.

She crossed her arms over her chest, glaring to the side.

"I'm all for your being unconventional, but taking a revolver
to dinner"—I shook my head—"that is much too much."

She huffed. "I didn't take the revolver with me into dinner,
nor did I place it there."

I frowned. "You found it in your chair?"

She shrugged.

"Doesn't that . . . trouble you?"

"Not really. Rockham has any number of guns."

"Yes, but surely he doesn't just leave them lying about the
place?"

Again, she shrugged, unconcerned. "But it was a rather good
quip I made."

My sympathy wearing thin, I cast her a withering stare.
"*Good* is not the adjective I would choose."

She rolled her eyes. "Oh, don't be such a drag. Everyone knows
it was only a jest," she declared over her shoulder as she strode off
toward the salon.

"No, they don't," I said to myself, unwilling to raise my voice
and risk being overheard. Not when Ada wouldn't listen anyway.

I stifled my aggravation and followed her, trying to brush
aside my concerns. If Ada was determined to damage her reputation and ruin her marriage, so be it. There was nothing I could
do about it. I'd already helped her as much as I could to learn
how to manage an aristocratic household, much good that had
done.

I paused at the threshold. And now I sounded like my mother.
She had forever been berating me for my choices, insisting I was
courting disaster. In some ways, she had been right. But that
didn't make her comments, delivered in that sanctimonious
voice she used, any less infuriating.

Vowing to stifle my censorious impulses—after all, it was
considered vulgar to care about the infidelities of others—I re-

joined the ladies. But rather than immediately make for the group of Ada's friends, I moved toward a cluster of less flamboyant aristocrats seated near the hearth. Most of them sipped coffee, though a few indulged in something stronger. After all the wine, champagne, and Madeira at dinner, I decided it would be best to keep my wits about me, and poured myself a strong cup of coffee from the silver carafe one of the footmen held on a tray.

However, there was only so much discussion of which noblemen had been forced to either sell the contents of their country home or put the manor itself up for sale in order to retrench that I could stomach. Such matters were, of course, on everyone in the upper class's mind, but the details did not need to be rehashed, and with almost spiteful relish by those whose fortunes seemed secure.

So, I disengaged myself to cross the room toward the corner, where the gramophone quietly played "Swanee." There, Ada lounged at the end of a snowy-white settee, one arm draped languorously along the low back while the other hand cradled another cocktail. Several of her friends were gathered around her, discussing the latest fashions. A conversation that was unquestionably less fraught.

I perched on the arm of the opposite settee, mostly to listen. When I did venture a comment, it was met by a tiny gasp from the young woman seated next to me. Her eyes widened in recognition. "Oh, my! You're Verity Kent."

"I am," I replied in gentle amusement.

"You're even lovelier in person than in the pictures I've seen in all the papers."

"Yes, well, the photographers rarely capture you at the most opportune moment or angle." Especially when they were intent on surprising you, hoping you would reveal something titillating.

"And your husband," the brunette beside her gasped. "He's so handsome."

Several of the other ladies cooed in agreement as Ada lifted her glass in a toast. "The dashing war hero and his intrepid, blushing bride. The papers simply can't resist a story like that."

I shrugged, unable to tell whether Ada was being in earnest or subtly mocking us. "Scandal and adventure sell newspapers."

And Sidney's sudden return from the dead, not to mention our unmasking of a nest of traitors, had certainly been both of those things.

Throughout June and early July, our steps had been dogged by tenacious reporters and photographers eager to document our every step for the rabid public's consumption. Our trip to Belgium and then retirement to our Sussex cottage had granted us a reprieve, except for the newsman who'd been caught trying to sneak over our fence one evening. But since our return to London a week before, our photographs had been snapped only half a dozen times, including as we arrived at Grosvenor Square for Rockham and Ada's party. The press's interest must finally be waning.

A moment later the gentlemen rejoined us, and I excused myself to search for Sidney. His expression when he entered the room was genial, but I could sense the impatience and irritation simmering below the surface.

"I take it the conversation around the dinner table was no more stimulating than it was in here," I murmured, smelling the spicy smoke from his Turkish cigarettes still clinging to his dark suitcoat.

He turned to survey the room, sliding one hand into his pocket. "Not unless one is interested in shipping ventures or a fan of horse racing."

Though I knew he enjoyed a good gallop through the country as much as any gentleman, and in fact, had been a capital polo player at university, motorcars were now much more his passion.

"Doncaster?" I guessed, knowing the races there were only a few days away. It had been one of the events the ladies had mentioned when discussing what clothing they intended to wear.

Sidney nodded. "Apparently, Rockham has a few thoroughbreds racing, and one is favored to win the St. Leger Stakes."

"Yes, I believe Ada said he's leaving for Doncaster in the

morning, but she's not taking the train up until Wednesday," I replied, stifling a yawn.

His eyes lit with amusement. "Did something happen?"

I looked up at him in confusion.

"Not that I don't appreciate the attention," he elaborated. "But you're usually circulating the room, moving from person to person like a honeybee gathering nectar."

I sighed, watching Ada's progress across the room toward Lord Ardmore as one of the footmen changed the music on the gramophone. "This evening has not gone as I expected."

"Thirty minutes more, and then shall I find a way to politely extricate us?" he offered as the ragtime strains of "Oh!" burst forth from the grammy.

Propriety stated we remain for half an hour after the gentlemen joined the women, but after that one could make a gracious exit.

"You would do that?" I asked, feeling a desperate urge to escape, despite my friendship with Ada.

"Of course."

"Then, yes. Please do."

In the end, it didn't truly matter what our excuse was, for Ada was nowhere to be found. Rockham stood in deep conversation with several men in the corner and merely flicked a hand at the half dozen of us who had stepped forward to take our leave.

We chatted softly as we crossed the echoing hall, lest our voices carry farther than we wished. But at the doors, I couldn't resist the urge to turn back.

Despite its magnificence, there was a solemn loneliness to all the gilt and stucco; its corners wreathed in shadows despite the electric sconces. I felt in indescribable sadness for Ada, wishing things could have been different for her and Rockham. But love was easy in the first flush. It was only later that the struggle began. How well I knew.

CHAPTER 3

Our cab slowly rounded the leafy shadows of Grosvenor Square and headed south toward Berkeley Square. Even in Mayfair, the enclave of the wealthy and well connected, the evening was alive with the growls of motorcar engines, the short blasts of their horns, and the shouts of passing voices. Most were headed deeper into the city en route to the clubs, restaurants, and theaters. On any other night, Sidney and I might be headed that direction ourselves, to drown our cares and our memories of the war in a quick rag and a glass of overpriced champagne or cheap gin, depending on our chosen destination.

Before I'd known my husband was still alive, I'd employed the same methods of distraction, though each night's revelry had been more desperate, each morning's waking racked with more guilt. Now, the pain and guilt were still there, but for a different reason. One I suspected all of us who had survived the war shared to a certain degree. I glanced at Sidney out of the corner of my eye. I knew he did.

A cool breeze wafted through the open windows and riffled the hair at my temples, rife with the scents of exhaust, cooking onions, and the lingering stench of hot asphalt. "Did you wish to visit the Embassy Club or Ciro's?" I asked listlessly, for once having no desire to dance at one of our favorite nightclubs, but sensing the restlessness of his mood.

Rather than answer me, he asked a question of his own. "When did you first meet Ada?"

The question was simple, his voice unconcerned, but I knew there must be a reason he had ignored my query in pursuit of his own.

I let my wrap slip lower down my back, the heat of the day still pressing in around us. "We were introduced at a club—Grafton Galleries. A somewhat calculated maneuver on my part."

Sidney turned to meet my gaze, letting me know he understood what I was implying. Perhaps he'd already suspected it.

I shrugged a shoulder negligently. "She and her friends were rather in the thick of it. Wined and dined, courted, and, in some cases, bedded by some of the government's highest-placed men. The things they heard could prove invaluable to those of us in the Secret Service, or catastrophic if they fell into the wrong hands."

"And yet you've remained her friend."

I glanced at him, trying to decipher the stilted note I'd detected in his tone.

"I know she's not from our normal world, but I like her. She's smart and forthright. She speaks her mind. And she never asks me to be anything other than I am." I searched his face, and though it was maddeningly impassive, I could tell one thing. "You don't like her."

He glanced toward the cab driver, who seemed not to be listening to us, but one could never tell. "I wouldn't say that. I don't really know her." His gaze settled on me again, penetrating even in the gloom. "But she seems to be getting rather more benefit out of your friendship than you do."

I frowned, trying to squash the misgivings that had been spreading through me all evening. "Well, as you said, you don't know her. And you certainly didn't know her during the war. So how can you say?"

He ignored the challenge in my voice and lifted his hand to untangle the strands of hair caught in my earring, using it as an excuse to lean closer. "Yes, you wrangled intelligence out of her," he murmured in a low voice. "Just as it was your job to do. And I can tell you feel guilty about that, though you shouldn't."

"I know that," I whispered back fiercely, even though he was spot-on in his assessment. "There was a war on, and I was merely doing my bit."

"That's putting it rather mildly."

I scowled as the knowledge of all the dangers I'd undertaken by slipping through the electric fence from neutral Holland into German-occupied Belgium multiple times during the war passed between us. As I'd only shared the exact nature of my war work and involvement with the Secret Service six weeks ago, having been forbidden to do so during the war, he was still struggling to adjust. After all, he'd spent most of the war believing I was safe at home in our flat, working at a firm of shippers and exporters that helped deliver supplies to the troops.

There were few people outside the friends and colleagues I had made during my time with the Secret Service who knew about my wartime activities. And only Sidney and our friend, Max Westfield, the Earl of Ryde, knew any details. The rest of my family and friends would likely never know, and that included Ada. But I felt certain of her reaction even if she did.

"I know Ada would understand," I insisted, trying to convince myself as much as him.

"Was she useful?" he asked casually as the cab reached the north side of Berkeley Square.

I studied his face, cognizant of where his mistrust came from. After all, the nest of traitors we had uncovered in his battalion had been instigated and directed by a seemingly flighty society girl back in London.

"Yes and no," I replied, as he helped me from the cab.

Linking my arm with his, he arched his eyebrows in curiosity but didn't voice his question as he led me toward the building that housed our luxury flat. With its Portland stone elevations, Neo-Grec detailing, and Parisian-style ironwork, it was a lovely piece of architecture, if slightly out of place next to the neighboring Georgian-era buildings.

I smiled at the doorman in his crisply pressed uniform. "Good evening, Sal."

"Evenin', Mrs. Kent, Mr. Kent," he replied, touching his fingers to his hat. Then his teeth flashed white in his dark face.

"Will you be needin' a cab again shortly, or are you callin' it a night?"

Sidney's gaze dipped to mine. "An early night, I should think."

Accustomed to our night-owl tendencies, this uncharacteristic answer nonetheless didn't faze him. "Right-o," he declared. "Have a lovely evenin'."

We rode silently up in the rattling lift, Sidney's warm hand on the small of my back, waiting until we entered our fourth-floor flat before we resumed our discussion.

"Ada didn't provide us as much information as some of the women I befriended," I informed him, dropping my clutch on the bureau next to the telephone. "But I can't tell you whether that's because she didn't know it or she was simply more circumspect." Spinning about to face him, I began to pull the tight-fitting gloves from my fingers one by one. "Whatever the case, there's not one bit of evidence to suggest she ever had any nefarious intentions for the secrets she may or may not have been told, so there's no use suspecting her, darling."

He shrugged. "Maybe not about her activities during the war, but I do suspect she's trying to convince Rockham to divorce her."

I sighed. "I admit, I had a similar thought." Sliding my second glove from my arm, I turned to lay them on the bureau. "It's rather disillusioning. Especially when I thought she was happy."

Sidney stepped closer to stand behind me, resting his hands gently on my upper arms. "Well, it takes two people to sustain a marriage, and two to usually wreck it."

That had certainly been the case with us, and I was heartened to hear him speak of it so, despite our own continued struggles to forgive each other's mistakes and adjust to living with each other again after four and a half years of separation.

"I suspect Rockham may be equally to blame, even if perhaps he's a bit more discreet in his dalliances."

"Yes, I'm certain you're right," I replied, recalling what Etta had told me. My gaze fell to the slip of paper tucked next to the telephone, and I lifted it.

Sidney's lips pressed to my temple. "But enough about them. What's that?"

"It's a note from Sadie." Our maid must have left it before departing for home earlier that evening. "My friend Irene Shaw telephoned."

"Do you need to ring her back?" he asked, continuing to nuzzle my skin.

"Not tonight. Irene never kept late hours," I replied, though I was intensely curious as to why my old colleague from the Secret Service had contacted me. We hadn't spoken in months, not since we'd both received our demobilization papers. The last I'd heard, she'd found a job as a typist—one for which she was undoubtedly overqualified, as all the best positions went to returning soldiers. It was difficult to know how to feel about such a situation. Those soldiers needed jobs, but so did my friend.

Unaware of where my thoughts had gone, Sidney's mouth continued to drift lower, as did his hands. "Well, then, whatever shall we do with ourselves the rest of this evening?" His lips skimmed across the sensitive skin behind my ear, riveting my attention to what he was doing. "How can we possibly occupy ourselves?"

I gave a little gasp as his teeth grazed my neck and I felt his lips curl into a satisfied smile.

"I do love this dress." His hand brushed over the exposed skin of my back, sending tingles down my spine.

I turned in his embrace, draping my arms over his shoulders. "Then perhaps we should remove it before you wrinkle it."

His eyes flashed roguishly. "I thought you'd never ask."

I wasn't certain how long I'd slept after Sidney's exhaustive attentions before I was awakened by the sound of the telephone. He was already seated upright, his nerves far more attuned to any noise after having spent nearly three and a half years in the trenches. So perhaps it was his movements that woke me and not the muted jangle of the telephone in the entry hall.

"Who is it?" I murmured blearily.

His stiff muscles relaxed as if recognizing where he was, or more accurately, where he wasn't, and he settled back under the blankets.

"Who cares? It's three o'clock in the morning."

"Yes, but if they're calling at this hour . . ."

"If it's important, they'll ring back."

At these words, the telephone silenced, and I closed my eyes, sinking my head deeper into the pillow.

A moment later the ringing began again.

Sidney leapt out of bed, throwing his dressing gown around his shoulders as he strode barefoot toward the hall. "This is why we need live-in servants," he muttered.

I refrained from pointing out that if we had live-in servants, he could not have done half the things he'd done to me the night before without shocking them dreadfully.

Reaching for my own silk dressing gown, I padded over to the door, gazing down the long length of the hall toward the entry. He stood with his back to me, speaking sharply into the telephone, though I couldn't make out his words. I knotted the belt, the uneasy feeling that had settled over me sharpening into dread as the timbre of Sidney's tone changed.

"You're certain?" I thought I heard him ask as he turned to glance down the hall toward me.

I moved forward hesitantly at first, then with more determination. "Who is it?" I asked as I drew close enough to see the resignation in his eyes where he stood in the dim light cast by a streetlamp shining through the windows in the drawing room.

"It's Ada." His gaze searched mine. "Rockham is dead."

"What?!"

I stepped forward, reaching for the telephone. I could already hear Ada shrieking through the earpiece, demanding that he put me on.

"Ada, it's me," I spoke quickly. "Is it true?"

"Oh, thank God!" she gasped. "Verity, you must come. Please! The police are here, and I . . ." Her voice broke on a sob. "I don't know what to do."

If the police were already there, it must be true indeed. And very serious.

"I'll be there as fast as I can. And, Ada?" I added as an afterthought as the previous evening's events came rushing back to me. "Be careful what you say. The police will use whatever you say . . ."

"I know," she murmured.

There was something in her voice, something that made me want to ask how *she* knew that, but now wasn't the time. "I'll be there as soon as I can."

I rang off and then hurried back down the corridor toward our bedchamber, turning on the lamps. Sidney followed more slowly, but when I turned from the wardrobe with my sap-green crepe dress, it was to find him stepping into a pair of trousers.

"You're not going to object?" I asked, having expected him to do so at any moment.

He glanced up at me, the same dark wayward curl that always seemed to resist being tamed having fallen over his forehead. "Would it do any good?"

"No."

"Then why bother," he muttered, resuming his task.

I pulled a chemise over my head and then sat on the edge of the bed to don my stockings. "You're coming with me, I see."

"Of course."

I stilled for a second, arrested by his response. For while he'd stated it as if this was a given, we both knew it was far from it.

After all, I'd been largely on my own since the three days after our wedding nearly five years ago when he headed off to the front. The three months since his return had not erased that. And the last time I'd set off on a mission to help a friend, he'd balked at accompanying me. Granted, the situation had been far more fraught and complicated than those words conveyed, but the point remained. I had not been able to rely on Sidney in the past, even if most of the blame for that lay with the war and his duty to the army and the men under his command.

Sensing the impact his words had on me, he looked up from the buttons he was fastening on his shirt. Thoughts flitted through his gaze, too numerous to name, before settling on something akin to regret.

I turned away, rolling my stocking higher up my leg. "You'll be ready before me," I said in a voice that sounded slightly hollow. "Will you ring down to Sal and ask him grab us a cab?"

"I was already planning on it."

"What will he think of us now, dashing off at a quarter past three in the morning?" I attempted to jest, though it fell flat.

"I'm sure he's witnessed odder things," he replied mildly.

Now, that was something to which I could attest, though I thought it best not to admit so to Sidney.

"Oh, Verity," Ada exclaimed, leaping up from the sofa where she perched. "Thank heavens you've come." Her cheeks were streaked with tears, her eyes rimmed with red. She immediately stepped into my embrace when I lifted my arms, burrowing into my shoulder as she continued to weep. "It's just . . . so awful," she blubbered. "Poor Rocky."

I nodded to Sidney over her shoulder, and he backed out of the morning room to go confer with the police, just as we'd planned. I guided Ada back over to the blue toile sofa and passed her a dry handkerchief. "What happened?" I asked as we settled back into the cushions.

At half past three in the morning, this room was cold and gloomy, even with a fire burning in the hearth. In a few hours, the sun would rise and shine through the large windows onto the pale-pink walls and dainty cream scroll-footed furniture. But until then the drapes remained closed, and the chamber sat wreathed in gray shadows.

"I don't know," she sniffed, shaking her head. She flung her hand out toward the door. "That dreadful man woke me."

"Which man? Deacon?" I guessed.

She nodded. "He started making all sorts of dreadful accusations. I thought he was canned, waking me up in the middle of the night with such insolent nonsense. It took me several minutes to realize he was saying that . . . that Rockham is dead." She began to blubber, and I squeezed her fingers to try to help her pull herself together.

"Did Deacon find him?" I asked.

She dabbed at her nose. "I suppose. Maybe *he* did it, and he thinks to blame *me*." A vicious gleam lit her eyes. "Well, I won't let him get away with it. I won't!"

"I think we're getting ahead of ourselves," I cautioned her before she could utter any more impassioned pleas. "Do you know how Rockham died?"

Her chin dropped to the handkerchief she was worrying between her fingers in her lap, her dark bobbed hair shielding her face. It was such a shift from her vehement declarations a moment before that a sinking suspicion settled in my gut.

I tilted my head so that I could see her face. "Ada," I stated firmly, demanding she tell me.

Her dark eyes when they lifted were clouded with fear. "He was shot."

CHAPTER 4

I swallowed my own dismay and tried to focus on the problem at hand. "Was it with the same revolver you brought to the dinner table last night?"

She shook her head. "I don't know. I . . . I haven't entered the study. I only know he was shot because Deacon accused me of pulling the trigger."

"So it happened in the study?"

"Yes." She glanced toward the open door. "That's where most of the bobbies are. One of the older chaps, a chief inspector or something, told me to stay here."

I followed her gaze toward the hall, where beyond we could hear the sounds of people moving about and the low murmur of voices. I trusted Sidney had located this chief inspector or whoever was in charge by now. Given his war record and his commanding presence, when he wished to exert it, I hoped they would share much of what they knew with him.

"And you were in bed? You didn't hear any gunshots?"

She rubbed her fingers over her right temple in circles. "I was rather sotted when I stumbled into bed. I'm not sure I would have even heard that odious butler had he not been standing over me shouting."

Whether because of her hangover or the night's shocking revelation, her face *was* very pale. Swathed in a loose-fitting gauze dress and a voluminous cardigan, she looked frail and weak, her shoulders bowed with either grief or guilt or pain. Perhaps a combination of all three.

I vacillated, but the fact was the question had to be asked. "Ada." I waited until she looked at me. "Why on earth did you say what you did at dinner?"

I expected her to take umbrage with me, as she had the night before, but instead she seemed to wilt, curling further into herself. "I don't know. At the time I was just so angry with Rockham, and I suppose I thought it would be funny." She heaved a sigh and sank back into the sofa cushions. "If I'd stopped to think for longer than two seconds, I would have realized how in poor taste it was." She gestured vaguely toward the door. "And now this."

"Yes, but Deacon removed the revolver from the table in the middle of dinner. Do you know where he put it?"

She surged upright, her voice brightening. "You're right. I'd forgotten that." She sank back again. "But it's no use. Deacon would have put it back in Rockham's gun cabinet, which I have access to, should I really wish to get my hands on a weapon."

I drummed my fingers against my knee. "I don't suppose you discovered why the revolver was in your chair to begin with?"

She shook her head. "Honestly, I never gave it another thought." Her expression was grim. "Not until my rude awakening."

I sat staring at the medallion-patterned carpet, ruminating over everything she'd told me, everything I remembered from the night before, when she suddenly grasped my arm.

"They're going to think I did it, aren't they?" Her eyes were wild, her voice strangled with panic. "But I *didn't*. I didn't, Verity! I know I behaved badly last night. This life, this marriage, well . . . it wasn't what I expected. But I didn't wish Rockham dead! I just wanted him to be as unhappy as I was."

For all that her words did not speak well of her, they did have the ring of truth. Perhaps precisely because of that.

"*Please*, you have to help me! Tell me what to do."

I rested a hand over hers where it gripped my sleeve. "First of all, take a deep breath. It will not help you to be seen in such a state."

She inhaled a shaky breath, swallowed, and nodded.

"Now, you're right. You're bound to be a suspect. But you were, anyway. The spouse always is. And you *were* here when it happened."

She blinked her eyes rapidly, as if inwardly flinching at these facts.

"But before we can make any assumptions, we need more information." A few points of contention flitted through my mind, but I didn't mention them. Not then. "In the meantime, when they question you, stick to the facts. Tell them the truth, but don't elaborate unnecessarily. And if you think they're fishing for information, something they can use against you, refuse to answer."

"But won't that make me look guilty?" she argued.

I grimaced. "If they're doing that, they already think you are."

She blanched.

My gaze shifted past her to where a tall, bronze-skinned man now stood in the doorway, and just beyond him Sidney. The man paused, sizing up the situation in one efficient glance before advancing into the room. Dressed in a simple but well-tailored suit, he seemed a cut above the average Scotland Yard inspector, which could either be a positive thing for us or a negative. My gaze darted to Sidney, who followed more sedately, his hands tucked in the pockets of his trousers. From what I saw reflected in his eyes, he was still reserving his judgment on that fact.

"Lady Rockham, my apologies again for your loss," the policeman told Ada, stopping before her on the sofa. "Do you feel up to answering a few questions?"

"I suppose," she answered uncertainly.

His coal-black eyes flicked to meet mine. "If you would like, your friend may remain. I understand Mrs. Kent attended the dinner party you held last night."

"I did," I replied, offering him my hand. "How do you do?"

"Detective Chief Inspector Thoreau," he stated, accepting it and bowing his head perfunctorily toward me.

Ada clutched my skirt. "Would you stay, Verity? It would be ever so reassuring."

"Of course. Would you mind if Sidney also remained?"

"Not at all." She cast an almost bashful glance at my husband. "Hullo, Mr. Kent."

"I'm terribly sorry for your loss," he said.

Ada dipped her head, dabbing at her eyes as she fought back another wave of tears. "Thank you."

A third man slipped into the room then, settling into a chair a short distance away and removing a notebook and pencil from his pocket.

"This is Constable Stephens. He'll be taking notes of our conversation."

Ada nodded hesitantly and then looked to me. I tapped her hand in reassurance, letting her know this was standard procedure.

The inspector sat in the chair across from us, his posture relaxed and his voice soothing. This was definitely not his first encounter with the aristocracy or a weeping widow. "Now, walk me through the events of late last night and this morning."

It was a leading question, and a dangerous one at that, for the witness might very well let more information slip than was necessary. I had employed a similar tactic often enough in my work for the Secret Service. But Ada heeded my instructions, laying out merely the bare facts with just the slightest embellishment, which made clear the contentious relationship between herself and Deacon.

"What time would you say you retired?" Thoreau attempted to clarify.

"Not long after the last guests departed." She sighed wearily, rubbing her temple. "I should say half past one." Her gaze met mine for a second before looking away, and I could tell what she was thinking. That was rather an early ending to one of her parties. Apparently, the tense atmosphere had not improved even after Sidney and I left.

"And what time did your butler wake you?"

"Around a quarter to three."

"And you heard nothing out of the ordinary?"

She shook her head before adding, "But I was rather zozzled."

"Did you take any of your sleeping pills, as well?"

A slight furrow formed between her eyes, clearly displeased someone had shared this with the inspector. "Not last night, no," she replied more crisply. "I didn't need them."

He searched her face, marking the lines of strain, and then nodded. "Where was Lord Rockham when you retired?"

She shrugged. "He had gone off to the billiard room at one point with a few of his chums from Parliament, and I never saw him again after that."

"So you don't know whether anyone else was present with him when you retired?"

Ada paused, and I could tell she was choosing her words with care. "I thought the last of our guests had departed, but I didn't inquire."

This wasn't necessarily odd for members of the nobility, where wives and husbands often went their separate ways much of the time, and Thoreau seemed to realize it. At least, he didn't remark on it or her indifference to what he'd been doing.

However, he did not miss the opportunity to inquire about the most remarkable incident of the evening.

"I hear you brought a rather interesting accessory to the dinner table."

I had to give him points for not sounding either snide or disapproving. In any case, it appeared Deacon had definitely been talking to the inspector if he'd already discovered this choice tidbit.

She scowled. "I didn't bring it with me. I found it tucked in the seam of the cushion of my chair." Her gaze dipped to the handkerchief she had flattened over her lap, running her fingers along the lace edges. "I admit I made a rather unsporting jest in poor taste." She could hardly deny it with so many witnesses. "But heavens, I never actually intended to do anything about it. I was merely cross with him."

"Cross enough to shoot him?"

Ada glared at Thoreau, who showed no remorse. "No." She arched her chin. "Besides, Deacon removed the gun from the table soon after, and I haven't seen it since." Her bravado faltered as her eyes searched his stony face. "Is . . . that . . . what killed my husband? That revolver?" She nearly choked on the words.

"Yes."

For a moment, I thought she might faint or become ill, such was the paleness of her complexion. But she swallowed and forced a breath into her lungs. "You're certain?"

"We will be verifying with others, but yes, fairly certain."

"Do . . . you need me to look at it?"

He shook his head. "No, I don't think that's necessary."

She nodded, her arms stealing around her middle as she stared at the floor. "I'm afraid I'm not feeling very well. Is that all? May I go lie down?"

His penetrating gaze scrutinized her features. "Of course, Lady Rockham. I'll let you know later if I have any further questions."

That there would be further questions was never in doubt, but I appreciated the tact he must exert, especially in such situations.

I helped Ada to her feet and Sidney stepped forward to assist her as she wobbled toward the door. "Shall I ring for McTavy?" I asked, but before she could reply, Thoreau interjected.

"If you're speaking of her ladyship's maid, I asked Miss Mc-Tavy to wait in the hall for her mistress. That she might have need of her."

That he had anticipated this spoke much of his experience. What I couldn't tell was whether he was cynical of a lady's need for her maid, or merely aware of the proprieties that dictated a gentlewoman's life. Proprieties young noblewomen were just beginning to balk at in large numbers after the comparative freedom they had enjoyed from such restrictions during the war years.

I turned to face the chief inspector, who had risen from his chair with the rest of us. He was nearly a head and a half taller than me, forcing me to crane my neck to look him in the eye. I suspected his size came as an advantage, but he didn't try to use it to intimidate me. Perhaps he realized that would never work, or that he had no need to resort to such tactics. Whatever the case, his expression gave nothing away except mild curiosity.

"Mr. Deacon told me Lady Rockham had called you in to run interference for her. That you often do such a thing for her."

"I wouldn't need to if Deacon wasn't such a snob," I retorted.

Perhaps it was a trick of the light, but I was fairly certain I saw a flicker of a smile cross Thoreau's face at this comment. So he'd taken the butler's measure as well.

"Are you going to make trouble for me?"

"Not if you do your job thoroughly and objectively," I challenged back.

He glanced at Sidney as he returned to the room. "With a war hero and his daring wife breathing down my neck, I suppose I shall doubly be made to do so," he muttered dryly. He arched his thick eyebrows. "But you do realize we must consider Lady Rockham a suspect?"

"I do. It would be improbable for you not to." I tilted my head. "And . . . as much as I don't want to think my friend could murder her husband, as much as I don't *believe* she did, I am willing to concede there is a slim possibility of it." If he was willing to be reasonable, so could I.

"Then would you mind telling me what you remember about the incident with the revolver last night? I understand you were seated close to Lady Rockham." He tipped his head toward Sidney. "Closer than your husband."

We settled in our seats again, though this time Sidney aligned himself with me, sitting in the place on the sofa Ada had vacated. I told the inspector what I recalled, as well as a few of my own impressions. I decided there was no point in withholding any information. Thoreau was certain to interview most of the guests from the dinner party, and some of them would be far less kind in their opinions of Ada and her bizarre behavior than I would. He would discover soon enough how tense the evening had been and how the Rockhams had squabbled. If I left any of that out, he was certain to question my objectiveness.

"So it was you who suggested Deacon should remove the revolver?" Thoreau wanted to clarify.

"Yes, having it at the table was awkward, to say the least. He tucked it into his pocket, and then I thought no more of it. I assumed he would return it to the place where it was usually stored. Did he?"

Thoreau didn't reply at first, plainly weighing how much to share. "He says he put it back in the gun cabinet in Lord Rockham's study, and that was the last he saw of it before finding his employer dead in his chair some hours later."

"Do they keep the gun cabinet locked?"

"No."

I glanced at Sidney. "Then anyone could have taken it from the cabinet after Deacon replaced it. Anyone who was in the house either during the party or after."

"Feasibly, yes."

"And you are certain the gun that killed Lord Rockham is the same one Lady Rockham found in her chair at dinner?"

"Given the fact that the revolver Deacon claims he returned to the cabinet was no longer inside it, and one that had recently been fired was lying on the floor next to Lord Rockham's body, yes. But I hoped you might be able to confirm it."

"I can tell you that it was a Webley revolver, but I couldn't tell you if it was that particular gun, only one of its type."

"Well, I shall have you take a look at it regardless, simply to verify what you can."

"Of course."

He nodded to the constable, who rose and exited through the door to speak with someone before returning a few moments later.

While he was in the hall, I ventured a question of my own. "If I may, you said Lord Rockham was found in his chair in his study. I presume the one behind his desk."

"That is correct."

"And there's no chance this could have been a suicide?"

I did not myself believe it likely, but the position of the body and the wound was suggestive of one, so I decided the question must be asked.

His already perceptive gaze seemed to sharpen even more. "One would think such a possibility should be considered, but for two things. There was no suicide note. And I've been informed that his lordship was left-handed."

"And yet he was shot in the right temple," I surmised.

"Correct."

Which was something that surely his wife would have been aware of.

"Do you have reason to believe otherwise?" Thoreau asked, his eyes narrowing.

Sidney made a snorting noise under his breath, making us both turn to look at him. "Rockham was too arrogant to ever commit suicide." He tapped his fingers on the arm of the sofa and turned to the inspector in query. "Unless you have evidence he was in dire financial straits and he was about lose his power and position?"

"Not that I'm aware of."

"Then I should say such a thing is highly doubtful."

I had to agree. "He wasn't in the right frame of mind. He was annoyed and cross, but not despondent." I pressed my lips together a moment in thought. "But that doesn't mean the shooter didn't wish us to think he'd killed himself. If he was shot deliberately in that manner, then the person who did it must not have realized he was left-handed."

"Or they'd forgotten," Thoreau remarked pointedly.

I wanted to argue, but I couldn't. He was right. In the heat of anger, or the fog of nerves, it would be all too easy for an inexperienced killer to overlook such a detail.

Another police officer entered then, carrying the revolver in a dark cloth. Thoreau directed him to show it to me, and I studied it carefully. Though I'd expected it to match the gun Ada had brought to the table, my heart still sank at the evidence before me.

"Yes, it's the same type. Though, as I said, I did not view it closely enough to be able to say with certainty this is the exact same revolver."

I was aware I was being pedantic, for in all likelihood they were one and the same, but I couldn't help wanting to be precise. Not when Ada's fate hung in the balance.

Thoreau nodded once, and I was certain he understood far more than I would have liked. "We'll know soon enough," he declared, dismissing the other officer. "If it's the same weapon, her fingerprints will be on it."

Which was both a point in Ada's favor, but also a pitfall. They wouldn't be able to say definitively that her fingerprints didn't get there from handling the gun at dinner, but they were also bound to be on the weapon, linking her to the crime.

"I understand Lady Rockham was his lordship's second wife," the inspector said. "That he divorced his first wife."

"Yes." This was common knowledge.

"Was it a happy union?"

I couldn't withhold a wry glare. From everything he'd already heard, he could evidently tell it was not. "They had their difficulties, the same as any marriage."

His gaze glinted with challenge. "Perhaps, but I cannot imagine you believe it's typical for a wife to threaten to shoot her husband in front of a table full of guests."

"It was a quip, not an actual threat. Though one made in horrible taste. Besides, it would be perfectly idiotic to make such a jest in front of dozens of witnesses and then follow through with it later. And I assure you, Lady Rockham is no idiot."

"Unless she counted on us discounting her for that exact reason."

I briefly considered this suggestion and then shook my head. "No, I don't believe it. That would be a terrible gamble. And in any case, she had no motive to kill him. All of Rockham's wealth and titles pass to his eldest son and heir. She would have received more money from him in a separation than upon his death. If she wished to be rid of him, she could have asked him for a divorce."

Sidney's hand tightened where it rested on my knee, and when

I looked at his face, I could tell he knew something I didn't. Something I wouldn't like.

Thoreau plainly shared in this knowledge, for he sank deeper in his chair, his gaze raking over my features as he deigned to enlighten me. "She couldn't if it's true that Lord Rockham wished to convert to Roman Catholicism."

CHAPTER 5

By the time we departed Rockham's townhouse, London was awash in a watery gray. The pavements of Mayfair were thronged with people huddled under black umbrellas, hugging the buildings as they attempted to avoid the spray of foul gutter water thrown up by passing motorcars. That we'd even been able to nab a taxi in the rainy morning bustle was thanks to Deacon. Despite my dislike of the butler, I had to admit he performed his job admirably. When he wished to.

"You didn't know, did you?" Sidney remarked, pulling me from my frustrated musings.

I shook my head and glanced at the rearview mirror to see if the driver was listening. "She never told me," I murmured.

Which had made the fact that Thoreau had been called away after revealing Lord Rockham's intended religious conversion rather fortunate, even though I had a sinking suspicion I'd not adequately hidden my shock. I had wanted nothing more than to march straight up the stairs to Ada's boudoir and demand she tell me if it was true, but I had known how that would look to the inspector.

"How did you learn of it?" I turned to ask him.

"I overheard Deacon telling the inspector."

I scoffed. "Of course."

We fell silent as the cab pulled up to our building, and remained so until we entered our flat. I could hear Sadie, our maid of all work, moving about in the kitchen and went to ask her to make us some breakfast. If the slip of a girl—who was no older than my almost twenty-three years—found it odd her employers were both awake when normally we had just collapsed into bed only hours before, she didn't show it. And the fact that her features were dominated by a pair of heavily lashed doe eyes made it difficult for her to hide anything. At least from me. It was part of the reason I'd hired her. That, and the fact she was also a war widow, though one who had been left in far less auspicious circumstances.

When I'd returned to London in June with a suddenly very-much-alive husband, I had been able to tell how stunned and unsettled she was. For a week after, I'd met each morning expecting her to give me notice. But then I'd also known she desperately needed the income we provided, as well as the freedom to live outside our flat. Few employers paid as well as the rate I'd given her, or allowed such a concession. I'd long suspected she cared for someone who could not care for themselves, be it an invalided soldier or an elderly family member, but I did not pry. I valued my own privacy too much to meddle in hers.

I entered the drawing room to find Sidney gazing out through one of the tall Georgian-style windows streaked with rain. One of his specially blended Turkish cigarettes dangled between his fingers, and his eyes narrowed in thought. As such, I approached slowly, not wanting to startle him on the chance he might be lost in one of his memories from the war. Normally, he did not struggle during the daytime. Only at night, when his nightmares could sometimes be vicious.

His gaze dipped to meet mine as I perched on the deep ledge before the window, and I could tell from the sharp glint of his deep blue eyes he was not wandering in the past, but firmly in the present.

"What did I miss, then? Did the inspector allow you into Rockham's study?"

He inhaled another drag from his fag and nodded. His lips quirked into a cynical smile. "I suppose there are some perks to being such a celebrated war hero."

That much of the time this status did not appeal to him said much about his experiences during the war and the weight they still carried. I felt a twinge of guilt for asking him to use it to gain information, even though he'd been the one to offer to speak to the inspector.

"But you were correct," he continued. "The chief inspector is rather of the old-school variety. Despite your daring reputation, he would never have let you near Rockham's body."

He took one last puff from his cigarette before stubbing it out in an ashtray on the low table positioned between our emeraldine sofas. I followed him, sinking into the cushions of one of the sofas and swiveling to face him as he joined me.

"Then everything was as Inspector Thoreau implied, more or less?"

"Yes, that single shot to the head killed Rockham." His expression was grim.

"And he was sitting at his desk, either forced to do so or completely unaware of what was about to happen," I surmised, trying to picture the scene. "Was there any evidence of what he might have been doing while seated there before he was killed?"

Sidney shook his head. "Not that I saw. Though Scotland Yard might have removed it before we arrived."

"What of the gun cabinet? Where is it located in relation to Rockham's desk?"

"To his left if he was seated at the desk."

I frowned. "Then he must have seen them opening it. Unless he was distracted somehow." I bit my lip, considering. "Was there a sideboard in his office?"

From the glint in his eyes, I could tell he was impressed I'd thought of this. "Yes, on the opposite side of the room. But all of the glasses were accounted for, and none of them had been used." He tipped his head. "Unless the killer took the time to clean up after themselves. But that's unlikely given the fact Deacon said he heard the gunshot and ran upstairs to investigate. That's when he found Rockham."

I could tell Sidney had already had the same thought I did,

but I spoke the words anyway. "Unless Deacon himself is the killer. But then I can't imagine Rockham sharing a friendly drink with his *butler*."

"No, but it might explain why Rockham wasn't alarmed by someone extracting the revolver from the cabinet. Perhaps Deacon had never replaced it."

"That does make sense." I tapped my fingers where they lay against the cushion along the back of the sofa, then lowered my arm. "But even though that theory is far easier to accept, I can't conceive what Deacon's motive can possibly be for killing Rockham. I *can* imagine him attempting to frame Ada, and I'm sure whatever he told Thoreau was certain to paint her in the worst possible light, but I simply can't comprehend why he would kill Rockham in the first place."

"Perhaps he was worried Ada would see him sacked."

I shook my head. "There was no chance of that happening. You heard Rockham tonight. He gave his wife no support when it came to domestic matters." I scowled. "In truth, I think he rather approved of Deacon's treatment of his wives. Maybe he thought it proved the butler's loyalty to him." I sighed. "What of the other servants? Did they hear the gunshot? Can they corroborate what Deacon said?"

"I don't know. But I suspect Thoreau will be able to discover that soon enough and establish a firm timeline. Which means you may need to consider the possibility your friend *did* do it." Sidney reached across to brush a wayward curl behind my ear. "I know you might not wish to think so, but she does appear to have a temper. And she does have motive if what Deacon told us proves to be true. His Holiness the Pope might be willing to grant an annulment of the marquess's first marriage in order to secure the conversion of such a high-ranking individual, but I can't imagine him endowing two."

Divorce was not allowed in Catholicism, but sometimes the Church could be convinced to annul a marriage. However, Sidney was right. I doubted there was any price Rockham could pay that would persuade the Pope to grant two. One could be written off as a mistake. Two was a habit.

Instinctively, I wanted to reject the possibility of Ada being the culprit, but experience had taught me not to rush to any conclusions, especially when one was personally involved. So I forced myself to consider the painful prospect that my friend was a killer. That she'd murdered her husband in cold blood and preyed on my friendship and loyalty to convince me she hadn't done it. Except my mind simply would not accept it.

"I know she's the likeliest suspect, but . . . I just can't believe she did it," I told him. "Maybe she had motive, but the way in which it was done . . . It doesn't sound like Ada."

"What do you mean?"

I turned to stare at the Impressionist painting hanging above the hearth, its blurred lines and hazy edges, as I tried to put my thoughts into words. "I know few people mark it, but Ada is incredibly clever. Of all the friends and contacts I cultivated for information during the war, she was one of the ones I most feared would realize what I was doing."

"Did she?"

"If she did, she never let on." I turned to look at him, curious if he knew he had been the other. And he *had* figured it out, though I hadn't known it until after his return. "If Ada truly wanted to kill someone, she would be far more cunning. She would devise a way so that either the murder wasn't even detected, or the blame was unlikely to fall on her. She would *not* shoot the victim with the same gun she had just jested in front of several dozen guests that she would kill him with only hours before, and with no one else but the servants in the house to take the blame." I arched my eyebrows in emphasis. "She might have a temper, but she's not a fool."

Sidney shifted, slouching deeper into the cushions. "I see your point."

"The way I see it, her finding that revolver at dinner, and making such a poor jest, might have been the impetus for someone else to carry through with it. They could have decided they would never find a more perfect scapegoat."

He squinted at something across the room. "All right, then," he conceded. "Who else could have done it? Who else could have wanted Rockham dead? Other than Deacon. One of the other servants?"

"Possibly," I hedged, though I couldn't begin to speculate who or why. I wouldn't know that until I spoke to them, but I doubted it.

"Maybe someone unseen found a way to access the house?" He glanced sideways at me. "What about his first wife? Maybe she's still angry about the divorce."

I couldn't withhold a wry smile. "I can assure you, Calliope is not angry. She was more than glad to be rid of Rockham. She never wanted to marry him in the first place." The corners of my mouth tightened in disapproval. "A more mercenary transaction I've never heard of. He wanted her father's American money, and her parents wanted an English title for their daughter. Calliope's feelings didn't factor into the equation."

"You're acquainted with Calliope Tennyson?"

That this should surprise him amused me. "Yes, and she's a lovely person. But she didn't mourn her divorce from Rockham in the least. In fact, she celebrated it. Quietly, of course, mindful of decorum. But she's much happier now than she was before. Not to mention the fact she's engaged to be married in a few months, to a man of her own choosing this time."

I reached out to touch Sidney's hand where he sat ruminating. "Have you been blaming Ada for Rockham's failed first marriage? Darling, it was on the rocks long before she ever met him. And she certainly wasn't his first mistress."

He looked up to meet my gaze. Given our recent difficulties, I wasn't surprised to discover he'd harbored such disapproval of Ada. But the Rockhams' marriage had been quite different from our own.

"What of Rockham's son?" he suggested. "He does stand to inherit everything, and if memory serves, he's rumored to be somewhat of a wastrel."

"I think it's less an indication of his character than the shame he feels that he wasn't allowed to serve in the army." Because of a bad fall when he was a boy, Lord Croyde walked with a distinct limp, which had rendered him unfit for active service.

"Though he didn't realize she knew it, Calliope said he tried multiple times to sign up, even attempting to use a fake name. But he was turned away every time."

"I can't imagine Rockham was best pleased by this."

There was no need to respond, for the answer was apparent. The vainglorious marquess had been disappointed his son was not able to cover himself with glory on the battlefield, and I imagined he never missed a chance to let Croyde know it.

"What about his new stepmother?" Sidney arched his eyebrows. "Did Croyde and Ada get along?"

"They largely avoided each other," I admitted. "He didn't approve. And although, at first, she attempted to befriend him and his sister, eventually she stopped trying. After all, it was well within their rights not to like her, and she realized it would be best not to force the issue."

"Do you think she was truly so unaffected by it?"

I glanced over at him, surprised by his perception. "Of course not. But what could she do?"

Sidney dipped his head in acknowledgment.

Agitation simmering under my skin, I pushed to my feet, gnawing on the tip of one fingernail as I paced toward the window before turning back. "Deacon said he locked up for the night?"

"Yes, he said he showed the last guest out at half past one."

The same as Ada had recalled. So why had Thoreau made a point of asking her again whether all the guests were gone when she retired?

"And he's *certain* no one was closeted with Rockham?"

Sidney stretched out his legs as he appraised me. "Thoreau didn't press the point. Not with Deacon," he added, clearly having noted the same thing I had. "Are you suggesting you think there was?"

"I'm saying it's a possibility." I turned away, crossing my arms over my chest in thought. "But if so, it must have been someone the butler was accustomed to seeing there at such odd hours. Even then, why wouldn't he have mentioned their presence?" I frowned. "Unless . . ."

"Rockham hadn't wanted his butler to know they were there," Sidney stated, finishing my thought.

"The question is, why?"

"Shady business dealings, shadowy politics. With Rockham, who knows?" Sidney remarked cynically as he stared at the gleaming biscuit toes of his shoes. "Or it could have simply been his latest mistress."

I didn't remark on this, for a more intriguing thought occurred to me. "What if it was Lord Ardmore?"

This suggestion was met with silence, and I looked up to find Sidney studying me with a veiled expression. "Ada's lover," he finally said.

"Yes, I know perhaps that doesn't make sense," I hastened to say, trying to explain. "But there's something about that man. . . ." I faltered, not knowing how to put into words what my instincts told me about him.

Fortunately, Sidney had recognized the same thing I had, at least partially. "He's a bounder."

"Yes, but it's more than that." I scowled. "I don't trust him."

"Well, I can't say I like the man, either, but that doesn't mean he's a murderer."

I nodded, conceding this point, but I wasn't yet ready to cross him off my list.

"Besides, why would he have wanted to meet with Rockham?" Sidney arched a single eyebrow mockingly. "Surely you're not going to tell me it was a duel for Ada's honor."

"No, of course not," I snapped. "Don't be absurd. And I can't tell you exactly why they would have met secretly. Except there was something between them, something more than Ada." I lifted my hand to brush the issue aside. "Whatever the case, we need to speak with Deacon again and find out if there's anything he neglected to tell the police. He was obviously dead set on Ada taking the blame."

Sidney began to chuckle.

I turned to him in surprise. "What's so funny?"

He rose to his feet, shaking his head. "Nothing." But the wry smile curling his lips belied this answer. "Didn't I tell you that you weren't done dragging me into your exploits?"

I recalled those were almost his exact words following our last adventure in Belgium. An adventure that had almost ended with him being blown up. "I wouldn't exactly call this an exploit," I argued.

"Maybe not yet," he conceded, moving to stand before me. "But give it some time. I'm sure you'll find some way to tumble us into a situation where I'll be shot at."

His words caused me a moment of qualm, worried he disapproved of my actions. Until I noted the twinkle in his eyes and realized he might actually be looking forward to such danger.

"You don't have to follow along, you know." I clasped my hands behind my back coyly. "I *can* look after myself."

"Oh, no." He grasped me around the waist and pulled me to him. "I'm afraid you'll get into far too much trouble without me."

"Is that so?"

His gaze flicked over my features. "Besides, I like trouble. Especially when it involves you."

He would have kissed me then—I could see it in his eyes— had Sadie not rapped on the open door and announced in a timid voice, "Breakfast is ready."

"Thank you, Sadie," I replied. She hurried away, and I urged Sidney to follow me. "Come on, darling. I can't think on an empty stomach." I tossed a saucy glance over my shoulder at him. "Or do anything else, for that matter."

Quickly catching up, he leaned forward to murmur. "Lead on, then, dearest."

CHAPTER 6

After breakfast, I returned to the drawing room while Sidney moved toward the entry hall to use the telephone. I could hear the rumble of his voice directing the operator to connect him to Scotland Yard. A friend and former soldier from his company happened to work in the Criminal Investigation Department (CID), and he'd proven willing to share information with us in the past. We were both curious what Chief Inspector Thoreau might have elected to omit when he was speaking to us. At the least, we knew we could count on Rawdon to inform us of any developments.

I crossed to the set of inlaid oak bookshelves and arched up on my toes to reach our copy of *Debrett's Peerage*. It had been some time since I'd cracked it open, and even now I was hesitant to do so out of dread that the pages might fall open to the name of one of the hundreds of casualties from the war.

Cradling the book in my lap, I turned my head aside to sneeze as I flipped open the volume to the middle. While Sadie had dusted the outward-facing spines, a fine layer of dust had settled over the tops of the pages. Leafing swiftly through the crisp pages, I searched for the Marquess of Rockham's entry. Although I was acquainted with the family, I wanted to refresh my memory of their lineage and estates. Perhaps within those particulars would lie a clue as to who else might wish to see Rockham dead.

I had just finished skimming over the entry when I glanced up to find Sidney reading over my shoulder, his hands tucked casually into the pockets of his dark brown trousers.

"Find anything of interest?" he asked, rounding the sofa to settle into the bergère chair across from me.

"I'm not sure," I admitted, closing the book. "Nothing overt, at any rate. But did you know he owns estates in Ireland?"

He arched his eyebrows in interest.

"Apparently, some of his ancestors were part of the Protestant Ascendancy, taking over a large tract of land, undoubtedly from some penalized Catholic landowner, in the late seventeenth century." I frowned. "I don't know if that has anything to do with what happened to him, but I do find it curious given the current state of unrest in Ireland, and the fact that Rockham was allegedly converting to Catholicism."

The question of Ireland and what had been done to her people by the British troubled me. As an agent of the Secret Service during the war, I was to treat anyone with sympathies for Ireland and their quest for independence as a potential threat to the union, but privately I thought the Irish made some valid points. In addition to their land, the largely Catholic population had been stripped of many of their rights by the conquering English, and only through much struggle and turmoil had they steadily begun to gain it back over the course of the last century. Now they were pushing for their independence, and willing to fight for it, even using violent means if necessary. But no more violent than the British were using to keep them.

"It's a dangerous time to be a Protestant landowner in Ireland." The ironic lilt to his voice did not escape my notice.

"You think Rockham's 'conversion' is a calculated maneuver?"

He tilted his head, considering the matter. "Perhaps. Though it does seem a rather extreme measure to take simply as a bid to keep his land. Especially when it might burn bridges elsewhere."

I traced the gilt lettering on the cover of the *Debrett's*. "I wonder what his politics on the matter really were."

"I wonder if anyone truly knew."

My gaze lifted to meet my husband's, grasping what he meant. Rockham would not have been above playing both sides.

I slid forward to set the book on the low table before me, scowling at the hypocrisy of such men.

When it had become clear that Germany was crumbling from within, her threat to us all but extinct even before the armistice was officially signed, the chief had turned his eyes toward Russia and Ireland as our next biggest threats. C had known we were on the brink of civil war, and he had been proven right in January when the Sinn Féin candidates elected to Parliament instead formed a separate government and declared independence from Britain. While the agents C had sent into Ireland and the citizens of that island grappled with the life-or-death implications of the struggle, men like Rockham played word games, saying whatever was needed to gain what they wanted.

"Well, if I were Croyde, I would sell that property now before the house is burned to the ground or it's taken from him by force," Sidney remarked, and I couldn't disagree. A number of manor houses had already been burned or sacked by the rebels, and the number was certain to increase as the unrest grew.

"The question is whether he will allow himself to be advised by cooler heads in this matter, or whether he'll follow in his father's footsteps and insist on hanging on to what he believes is rightfully his. For all that they didn't rub along well together, they are remarkably alike."

Before he could respond, there was a rap on the door to the flat. From where I was seated, I couldn't see into the entry hall, but I heard the low rumble of a man speaking to Sadie. A few moments later, Crispin appeared in the doorway still wearing his evening clothes from the night before.

"Is it true? Did she really shoot Rockham dead?"

I rose from my seat to greet him as he advanced into the room. "Good morning to you, too, Mr. Ballantyne. Or is it still 'good evening'?" I teased, pointedly taking in his attire and tousled red hair.

He flashed a wide, sheepish grin before leaning down to buss my cheek. "Don't scold me too harshly, Ver. Phoebe's off in the country, and I can't sit home alone every night."

Given the fact he smelled strongly of cigarette smoke and gin, and not ladies' perfume, I suspected I needn't worry about his having been unfaithful to his new fiancée. In any case, Crispin would never have shown up at my door in such a state if he was rising from another woman's bed.

Even so, I reached up to straighten his tie, lest his rumpled appearance lead to nasty rumors. "As to the other, yes, Rockham was shot dead. But no, we don't know that Lady Rockham did it. Is that what everyone is saying?"

"Yes, but it's only natural given that stunt she pulled at dinner," he replied in his defense.

"Well, it may be true, but it may not," I replied matter-of-factly. "Let's not jump to conclusions. Unless you think Lady Rockham would be so foolish as to announce the precise manner in which she planned to kill her husband only hours before she did so."

This seemed to give Crispin pause.

"There," I declared, tapping his shoulder as I finished with his tie. "Now, have a seat. If I know Sadie, she'll be along with coffee shortly." I tipped my head toward the sideboard. "Unless you prefer the hair of the dog instead."

"I'm not as bad as that," he protested, though his bloodshot eyes and the pale cast to his skin belied such an assertion.

Sidney's lips sported a knowing quirk. "Who told you about Rockham?"

"Langham heard it from Beecham. You remember Beecham, don't you?"

"Gassed at Passchendaele in '15, wasn't he?"

"Yeah, and then sent to Blighty, the lucky sod." Crispin's gaze darted to me. "Not that I'd want to take his place. Phosgene. That's a nightmare."

For all the feeling in his voice, I'd been around enough soldiers to recognize he hadn't meant to disparage him, and I waved it off.

"Which reminds me. Did you hear Rogers died?"

Sidney stiffened. "Albert Rogers?" he asked in disbelief.

He nodded.

"But I thought he was recovering from his wounds."

"He was. Langham saw him not more than a fortnight ago

and he seemed to be doing well. But then they found him in his room one morning. Passed away sometime in the night without anyone realizing." His expression became guarded. "No one knows exactly how."

I'd seen that look before. Had heard those words, too. It's what was said when suicide was suspected, whether it could be proven or not.

Though he strove not to show it, I could tell this news had a profound effect on Sidney. His calm insouciance had been rattled, and lines of strain etched his forehead. "When did this happen?"

"Two . . . no, three days ago."

Sidney's gaze shifted, and he seemed to stare unseeing at the wall to my right. His fingers tapped a nervous beat against the arm of his chair.

"I'm not sure I've met Mr. Rogers," I said. "Did he have a family? A wife?"

Crispin nodded. "And two young children. Both boys, if I recall."

"A boy and a girl," Sidney corrected as he rose from his chair.

"That's right. He was always talking about what a scrapper she was."

I watched as my husband proceeded to pour himself three fingers worth of whiskey neat.

"Where did they live?" I asked, trying to tamp down my growing concern. "Here in London?"

"Surrey." Crispin rubbed his chin. "Guildford, I believe."

"We could travel down to pay our respects, if you wish," I told Sidney as he turned to face us. "The rail lines must run through Guildford, or I'm sure someone has a motorcar we could borrow for a day."

"Still waiting on your new Pierce-Arrow to be delivered?" Crispin interjected.

Sidney's prized motorcar had recently suffered a minor mishap during our last investigation. That is, if you considered being burned to ashes by a revengeful madman to be minor. Having adored his Pierce-Arrow, he'd swiftly ordered another one, ecstatic about the new features available on the more recent models, including an electric starter. But Pierce-Arrows were manufactured in America. So he not only had to wait for it to be built to his specifications, but then shipped across the Atlantic.

"I've been told it'll be a few more weeks," he replied before taking a drink from his glass. Then he leaned back against the sideboard, crossing one ankle over the other, for all the world as if he hadn't a care. But I hadn't missed the fact he hadn't answered my question.

Deciding now was not the time to press the issue, I turned back to Crispin and the initial reason for his visit. "How long did you stay at the Rockhams' party last night? You were still there when we left."

"Another hour or two." He grimaced. "Honestly, it was a complete drag. Lady Rockham was so zozzled she could barely put one foot in front of the other, and Lord Rockham basically stood against the wall scowling at everyone. That is, until he took himself off somewhere." He crossed his arms over his chest. "If I wanted to spend my evening being glared at, I'd go visit my old man."

"Did anyone leave with Lord Rockham?" I persisted.

Crispin shrugged. "Not that I recall. But then, I was just glad to see him go."

Sadie slipped through the door then, and I gestured for her to set the tray she carried on the low table before me.

"Coffee?" I offered our guest, then gestured to the plate of sultana scones next to the silver urn.

He glanced at his wristwatch. "No, thanks. I'm running late, and I shouldn't have dropped in, as it is. But I had to hear the truth about Rockham, and I knew you would have it." He flashed me an impish grin. "Offer Mrs. Rogers my condolences if you see her," he called over his shoulder as he exited.

I waited until I heard the outer door to our flat close before meandering over to the sideboard. "Are you going to pay Mrs. Rogers a visit?" I asked while I poured a drop of whiskey into my cup of coffee.

"Maybe," Sidney murmured.

"I take it Mr. Rogers was a friend." Although I'd tried to state it as casually as I could, Sidney wasn't fooled.

He turned his head to the side to regard me as I lifted my cup to take a sip. There was something dark swimming in the back of his eyes, some shadow of grief or pain.

"Yes," he finally said, but then turned away, as if he was determined to ignore it. "It sounds like Lord Rockham was rather brusque with everyone last night. Not that that would be motive enough to kill him. But if someone were already angry with him about something else, and also imbibing rather too much, that rudeness might have been the straw that broke the camel's back."

The fact that my husband was willing to indulge in such wild speculation told me how badly he didn't want to discuss his friend or his reaction to his death. However, he did have a fair point. Rockham hadn't exactly been a gracious host, which meant he *could* have infuriated the wrong person.

He stepped away from the sideboard, turning to face me. "Moreover, Crispin seems to confirm what Ada claims about being too drunk to have committed the murder."

"Yes, there is that," I replied, though Crispin's words hadn't reassured me like Sidney assumed they had. For one, I had seen Ada thoroughly embalmed and too primed to stand. The idea of her being able to descend a staircase without falling down it was laughable, let alone firing a revolver straight. But if she had been that corked, then how had she been able to clear her head fast enough to receive me and Chief Inspector Thoreau? The murder of one's husband would most certainly have a sobering effect, but I felt a frisson of uneasiness all the same.

Sidney must have sensed my ambiguity, for he turned to me in question.

But I had no intention of sharing my doubts, so I decided to borrow a maneuver from his repertoire and change the subject. "Did Mr. Rawdon at Scotland Yard have any information he was willing to share?"

His eyes gleamed, recognizing the ploy for what it was, but

given his evasiveness, he couldn't precisely call me on it. I arched a single eyebrow in challenge to let him know it.

The corners of his mouth curled upward for a second in acknowledgment before falling back into more somber lines. "He said he hadn't been briefed on the matter yet, but he is familiar with Chief Inspector Thoreau."

"Well, that sounds rather ominous."

"Quite the opposite, in fact. Rawdon said he's sharp and thorough, but he despises sentimentality. So if Ada thinks to convince him of her innocence that way, she's sadly mistaken."

It was a valid observation, for Ada was not above using histrionics to try to get her way. I nodded, realizing I would have to counsel my friend again against using such tactics. In truth, it was partially her histrionics that had landed her into this situation in the first place—with her husband, her staff, and during her dramatic outburst at dinner the previous evening. I knew she was capable of showing restraint. The question was whether she was willing to.

Not one to sit idly by twiddling my thumbs when there was something to be done, I'd decided to pay a few discreet calls on some of the other guests who had attended the Rockhams' dinner party. However, I never made it past our entry hall because providentially they'd come to me.

Apparently, my friendship with Ada was almost as widely known as my and Sidney's turn as investigators when we unmasked a group of traitors several months prior. Our dashing bit of derring-do had been splashed all over the newspapers. If society was already anticipating our involvement in investigating Rockham's death, then it was only a matter of time before photographers and reporters began hounding our steps again.

Fortunately, Sal knew better than to let them in the building, but London's worst gossips were another matter. They blended in with the rest of the smart set, flocking to us in search of fodder. To a certain extent, I was happy to give it to them, for then at least I controlled the tone of it. But I was also wary of revealing too much, lest we let some crucial bit of information slip that might have helped us or the police trip up the murderer.

Unfortunately, no matter how I prodded, no one offered up a better suspect or motive for their killing Lord Rockham than Ada. That being said, no one seemed to be aware of the marquess's sudden religious conversion, either, whenever we speculated on the funeral proceedings or which church it was likely to take place at. But they were more than happy to share their opinions of the infamous couple. They were all "frightfully fond of them, of course," but that didn't stop them from wielding their tongues like blades, displaying their evident animosity, particularly toward Ada.

I did my best not to roll my eyes whenever these trite refrains were uttered, though as the afternoon wore on, this grew more and more difficult. I couldn't resist glancing at Sidney in shared frustration. For his part, though he tried to be charming and coax information from our guests, I could tell what a strain this socialization was for him. Especially on the heels of learning of his friend's death. The flippant, witty remarks that had come so easily to him before the war now seemed forced. That is, when he bothered to reply with more than a nod or a single word at all.

Not that that stopped the ladies from fawning over him regardless. If possible, his brooding melancholy and intense reserve might actually be more appealing, particularly when coupled with his dark good looks. He was certainly more tolerant in hearing them out when they expressed their alarm over the murder, where before he would have excused himself, having little time or patience for what he would have classified as feminine melodrama.

By the time Sadie had ushered the last of our guests through the door, I was ready to scream from the pointless tedium. Everyone seemed to have the same questions, the same spiteful tidbits to share, and no one had anything of use to tell me. As the latch clicked shut, I swiveled to face Sidney where he lounged in one of the bergère chairs. He was watching me with a glimmer of amusement in his eyes. Apparently my exasperation had not gone unnoticed.

"Please tell me you gleaned some valuable piece of information from all that nonsense."

"I'm afraid not, darling."

With a frustrated sigh, I sank down onto the edge of the sofa across from him.

"Not unless you want to know how terribly frightened half the female population of London is that the killer will come for them next."

I glared at him before quipping, "Only half?"

The corners of his mouth flexed. "Yes, well, I suspect many of them are merely starved for care and attention, and willing to feign a greater fear than they feel in order to get it."

That he'd been this insightful surprised me. Not that he was incapable of such thoughtfulness. He'd never been an unfeeling boar. But he'd also never paid much mind as to why women, in particular, might behave the way they did. That he did so now testified to the fact that not all the changes in him were bad.

"I did have another thought," he remarked before I could form a response. "Not that any of them were his greatest friends, but none of the people here today mentioned anything about his conversion to Catholicism whenever we prodded around it. And you would think such a juicy morsel of gossip would not have gone unnoted. They were more interested in discussing whether his bloody horses would still run at Doncaster tomorrow."

"I had a similar thought," I admitted, crossing one leg over the other. "Still, I find it difficult to imagine Deacon fabricated the entire matter. Not when it could so easily be disproved."

"If anyone knows the truth of the matter, I suspect it would be his first wife. Wouldn't Rockham have needed to inform her of the annulment?"

"Not necessarily. Rockham was never that considerate about anything else. But you're right. She is far more likely to know something than anyone else." I contemplated the matter for a moment longer before glancing at the clock. "I'm going to pay her a call," I declared, rising to my feet. "The hour is not yet so late, and I know Calliope will agree to see me even if it is."

"You'll also avoid that flock of well-wishers," he added drolly.

Yes, there was more than one advantage to visiting outside of society's proscribed calling hours.

I leaned down to press a kiss to his cheek, catching a whiff of his musky cologne. "I won't be long."

I straightened my appearance in the mirror and tossed a few things in my handbag before popping into the kitchen to have a quick word with Sadie. My steps were brought up short by the sight of her seated at the table, her shoulders slumped wearily. A twinge of guilt moved through me at the realization all of our unexpected guests had run her ragged this afternoon, fetching and preparing, in between answering the door and the telephone. And I'd not given her a single thought.

When she lifted her head to find me arrested in the doorway, she leapt to her feet. "My apologies, Mrs. Kent. I didn't mean—"

"Heavens, no, Sadie," I interrupted her, moving forward. "*Please,* sit down. You've unquestionably earned a respite."

When still she hovered uncertainly, I realized there was nothing for it but to sit myself; then she would have to follow suit. "I'm the one who should be apologizing. I had no idea we would be descended upon by the droves." I sighed. "Though, in hindsight, I should have expected it."

"It's no bother, ma'am."

But it was. It had been selfish of me not to hire additional staff now that the war was over and Sidney had made his miraculous return. She was doing the job of several servants—cleaning, cooking, maintaining my clothing, answering the door and telephone. I had even seen her ironing and brushing Sidney's suits.

"Sadie, I believe it's time we hire some additional staff."

Her eyes widened with sudden panic. "Are you not happy with me? Have I not met your standards?"

"Oh, no, no, no," I forestalled her. "That's not what I meant. You have been exemplary, and so very patient. There's no doubt of that. And I shall continue to leave the cleaning and the running of the kitchen to you, for that is what you would like, isn't it? But it is past time for me to find a separate lady's maid, and Mr. Kent most certainly needs his own valet."

At first Sadie didn't speak, merely stared at the table before her, her hands pleating the fabric of her apron in her lap. When she did dare to lift her gaze, it was with some trepidation. "Will you expect me to manage them?"

"No, but I also don't want you allowing them to boss you about. You'll each have your separate domains. Though I do expect them to be willing to lend a hand and prepare tea or fetch and carry when necessary, and I'll make that clear to them." And perhaps I should start addressing her by her last name, as well, as a sign of respect. Sadie had worked fine when it was just the two of us, but now it would be more appropriate to call her by her surname.

She nodded, and I guessed at the source of her continued uneasiness. "You needn't share anything about yourself you don't wish to," I said. "Heaven knows, I value my privacy." A corner of my mouth curled wryly. "Not that having my photograph splashed all over the papers affords me much of it. But I empathize nonetheless."

She reached out to straighten the fold of the towel resting on the table before her and cleared her throat. "Will you wish me to live in?"

Ah, so that was her chief concern. "No, our arrangement can continue as it always has. You'll simply be relieved of some of your duties."

Her shoulders seemed to lower in relief, and I felt a renewed stirring of curiosity, wondering exactly what or who she returned to every night. But I tamped it down, unwilling to pry. Not when I'd just promised her I wouldn't.

Before I could give in to the urge, I pushed to my feet and glanced around at the trays stacked with cups and plates. "Once you've finished, take the rest of the evening off. Mr. Kent and I can dine out." In truth, we did so more often than we stayed in, and I didn't smell anything cooking, so it seemed safe to assume in all the hubbub she'd had no time to begin preparing it.

"Thank you, ma'am."

"And, Sadie," I turned back to say, but then hesitated, wondering if I was about to overstep. "In the future, please let me know if you need anything, either here or . . . elsewhere."

A guarded look entered her eyes, and I smiled softly, trying to ease her worries.

"For all that I'm said to be remarkably observant, sometimes I overlook the things I shouldn't."

She nodded, and I trusted she understood what I meant.

CHAPTER 7

Calliope lived in a tastefully elegant house on a quiet street in Belgravia. One that was about a quarter of the size of her former residence with Lord Rockham on Grosvenor Square. But for all its loss of grandeur, her new home far exceeded the old in comfort and charm. It was a genuine reflection of its owner, and far more to her liking, I knew.

After hustling me inside, past the pair of photographers standing along the pavement, her butler left me waiting in the drawing room for less than a minute before ushering me up to the sitting room attached to Calliope's boudoir. From her appearance—devoid of jewelry, her dark hair partially undone, and her feet tucked into slippers—I knew I had interrupted her as she began to prepare for some evening engagement, but she came forward eagerly to embrace me.

"I've been waiting for you to call." She stepped back to survey me with warm amber eyes. "But you were wise to wait."

"A flood of condolence callers? I suspected as much." I tilted my head to study her features for any sign of strain. "I'm sorry for your loss."

Her mouth curled into a humorless smile. "But that's not why you called. I know." She led me over to the dainty Italian-painted settee tucked between two Kent side tables, each one holding a vase filled with gardenias. Their pleasing scent perfumed the room. Above us on the wall hung a Canaletto painting of Venice.

She sank nimbly down onto the settee, lightly draping an arm across its back. For all that Calliope was one of the tallest women I'd ever met, she was also one of the most graceful. "I can hardly believe it." She lifted a hand to her forehead. "Rockham shot dead? It seems impossible."

I could appreciate her shocked disbelief. "How did you find out?" I hoped the news hadn't been delivered by one of her callers.

"Croyde returned home with the news this morning," she said, referring to her son. "I thought at first he was playing one of his horrible jests, but he was so very pale, and obviously shaken. I don't think he's ready to become the marquess. His father hadn't prepared him for it."

I noticed she didn't ascribe feelings of grief to her son, but then I wasn't surprised. There had been little love between the marquess and his heir. Still, he must be feeling some sense of loss. For ill or for better, Rockham *had* been his father.

"And then a Chief Inspector Thoreau came to visit me this afternoon." Delivered in her flat American accent, the words were even more leading.

"Did he?" I murmured, admiring the inspector's speed.

"Indeed. I had to excuse myself from my guests to speak with him in the back parlor, and you can imagine the amount of speculation that stirred." Her finely shaped eyebrows arched. "I take it you're already acquainted with the man."

"I met him at Rockham House this morning. He seems competent. And discreet. At least, as far as his position allows him to be."

"Yes, well, competent or not, I trust that's not going to stop you from doing a bit of your own inquiring."

"What makes you say that?"

Her mouth tightened into a moue as her gaze flicked up and down my form. "You're here now, aren't you?"

I could have insisted I was there merely as a friend, but she happened to be correct, and I wasn't about to insult her by denying it. "You don't mind, do you?"

Her expression softened and she reached out a hand to touch

mine where it lay on the chintz cushion between us. "On the contrary, I'm very glad you are."

I blinked in astonishment. "You are?"

She nodded. "Oh, I know you are almost certainly investigating at the behest of Ada, and I don't begrudge you that, for it sounds as if she needs *someone* assisting her. From all accounts, the facts point squarely at her as the guilty party, and heaven knows, I myself would have liked to shoot Rockham a time or two when I was married to him. He is . . . *was* a very provoking man, to put it mildly."

For all that her words were empathetic, her eyes were sad, her face drawn, telling a tale of their own as she turned toward the window, where the evening sun pierced through the pale azure curtains. She might not have liked Rockham. She might be glad they were divorced. But she still mourned his loss. I supposed after twenty years of marriage and bearing two of his children, it would be impossible not to feel *something* at his passing.

She inhaled a deep breath. Her normally bright eyes were now dull. "But I know you will be fair, whatever the truth may be." Her gaze dropped for the briefest of moments before daring to meet mine again. "And I suspect there are things we do not yet know, things that might still come to light that could change our thinking."

I leaned forward, trying to read between the lines of what she was saying. "You know something."

"I know many things," she replied evasively, but then checked herself with a sigh. She closed her eyes, almost as if to hide from whatever truth she held. "But yes, I know some things that make me quail at the possibility of a competent Scotland Yard inspector prying into them."

When she lifted her gaze, I could see fear reflected there, but not for herself. And I could easily guess who.

"Lord Croyde," I guessed.

She nodded slowly. "Yes, my son has a temper, and he very nearly hated his father."

My brow furrowed, surprised by this calm reply, for it did not suggest the same level of anxiety as her previous statement. I was about to question her further when the door to her sitting room burst open.

"Fanny is refusing to dress me," her daughter sniped as she rushed forward in a flurry of rose-scented satin. "She says you gave orders that I would be staying in. You cannot actually be insisting that I remain at home and pretend to grieve? No one would believe it, anyway." The young lady's eyes flashed with fire, but I could tell by the lines across her forehead and the brackets around her mouth that she was lying. She might not wish to mourn her father, or for others to think she was, but deep inside she was still distraught.

Calliope's gaze slid toward me, as if to remind her daughter they weren't alone, but Lady Gertrude merely cast me a look of annoyance, her scowl deepening.

"Yes, I can," Calliope replied calmly. "It's only proper."

"What rot!" she snapped. "*You're* going out."

"To a private dinner with Armand and his parents," she said, naming her fiancé. "Not a ball with hundreds in attendance. No one can question the decorum of my intentions. But there will be outraged gossip if you present yourself at the Cowper's."

Gertrude stamped her foot. "I don't care what a few stuffy matrons think I should or shouldn't be doing. Gerald is going to be there, and I want to go."

"Mr. Waters will understand, dear. I doubt he expects you to attend."

"Yes, he does. I told him I would."

A deep furrow formed between Calliope's eyes, though her voice remained even. "And when precisely did you do that?"

"This afternoon." Gertrude's mouth clamped shut, realizing she'd revealed more than she'd intended to. Then she arched her chin upward. "I met him in the garden. He was concerned about me."

"Then why didn't he call at the front door as everyone else did?" her mother challenged.

"Because we knew you'd never allow us to be alone."

"For good reason."

She rolled her eyes. "Mother, you're such a flat tire. No one cared during the war whether I saw him alone."

"Yes, they did. But there were more pressing matters to be dealt with than your flighty tendencies." Calliope frowned. "And this is what's become of it."

I felt some sympathy for Gertrude. To be granted such freedom during the war and then have it taken away again, to be expected to return to the prewar world of rules, restrictions, and chaperones was difficult. But another part of me was appalled by her behavior. The difference in our ages was only four years, but in terms of experience it seemed a lifetime. Gertrude had been sheltered, cossetted, and frankly spoiled. I couldn't blame Calliope and the other mothers for wishing to protect their daughters, but in some cases it might have been better had they not.

Gertrude cast her a withering glare before turning to march back through the door. "I'm going."

"No, you're not." Her mother's voice brooked no argument, but her daughter whirled around to do so, anyway.

"Yes, I am!"

"Your father just died. A week or two of circumspection is the least you owe him."

Her heavily lashed eyes flared wide. "A week! I am not sitting around in this house for a week!"

"Darling, it's not so very long."

"Yes, it is. And how can you even suggest I owe him anything after the way he treated you. The way he treated Gerald!" Her hands clamped into fists. "I *hate* him. And I shall never forgive him for the way he treated all of us."

Calliope exhaled a weary breath, making me guess this was a familiar refrain. "Never is a long time, darling. And your father is no longer here to care how you feel."

If he ever did, I added to myself silently. At least, *I* had never seen Rockham display the least bit of concern for other people's feelings.

Gertrude's lip quivered, and I thought she might begin to sob, but she inhaled a swift breath, her eyes rekindling their fury. "And he's no longer here to stand in the way of my marrying Gerald." With that, she turned on her heel and strode through the door, closing it with a slam.

Calliope closed her eyes wearily before offering me a strained smile. "I apologize for that." Her gaze dropped to her lap, where she smoothed a hand over the burgundy silk. "Gertrude is taking her father's death harder than she would like to admit."

I nodded. Gertrude was very angry. And she was trying to mask her hurt and grief with even more anger. But had that anger also driven her to do something she might regret? Was her anger also masking something else?

"That's what you meant, isn't it?"

Calliope slowly lifted her gaze to meet mine.

"About other things coming to light. Her father didn't approve of this Mr. Waters."

She nodded. "Rockham told Gertrude he would never allow the marriage. And Gertrude . . ." She lifted a hand to her temple. "Well, she has her father's temper."

When she hesitated to say the words, I guessed. "She said she'd kill him if he refused Gerald's request for her hand."

She slumped. "Something like that." But then she sat upright again. "Oh, but I don't believe Gertrude would ever actually hurt her father. Mr. Waters either." Her brow furrowed. "He hasn't the spine." Her eyes turned anxious. "But if Inspector Thoreau should learn of it . . ."

"He might not come to the same conclusion."

She seemed reassured by the fact I understood. However, I was not. And her next words did not ease my concerns any further.

"So, you see why I'm glad you're looking into the matter. Maybe you can direct the inspector away from us as well. As you're doing with Ada."

I frowned, feeling vaguely insulted that was what Calliope thought I was doing. "I'm not directing the inspector away from Ada. And I won't direct him away for you, either. A man like Inspector Thoreau would not take kindly to such interference. If anything, it would only make him more determined to uncover what I was trying to hide."

"Oh, yes. I suppose you're right." She pressed her fingers to her lips, considering what I'd said. Then her expression turned wary. "Oh, but you won't tell him what I've just told you, will you?" she pleaded, grasping my hand. "It was spoken in confidence. I thought you might help me. Please, Verity."

I pressed my other hand firmly over hers where it clung to mine, silencing her. "Have you told me all?"

She hesitated, and I arched a single eyebrow in challenge. Our friendship and my empathy for her predicament would guarantee my silence only so far. In truth, I should share everything with Inspector Thoreau immediately, but I also knew the damage any whiff of scandal could cause to a debutante's reputation. It sounded as if Gertrude was already courting it, but being caught alone with a man could easily be remedied if an engagement swiftly followed. Being linked to an inquest of murder could never be undone, even if the suspicions were later proved to be false.

However, if Gertrude or Gerald Waters could be the culprit, I wasn't about to shelter them from Scotland Yard. Not when Ada could be forced to take the fall for their crime.

"Where was Lady Gertrude last night between midnight and three o'clock?" I pressed.

"We returned from a dinner party around one o'clock, and then she went to bed," Calliope replied.

"And you're certain she stayed there?"

"Well, I didn't look in on her, but . . ." She inhaled, cutting off her own dithering words. "Yes," she stated decisively, drawing herself up taller. "Yes, she stayed there until I summoned her at almost nine o'clock to tell her the news of her father's passing. You can check with her maid, but I'm sure she'll confirm everything I've told you."

I nodded, knowing she was correct about that, even if what her maid told me wasn't the absolute truth. Calliope was a good and fair employer, and that usually inspired a loyal staff. Her maid would repeat whatever she was instructed to.

"Then, as long as you've been completely forthcoming with me," I qualified, allowing her the opportunity to correct herself or further elaborate, but she gazed back at me resolutely. "Then I will keep the matter of Lady Gertrude's temper to myself. Mr. Waters, on the other hand . . . I don't suppose you know what his whereabouts were."

"No, but he resides with his elder brother, Lord Larchmont." Her voice was crisp. "I suspect he shall be able to tell you what you wish to know."

"Then I shall do my best to establish whether Mr. Waters has an alibi before doing anything hasty."

Recognizing my presence was no longer welcome—not after I'd refused to accept her children's innocence purely based on her word alone—I knew it would be best to leave. Unfortunately, there was still another matter I needed to address.

"This may seem like an odd question, but do you know whether Lord Rockham intended to convert to Roman Catholicism?" I searched her stony face for any reaction. "Mr. Deacon claimed he was in the process of doing so, but I haven't been able to corroborate it." When her posture relaxed and she turned aside, I pressed her further. "I have no greater liking for Deacon than you or Ada do, but I have a hard time believing he fabricated such an assertion whole cloth."

She chuckled mirthlessly. "No, Deacon might be an old carbuncle, but he would never lie about something like that." She sighed, glancing back at me. "Yes, Rockham was in the process of converting."

I felt faintly stunned to have such a revelation confirmed, and the implications of it.

"I'm sure there must be some sort of correspondence about it in his effects—letters to a bishop or the Pope, something of that nature." She waved her hands. "I don't know how it all works. And I'm sure you've correctly guessed that the only reason I'd been informed of it was because of Rockham's intention to have our marriage annulled by the Catholic Church. Though, of course, he could not do so civilly. Croyde remains his son and heir."

"Do you know who else knew about it?"

"His solicitor and private secretary," she speculated. "Whomever he was corresponding with in the Catholic Church. But if you're asking me whether he'd told Ada"—she shook her head—"I don't know. It's true, he was never the most forthcoming of husbands, and I doubt that's changed. But one would have hoped he'd shared something of such magnitude with her."

"Yes, one would have hoped," I muttered, wondering again if Ada had known. And if she would admit to it if she had.

"I'm sorry," Calliope murmured, drawing me from my troubled thoughts. "I suppose that doesn't help Ada's case, does it? Which I'm sure was Deacon's motivation in telling you. He never liked me, but he absolutely despises Ada."

"And he takes no pains to hide it," I added, sliding forward to rise to my feet.

She surprised me by pressing a hand to my sleeve to halt me. "Be careful of that one, Verity."

I searched her shadowed eyes, wondering what she meant.

"Deacon was unfailingly loyal to Rockham. He would lie for him in life." She lowered her hand. "And I can't imagine that has changed in death."

I nodded, though I didn't grasp how that would impact all of this. Wouldn't Deacon wish his employer's killer be caught?

Unless the truth would reflect poorly on Rockham. What then? Would he frame Ada?

Whatever the case, a chat with Deacon was undoubtedly in order.

CHAPTER 8

I returned to our flat to find Sidney waiting for me.

"Ada telephoned."

I paused in removing my gloves and turned to face him where he lounged in the doorway to the drawing room, his hands tucked into the pockets of his trousers. From the sardonic expression on his face, I knew this announcement did not herald good news. "Did Inspector Thoreau return?"

"Yes. From amidst her frantic monologue, I managed to glean the fact her fingerprints had been taken, and attempted to reassure her on that point, since such a thing was bound to happen."

I opened my mouth to thank him, but he wasn't finished.

"But that's not why she called."

I gazed at him in question, wondering what could have brought such a cynical glint to his eyes.

"She wished to postpone our engagement to attend the Embassy Club this evening until tomorrow."

I blinked in shock before blurting. "Is she mad?! She can't venture out to a nightclub on her lover's arm the night after her husband was murdered? Or even the night after that? Does she *want* Scotland Yard to arrest her?"

"I wouldn't know, darling. You're far better acquainted with her than I am."

Ignoring this quip, I turned to face the entry table, wondering if I should ring up Ada and try to talk some sense into her. But then I caught a glimpse of my drawn expression in the mirror hanging above it and decided tomorrow would be soon enough for that. I'd frankly had enough of Ada and her troubles for one day. Particularly if she couldn't exercise an ounce of common sense.

I dropped my gloves on the tray and turned to stride past Sidney into the drawing room. He didn't speak as I passed him, merely followed me inside, waiting until I'd poured myself a drink before commenting further. Not so long ago, I would have needed any number of drinks to pass an evening and numb the pain. Something I had been ashamed for my husband to discover. Now, I didn't crave the same forgetfulness, though I still welcomed the cool edge a gin rickey could give me at moments like this. And thankfully, Sidney had considerately filled the ice bucket.

"So what did Rockham's first wife have to say?" he asked as I took an experimental sip, then added another splash of gin.

"More than I expected. Including adding another suspect to our list."

Sidney's eyebrows arched in interest as he sat down on the sofa, and I shared what I'd learned about Lady Gertrude and her fiancé, as well as the fact that Calliope had confirmed Rockham's intentions to convert to Catholicism.

He listened in silence, his fingers rustling the pages of the book he must have been reading before I returned. When I finished, he carefully voiced another question. "Do you still believe Ada didn't know?"

I sighed heavily, sinking deeper into my chair. "I don't know what I believe. Not if she's prepared to make a spectacle of herself by going to the Embassy with Ardmore less than forty-eight hours after Rockham was killed." I stared up at the pomegranate damask wallpaper and then shook my head. I didn't want to contemplate Ada's integrity, or lack thereof. Not when my feelings about her were so muddled. "What of Gerald Waters?" I asked him. "Are you acquainted with him? Or his brother, Lord Larchmont?"

"Larchmont's a few years my senior. Capital tennis player." His voice stirred with enthusiasm. "But I can't say I know the chap by more than a passing acquaintance. And I only know his younger brother by sight." He tilted his head. "But Crispin is friendly with Larchmont."

This did not surprise me. "Yes, well, Mr. Ballantyne seems to be friendly with everyone."

His eyes warmed with humor. "I'll see if Crispin can help me scrounge up an acquaintance to Waters if that will help. Find out if the man is a likely culprit." His brow furrowed. "Though I can tell you that at least part of his interest in Rockham's daughter is probably monetary. The Larchmont finances have been strapped for some time, and I can't imagine the war helped. As a younger son, Waters won't be receiving much of an income, if any."

"Maybe that's why Calliope didn't seem happy about her daughter's fixed interest. She never said so in so many words, but I could tell she wasn't best pleased by the possible match. If Waters is a fortune hunter, then that would explain it."

The ice clinked in my glass as I drained it of the remainder of my cocktail. My skin flushed as it always did when imbibing in my first drink—a curse of my auburn locks—and my head began to swim pleasantly as I reached over to set my glass on the table beside me. I hadn't eaten since almost midday, despite all the food Sadie had prepared, so it wasn't surprising, but now I felt famished.

"I gave Sadie the evening off, so I suppose we should go in search of our dinner," I told my husband, though the last thing my limbs felt like doing was moving. "By the way, I told Sadie, or rather Mrs. Yarrow, that we would be hiring some additional staff. At least, a lady's maid and a valet."

Sidney nodded. "I suppose it's past time we did so."

He didn't question my failure to hire a new maid over a year ago, after I sent the last one back to my parents when I could no longer tolerate her spying for my mother. He didn't need to, for he knew enough now about my life during the war, and the dark days that had followed my receipt of the telegram informing me of his death, to know why I'd desired solitude. The same as I didn't question his failure to hire a valet upon his return three months prior.

He lifted his gaze to the Morisot painting above the hearth. "I wonder how old Nimble is getting on."

His batman during the war was neither old nor nimble. Nor was that his real name. But I'd never heard my husband, or anyone else for that matter, refer to him as anything else. I'd only discovered it by chance when he called on me a few months after Sidney's death to pay his respects, and even then he'd assured me that everyone called him Nimble. Had his visit not been to mark such a solemn occasion, I would have asked him how he'd come by this sobriquet, for there was obviously some story behind it. The young man was about as far from sprightly as I could imagine. I had heard his footsteps clumping down the hall to and from our flat, and he had that habit that polite, large men often do of trying to confine themselves to the smallest space possible, as if they live in constant fear of breaking something or knocking something over. Or perhaps it was a by-product of the war, where the dugouts and trenches were small and narrow, and showing one's head above the parapet could earn you a sniper's bullet.

I'd thought him an odd choice for my husband's personal servant, but after speaking to him for a few moments I better understood. Sidney could never abide idle chatter, and Nimble was spare with his words. However, I also detected a wry sense of humor lurking beneath his reserve. One I knew Sidney would appreciate. And given the fact I'd never heard my husband complain about his batman, I assumed Nimble performed his tasks adequately.

He was also loyal to Sidney—a trait he and I both prized. For a moment during that visit, I'd thought Nimble was going to give way to emotion, which would only have made me do so as well, so I had quickly turned the subject, for both our sakes.

"I don't know," I told Sidney. "But I'm sure he'd like to hear from you." He'd been just as misled as the rest of us, believing Sidney dead for fifteen months.

His voice was quiet, perhaps reflecting on the same thing. "I'll have to track him down."

I wanted to ask why he'd not done so before, but hesitated, not wanting to add any more strain to the evening.

"Did you wish to hire anyone else?" he said.

Like most gentlemen, who preferred to leave the hiring of staff to their wives, butlers, and stewards, I knew he had little interest in such matters. So for him to inquire such a thing either meant he was trying to make an effort to please me, or he was determined not to discuss his former batman further. Knowing my husband, I suspected it was the latter.

"Well, that depends on whether we intend to do much entertaining," I answered. "If so, we should probably consider engaging a butler, as well as a maid to assist Mrs. Yarrow."

"Whatever you wish, darling."

I nodded and lowered my gaze to my feet, ostensibly to check the lace of my navy leather Derby shoes, but the truth was I felt vaguely disconcerted. I hadn't much considered my life after the war, or what I wished to do with it. When I'd still believed Sidney to be dead, it had merely yawned before me like a great gaping maw—something to be blotted out and forgotten by whatever means necessary. But now that Sidney was returned, now that our marriage was no longer in immediate danger of crumbling to ashes, I should have been making plans for our future. Instead, I was almost as determined to ignore it as before.

The idea of filling my days and nights with nothing but an endless round of tedious teas, morning calls, and society events—as I'd expected to do before the war—no longer appealed to me. I supposed my time with the Secret Service was to blame for that. I was no longer content with such a life now that I'd known adventure and made important contributions. I wondered how many other women were chafing under their enforced return to their prewar life. How many soldiers were missing the excitement and comradery of the battlefield, no matter its danger and deprivations, when faced with the drudgery of their normal life?

I glanced up at Sidney, finding him watching me. Was he?

I summoned up a smile. "Dinner?"

He pushed to his feet and then crossed to help me rise. "I suppose we could still join the Summerville party at the Savoy," he suggested. Our original plans for the evening.

"No, let's go somewhere quiet." I lifted a hand to my temple. "The last thing I feel like doing is changing into an evening gown and rehashing Rockham's murder with another three dozen people. Particularly when there are certain to be reporters and photographers hanging about." I didn't trust Freda Summerville not to have informed them of our place on her guest list simply to ensure her party made a splash in the society papers.

He pressed a reassuring hand to the small of my back. "Spiro's, then," he stated, naming a small restaurant only a few blocks away that had become one of our favorites—the food being excellent, and the staff and location discreet.

We walked arm in arm to the entrance hall, where I paused to check my appearance in the mirror. He'd just reached for his hat hanging on the hook on the wall, when there was a sudden knock on the door.

I turned to him in question, curious who could be paying us a visit at this hour. His eyes reflected the same puzzlement as he reached for the handle.

A petite woman stood on the other side of the door attired nearly from head to toe in a rich shade of brown, grasping a handbag tightly in front of her body. The wide brim of her hat forced her to tilt her head upward to peer at Sidney. "Good evening," she murmured uncertainly. "Is this . . ." Her gaze shifted to me, where I stood beyond my husband's shoulder. "Verity," she gasped in relief.

Sidney shifted to the side as I moved forward. "Irene, is that you? Well, come inside, darling." I took hold of her arm, pulling her nearer as my husband swung the door shut. "I received your message, but I'm afraid in all the hubbub I completely forgot. But what has brought you here at this hour? *Not* that I'm not pleased to see you."

"Daphne suggested I call on you, that you wouldn't mind,

and . . . oh! Were you just leaving?" she exclaimed, seeing the hat in Sidney's hand. "Oh, I'm so sorry. I knew I should have called first. I'll come back tomorrow."

I pressed a staying hand to her arm, startled to see her so flustered. The Irene Shaw I knew had always been cool and confident, even with a colonel breathing down her neck demanding information on a suspected German spy from counterintelligence's Registry, where she worked in MI5 with Daphne during the war. Something must have truly upset her to ruffle her so.

"Now is fine," I assured her, wrapping an arm around her shoulders. "Come into the drawing room and tell me what this is all about."

I shared a swift speaking glance with Sidney, who appeared to have already sized up the situation and was returning his hat to its hook. He followed us into the room, crossing toward the sideboard to pour Irene a drink while I settled her on one of the emeraldine sofas.

"You're certain?" she demurred. "Because I don't want to ruin your plans."

"There are no plans. So tell me." I darted another look at my husband. "Or would you rather do so privately?"

She followed my gaze to Sidney as he moved forward to hand her a drink—two fingers of brandy from the looks of it. "Oh, well." She scrutinized his placid expression. "Seeing as how you both exposed those traitors on Umbersea, I suppose he now knows something of what you really did during the war?" She arched her eyebrows in question.

"Yes, more or less," I replied vaguely, uncertain whether she approved.

She nodded. "Then he can stay."

I watched as she took a fortifying sip of the amber spirit, nerves stirring in awareness throughout my body. If Irene was concerned with how much Sidney knew about my service during the war, then that meant whatever had unsettled her somehow harkened back to it. Her gray eyes darted around the room, landing on almost anything except us.

Cradling the glass between her two hands in her lap, she ventured to speak. "You may or may not recall, but I had a half sister. Esther."

Not having worked closely with Irene, I had not known this. In truth, she was more Daphne's friend than mine, though we had dined together on occasion at the members-only restaurant near Waterloo House that offered discounted meals to those of us working for military intelligence.

Her eyes flicked upward to meet mine before dropping again, the fingers of her right hand anxiously circling the rim of her glass. "She was killed about a fortnight ago."

"I'm so sorry," I murmured, taking note of her choice in verb.

She nodded once before pressing on. "The police say it was a burglary. That she must have come home and surprised the thief, and he struck and killed her."

Her words broke off as her lips clamped together, her throat working as she struggled to control her emotions.

"But you don't think so," I guessed.

She shook her head. "Nothing was taken. At least, nothing that I could tell. Her bureau was overturned and a few boxes in her wardrobe were dumped out, but the jewelry in the case on her dresser was untouched, and her silver-backed hairbrush and comb lay tangled in the mess on the floor." Her voice grew stronger with each sentence. "If it was a burglary, wouldn't they have taken *something?*"

"She might have startled them before they could," Sidney answered. "If they struck out to stop her from catching them, and unintentionally killed her, they might have panicked and fled." His brow furrowed. "But then why would the bureau have been toppled and the boxes in the wardrobe be tipped over? Not when any common burglar worth his salt would have gone straight for the jewelry case."

"It sounds more like they were looking for something specifically," I ventured carefully, uncertain how Irene would react to such a suggestion. "Something they may or may not have found."

Irene sat up taller. "I wondered the same thing. And I've searched her rooms. Multiple times. But if they left whatever it is behind, I haven't found it."

"Do you have any idea what it might have been?"

She shook her head, lowering her gaze again to her glass. "Except . . . well, I did wonder if it had anything to do with her war work." Her eyes when she lifted them to meet mine were guarded.

"What did Esther do during the war? Was she . . . one of us?" Part of the Nameless Club of women who staffed the halls of military intelligence and other civil service bureaus, but were pushed aside and almost shunned by the government who had employed us in such droves during the war, eager to replace us with the returning men.

"She worked for the Royal Mail," she began tentatively, more from habit, I suspected, than a reluctance to tell me.

"In the censorship department?" If her position with the postal service was sensitive, then it was likely that's where she worked.

"Yes and no." Her gaze darted to Sidney. "It was her job to read the green honor envelope letters sent home by soldiers from the front."

If she'd expected my husband to react adversely to this, she had no need for concern. As an officer, he was well aware of the system. After all, it had been part of his job to censor his soldiers' letters home to be certain they hadn't allowed information to slip through that could put their company, or the army in general, at jeopardy, or hurt the country's morale. If, for whatever reason, a soldier didn't want their letter to be read by their commanding officer, they had been allowed to place it inside a green honor envelope. By doing so, the soldier was supposed to give his solemn word that nothing of a sensitive nature was contained within. But he would have been a fool not to expect someone was going to check the contents before forwarding it on to the recipient. And if what Irene was telling us was true, then Esther Shaw had been one of those special censors.

"How could that have gotten her killed?" Sidney asked calmly.

"She confided in me once how bizarre some of the information contained in those letters was. She said most of it was very routine—private matters or complaints that made it obvious why the soldier did not want such information read by his commanding officer. But once in a while the contents contained within could be disturbing, or almost nonsensical. The nonsensical ones she passed on to her superiors on suspicion of a hidden code. But the others were more difficult to determine, and it didn't help that her managers didn't want to be bothered by matters of little consequence. When there was any doubt, she was merely supposed to black out the suspicious words and move on. I know she worried constantly she had missed something."

I frowned. "Did she give you any examples of what she meant by 'disturbing'?"

She lowered her glass after taking another sip. "No, she'd already revealed more than she was supposed to, but she balked at telling me specifics."

I glanced at Sidney, curious what he thought of the matter, but his expression betrayed only polite interest and nothing more. "What type of person was Esther? Was she very staid and refined? Was she shocked easily?"

"No more than most of us with proper upbringings were when the war began." She chuckled under her breath. "And that certainly wore off quickly."

My lips smiled reflexively in agreement. The very idea of our having this conversation five years ago was unthinkable. Even now, if my mother ever heard me speak the words I was about to utter she would faint dead away. "So when Esther speaks of 'disturbing' things, you don't think she means infidelities or body lice or venereal disease?" All three problems had been rampant in the trenches and the garrison towns with their brothels.

"No, and that wouldn't have kept her awake at night, making her wonder whether the information would cost our soldiers their lives or tip off the enemy."

Sidney sank deeper into the sofa across from us. "But you think something she read got her killed?"

She exhaled a heavy breath, leaning forward to set her drink on the low table before us. "I don't know. Maybe?" She scraped a hand across her brow. "All I know is that *someone* murdered my sister," her voice was strained, but vehement. "And Scotland Yard's explanation doesn't make any *sense*. Esther wasn't the type to court trouble. I can't think of any reason someone would attack her. *Unless* . . . she read something she wasn't supposed to." She waved her hand, clearly having given this a great deal of thought. "Or censored some piece of information that someone had desperately needed to get through."

"But how would they know she was the one to censor it?" I pointed out, knowing such things were all done anonymously. "And why now? The armistice was called ten months ago."

Her face was etched with lines of frustration.

"It's not that I doubt your intuition," I assured her. "But I don't apprehend how it could be possible."

"Maybe they just found out," she suggested. "Maybe she told another colleague, and they told someone else, thinking it was of no consequence. There are always people who talk. People who think they know what actually requires discretion, and with who, and what does not."

My gaze met Sidney's, for I knew this all too well. It was from one such colleague at the Secret Service that Sidney inveigled the true nature of my war work. I'd been forbidden from telling anyone about my role with military intelligence, even my husband. But this chap, having been a friend of Sidney's from Oxford, had decided it would do no harm for Sidney to know. Providentially, he was right, though it had made Sidney question whether my ultimate loyalty would be to him or to my country. Even so, I was still furious that my husband persisted in protecting the fellow's identity.

"Whatever the case, I know it's a long shot." Irene leaned toward me, grasping my hand. "But will you please look into it for me. I know it's more likely than not that you won't find anything, that maybe I'm clutching at straws. But I'll feel better, I . . ." She swallowed before continuing. "I'll feel like Esther will rest better if I know someone else inquired about it." Her eyes pleaded with me. "Please, Verity."

Faced with such a fraught entreaty, I couldn't very well say no. Not when my dearest friend Daphne had sent her to me. Not when Irene was one of us. So I nodded.

Her shoulders slumped in relief. "Oh, thank you." Her voice broke, and I worried that this, of all the things spoken between us, would make her dissolve in tears.

"I can't promise anything," I warned her.

"Of course," she replied, dabbing at her eyes.

"But I'll see what I can uncover."

I felt my husband's gaze on me, compelling me to look at him, but I kept my eyes locked with Irene's. It was safer that way.

"Have her rooms been rented?" I asked.

"No, I paid the rent for another fortnight, just in case . . ." She didn't finish that sentence, but it was clear she'd already been planning ahead.

"Then I'll visit them tomorrow and have a look around."

I gleaned several more details from Irene, as well as her address and how I might contact her, and then showed her to the door.

When I turned around, Sidney was hovering behind me. "Two inquiries in one day. My, aren't we enterprising."

There was no bite to his jest, but I felt my hackles begin to rise nonetheless. "Well, you heard her. I couldn't very well refuse."

His gaze softened. "Actually, you could have. And many would have. But I'm well aware that's not your nature." He arched his eyebrows. "Nor did I say you should have."

My defensiveness began to dissolve in the face of such calm acceptance, though I didn't know how to respond.

He stepped forward, wrapping his arms around my waist. "But I *am* saying that I'm not going to let you do this alone. Nor am I going to let your inclination to help and protect your friends beyond what is reasonable override your good sense."

"I exercise good sense," I protested.

"Usually," he agreed. "But you're also extremely loyal, and sometimes you place your dedication to others above your own safety." That he was speaking of the events in Belgium, when we'd both almost been shot, incinerated, and blown up, all in the pursuit of assisting a friend, was obvious. "I'm not saying that's a fault. But what kind of husband would I be if I didn't insist you also look after yourself?"

I flushed. "Well, when you put it that way . . ." I could hardly argue with him.

His lips curled into a smile. "Now, let's go find some dinner. Before someone else comes around asking you to solve a murder."

CHAPTER 9

The calendar might have turned over into September a week before, but summer, it seemed, had no intention of relinquishing its hold on the British Isles. And a warmer summer, I could not remember. It was only mid-morning, and I could already feel sweat gathering at the back of my hairline as the sun beat down through the open window of the cab as it rounded Grosvenor Square.

I exhaled a sigh of relief when a welcome gust of wind rustled the charcoal gray serge of my skirt as I climbed out of the motor-car under the shade of the Ionic-columned portico of the Marquess of Rockham's palatial mansion. Its white-gray façade of Portland stone shimmered in the light, while the drapes and curtains in the open windows on the upper floors billowed in the breeze. Here was one sign of the changes that Rockham's death had wrought.

I remembered Ada complaining some months past how the marquess had despised open windows. He absolutely refused to allow the sashes to be thrown back, even on the most stifling of days. For a woman like Ada, who had spent half her childhood along the Côte d'Azur, breathing in the sea breezes, this had been torturous. But now that he was gone, she could do as she pleased. At least, until her stepson took possession of the property.

Having been so thoroughly entrenched in his former employer's pocket, I doubted Deacon approved of this new development.

I glanced at the footman who had assisted me from my cab, wondering what the other servants thought. Dressed in a heavy, double-breasted coat, waistcoat, black tie, and trousers, I could only imagine how warm such attire must be in this weather. Surely the open windows were a welcome change.

The footman had noted me observing the windows and I smiled, not wanting him to think I objected. Not that it was any of my business either way, but members of society did have a tendency to think their opinion always mattered even when it didn't.

"Am I the first caller this morning, or have you been turning them away in droves?" I quipped, as we climbed the steps to the door, careful to keep my face forward, lest any photographers be lurking in the square across the street.

At first, he didn't seem to know how to respond. I judged him to be in his upper twenties—old enough to know better than to indulge in idle gossip, but still young enough to unbend a little. He followed the traditional mold of the best footmen, being tall, dark haired, and handsome, but not so handsome that a gentleman risked the females in his household falling in love with him upon first sight.

Once inside, I passed him my gloves and wide-brimmed hat, still waiting for him to reply. In the end, he chose not to answer my question directly, but still managed to communicate the answer.

"Her ladyship is not receiving visitors yet, but I can inquire."

"If I know Ada, she's still a slug-a-bed. No, there's no need to wake her. Actually, you're just the person I wished to speak with."

"Me?" he stammered.

"Yes." It had been a stroke of luck that Deacon had not been minding the door when I arrived, and I was not about to waste it. Not when he might forbid me from questioning the staff, or hover over us while I did. "I need to know if there was a footman on duty the night Lord Rockham was killed? I was led to believe Mr. Deacon had retired, but was anyone else left to mind the door?"

"Ah, no, ma'am," he stammered a response. "Mr. Deacon informed us that since his lordship and her ladyship were already home, there was no need for one of us to remain on duty. We were all right tired from the party that evening, and none of us were about to question the chance to catch a bit of extra kip."

His use of soldiers' slang made me suspect he'd served some time at the front, like most men his age and fitness. It was also something of an indication of his comfort level in speaking with me, even if initially I'd caught him off guard.

"Was Mr. Deacon the first to find the body?" I spoke softly, lest someone overhear us. Namely Deacon himself.

"Several of us heard the gunshot. It's not something you sleep through. Not after the war. But Mr. Deacon was the first to reach the study."

"He went directly to that room?"

"Yes, ma'am. We could see a light was on beneath the door."

"Did you see into the chamber?"

He shook his head. "Mr. Deacon wouldn't allow anyone else into the room. Told me to get dressed and go fetch Scotland Yard. That's how we knew his lordship had clicked it."

Deacon's insistence that the staff not trample all over the room and the evidence within was both admirable and suspicious. For if no one else was permitted to enter the study after him, what was to stop him from making changes to it?

"So you never saw into the room?" I confirmed.

"No."

A door opened somewhere on the floor above us, and we both glanced toward the landing at the top of the stairs on the other side of the cavernous hall.

"But Maisie did."

I glanced back at him in interest.

"She was at the head of the pack following Mr. Deacon. Would've gone in after him had he not stopped her."

I noted this, determined to talk to this Maisie later. I was curious whether she'd seen enough to be able to either confirm or deny the butler's description of the scene.

"Did you notice anything odd at the party? Other than Lady Rockham's distasteful jest at dinner," I qualified, the guarded look that entered his eyes plainly communicating what he was thinking of. "Any quarrels or glimpses of guests in places they shouldn't be?"

He shrugged. "Nothing beyond the normal gin-soaked squabbling and canoodling."

And almost every dinner party could claim those.

His eyes narrowed as he thought back. "But there was a gentleman who visited his lordship a few hours before the party. From the sounds of their raised voices they were arguing over something."

"Do you know what?" I asked eagerly.

We could hear the sound of footsteps approaching from the rear of the house; then Deacon turned the corner. Catching sight of us, his footsteps checked before he strode more determinedly toward us.

"I couldn't make it out," the footman replied hastily. "But Mr. Deacon announced him, and he stayed nearby. I'd wager he heard some of it."

Yes, but would he admit to it?

"One last question," I murmured as the butler was bearing down on us. "The revolver. Does anyone know how it ended up in Lady Rockham's chair at dinner?"

"No, ma'am."

"William," the butler intoned. "Lady Rockham has rung for a breakfast tray. See to it."

"Yes, sir."

"And after that, see to the silver. There are spots on it, and if you think I will allow such lax behavior just because his lordship is now deceased, you are sadly mistaken."

A corner of the footman's jaw leapt, but he responded evenly. "Yes, sir."

I watched him walk off stiffly toward the door to the servants' domain belowstairs, empathizing with his anger. There had been no reason for Deacon to speak to him that way in my presence. No reason other than to put the younger man in his place and perhaps punish him for speaking to me. If so, the butler had made a miscalculation, for I suspected William would be even more eager now to answer my questions about the household purely to spite Deacon.

The butler cast a gimlet glare over my appearance. "I'll show you up to her ladyship."

"Actually, I would rather speak with you first."

My words halted him midturn and he swiveled back around to meet my gaze. "Of course," he responded, though I could tell he would rather have declined.

I glanced to my right. "Let's step in here, shall we."

Deacon reluctantly moved forward to open the dining room door. As he did so, I glanced upward to catch two maids peering down from the landing above. They swiftly retreated, but not before I caught a glimpse of their curious faces.

The wood of the dining room table gleamed in the light spilling through the open windows. Outside I could hear traffic passing on the street, and the occasional burst of birdsong from the trees in the square. I strolled down the long table, trailing my hands idly over the backs of the chairs, while Deacon came to a halt at the foot of the table, his chin arched in the air. I'd chosen this room specifically, and he must have known it.

"I know you do not approve of Lady Rockham. In fact, I would say you outright despise her," I said, nearly quoting Calliope. I hoped by being direct, he might be goaded into revealing something he otherwise wouldn't. But I never expected him to be so forthcoming.

He sniffed. "Despise is too strong a word for the likes of Lady Rockham. She is an interloper and therefore unacceptable, but my feelings do not factor into the equation."

I turned to stare at him as he made this speech, never once removing his gaze from the wall straight ahead. "You, Mr. Deacon, are a snob," I said with a shake of my head. "And you're lying."

At this comment, he was startled into looking at me, and I arched my eyebrows in emphasis before resuming my saunter down the table.

"I hope you haven't allowed your aversion to Lady Rockham to cloud your perceptions, or altered anything in your resolve to see her found guilty of her husband's murder."

"She *is* guilty of Lord Rockham's murder."

"Perhaps." I glanced over my shoulder at him. "I'm willing to concede that's possible. She had the means and the opportunity, as well as a potential motive." I turned, placing my hands on the back of the chair before me to stare down the table at him. "But what if she didn't? What if someone else killed Lord Rockham, and your determination to see Lady Rockham named the culprit allows them to get away with it." I narrowed my eyes. "Or is that your intention?"

His head reared backward.

"Are you protecting someone? Perhaps even yourself?"

His eyes bulged with suppressed anger. "No, madam, I am not. Nor do I need to stand here and listen to this nonsense. I have already spoken with Scotland Yard and told them everything they need to know. You are meddling where—"

"Did you tell them about the gentleman who called upon his lordship the afternoon before the dinner party?"

He exhaled in frustration. "No, I did not. I did not believe his visit to be relevant."

"Not relevant?" I stated in disbelief. "He argued with Lord Rockham just hours before he was murdered."

"Yes, but it would have been impossible for him to shoot his lordship. He wasn't even in the house."

"The possibility or impossibility of such a thing is not for *you* to decide. That's the job of Scotland Yard."

He didn't respond, simply scowled back at me, evidently believing his opinions were unassailable. It made me want to slap him.

"Who was he?"

His response was clipped. "I don't know."

"Come now, Mr. Deacon. You had to. announce him, didn't you?"

"He wouldn't tell me."

"And yet you still presented him to your employer?" I muttered doubtfully.

His hands twitched at his sides. "Lord Rockham heard me speaking with him. He recognized him and told me to show him in."

I scrutinized him. His affront was genuine. He disliked the fact that his employer had intervened before he could force the visitor's identity from him. But that didn't mean he hadn't discovered it later. Perhaps while he was eavesdropping on their conversation.

"Then what did he look like?"

He lifted his chin even higher, staring down his nose at me. "I didn't notice."

At this, I nearly lost my temper. Indeed, it took everything within me not to shriek back at him. But a butler as pompous as Deacon would never respond to such histrionics. That's what Ada had never learned. Instead, I retreated deeper into icy disdain.

"You didn't notice the appearance of a man who refused to tell you his name and then quarreled with your employer?" I allowed my gaze to flick over him scornfully. "I knew you were a punctilious prig, but I never took you to be inept." I tilted my head. "Or are you becoming dodgy in your advanced age?"

His sharp features turned as rigid as stone. "I suppose he was of average height. Brown hair . . ."

I scoffed and turned away, not trusting anything he was describing to be accurate. Deacon either knew who the man was, or was being deliberately evasive about his appearance. I only hoped he was more forthcoming with Inspector Thoreau after I told him what I'd learned.

Regardless, it was evident that Deacon was unreliable and possibly pursuing his own vendetta. He would never tell me if another person was closeted with Rockham in his study when he retired, contrary to what he'd already told Scotland Yard. He would also never reveal to me if another guest had slipped into the dining room while they were making final preparations for the evening. Someone who might have placed the revolver in Ada's chair.

So I decided to wash my hands of him, at least for the moment. There were more promising sources of information to be explored.

I swiveled to face the window, watching as a green Riley whipped by on the street below. "Send the other servants in to me in groups of two or three. Begin with the maids."

When he didn't comply, I turned my head to glare at him.

"You have no authority to speak to them," he argued. "Nor to command me."

If he thought this would naysay me, then he was mistaken. I had interrogated and overridden more recalcitrant suspects and witnesses during the war, and with far more perilous stakes.

I crossed my arms over my chest. "No, but Lady Rockham does. Shall I ask her ladyship to order the staff be sent up to her private parlor instead? I'm sure she would be more than happy to listen in on our conversations." Though such a situation would not be ideal—for the servants might be more reluctant to share what they knew in front of the marchioness—I was prepared to go to Ada if Deacon persisted in defying my wishes.

The butler recognized he had been routed. At least temporarily. He dipped his head once and strode from the room, his spine bristling with fury. I had counted on the fact that Deacon would not wish to be forced into a confrontation with Ada that he could not win, and I was certain that only added fuel to his anger.

A few minutes later I was joined by a pair of maids. Neither of them was Maisie, and neither of the fretful girls was in any way helpful. But I hadn't expected them to be. I knew the butler's game. He would send up the servants who were the least likely to be able to provide me with pertinent information. Perhaps he hoped I would grow weary of the exercise and give up, but I suspected he had another ploy in mind.

My suspicions were proved correct when William the footman poked his head into the room as I was dismissing a second set of maids who knew nothing of use.

"Mr. Deacon sent one of the other footmen for Scotland Yard."

I glanced toward the window. "I anticipated as much. Can you be certain he sends Maisie in with the next group of maids?"

He flashed me a grin. "I'll do what I can."

He disappeared from sight, and I smiled at his eagerness to thwart the butler. It was good to have an ally.

Whether William had contrived it or Deacon had sent her of his own accord, I was relieved when a sandy-haired maid stepped forward from the trio before me to introduce herself as Maisie. Rather than waste time making general queries as I had with the others, lest Inspector Thoreau arrive to interrupt me, I addressed the scullery maid directly.

"I understand you were at Mr. Deacon's heels as he reached Lord Rockham's study."

Her eyes rounded at my knowing this information. "Y-Yes, m'lady."

I wasn't a lady, but I didn't correct her.

"I were still finishin' the washin' up from the party," she hastened to add, as if she worried I might question why she had been there. "Nearly dropped a platter when I heard the shot."

"So you followed Mr. Deacon upstairs to see what had happened?"

"Well, nay. I were there first."

My eyebrows lifted in surprise.

"At the top o' the stairs, that is." She shrugged one shoulder. "I knew what it meant. I were part of the WAACs over in France." A domestic worker, I presumed, cooking for the army. "'Twasn't till I reached the hall that I realized maybe I shouldna rushed toward it." She crushed the apron she'd been pleating between her hands. "That's when Mr. Deacon pushed past me, and I could hear the footmen poundin' down the stairs from above. So I figured 'twas safe to follow."

I nodded, leaping in before the voluble girl's words ran on. "And did you see anything? Inside the study, that is. Before Mr. Deacon sent you away."

"I didn't see the body, if that's whatcha mean."

One of the other maids cringed.

"Mr. Deacon were standin' in the way. But I did see the gun lyin' on the rug, and I could smell the shot."

I was skeptical of the last, for the sharp, almost-sweet stench of cordite from one gunshot usually did not linger for long, especially if one was not standing within a few feet of where it was fired, but I did not refute her. Her mind had likely supplied the smell, expecting it to be there, and wanting to be helpful, she'd recounted it.

She twisted her lips regretfully. " 'Fraid I didn't see much else, not afore Mr. Deacon shut the door in my face. But the room gave me a right chill, I can tell ye that. And it wasn't just from the open window. Somethin' evil happened there."

"Wait." I held up a hand, forestalling her poetic embellishments, my heart beginning to beat faster. "You said the window was open?"

"Yes, m'lady," she replied, before being distracted by the sound of raised male voices in the hall outside.

I had a strong suspicion whom those voices belonged to, but I wanted confirmation of what she was saying before they burst through the door.

"Maisie," I stated firmly, making her head whip around to look at me. "Are you *certain* the window was open?"

She blinked at me and would have turned her head again to look at the door if I hadn't snapped.

"This is important. I need to know if you're certain the window was open."

Her brow furrowed as if thinking back; then she nodded decisively. "Yes, m'lady. It was."

I thanked her just as Mr. Deacon whipped open the door to admit Chief Inspector Thoreau.

CHAPTER 10

"Mrs. Kent, I understand Lady Rockham is a friend of yours," Chief Inspector Thoreau began in a low voice, having stepped aside with me next to the window looking out over the square. "And while it's quite admirable you wish to help her, I'm afraid I really must insist that you not interfere with Scotland Yard's investigation into the matter of her husband's death."

I couldn't halt the trickle of amusement I felt at witnessing his strained politeness from curling my lips. "While I do appreciate the consideration, there's no need to treat me with kid gloves, Inspector. Not when I can tell you are silently wishing me to the devil."

His heavy eyebrows arched; then his rigid expression relaxed. "Well, perhaps not so far as that," he admitted, making my smile widen. "But I can tell you I was not best pleased to receive Mr. Deacon's message. Particularly as I was meeting with my superintendent at the time."

I glanced toward the butler where he stood on the opposite side of the room next to Constable Stephens. His smug expression made it clear he thought he'd won the day.

"Well, I do apologize for the inconvenience, and I shall now leave the matter in your capable hands."

He seemed surprised, and perhaps a little suspicious, of my easy capitulation. "Thank you."

I tilted my head toward the trio of maids where they whispered together. "But I do think you'll find it interesting that the sandy-

haired maid—her name is Maisie—saw into the study before
Mr. Deacon shut the door in the other servants' faces. And she
recalls quite clearly that a window was open." I turned to stare
into the inspector's dark eyes, wondering how he would react to
such a revelation. "I was under the impression the windows
were closed."

His gaze shifted over my shoulder toward the butler. "As was I."

I'd been right, then. Deacon *had* closed the window before
Scotland Yard had arrived, and yet he was supposedly preserv-
ing the scene for the police. This could be a critical piece of evidence. For one, it called into question the butler's reliability and
made me wonder what else he might have tampered with in the
room. And two, it showed that the murderer could have entered
and exited through the window. That the culprit might not have
been someone within the marquess's household.

Rockham's study was not on the ground floor, but if I remembered correctly, the roof of the portico ran beneath his window. Someone could have feasibly climbed down from the
portico with the aid of a ladder or by some other means and escaped through the garden. There was no need to point this out
to the inspector, for I knew he would discover it in short order.

Of course, there was always the possibility the killer had
opened the window simply to confuse matters, so Ada was not
cleared, but now there was doubt.

I could tell by the hard line of Thoreau's jaw that he was displeased. And he was about to be more so.

"I also learned from the footman, William, that Lord Rockham received a visitor a few hours before the dinner party. Apparently several members of the staff heard them quarreling
rather heatedly. Including Mr. Deacon."

The inspector's eyes kindled with anger. "I see."

I expected some of his irritation to be directed at me for stealing a march on him, but I knew most of it was reserved for Deacon. Though one would never have known it from the way he
kept his glare pinned on me.

"Well, I wish this footman had seen fit to inform me of this
quarrelsome visitor when I spoke with him yesterday, and I

should hope the maid would have revealed as much when we returned to question her today. But nonetheless, you have ably loosened their tongues."

Recognizing when retreat was the better part of valor, I lowered my gaze to the row of dainty shell buttons along the left sleeve of my slate-blue voile blouse, straightening them before I clasped my hands demurely before me. "I shall go visit Lady Rockham in her private parlor. Or will that be too intrusive?"

His lips quirked cynically. "Mrs. Kent, I suspect her ladyship is already aware of your presence, and should I try to speak with her before she sees you, she would undoubtedly refuse."

"Probably," I conceded.

He scrutinized my features. "If I agree to allow you to speak with her, will you promise not to tell her any of the details you've just relayed to me?"

I considered his request and decided it was more than reasonable. If Ada was as innocent as I believed, then she wouldn't know anything about the window. And if she knew about her husband's angry visitor, then Inspector Thoreau could glean that from her. "Yes, you have my word."

He nodded his head toward the door. "Go on."

Deacon's smug expression had turned to one of misgiving, and when I strolled past him to exit the dining room, I couldn't resist offering him an untroubled smile. His eyes narrowed, and he would have followed me had the inspector not called out and asked him to remain.

I found Ada lounging on the green velvet chaise in her private parlor, idly twirling the sash of her vermillion silk dressing gown. It was rare to catch her in such an unguarded moment. Normally she was much like an actress on the stage, playing some part, be it marchioness, coquette, muse, or jeune fille. But in that moment, she was none of those things.

Her eyes were troubled and ringed with shadows, indicating she'd endured a restless night. One of many, if the sleeping pills Inspector Thoreau questioned her about were any indication. Though still undeniably lovely, her complexion bordered on sallow, and in the harsh sunlight glinting through the windows I could pick out fine lines at the corners of her eyes and around her mouth. Lines that seemed to deepen in contemplation of some unhappy topic. Whatever the truth of the murder, one thing was evident. Before me sat an uneasy woman.

The moment passed before I could form more of an impression than that, and she turned to me with a sad smile, her features conforming once again to some mask.

"Verity, there you are." She tilted her head upward as I came forward to buss her poppy-scented cheek before sitting in the Hepplewhite chair beside her. "McTavy told me you were interviewing the staff." A spark of mischief lit her eyes. "Much to Deacon's chagrin."

"Yes, well, I *was* doing so until he sent for Scotland Yard."

The amusement fled from her face. "Odious man."

"But not before I uncovered one or two things that have caused Chief Inspector Thoreau to question Deacon's veracity. And more importantly, your viability as a suspect."

Her eyes widened with shock and then delight. "Truly?"

I nodded.

"Oh, Verity, you are an absolute doll! I *knew* you were sharper than these coppers. Though I imagine that inspector wasn't pleased to discover you'd outwitted him."

"I don't think it's a matter of outwitting," I demurred, not wanting to give her the wrong idea. "I'm sure the police would have uncovered the same information eventually." So long as William and Maisie had been comfortable confiding in them.

But Ada wasn't even listening. "It's too bad you're so devoted to your husband. Otherwise the inspector might be even more persuaded by your charms. I think he rather fancies you."

I scowled at this suggestion, not only finding it to be in poor taste, but also rather insulting. I did not use physical intimacy as a means to gain information or to get my way. Facts and evidence should be enough to persuade Thoreau.

"Oh, don't look at me like that," she retorted. "I was merely suggesting a bit of flirtation, not letting him tumble you." She tilted her head. "Though, the inspector is rather intense." She arched her eyebrows. "And you know what that means."

"Ada, do not be coy with Inspector Thoreau," I warned her.

She smirked, stretching her arms overhead and sinking deeper into the chaise. "Oh, darling, I know better than to do that."

But the glint in her eyes told me she was considering doing just that.

"I mean it. Sidney and I have done our research, and the chief inspector is not one to indulge in idle flirtation. And he absolutely despises sentimentality. If you don't want him to take a crotchet into his head against you, you'll be discreet and restrained."

She sighed. "Well, that's no fun. I was so looking forward to playing the grieving widow—wailing and gnashing my teeth."

I knew she was being sarcastic, but her jest was decidedly out of place.

"That goes for your evening excursions as well."

Her gaze dropped to meet mine, wide with alarm. "You don't know what you're asking of me! I can't sit here night after night with only myself for company."

I gripped the arms of my chair, leaning toward her. "You can and you *must*. If you begin parading through London's nightclubs on the arm of your lover less than forty-eight hours after your husband's death, it won't matter what the evidence says. People will assume you did it. And Scotland Yard will be more obliged to make it so. You don't need any more strikes against you."

She crossed her arms over her chest and glared at me. "Why should I care what they think? They can't convict me of something I didn't do."

"Yes, they can," I bit out sharply, having had enough of her foolhardiness and defiance. "With enough evidence and a poor enough impression, they can hang you for this, regardless of the truth."

Her face blanched.

"You asked me for my help, but I can't help you if you won't help yourself." I pushed to my feet and turned to go, but Ada grabbed my hand, preventing me.

"No, Verity. Please, don't go," she pleaded, clutching my hand to her breast. "I'm sorry. You're right. I'll do whatever you say. Just please don't go." Her face was stricken with panic, and even knowing what a talented actress she was, I had difficulty believing it wasn't genuine. It was perhaps the first genuine emotion I'd seen her display in the past three days.

She swallowed. "I'm . . . I'm frightened, Verity." Her voice was naught but a raspy whisper.

In the face of this admission, I couldn't walk away. I sank down beside her on the chaise and gathered her to my side. Perhaps the words had been a ploy, but I didn't think so. Not when I could feel how she trembled. She truly was terrified.

When the worst of her shaking had subsided, I voiced the question I had originally come here to ask. "Ada, were you aware that Rockham was converting to Catholicism?"

"Thoreau asked me the same question yesterday evening," she murmured so softly I almost couldn't hear her. "And I don't think he believed my answer." She pulled back to look up at me. "No, I didn't know." Her mouth twisted cynically. "He rarely shared anything with me." Her gaze dropped to the bronze-toned rug. "In the beginning, I thought that was because there was nothing to share. It wasn't until later that I realized he simply didn't care enough to do so."

Gazing at her stricken expression, I wondered how much of her previous behavior had been an attempt to deny the truth. After all, I'd also used my fair share of bravado and outrageous behavior to mask the pain and fear I was feeling, not only from others, but also from myself. Upon occasion, this had served me well, particularly during my time with the Secret Service. But that didn't mean it was always the best course of action—for myself or for Ada. In this case, all I could do was hope she listened and heeded my counsel.

Though we'd traveled just the distance of two blocks, I'd already counted three stifled groans from Sidney. In all honesty, I couldn't blame him for his impatience. Our cabbie did appear to be the slowest and most cautious in all of London. In marked contrast, my husband was notorious for his speed and recklessness behind the wheel. He was chafing under his desire to get his hands on his new Pierce-Arrow, which would not be delivered for at least another three weeks, and this sedate drive was almost too much to bear.

"What of your errand this morning?" I asked, seeking to distract him. I had climbed into the cab to join him just moments before as we set off toward Bloomsbury. "Were you able to make Mr. Waters's acquaintance?"

He exhaled a long breath, suppressing his growing frustration with the cabbie. "Yes, though he was still abed at his brother's house when I dropped in to pay Lord Larchmont a call." A glint of something shimmered in his eyes. "Larchmont was only too happy to have an excuse to pull him from his slumber. I gather he's grown rather tired of his brother's indolent, spendthrift ways. Particularly when he doesn't have the means to support it."

"Did he vouch for his brother's alibi?"

"He did not. In fact, he seemed very certain his brother was not at home during the hours in question. Even went so far as to rebuke him for lying when Waters tried to claim he was."

I arched my eyebrows in surprise, at which Sidney's lips quirked in amusement.

"Told him he was an idiot to think we wouldn't catch him out in his lie." He shook his head. "So I think we can count on Larchmont not to fib for him. Or to stifle his own low opinion of his brother's activities. He certainly didn't hide his disapproval of his brother's marked attentions to Lady Gertrude Tennyson."

"Does he suspect his own brother of fortune-hunting?"

"Something like that. Larchmont cautioned him against doing anything that might harm the girl's reputation." He glanced sideways at me. "I gather it's a familiar refrain."

That his own brother did not appear to trust or respect him did not speak well of Mr. Waters.

"Then where was Mr. Waters during the time Rockham was murdered? Did he say?" I asked, referring back to the matter at hand.

Sidney's voice dripped with condescension. "He doesn't remember."

"Now *that* I don't believe for a minute."

"Neither did I. Or Larchmont. But neither do we have proof he was anywhere near Rockham House."

"But he could have been. And that keeps him firmly on my list of potential suspects."

Sidney nodded. "Mine as well. He's undeniably a shady character. I don't blame Rockham for sending him away with a flea in his ear."

The cab slowed as we merged with the heavy traffic at Oxford Circus. Large placards plastered the buildings, advertising everything from vitamin tonic to music lessons, while even more colorful signs festooned every bus trundling through the streets, urging me to buy Hudson's soap or Colman's mustard. Only buildings like Peter Robinson's department store remained untouched, a reminder of the days before such blatant advertisements became the norm. Along with the flower girls, who still stood next to the lampposts with their wicker baskets filled with bright, cheery blooms, as they'd done for centuries.

Although how anyone could enjoy their sweet perfume in such a place, I didn't know. The petrol fumes from so many motorized vehicles were nearly overwhelming in such heat. Those vapors and the stench of tar and flint being spread across the road from the repavement project begun farther along Oxford Street to the west burned the back of my throat.

My husband, whose approach to such congestion could be likened to a thoroughbred charging through a field of competitors, gripped the seat beneath him in an outward display of his exasperation as the cab inched forward.

I reached over to press a hand to his arm, lowering my voice. Not that the cabbie was likely to overhear me over the tumult of honking and growling engines. "Darling, recall. We're not in a Pierce-Arrow. Or even a Rolls-Royce." The speed and maneuvering one expected in those swank, precision motorcars was not possible in a lumbering vehicle like this.

He exhaled a long breath and nodded, though the tension in his shoulders did not ease. I had to wonder if some of the cause of his aggravation was not merely impatience, but also the loss of control. After all, for three and half years of war, and another year spent concealing his survival in order to catch a group of traitors, he had possessed very little control over what happened to him. He'd been beholden to the army's orders, or the limits of what he could risk without being caught or placing others in danger. Since his return, I'd noticed how he chafed under any sort of restriction.

"What about your morning?" he asked. "Did Rockham's servants have anything of interest to tell you?"

I filled him in on the day's revelations, including Deacon's decision to mislead the police by withholding two potentially crucial pieces of information. Sidney merely shook his head. His eyes clearly communicated he thought the butler a fool.

"Given the fact I uncovered both of those omissions rather quickly, I have to wonder whether the staff knows anything else that's pertinent. And if they'll be comfortable enough to confide them to Chief Inspector Thoreau and his officers." I breathed a small sigh of relief as the cab turned away from the busier thoroughfares onto a side street. The breeze blowing through the windows lifted the hair on my neck, drying some of the sweat gathered at my hairline.

"I suppose we'll have to hope your trust in the good inspector sets an example."

I tucked a curl that was tickling my nose back up under the brim of my hat. "Or their dislike of Deacon outweighs their reticence."

His mouth curled upward at the corners. "Yes, that. In any case, it appears your instincts may have been right, after all. At the least, all of this introduces some doubt whether Lady Rockham is the killer and forces Scotland Yard to look elsewhere for a possible culprit." He glanced at me. "Unless you think Deacon did it?"

I felt a vague stirring of unease at his words. One I hadn't expected. So it took me a moment to respond. "No, Maisie and William both recalled Deacon emerging from the servants' stairs leading to the lowest level, where his rooms are located, soon after the shot was fired. It's simply not possible for him to be the killer."

The cab slowed as we turned into another block, creeping along before the buildings as the driver searched for the right address.

"And I never said my instincts told me Ada was innocent," I added in a softer voice, gazing out at the rows of brick houses, their tidy window boxes filled with potted gardens—a remnant of the war when the government had urged people to grow food wherever they could. "My instincts aren't telling me anything. I merely want the truth."

The motorcar pulled to a halt, and before Sidney could prod further around that statement, I climbed out onto the pavement.

CHAPTER 11

The boardinghouse where Esther Shaw rented her rooms was located in a quiet street off Tottenham Court Road, not far from the Duke of York pub. The red brick was blackened with soot and the white trim worn and cracked with age, but the pavement before it was kept tidy, and the windows gleamed in the sunlight directly overhead. I stepped forward to knock, hoping that Irene had informed the proprietress of our intentions.

The door was opened by a tall, willowy woman with faded blond hair and tired eyes. The milky-white apron she wore over her dress was patched and darned, and had obviously seen better days. As had the faded green blouse and checked skirt beneath it, which I suspected had once been a vibrant emerald.

"Can I help you?" she asked hesitantly at first, taking in our expensive clothing and flush appearance. But then a glint of recognition lit her eyes, transforming her face. "Are you . . . the Kents?"

"Yes," I replied.

"Oh!" she gasped, her hands fluttering before her chest. "I've seen your pictures in all the papers. You always look so dashing."

There were times when being famous worked in our favor. We rarely had to wait for a table at a restaurant, and were courted by the owners of the swankest nightclubs. It also seldom required much effort to convince people to talk to us about a suspect or a crime. Unless they were themselves a suspect, and anxious to hide their guilt. But one couldn't have it both ways.

"And, Mr. Kent . . ." She flushed as she glanced at my husband, unable to finish her sentence. "Oh, well, oh my!" she stammered. "And here you are at my door. The girls will never believe it." She inhaled a swift breath. "Oh, but you must be here to see Miss Shaw's rooms." She reached up to smooth back her hair. "Her sister never told me it would be *you*."

This was stated as almost an accusation, and I could only guess Irene had foreseen the landlady's reaction and wisely chosen not to reveal our identities ahead of time. Otherwise, we might have been met by a complement of "the girls," as well as anyone else the proprietress had chosen to reveal our impending visit to. Or worse, they might have trampled through Esther's rooms, thinking to helpfully supply us with their own ingenious insights.

I stepped forward, hoping she would collect herself and invite us in. "It's a pleasure to meet you, Mrs. . . ."

"Worley," she gasped, accepting my proffered hand as she stepped to the side to allow us to enter.

The entry hall smelled of floor wax, and one glimpse at the linoleum seemed to confirm it had indeed just been polished. Benches and rows of hooks lined the walls in one corner, evidently for the tenants' use. A table next to the staircase held neat stacks of letters. I moved forward to gaze down at the names printed on them while Sidney politely declined the landlady's offer to take his hat.

"Is this the tenants' correspondence?" I asked.

"Yes, mail comes twice a day, and my tenants know they'll find it waiting for them there." She arched her chin proudly, clasping her hands before her waist.

"Did Miss Shaw receive any mail after she died?" Sidney inquired, following my line of thought.

"She did. And I passed it on to her sister." She tilted her head. "Well, I suppose Miss Irene Shaw is her half sister. But the difference is negligible, isn't it?"

"What about when she was alive?" I interjected. "Did you happen to notice whether Miss Shaw received any regular correspondence? Or whether there was anything out of the ordinary in the weeks leading up to her death?"

She dithered. "Well, now, I'm not one to pry into my tenants' lives. . . ."

"But you did sort her mail."

"Yes, and I know she exchanged letters with her half sister quite regular, as well as a Lucy Clark out in Chigwell. She loved her fashion magazines, as well. Though, Lord love her, she could never afford to dress that way." At this, her gaze dipped to my own chic ensemble, purchased in Paris. "And she got letters from somewhere in France every so often. As I understand it, she had cousins who lived there."

I nodded, doubting her cousins would have anything pertinent to tell us. But Miss Clark might.

"How are you managing since the break-in?" Sidney's mouth grimaced in sympathy. "It must have been quite a shock."

"Well, I . . ." She pressed a hand to her chest. "I've never had anything so awful happen in my life." Her face turned to the side. "Except for losing George, of course. My husband." She glanced back to explain before gesturing vaguely toward the English Channel. "But that was over there. Not in my *own* home. And poor Miss Shaw. That she walked in on them and they . . . they . . ." Her throat constricted as she swallowed, unable to get the words out. "Well, you know." She shivered. "It's perfectly dreadful!"

"This is the first time your home has ever been broken into, then?" Sidney asked.

"Oh, yes, indeed. I've never had a bit of trouble until this happened." She tilted her head. "There was one instance a few years ago, back before the war, when a few drunken fellows from the Duke of York broke a window. But George was here then, and he set them straight." She sighed, gazing forlornly into the distance. "My, I do wish he was here now."

I could only imagine it had been difficult for her, managing it all on her own. Forced to take in lodgers in order to make ends meet.

"How long had Miss Shaw lived here?" I ventured.

"She was one of the first to come to me. About a year before the war ended, I would say."

"Do you know what she did during the war?"

"Worked for the Royal Mail. Until they let her go, along with many of the other women. Since then, she's worked at Peter Robinson's department store in Oxford Circle. Though, I think she struggled a bit."

"Why do you say that?"

"Well, before she'd always been quite the sharp dresser, despite the restraints of the war. But after, she didn't purchase many new clothes anymore. Nor did she venture out with her friends to the dance halls and such as often. But she always paid her rent promptly. Never was a trouble there."

"And her rooms were on the third floor?" Sidney prodded, since it seemed she had no intention of budging from her spot.

"Yes." She extracted a set of keys from her pocket. "I'll take you up now."

"I understand nothing was reported missing from Miss Shaw's rooms," I said as we climbed. The stairs below us creaked with age. "But what of the other tenants?"

She glanced down at me through the railings. "Nothing. The police said he was probably one of those cat burglars. Climbed in through Miss Shaw's window and never made it farther into the house."

"Was anyone else home at the time?" Sidney called up behind me.

"No, the others were out enjoying their evening—it was a lovely one that night—and I'd just stepped out to my weekly bridge game with the girls. Miss Shaw left for the evening as well, looking bright as a brass penny. But for some reason she decided to come home early." Her footsteps halted on the landing. "If she hadn't, she might still be alive." She shook her head sadly and then moved on toward the second flight of stairs.

That certainly was curious. I wondered what had caused Esther Shaw to return to her rooms earlier than usual that evening.

Did it have anything to do with her death, or had it been purely chance? And rotten chance at that.

"Here we are," she declared as we reached the third landing. Lifting her key ring, she sorted through them until she found the right one and then moved forward to unlock the central door. "I haven't touched a thing, just as the elder Miss Shaw wished. Except to have the rug removed so it could be cleaned properly." She opened the door and stepped to the side to allow us to enter.

"And the other doors?" I nodded over my shoulder. "Do they belong to other tenants?"

"The one on the right did belong to Miss Teagarden. But I'm afraid it was all a bit much for her. Moved out a few days after it happened." Mrs. Worley sighed, perhaps contemplating how she had two more lodgers to find. "The door on the left is the lav the two girls shared."

Miss Teagarden's fright was understandable. The murder of one's neighbor would definitely rattle you, especially if you were a young woman living alone. But I also couldn't help but think that would also make a perfect excuse to leave if you had something to hide. Or knew something and were afraid the killer would realize it.

I tapped my chin. "You know, I was friends with a Miss Teagarden years ago, but we lost touch with the war."

"Oh?"

"I wonder if they could be the same."

The look she gave me, and the way her eyes flicked over my dress once again, communicated how unlikely she thought that suggestion. But what she didn't know was that I was quite a different person from who I'd been before the war. Before Sidney had swept me off my feet that last glorious summer. If not for him and my role with the Secret Service, I would have likely fit right in with these girls. That is, if I'd ever managed to escape the Yorkshire Dales and my controlling mother.

"Virginia," she replied finally. "Miss Virginia Teagarden."

"Oh, no. Not her," I murmured, feigning disappointment.

The glint in Sidney's eyes said he knew what game I was playing, but he did not give me away. However, he did halt Mrs. Worley before she followed us into the room. "Thank you for your assistance. We'll let you know if we need anything."

She nodded haltingly and had just opened her mouth to say something more when he closed the door in her face.

"Busybody," he mumbled under his breath.

I smiled at his gruffness. "Darling, I do think she was only trying to help."

He arched a single eyebrow. "Yes, help herself to a story she intends to sell to the nearest gossip rag."

I shook my head, though I suspected he was right. If Irene had hoped to keep our involvement in the matter a secret, that would not last much longer.

Pushing aside such concerns for the moment, I turned to focus on Esther's rooms. There were but two of them—a sitting room and a single bedroom. The sitting room was sparsely furnished, but what furniture it did contain was of excellent quality. A lovely Georgian sofa and chair perched atop an Aubusson rug on one side of the room next to a sturdy oak bookcase yawning with books, while an oak table with two Chippendale chairs held pride of place in one of the opposite corners.

"I wonder if Esther inherited these pieces," I ruminated as I ran my hand over the blue and white chintz upholstery of the chair. "They seem beyond the means of a postal employee or a shop girl, even one with the eye and appreciation for finer things, and the patience to save for them." I swiveled around to take in our surroundings, watching as Sidney opened the cupboard to find a hot plate and teakettle, as well as a few dishes and other kitchen items. "Unless she received a stipend from her family and her employment was more a means of occupation than a necessity." I shook my head. "But then why live here? This rooming house is certainly respectable, but it isn't exactly posh."

"Perhaps they were gifts," he suggested as he lifted aside the curtain to examine the window and the view of the alley below.

Understanding what he was implying, I considered the possibility that she might have taken a lover. "If that's true, then based on what Mrs. Worley told us, the relationship must have ended some time ago. Remember, she said she'd stopped dressing in sharp, new clothes and going out to the dance halls with her friends. That she seemed to be living under reduced circumstances." That would make sense if she'd once had a lover paying for many of her things.

Making a mental note to ask Irene about it, I moved toward the door leading into the bedchamber. From the information we'd been given, all of the altercation seemed to have happened there, so I decided to direct my attention there first.

However, I stiffened as I stepped over the threshold, shocked to find that the window was open. The soft white curtains billowed gently in the warm breeze.

I should have noticed the air was cooler in Esther's sitting room. The temperature had grown more stifling as we climbed higher in the closed stairwell, but once we'd stepped into Esther's rooms it had lessened slightly. Here was why.

I doubted Mrs. Worley had left the window open. Especially not after what had happened to her tenant, which meant only one thing.

And Sidney seemed to agree. "Stay here," he ordered, sliding past me into the room.

I watched as he systematically moved through the space, opening the wardrobe and crouching to peer under the bed. Rising to his feet, his shoulders lowered from their vigilant position. Whoever had been there was now gone. He crossed toward the window, leaning out to gaze left and right along the building and then down into the shadowed alley.

"Do you think we surprised him?" I asked. "Or did he simply not care about concealing the fact he'd been here? Again," I added, for it seemed almost certain the intruder must have been the same.

"I suspect it was more a matter of difficulty." He pointed down toward the roof of a shed below. "The cat burglar must have climbed atop that and then scaled the remaining distance using little more than his fingers and the crevices in the bricks. It would have been challenging enough to open the window to gain access, and undoubtedly the riskiest part of such a feat. I doubt he would have taken the added risk of closing it behind him. Nor would he attempt any of it during the day when anyone might look up or out their window and see him."

I nodded and turned to survey the bedchamber. "He must have come back to get whatever he was looking for when Esther surprised him. I wonder if he found it."

The jewelry case and silver-backed hairbrush and comb were now gone, but Irene had told me she'd removed those along with a few other small valuables. The floorboards were bare wood as Mrs. Worley had removed the blood-stained rug. But everything else was supposed to have remained exactly as it had been *before* the intruder had killed Esther.

I reached out to turn the key left conveniently in the lock at the top of the mahogany bureau and lowered it to study the objects on its surface and search the tiny drawers and slots, and even one secret compartment Irene had told me would be there. When nothing noteworthy leapt out at me, I moved on to the long drawers beneath. Likewise, Sidney searched the dresser before crossing to the nightstand. Between the two of us, we searched every piece of furniture and every square foot of the room, even going so far as to test the floor for loose boards and probe the bed posts for items hidden within.

When every possible place of concealment had been tried, I stood glaring at the contents of the room in frustration. "We should go over the other room in a similar manner, but it seems whatever the intruder was looking for, he found it."

"That, or we don't understand the item's significance."

I exhaled in dissatisfaction. "True. That's why I'm going to take Esther's journals and correspondence with me, and that sketchbook." I nodded at the items on the bed. "Perhaps they can tell us something."

"Didn't Irene already say she'd read through her sister's journals?"

"Yes, but maybe she didn't know what she was reading. She was MI5, after all."

His lips quirked.

I lifted my head. "What?"

He shook his head, but I could see the glimmer in his eyes. "What's so amusing?"

"I wasn't sure if that was supposed to be meant as some sort of disparagement against MI5."

My brow furrowed, trying to recall exactly what I'd said. "Of course not. I only meant that she wouldn't have been made aware of the broader implications of the war, nor did she have much awareness of the realities most soldiers faced. Her purview was strictly counterintelligence and managing the Registry of foreign connections and potential German operatives here in Britain."

"Oh."

I scowled at the humor still dancing in his eyes and gathered up the journals, sketchbook, and box of saved letters to transfer them to the table in the other room.

"Well, one thing is clear," he stated as he followed me a moment later. "Your friend Irene appears to be correct. This wasn't merely a simple robbery. If so, why would they hazard returning when they must know anything of portable value would already have been removed?"

I glanced over my shoulder as I began to remove books from the shelves next to the sofa to flip through them. "Yes, that occurred to me as well," I admitted, troubled by the revelation. It would have been far easier if Esther's death had turned out to be just what the police had decided—a house breaking gone wrong. Easier for me, in any case. But not necessarily for Irene.

I glared down at the cover of the book before me. "I also wondered if the method of entry might be indicative of something about the crime. Surely cat burglary must be a specialized trade. I can't imagine just anyone scaling a wall in such a manner."

"Why would someone with that particular ability go to all the trouble of gaining access to Miss Shaw's apartment and not steal the jewelry and other valuables laid before them?" Sidney queried, following my line of thought. "Why, unless they were hired by someone else."

"Precisely. It seems too great of a coincidence otherwise. That the person who wished to retrieve something from Miss Shaw should also be capable of such a climb."

Sidney began prodding the floorboards on the opposite end of the room. "I'm sure Scotland Yard already spoke with the neighbors about whether they'd seen anything suspicious, so I'll contact Rawdon and see if he can share any information they gathered from potential witnesses. I'll also ask him for a list of known cat burglars. If the thief has much experience, then he'll likely be a known quantity."

"I should hope Scotland Yard is already looking into those men." In my experience, the police were not always as imaginative as one wished, but they were undoubtedly competent. Of course, it depended somewhat on who was assigned to the case. And I couldn't imagine a shop girl in Bloomsbury, one who had been presumably killed during a house breaking, had been given much priority.

We spent another fruitless half hour searching Esther's rooms with no success before gathering up the possessions I wished to take and departing. Descending the darkened stairwell slowly, my attention focused on not missing a tread, I was startled when a woman's head suddenly emerged through the crack in one of the doors on the last landing. "Psst," she hissed. "If ye don't wanna be caught by The Whirly and her girls, then follow me."

Sidney and I paused, exchanging a glance. I realized what she meant, for we could hear them now—the excited voices chattering together below. I cringed. So Mrs. Worley hadn't even waited for us to depart before spreading word of our visit. Just how many people were waiting for us downstairs?

CHAPTER 12

Seeing my expression, the woman smirked, gesturing for us to follow her. "Come on, then."

Eager to escape without having to endure Mrs. Worley's attentions and pointed questions, I calculated it was a risk worth taking to see where this dark-haired girl proposed to lead us. So, I stepped through the door into a set of rooms much like Esther's above, though these were decidedly less tidy and filled with the type of secondhand furnishings one expected of a working girl.

She closed the door behind us and then flashed us a cheeky grin that made it evident how much delight she took in thwarting her landlady's aspirations. "Me name's Flossie Hawkins," she declared in a lilting Irish brogue before she tipped her head to the side. "This way."

She led us toward what I judged would be the bedchamber door, speaking over her shoulder. "I hope ye find 'im. The scum what did Esther in. I hope ye find 'im and he swings for it." Her jaw and voice hardened as she spoke.

"Were you close to Miss Shaw?" I asked as my nostrils were assaulted by the scent of cheap perfume. Miss Hawkins had evidently doused herself shortly before inviting us in.

"Aye. 'Twasn't right what happened to me girl." She pivoted to face us, her hand on the knob and her chin arching almost defiantly in the air. Tears gleamed at the back of her eyes. "She didn't deserve to die like that."

"No, she didn't," I agreed. "And, Miss Hawkins, we're going to do everything we can to find out who killed her and why."

She searched my face and must have found me to be in earnest, for her sudden truculence faded almost as quickly as it had appeared. "Call me Flossie." Her gaze lowered to the journals I carried. "I 'spose her sister sent ye."

"Irene? Yes."

"She said she knew someone who might be able to help. Didn't say it was two famous swells, though." The corner of her mouth lifted in teasing.

Sidney slid the hand not cradling the sketchbook and box of letters into his trouser pocket, and leaned against the arm of a thread-worn chair that had seen better days. "Then you were also suspicious of the police's ruling on Miss Shaw's death?"

Flossie scoffed. "You'd have to be either balled up or an eediot to believe such rubbish."

"What do you think happened, then?"

"I don't know. I wish I did. I really do. But Irene said she believed the thief was looking for somethin', and I can more easily believe that tan the other." She leaned toward us. "Esther had this way 'bout 'er. This . . . stillness and kindness. Made ye want to confide in 'er." Her mouth twisted. "Maybe someone who confided in 'er later regretted it."

"Do you know where Esther went that evening?" I asked, shifting the books in my arms. "Or why she returned early?"

She shook her head. "Irene asked me the same thing, and I be wishin' I knew. She was 'sposed to join me and Ginnie, but she never showed." She laughed humorlessly. "I was right put out with her for ditchin' us. All in all, Gin's all right, but she can be a regular Mrs. Grundy at times, and that night she was bein' a complete rag. I was all set to be givin' Esther an earful . . . when I heard what happened."

I could hear her regret that the last emotion she'd felt for her friend when she was alive was anger and resentment, but something else she'd said nabbed my attention. "Ginnie? Do you mean Miss Virginia Teagarden?"

She glanced up from where her gaze had dropped to the floor, her gaze widening perhaps in surprise that we knew her name. "Aye, she used to live in the rooms next to Esther till a week ago. Then she legged it back to her parents in Wood Green."

We heard the muffled sound of a woman's voice outside on the landing. Realizing it was probably Mrs. Worley headed up the stairs to check on our progress in Esther's rooms, Flossie pushed open her bedchamber door and ushered us through. Shutting the door after us, she hurried over to the far corner, where a faded quilt hung over the wall. When she pushed it aside, she revealed a hidden door.

"We, both of us, snuck out this way from time to time. Esther knew she could use it whenever she pleased." She wrinkled her nose. "Neither of us liked The Whirly knowin' our every move. She's a nice lady, but nosier than Big Willie's flyboys."

After this pronouncement, she disappeared through the door and down a rickety staircase lit only by a dusty, narrow window above. "Best as we could tell, 'tis an old servant staircase," Flossie told us, speaking over her shoulder. She snorted. "One I 'spose The Whirly thought I wouldn't notice was there if she hung a blanket o'er the door. Mind yer head," she called out as we neared the bottom.

I discovered this was for Sidney's benefit, for I could clear the low-hanging lintel with a few inches to spare. However, without the warning, my husband would have sported a sizable knot on his forehead.

We soon reached the bottom, and Flossie threw open another door with a flourish. This one led out into the narrow alley behind the building that we'd seen from above. "Here we are, then. Give me regards to Irene. And don't let The Whirly catch ye." She winked at Sidney. "She'll start suspectin' me of sneakin' beaus up into my rooms."

But before she could dismiss us entirely, I grabbed her hand. "Flossie, did Esther have a beau? Someone she was partial to?"

Something shifted behind her eyes, something that told me she knew something, but it took her a moment to reply. "It's funny ye should ask that. Because I been wonderin' the same thing."

I frowned in confusion. "What do you mean?"

Her gaze slid to the side, staring at the building opposite us. "Esther used to enjoy visitin' the clubs and dance halls as much as any girl, but o'er the months somethin' changed. It was kind o' gradual. She'd still go, though not as often as before, and she'd still dance, but I could tell me girl's heart wasn't in it, ye know?" She glanced at me to see if I understood. "I started to wonder if maybe she had a secret swell. One she couldn't be seen with."

"Did you ask her about it?"

"Once." She grimaced. "But all she did was laugh and say, 'If only it were that simple.'" She shrugged. "That's when I started to wonder if maybe he'd died. Ye know." She shrugged her shoulder vaguely in one direction. "Over there. That maybe she'd only found out a few months ago."

I supposed it was possible, even if it didn't sound exactly right. Wouldn't the discovery of such a death have caused a more immediate change, not one that was gradual? And wouldn't Irene have known something of the man? Unless she'd elected not to tell me.

"Thank you," I told Flossie, squeezing her hand and releasing it before Sidney and I hurried away. I glanced back to find her still watching us as we reached the corner. She lifted a hand and then disappeared through the door.

Rather than return the way we'd come, we turned our steps north and then east, hailing a cab near Middlesex Hospital. I thought nothing of it when Sidney directed the cabbie to take us home via Wigmore and Duke streets, being too absorbed in my own contemplation of all we'd learned. But when Sidney asked him to stop outside Selfridges, I turned to him in surprise.

"I've learned that Nimble has been working here."

"Already? Well, that was quick work."

"Yes, well, I figured someone from my company would know where I could find my old batman."

His voice was subdued, and I wondered if he might be nervous to speak to Nimble after all that had passed. But when I offered to accompany him, he cut me off before I could even finish my sentence.

"I'll meet you back at the flat," he proclaimed as he opened the door to the cab. Leaning forward, he relayed our Berkeley Square address to the driver before he stepped out onto the street and disappeared into the queue of people entering the department store.

I frowned after him, wishing he would share what troubled him rather than being so dashed reserved all the time.

Stifling my aggravation, I focused my attention on the items we'd removed from Esther's rooms. I cracked open the first journal, skimming over the entries from before the war and much of the early years. In truth, there was little of interest. Esther's hopes and dreams had been much like every other adolescent girl in Britain, and her emotions had swung in just as great of arcs. I thought of my own adolescent journal buried in a trunk somewhere, and cringed.

After the war began, and she started her work in the postal censorship division, I feared she might be less than circumspect, thinking her private diary safe from enemy eyes. But even in this, she kept true to the Official Secrets Act and wrote only in vague terms of the work she did for the Royal Mail.

Irene had spoken the truth. Esther *had* been concerned about the decisions she was forced to make, almost obsessing over the information she'd chosen to censor or not. Her anxiety leaked through onto the page, even if she didn't share the details.

I ruminated over this as I climbed from the cab and took the lift up to our flat. Sadie was there waiting for me, asking which dress I wanted aired for the evening. Which only served to remind me that I needed to be making my own strides toward hiring a lady's maid.

I didn't have much experience with such things. I'd met Sadie by chance, sitting on a bench in the train station, her hands wringing in despair. It had probably been foolish of me to hire her with no references. But it had been shortly after I'd learned of Sidney's supposed death and I'd finally gotten fed up with my old maid's betrayal and sent her back to Yorkshire. In all honesty, I'd been quite reckless and not thinking clearly. I was fortunate the situation had worked out as well as it had, for me and Sadie both.

I supposed this time I would have to contact an agency. Daphne was certain to know the best one. She would also have a decided opinion about the way it should be done. Perhaps I should just ask her to sort it out. Except, the girl would be *my* maid. I didn't want just anyone privy to my private bits, or my and Sidney's quirks and secrets.

I settled in a seat before an open window in our drawing room so I could feel the cool breeze on my cheeks, then dived back into Esther's journals. At first the pages contained much of the same, though I noticed there were larger and larger gaps between entries. It had begun to grow rather tedious, making my eyes droop. But then in the autumn of 1917 there was a sudden shift in her tone. It became lighter, more hopeful, but also more mysterious. And what followed puzzled me greatly. As did the box of letters.

Noticing the failing light, I began to rise to ready myself for the evening, still ruminating on what I'd uncovered—or rather, hadn't uncovered—when I heard the click of the front door opening. I'd forgotten about Sidney and his errand, and crossed the room toward the door to greet him after he'd hung his hat.

"You were gone longer than I expected," I teased. "Any luck?"

His eyes flared slightly and his features stiffened, as if he'd not been prepared to see me, before he arranged them back into apathetic lines. "Yes, Nimble was there. He's willing to start in a few days' time."

I searched his face as he strolled past me toward the sideboard, trying to figure out what it was he wasn't saying. "Was he surprised to see you?"

"Yes and no."

"Was he upset?"

"Of course not."

His voice had grown terse, making it evident *something* had

unsettled him about the encounter. Unless the disturbing incident had come later.

"Did you have other errands to run?" I tried to ask as con-
versationally as possible, reaching over the back of the sofa to
rearrange the pillows so I would appear distracted.

But Sidney wasn't fooled. He finished pouring his whiskey
neat and then turned to glare at me. "I hadn't known I needed a
nurse-minder."

I frowned.

"No, I decided to walk."

While he drank, I opened my mouth to ask why on earth he
would choose to walk in this heat, but then stopped myself. No
doubt this would only earn me another acid response. But this
only confirmed that something about his meeting with Nimble
had troubled him. I wished I knew why, but it was evident he
wasn't going to share it. Perhaps I would have to wait to find
out until Nimble himself joined us.

"I also stopped to place a call to Rawdon at the Yard," he
said as he lowered his glass. "He said he'd let me know what he
could discover about Miss Shaw's case. He hasn't telephoned
here, has he?"

"No."

He grunted, his lips quirking. "Well, I imagine he has his own
work to do. He can't simply be scrounging up information for us."

This was an attempt at humor to ease the tension that had
fallen between us, and a poor attempt at that. Still, I smiled faintly
as I turned to leave the room. "I need to dress, if we're still going
to Grafton Galleries."

I wandered down the corridor to our bedchamber, where my
Chinese blue chiffon gown hung on the outside of the wardrobe,
pressed and ready for me to wear. Its dark beads caught the light
from the small crystal chandelier above. Removing my skirt and
blouse, I settled on the bench before my vanity mirror in my
ivory lace chemise.

"What of you?" Sidney asked as he followed me into the room.
"Did you uncover anything interesting in Esther Shaw's journals?"

Gazing at our reflections in the mirror, I lowered the puff I'd been using to powder my nose, considering his question. "Yes and no."

From the manner in which the corners of his eyes narrowed, I could tell he thought I was making a jab at him by unconsciously echoing his earlier response to my query about Nimble.

I swiveled around to face him. "She redacted words, sentences, sometimes entire paragraphs from her own journal."

Sidney halted in the midst of removing his tie, his eyes reflecting the same bafflement I'd felt upon discovering this.

"She censored herself. And she did a thorough job of it, too," I added, having already strained my eyes trying to read through the bold black slashes.

"So you can't construe from the context what she might have been hiding?"

"In some instances, I can tell it's a name or a location, but in others I haven't any idea what she was censoring." I turned to drop the puff on my vanity. "I also don't understand why Irene didn't mention this. She said she read her sister's journals. Surely she didn't miss the fact that this could be connected to her theory that her sister knew something that got her killed."

He pulled his tie out of his collar and dropped it on the bed. "That is odd."

"What's more, I can tell there are letters missing from that box. Mrs. Worley said she received correspondence from her cousins in France, but there are none there."

"Maybe she didn't care enough to keep them," he suggested as he shrugged out of his suitcoat.

"Not a single one?" I retorted doubtfully. "I don't believe that for a second." I popped the top off a tube of lip salve, staring at the soft rose color. I was daring enough to wear it, but not daring enough to choose bright red. "Which makes me wonder whether *that* was what the intruder was looking for. And he found them."

"Unless Irene removed them."

I glanced up to see Sidney staring at me in the mirror. "I'll ask, but I already know she didn't."

He didn't argue, probably because he knew I was right.

I set the lip salve aside for last and then began to finger-comb my waves, adding a jeweled headband across my forehead. I swiveled left and right, checking my hair from several angles. "*If* the letters were their aim, now the question becomes, why? Why would someone want those letters from her cousins? What could they possibly contain?" Ceasing my primping, I gazed solemnly at the contents of my vanity table. "And were the contents worth killing over?"

"Things rarely are," was Sidney's unexpected reply.

When I looked up it was to see he'd turned his face aside to gaze at the wall. The lines and hollows of his features were more pronounced in the light cast by the lamp, the weariness and guilt that I knew still weighed on him evident in the stoop of his shoulders. It was like the shadow cast on the wall behind him, ever haunting him, when awake and at rest.

I slid my feet beneath me and made to rise, but as if he sensed I was about to come to him, he inhaled a swift breath and cast me a smile.

"Best hurry. Or even Miss Merrick will arrive at the club before us."

I knew he was avoiding speaking of things that I suspected it would be better he faced—if they could be faced at all—but now was not the time. Not when we were due in Grafton Street. So I let him change the subject without a fight, offering him a forced smile of my own. "You know she keeps insisting you call her Daphne, so why don't you?"

He shrugged one shoulder, studying the buttons on his shirt as a real grin hovered at the corners of his mouth. "Perhaps I forget."

I gave him a look that told him just what balderdash I thought that assertion. "I think you do it because it irks her."

"Perhaps," he hedged.

I shook my head. "Well, don't keep it up for too long. You've never seen Daphne irked, and you don't want to."

"Oh, no. Will she cut me dead?" he proclaimed with mock sincerity.

"No." I rose slowly from my bench and propped each foot

there in turn to check my stockings and garters. "But if Daphne is irked, then *I* will be irked." I cast him a coy smile from beneath my lashes. "And you don't want *me* to be irked." I gave the skirt of my chemise a little flip as I turned away from him.

"No, I don't," was his earnest reply.

I couldn't help but laugh as I reached for my gown.

CHAPTER 13

True to his assertion, Sidney greeted Daphne by her given name when she came forward to welcome us as we skirted around the edge of Grafton's dance floor toward the table where she and George sat along with a few of our other friends. From her high spirits and the flush of her peaches and cream complexion, I could tell she'd already indulged in a gin and tonic or two. Her blond hair bobbed about her face when she flashed me a grin of triumph, evidently believing Sidney now considered her a friend. Daphne had an insatiable need for everyone to like her—a very dangerous compulsion in a society as fickle as ours. So it was fortunate that she was also rather naïve, and sometimes remarkably thick when it came to her perceptions of others.

George Bentnick, on the other hand, was as rational and insightful as they came. A brilliant mathematician, he had worked in OB 40—Naval Intelligence's code-breaking department—during the war and had yet to be demobbed. Though he said he expected it any day. All the wartime departments had scaled back, demobilizing most of the women, and even some men.

Catching my eye over Daphne's shoulder, his eyebrows shot skyward, signaling, I suspected, that our friend was in top form tonight. She was perpetually trying to match him up with one girl or another, failing to grasp the obvious. That he wasn't interested, and never would be, in the type of people she was parading before him.

I often marveled at the fact that two of my closest friends

were so vastly different from each other. Even their looks were disparate. Daphne was all golden blond hair and limpid blue eyes, though her most arresting feature happened to be the pronounced hook in her nose. Meanwhile, George had his Indian grandmother to thank for his smooth caramel skin, brown eyes, and rich black hair. The only feature he seemed to have inherited from his mother's side of the family were the tight curls restraining his hair.

I looped my arm through Daphne's, guiding her away from George toward the opposite end of the table to greet some of our other friends, hoping perhaps she would direct her enthusiasm at them for a while. Fortuitously, Crispin was among them, and whether he'd intuited my designs, or merely was eager to spin a pretty girl about the floor, he leapt up to sweep Daphne into the mob of fox-trotters.

Though not as exclusive as the Embassy Club, Grafton Galleries on Grafton Street was one of the best nightclubs in all of London, and practically around the corner from Berkeley Square. It was also where I'd met Ada during the war, and where I knew she still preferred to spend her evenings, even though she could now gain admittance to the more exclusive Embassy Club. Because of this, it seemed the best place to begin in my quest for information.

The building had formerly housed an art gallery—hence its name—which had since moved to Bond Street. As such, the marble and white cornices and moldings around the ceiling were something to behold, but beyond that there wasn't anything noteworthy about its décor. There were some who complained that Grafton's was shabby, but in truth, it was difficult to compete with The Embassy's violet and jade-green color palette and walls ranged with looking glasses.

In any case, at Grafton's the real draws were the dancing and their performers, not seeing and being seen. The jazz bands they booked, mostly from America, were tip-top. And my friend, Etta Lorraine, always charmed the crowd with her rich, mesmerizing voice and teasing hips. Somehow Grafton's had also stolen a march on the other clubs by landing the new dance duo

Moss and Fontana for its midnight exhibition of ballroom and novelty dances. While I'd enjoyed seeing them demonstrate the shimmy and the tango, their elegant valse was truly a sight to see.

Having greeted the others, I retraced my steps to George, and pulled him out onto the dance floor, where we might have a modicum of privacy amid all the swirling, jazzing dancers to hold a conversation without interruption.

"You *do* realize it's the gentleman who usually invites the lady out onto the floor," he teased me.

"You did. I could see the idea forming in your head. I just saved you the effort of forming the words."

A smile hovered on his lips. "I see. Well, then, what is it you want to know?"

"Who says I want to know anything?"

His expression turned chiding. "When you're this determined for my company, you definitely want something." He twirled me, waiting to continue until I was facing him again. "This is about Rockham, isn't it?"

"This is why I like you. No beating around the bush."

This smile was genuine. "Unlike Daphne, who *only* beats around the bush."

"Which also has its uses," I countered, thinking of the time Daphne had unwittingly distracted a major so I could return a report I'd stolen earlier from his dispatch case. "But that is not of the moment. The fact that I'm fairly certain Ada Rockham is innocent of murdering her husband is."

"*Fairly* certain?"

I sighed. "Of course, you would latch on to those two words. I am *trying* to be impartial. And right now the facts are leading away from her."

The band began to pick up the tempo, forcing us to move our feet faster.

"Where are they leading?"

"I don't know. Not yet. But I wondered what you could tell me about Lord Ardmore." I slipped the words in as nonchalantly as I could between breaths, hoping he would be too distracted to disapprove, but I should have known better.

He scowled.

"I know he has something to do with *your job*," I pressed, knowing he would understand I meant Naval Intelligence. "And he's Ada's latest lover."

"That doesn't mean anything."

"No, except Rockham seemed to imply he might know some of his secrets."

George's frown turned troubled, as he appeared to consider my words, but then he shook his head. "I know what you're asking me, Ver, but I can't. You know I can't."

"Nothing?"

"No."

I nodded, having realized my questioning him was unlikely to yield results. George saw the world in a very black and white manner, and he took his oaths seriously. Sharing information about someone inside Naval Intelligence would be illegal and against his ethics. Even if I had still been an active agent of the Secret Service it was impossible, for the branches of military intelligence operated separately from Naval Intelligence, despite arbitrarily being lumped together recently under a new director by the Home Office. I valued his friendship too much to press him further on the matter, so I shifted targets.

"What of Ada, then?" I began to ask, but before I could elaborate, George interrupted me.

"You do know he's watching us?"

"Who?"

"Ardmore?"

My back stiffened under his hand. I knew he felt it, but otherwise I didn't react, allowing my experience to take over. "Where is he?"

George kept his eyes locked with mine. "Across the room. Near the entrance."

"Please don't tell me Ada is with him?" I murmured in misgiving.

"She's not."

I exhaled in relief. "Well, thank heaven for small miracles."

I'd been worried she wouldn't listen. She was one of the most stubborn people I'd ever met, after all. But perhaps this was a sign she wasn't completely intractable.

While George and I twirled across the floor, I cast my gaze over his shoulder, catching a brief glimpse of Ardmore. He was no longer watching us, and he didn't seem displeased or suspicious. But a man like him wouldn't.

When the song ended, George seemed to brighten, as if he'd been released from prison.

I laughed. "Well, don't look so pleased to be rid of me."

He smiled. "If you wouldn't insist on playing twenty questions, I wouldn't."

I shrugged one shoulder, knowing he wouldn't really fault me for trying. He knew what I was and what I'd done during the war. Perhaps not all of it, but enough.

When I would have turned away, he surprised me by clasping my hand. "Be careful, Ver." His gaze was earnest. "I know I say that entirely too much, but someone has to. And in this case, I'm not sure the person you're trying to help is worth the effort."

Before I could respond, an arm was thrown around my waist. "Verity. Dollface. Tell me you saved the next dance for me."

I looked up into the grinning mug of Dickie Bennett. Though he was reputed to be charming, and his features were undeniably handsome, I found the baronet's son to be rather cloying and smarmy, and his hands had a tendency to wander where they shouldn't. But he *had* been Ada's lover before she took up with Rockham, and he might know something useful.

All the same, I cast a glance Sidney's way, catching his eye at the same time I answered Dickie. "Of course."

He pulled me onto the floor of twisting and shimmying bodies, wending our way farther into the center than I would have liked. Then he turned abruptly, drawing me into his arms closer than a gentleman should. One strategically missed dance step remedied that.

"Ouch!" he exclaimed. "Jeez, Ver. I seem to remember you bein' a better dancer."

"That, or you forgot how long my legs are," I replied with a sharp smile, making sure he understood I wasn't averse to using them.

One corner of his lip curled upward wryly. "Yeah, well, word has it you're lookin' into Lord Rockham's murder."

I arched my eyebrows, surprised, but not displeased, that he'd broached the very topic I wanted to discuss. "And if I am?"

He glanced to the side, much of his gaiety draining from his face. "Well, if you are, I might have some information for you."

I waited for him to elaborate, refusing to be baited into confirming or denying my involvement.

"About Ada."

When I still didn't respond, he scowled, swinging us into the next step with more force than was necessary.

"Do you wanna know or don't you?"

"You could tell Scotland Yard," I murmured apathetically, continuing to toy with him.

However, this backfired, for his eyes sparked with malicious amusement. "Oh, I'm sure they're already aware of it."

Now I was intrigued, and he knew it.

"But it seems you're not." He leaned toward me. "What will you give me if I tell you?"

I felt my skin begin to flush with anger—the curse of my red hair and fair skin—and took a deep breath to calm my fury. "Careful, Dickie," I enunciated, moderating my tone. "My husband is dancing just over your shoulder, and I don't think he'd take kindly to you propositioning his wife."

He glanced over his shoulder to find Sidney watching us over his dance partner's head.

"I'm sure whatever you intended to tell me I can find out from someone else." I began to pull away, but he jerked me back into his arms.

"All right, all right. The gold digger's got a record," he hissed.

"For doing what?"

"For nicking cigarettes."

I cast him a withering glare. "And just how old was she? Ten?"

"*And* she was arrested for threatenin' a dame with a shiv."

I blinked in surprise. "She threatened someone with a knife?"

A smug expression spread across his face. "You didn't know that, now, did ye?"

"Who did she threaten?"

"I don't know. But I do know Rockham had the entire matter hushed up. Claimed it was some big misunderstanding."

I eyed him skeptically, uncertain whether I believed him. After all, it was evident he still had a beef with Ada for dropping him for Rockham.

"You don't believe me, ask Etta." He nodded his head toward the stage, where she stood in the wings, waiting to perform.

Given how easy that would be for me to do, I felt that vague stirring of uneasiness again. I'd sensed Ada was keeping something from me. Could this be it? If so, she'd been a fool to attempt to conceal it. If Chief Inspector Thoreau was as thorough as his name and reputation proclaimed him to be, he'd already discovered it.

"Believe me. Ada is a bearcat," Dickie sneered. "And not in all the good ways."

I ignored this comment, simply wanting the dance to be over.

When the last trumpet blast sounded, I stepped away from Dickie's obnoxious paws and was relieved to find Sidney at my side.

"You look like you could use a drink," he leaned down to whisper as we joined the others in applauding Etta's entrance to the stage. She waved to the audience, smiling in her saucy manner and swaying her hips to the beat as the band began to play "After You've Gone." I much preferred Etta's slightly up-tempo version to Marion Harris's recording.

I turned into his arms. "The drink can wait. What I need is to dance with someone who doesn't make my skin crawl."

His smile turned sympathetic. "Well, I'm glad I fill the bill."

I swatted his shoulder playfully, for he knew exactly how he made me feel, and the look in his eyes confirmed it. I moved closer, inhaling the musky scent of him and the sensation of being sheltered in his arms as he guided us around the floor and through the steps of the fox-trot. Sidney had always been a marvelous dancer, being naturally fleet of foot and attuned to the rhythm and flourishes of the music. I'd discovered these skills transferred to other undertakings, as well.

I'd planned to tell him what I'd learned, but the proximity of his body, the drive of the music, and the intimacy of the lyrics rendered me speechless. I had known the words to "After You've Gone," had known they touched a little too closely on the difficulties in our marriage, but I hadn't counted on Etta's ability to bring them alive. My heart seemed to throb in time to the timbre of her voice.

"Miss Lorraine really is magnificent, isn't she?" Sidney said, his voice sounding a tad hoarse.

I shifted my head to look up at him, his face being only inches from mine. "Yes, she is."

I could see in his eyes that he'd been affected by the music, too, and he cleared his voice to speak again. "You said you met her around the same time you met Ada?"

"Yes, Ada danced onstage here from time to time, more as a lark than an occupation. That is, until she met Rockham." I flicked my gaze to the side, curious whether my previous partner had stuck around. "Before that, she was attached to Dickie Bennett."

"I cannot say I'm impressed with her choice in men," he remarked flatly, making my lips twitch. "But now I understand your willingness to dance with the slacker."

Considering the fact Dickie's uncle had gotten him a cushy job with some government agency, so he wouldn't have to enlist, I couldn't fault him his derision.

"Yes, well, it seems my sacrifice was not in vain. He told me that Ada threatened a woman with a knife, and Rockham had to cover the matter up."

He searched my face, noting how this distressed me. "Do you believe him?"

"On his word alone, no. But he told me to speak with Etta. That she would confirm it."

He glanced toward the stage, where my friend was belting

out her last mournful note of the song. "That doesn't mean she killed Rockham."

My lips curled into a humorless smile, appreciating his attempt to mitigate the ramifications of such a discovery. "No, but it does indicate she has a temper, and a possible history of violence."

He threaded my arm through his to guide me from the floor, raising his hand to signal to one of the waiters. In short order we were back at the table with our friends, where someone had ordered food. A gin rickey found its way into my hand, and I nibbled on canapés while chatting with friends when they dashed back to the table between sets to devour the food and down their drinks.

It was the same every night at the clubs dotting London's West End. Dancing had become something of a fever, one fed by copious amounts of liquor. Every night, the dance floors were crowded cheek by jowl with tireless, eager bodies, their eyes sparkling and hairlines matted with sweat. A miasma of cigarette smoke floated overhead, mixing with the scents of perfume, cologne, and tightly packed bodies, while the air reverberated with laughter and frantic, driving music.

There were few better ways to pass an evening, and few better ways to forget the things one wanted to than to saturate one's mind and one's senses. And while I was too introspective to give myself over to it completely, I was fully cognizant that I'd also caught the fever. Better to dance and be merry than to remember and regret.

When Etta's first set ended, I'd planned to wait a few minutes before inching my way around the room to the stage door where Etta normally emerged to mingle with the patrons. I'd hoped to waylay her there, but I got trapped listening to a girl who had danced alongside Ada in her earlier days and wished to lament her friend's rotten luck. I'd paused to hear her out because I'd thought she might have something interesting to tell me either about Rockham or Ada, but I couldn't decipher much from her drunken rambling.

Fortunately, Etta found me first. "Oh, go on with you, Mary," she said, shooing the girl away. "You need to soak your head."

Mary scowled, but obeyed, stumbling into a man behind her.

Etta slid into the chair next to mine, draping one elegant arm across the back of mine. The bracelets on her arm jangled against the wood. "Lookin' good, *ma chérie*. I saw you out there dancin' with that husband of yours. Now, he looks like a man who can command the floor, not one of these puffed-up swells trippin' over they own feet."

I smiled. "You were marvelous, as always. Even Sidney said so."

"Thank you, doll, but I know you didn't come here just to hear me perform." She eyed me up and down, not in condemnation, but interest. "My guess is you're checking up on Ada."

I had no intention of trying to slip something past her. Etta was much too sharp. "She hasn't been here, has she?"

She drew back. "Heavens no." But then she paused, narrowing her eyes in contemplation. "But she told you she was thinkin' about it, didn't she?" She didn't even wait to hear my reply before she rolled her eyes. "Sometimes I think that girl lost her sense with her virtue."

"You've known her longer than I have. Has she always been this way?"

"What? Lacking in common sense? No, I suppose that's unfair. She has sense. She simply doesn't care to use it. That's the problem." She sighed. "She thinks the rules don't apply to her. And when it comes time to pay the piper, she turns feral." Her large teardrop earrings swung from her earlobes as she shook her head. "Marrying a lord sure didn't help her none there. Probably made her even worse."

I considered her assessment of Ada and realized she was right. I'd rarely had occasion to observe her being crossed—Deacon being the exception—but I'd witnessed how irate and flustered she could become. If possible, she preferred to brush aside the dispute as if she'd wanted it to turn out the way it had all along. But what if such an option wasn't possible? What if she'd encountered a situation where she couldn't flout the rules and get her way? A situation like her husband refusing to divorce her, or allow her to carry on with her lover.

"Did Ada threaten a woman with a knife?"

The leg Etta had crossed over her knee and was swinging to the beat of the music abruptly stopped. "Who told you about that?"

CHAPTER 14

Etta held up a bejeweled hand. "No, never mind. I already know. It was Dickie Bennett."

"Then it's true?"

"*Oui, chérie.* But I'm sure that bounder painted her in the worst possible light, and Ada's actions weren't without provocation."

"What do you mean?"

"The woman was some cheap floozy who'd taken up with a bawdy picture fellow." She leaned closer to murmur, "She got her hands on some photographs Ada had been convinced to pose for by some pervert when she was practically a child."

"That's terrible!"

She nodded. "This was just after Rockham had announced his engagement to Ada, and the woman was threatening to show the photos to Rockham if Ada didn't pay her a hefty sum. Well, Ada knew enough to recognize that woman never intended to give up those pictures, that she meant to keep up her blackmail scheme until she bled her dry. She agreed to meet the woman in the alley, intending to force her to give up the photos, when of all the rotten luck, a bobby happened by."

"Dickie said Rockham hushed it up."

"*Oui.* Truth be told, Ver, 'tis the most decent thing he did for her. Whether he paid the woman or merely demanded the photographs from her, I don't know, but he had them destroyed.

The negatives, too. And he convinced the police to drop their charges against Ada and look the other way about the rest."

I agreed that *decent* was the right word, given the fact he must have been just as eager to see the images destroyed to salvage his own reputation as for Ada's sake. But regardless of his motives, it did speak well of him that he'd not broken the engagement, and suggested he'd cared for her at least to some degree.

A pair of young gentlemen sidled over to speak to Etta, and I listened in amusement as they tried to impress her with their sophistication. What they failed to realize was that Etta didn't give a fig for such pretensions. After all, Goldy, her current beau, was one of the most artless fellows I knew.

The man in question leaned back against the wall nearby, smoking a cigarette as he talked animatedly to Sidney, about his latest business venture, I wagered. However, Sidney didn't seem as enthused about it as he had at the Rockham's dinner party. There was a strain around his eyes, and he seemed to be brooding more over his own fag than listening.

When the young saps finally moved on, Etta began to push to her feet. "I've gotta get back to the stage." She took one look at my face and tsked. "Have another drink, *chérie*. And then make that delectable husband of yours take you back out on the floor. Ada would be the first person to tell you she doesn't want you sitting here all glum-faced on her account."

I offered her a tight smile as she stood.

She pointed a finger at me. "I mean it." And then she was off with a toss of her fringed skirt.

I decided to follow her advice, making my way over to the bar to order another cool drink. This took longer than I would have wished, for I hadn't been minding the clock, and the hour was inching toward eleven. With the wartime licensing restrictions still in place, drinks had to be served with food after eleven o'clock. As such, there was always a run on the bar just before eleven. Then after, the tables were littered with unwanted sandwiches and hors d'oeuvres, all purchased in order have their drinks replenished.

With gin rickey in hand, I inched my way through the horde of bodies toward where I'd last seen my husband. The club had grown more crowded as the evening wore on, and wouldn't ease until twelve thirty, when the glasses were removed and the bar forced to stop serving for the night. Then one either went home or moved on to one of the less respectable establishments that flouted the law. These were usually housed in damp, overcrowded cellars off alleys and back streets, and were prone to police raids, but that didn't stop people from going.

"Verity, there you are!"

I swiveled to face Daphne, who panted from the exertion of her latest dance.

"I've been wanting to talk to you all night. Can I have a drink of that?"

I passed her my glass. "I saw you dancing with Stephen Powell. Has he forgiven you for ditching him for that séance?"

"Oh, that. Of course. Ages ago," she assured me, returning my drink.

I arched my eyebrows in skepticism.

"Did Irene Shaw come to see you?"

"Actually, yes. She said you suggested she speak to me."

She clasped my wrist. "Are you looking into her half sister's death? Tell me you are?"

"Well, yes," I admitted. "It certainly seems suspicious."

"Oh, good." She blinked. "*Not* that it seems suspicious. But that you agreed to help her."

"I understood," I assured her.

"I've never seen her so rattled. Not in all our years working—" She halted her words abruptly, glancing around us. "Well, you know. Not even with shells dropping from the sky. It's heart-wrenching."

We crowded together, being jostled about in the mob. "I'm going to do what I can to help her find answers, but you know there's no guarantee."

"Oh, I know. But if anyone can do it, it's you, Ver." Her eyes glistened with hope.

I smiled weakly. "Did you know Esther?"

She dipped her head toward her shoulder as she shrugged. "Not really. Irene introduced me once when we bumped into her and her friend one night at a club. I can't recall which one." She frowned in thought and then shook her head. "Truth be told, I remember her friend much better than I recall her."

"What was her name?"

"Florrie? No. Flossie! That's it. I think they might have been roomies or something."

"I met her today. And you're right. She was certainly memorable," I ruminated.

"Sorry I couldn't be more help."

I nodded and then recalled my earlier decision. "There is one thing you can help me with. I've decided I need a proper lady's maid, but I haven't the foggiest idea how to go about it." This was an exaggeration, but I knew such a task would give Daphne pleasure.

True to my expectation, her eyes lit with enthusiasm. "Shall I come by tomorrow and we can discuss it?"

"Yes, please, do."

"Capital! I'm going to find you the best maid in all of London."

"Simply an adequate one will do," I protested as she backed away, though I knew there was no use. Once set upon such a charge, she would soon be drawing up lists and scouring domestic servant listings. Which, of course, was the reason I'd asked for her assistance in the first place.

I shook my head fondly, glad I could gratify at least one person that evening.

I blamed my good humor for my distraction, for it took me several moments to realize I was no longer standing in the midst of the crowd alone. I glanced up into the face of Lord Ardmore and struggled to keep the smile from freezing on my face.

"Mrs. Kent, how delightful to see you," he murmured, as if

for all the world he hadn't been plotting this move since the moment he stepped into the club and saw me dancing with George.

"My lord," I replied with the briefest nod of my head. "I confess, I'm surprised to see you here. I thought you might be aiding Lady Rockham in her bereavement."

That he understood precisely what I meant was evident in the way amusement flickered over his features like the tiniest ripple in a pond.

"You don't suffer fools gladly, do you, Mrs. Kent?"

"Only when they can't help it."

This time he actually allowed his lips to curl into a smile. He glanced briefly toward the stage as the band began to play a more measured tune, before he held his hand out to me. "Shall we dance?"

I felt my heart kick in alarm, though I willed myself not to react. Nor would I be rushed into making a decision. Let him wonder for a moment or two whether I would accept him.

Engaging in repartee of any kind with a man like Lord Ardmore was riddled with potential pitfalls. But doing so while taking part in something as intimate as dancing was particularly dangerous. Not only would I have to maintain complete control of my facial expression, but also every muscle twitch, every inhalation—and all without seeming to exert the least amount of effort to do so. On the other hand, the same could be said for Ardmore. There would no greater opportunity for me to try to gain information from him and gauge his reactions even in subtle, nonverbal ways. So, I ignored the voice inside me that warned me to stay far away from the man, and nodded my assent.

He swept me masterfully into the steps of the slower moving fox-trot, succeeding in surprising me from the start, even though I'd sworn I wouldn't let him do so.

"You are an excellent dancer, my lord."

He grinned at the astonishment evident in my voice. "Well, I would have to be to dabble in Lady Rockham's company, now wouldn't I?"

He made an excellent point. Ada had never taken pains to

hide her derision for men who couldn't dance. She insisted it indicated a lack of rhythm and finesse in other aspects of a man's abilities.

My mind shied away from contemplating such a matter in regards to Ardmore, especially not while I was trying to remain focused while dancing with him.

"I must thank you, by the way."

I blinked up at him.

"Ada tells me you were the one with the good sense to convince her to abandon her foolish insistence on patronizing the London nightclubs tonight." He shook his head. "I visited her this afternoon with the express purpose of doing the same thing, but was spared that necessity when I saw your guidance had already persuaded her to change her tune."

"I'm surprised you were able to tear yourself away from her lovely side," I probed as we emerged from a tight spin.

"Regardless of how lovely her side is, my presence at Rockham House beyond a certain hour would not go unnoticed. And the last thing Ada needs right now is more scandal attached to her name. She might not be capable of portraying the bereaving widow, but she can be a circumspect one."

The fact we agreed on this point did not stop me from being suspicious of his motives or his fidelity. He could just as easily be distancing himself from her for his own benefit, either temporarily or permanently.

His eyes searched mine with interest, their mossy-green hue so brilliant that even in such dim lighting the color was evident. "Ada tells me you've agreed to look into the matter of Rockham's death. To pit your wits against Scotland Yard." His voice was pitched so that it wasn't so much a taunt as a reflection.

"Oh, I wouldn't say that. It's more of a desire to ensure every avenue is explored fairly."

His uncomfortably direct gaze sharpened further. "I see. Then you're not certain of Ada's innocence?"

I smiled at this too pointed attempt to trick me into betraying my perceptions. "Why would you suggest such a thing?" I tilted my head. "Unless you yourself have doubts?"

"Of course, I do."

I struggled not to react to his lightning shifts in demeanor, his seeming candor.

"I would be a fool not to. After all, she was in the house and she had motive."

I scrutinized his features, wondering just how much he already knew. "And what motive would that be?"

He chuckled. "Come now, Mrs. Kent. Don't try to tell me you don't already know about Rockham's conversion to Catholicism."

"And how do you know about it?"

"Ada told me, of course."

And yet, just hours before she'd denied knowing anything about it until Chief Inspector Thoreau had informed her. Keeping this unsettling revelation to myself, I resorted to impertinence. "Why? Do you wish to marry her?"

He shook his head. "No, Mrs. Kent. I am a confirmed bachelor. But . . . Ada might have been under the delusion otherwise."

"Did you tell her that?"

This question seemed to amuse him. "Not in so many words. But I communicated to her that I was content to leave matters the way they were."

But that didn't mean *she* was.

He seemed to recognize this, for his expression sobered. "All that being said, I think it doubtful Ada killed her husband. Mainly because her widow's portion is such a pittance. Better to make Rockham's life such a torment that he finally agreed to divorce her."

"Then you don't believe his religious conversion was genuine?"

He arched a single pale eyebrow. "Do you?"

I allowed my gaze to wander across the room as I focused on completing a set of more intricate steps while Ardmore guided us around a couple who had nearly dissolved into fits of laughter. Those of us nearby were not privy to what it was they found so funny, but I suspected it was largely the gin.

I wasn't astonished to hear that others suspected Rockham's

conversion wasn't altogether one of the heart, but I was surprised to hear it from Ardmore. Of course, he might be covering for Ada, attempting to convince me a divorce would have been possible. But I didn't think so. For one, he didn't actually seem that enamored of Ada. Not when he'd willingly left her side this evening—whatever his protestations that he was protecting her reputation—spoke of her mercenary motivations, and baldly stated he had no intention to wed her.

Then again, I couldn't really trust anything he was saying. Any part of it could be half-truths or outright lies.

I gazed up at him while he seemed distracted by the couple next to us, deciding to attempt a ploy of my own. "What of you? Do you have any motivations for killing Rockham?"

He glanced back at me, a subtle gleam in his eyes that made my nerves stand on end. Not that he was upset or insulted I'd asked it. No, to the contrary, he appeared almost glad. At the least, he had anticipated it.

"None. Unless you think I'm lying when I say I'm a confirmed bachelor?" he added silkily.

But of all the things he'd said, that was the one thing I was most certain he'd told the truth about. He had no plans of making Ada his Lady Ardmore.

Undeterred, I pressed harder. "Then why did Rockham seem to imply you had secrets to keep?"

"Well, now. Who of us doesn't have secrets?" The look in his eyes made it clear he was speaking of me. "Particularly when it comes to the war." His gaze flicked toward where Sidney watched us from the edge of the room. He leaned against the wall, taking slow drags from his cigarette, but something in the set of his shoulders communicated his vigilance. "Secrets maybe even our loved ones aren't privy to."

I wanted to tell Ardmore there were no secrets between me and Sidney, but of course, there were. Thoughts that had remained unspoken, details of missions I'd undertaken that I wasn't sure I would ever share. I was also certain Sidney was still keeping things from me. Things he couldn't seem to bring himself to speak of. Things for which I hadn't pressed.

So I swallowed the protest, reminding myself this must be the reaction he had hoped for. To distract me. Perhaps even to trick me into betraying myself. Sidney might be a war hero, but he hadn't officially been given permission to be told all the things I'd disclosed to him about my time with the Secret Service.

Though he hadn't stated so directly, C clearly trusted my discretion and my decision to divulge what was necessary to Sidney. However, Ardmore might not look so kindly on such an action. And given the shadowy nature of his position with Naval Intelligence, he could be capable of having both me and Sidney brought up on charges for violating the Official Secrets Act.

"Yes, and I'm sure you hold more than your fair share," I replied pointedly, turning the matter back on him. "But I wonder which of them Rockham could have been privy to?"

Something dark flashed in his eyes. It lasted for merely a fraction of second, but I could have sworn I'd seen either fury or frustration constrict his features before they were smoothed into the perpetual mask of cool indifference he seemed to wear in my presence.

"I imagine I must be an obvious suspect given my relationship with Rockham's wife, but the fact of the matter is, I was nowhere near Grosvenor Square when Rockham was killed. Ada was growing rather potted, so I left the party early. Not long after you and your husband, if I recall rightly. I went to Dalton's in Leicester Square. I'm sure someone will recall my presence there."

If he asked them to.

I struggled to control my irritation and bemusement at such a confession. That a man of such a distinguished reputation as Lord Ardmore should patronize one of the seedier, license-flouting nightclubs was not a great surprise. I had witnessed dozens of peers and Members of Parliament doing the same. But that he should freely volunteer such information, and even cite it as his alibi, was shocking. And suspicious.

His assertion that someone would vouch for him was equally as puzzling. Most patrons, and certainly the employees, of such a club would never officially admit having anything to do with the establishment, let alone share who else had visited. For him to be certain others would confirm his presence meant he would have given them permission to do so. Which meant they could just as easily be lying.

Essentially, the alibi was worthless.

Unless someone I knew and trusted could attest to it. Someone like Crispin Ballantyne, who had already admitted he'd visited a club or two after the Rockham's dinner party. And one that operated at a late hour, like Dalton's.

Given Ardmore's attentive expression, I wondered if he'd already anticipated this. After all, Sidney and Crispin's friendship was common knowledge. But then why didn't he simply say so?

Because it was bloody Ardmore.

The band neatly slipped into the tag of the song, bringing it—and our dance—to an end. And not a moment too soon, for I could feel my self-composure beginning to crumble under the weight of Ardmore's exasperating answers.

However, Ardmore, it seemed, was not finished. "A small tip. Have a look into Rockham's shipping concerns during the war. You might find one or two items of interest, and consequently a few suspects."

I scowled, not bothering to hide my annoyance at such a cryptic statement. "If you know something, you should report it to Scotland Yard."

"Oh, come now, Mrs. Kent. I can't do that." He smirked. "Besides, it would deprive you of the opportunity to outdo them."

I narrowed my eyes, stepping back out of his arms at the last trill of music. But one of his hands wrapped around my upper arm, detaining me before I could turn away.

He lowered his voice and spoke directly in my ear. "You have fine instincts, Mrs. Kent. Do not discount them. Sometimes things are exactly as they seem." He hesitated. "And sometimes they are not."

CHAPTER 15

Before I could reply, Ardmore released me and moved away, leaving me to stew over what in the blazes *that* meant. What a pointless and ridiculous assertion! Obviously things were either what they seemed or not. They couldn't be anything other.

I blew out an aggravated breath and began to push my way through the mass of bouncing, gyrating bodies that had already launched into the next song.

Sidney met me halfway through the throng, spinning me into the quickstep of the dance. "Are you all right?" he shouted in my ear.

It took me a moment to acclimate myself to the speed of the dance before I could respond. "Yes."

"What did Ardmore want?"

I shook my head, my breath already coming fast. "I'll tell you later."

His eyes met mine in concern, but he knew better than to press. Instead, I gripped him tighter and dived into the music, directing all my stifled anger into the steps of the dance. Sidney matched my fervor with his own, until there was nothing but us and the driving beat and blasting saxophones. By the end, I even found myself smiling through my gasping breaths.

When I would have turned to retreat to the tables and sofas at the edge of the room, he kept his grip firmly locked with mine, urging me to dance another. I lost count after three or four, but we remained on the floor until midnight, when Moss and Fontana began their exhibition. Then we retreated toward the bar, planning to order two unwanted sandwiches so that we could get our late-night drinks. But Crispin, Daphne, and George headed us off.

"Anyone up for a change of venue?" Crispin shouted, raising his voice to be heard over those nearby who were yelling their food and drink orders to the barmen. "I hear Rudy's Syncopated Orchestra is playing at Café Coco."

"Do come, Verity," Daphne urged. Her bright eyes cut toward Crispin, her cheeks flushed with excitement. "I'm not ready to go home yet."

I stifled a wince, for I knew that look. Daphne was swiftly developing a crush on Crispin. Which meant she wasn't aware that he was engaged to Phoebe Wrexham.

What had happened to Stephen Powell? I thought he was the chap she was interested in.

I sighed inwardly. Best to head that off before it developed into something serious, at least on her end. Or Crispin did something he might regret.

"What of you, George?" I asked, wondering if he would be willing to play fire extinguisher.

He shook his head. "Not tonight."

Given his earlier mood, I'd expected not, but it had been worth a shot. After all, Daphne and I hadn't always been the ones dragging him to Grafton's or Ciro's Club after curfew during the war. Sometimes George had been the instigator.

I glanced at Sidney, who seemed to be awaiting my decision. Though our dancing had done much to smother the irritation I'd felt at Ardmore, I hadn't forgotten my conversation with him. Or what he'd revealed. "How about Dalton's?"

Crispin considered this a moment and then shrugged. "Suits me."

Daphne grinned when he turned to her. "Let's go."

Being a warm night, there was no need for coats or wraps, but I insisted on pulling Daphne into the ladies' cloak room before we departed. For one, I had visited Dalton's lavatory, and I had no desire to do so again. But this also presented me the perfect opportunity to inform my friend of Crispin's previous attachment.

Daphne's shoulders sank, but being the kindhearted soul she was, she proclaimed Phoebe a lucky girl. Then she inhaled a deep breath and reaffixed her smile. "He's great fun anyway. And now that I know he's spoken for, I won't get my heart bruised."

I reached out to hug her from the side. Daphne was such a lovely girl. I wanted to believe there was someone out there for her. But the truth was, so many of our young men had died during the war, or had been left far too damaged to ever sustain a relationship. That I knew almost the same number of men who were dead as living spoke to the gravity of the situation.

And was much too depressing a thought for what was supposed to be an evening of fun and amusement.

I squeezed her again. "I could make your excuses."

"No, I'm well," she assured me, brightening. "Besides, Stephen was becoming rather too cheeky for my taste. He needs to be taken down a peg or two, and watching me leave with another man should do the trick."

"Cheeky, you say? Well, we certainly can't have that." I smiled. "Come on."

One potential crisis averted, we strolled through the golden doors of Grafton's to find Sidney and Crispin standing on the pavement, nursing cigarettes. A misty rain had begun to fall, dusting their dark evening attire with water droplets and driving off any lingering photographers. At the sight of us, Sidney stubbed out his fag and came forward to take my arm, escorting me toward a cab that sat waiting along the curb. Once the four of us were cozily ensconced in the rear seat, it took off toward Leicester Square, water shushing beneath the tires.

"Crispin," I murmured, lifting my head to see around Daphne. "What club did you say you visited after the Rockhams' dinner party?"

Sidney's hand tightened where it rested against my hip. Seated on my side as I was to make room for us all, I was practically perched on his lap. He knew I was aware that Crispin hadn't said, but it seemed the perfect way to broach the question I really wanted to.

"Café Coco's, and then Dalton's, actually," he replied, and I felt a surge of triumph. "It was hopping that night," he confirmed. "Someone told me there were rumors that the police were going to raid the Titan Club, so I suspect many of them were from there."

I nodded in understanding. Late-night revelers ignored these rumors at their own peril, even when they were sometimes begun by one club trying to capitalize on another. I certainly didn't enjoy scrambling up rickety ladders in my glad rags or down dark, dank passageways, uncertain what unmentionable thing I'd just stepped in, all in an effort to evade Scotland Yard. Many of the law-flouting clubs' front entrances were seedy enough, let alone their hidden back exits.

"Do you remember if anyone else from the Rockhams' party retired to there as well?"

He tilted his head against the rain-streaked glass, contemplating the question. "A few." He listed the names of three people whom we both knew had attended the soirée, but then he dissolved into guessing, plainly not recalling who had dined with us and who had not.

Realizing that beating around the bush would get me nowhere, I asked pointedly, "What about Lord Ardmore?"

Daphne's eyes darted up at me in startlement from where she'd been searching through the contents of her handbag. She didn't lift her head or otherwise alert Crispin that anything was amiss, but the gaze she directed at me through the fringe of her lashes communicated she knew something of Ardmore's reputation among the intelligence agencies. Her scrutiny shifted to the side, beyond my shoulder to where Sidney sat, and then dropped.

"Ardmore. Ardmore." Crispin kept repeating his name, as if attempting to conjure him to mind.

"Do you know who he is?"

"Yes, distinguished-looking fellow. Pale hair going gray. Rather cagey, without seeming to be."

"Yes, that's him." Cagey might describe him to a T.

The cab pulled to a stop at the edge of a dim alleyway. Light illuminated the opening, but then was swallowed up by shadows. But the high-pitched tinkle of a drunken woman's laughter rather ruined any illusion of fright. We climbed out of the car and began picking our way over the broken cobbles and around muck-filled puddles. The rain had stopped, but the streets were still damp.

Once we'd reached a portion of relatively dry ground where I wasn't in imminent danger of ruining my dance pumps, I glanced over at Crispin, still waiting for his answer.

He shook his head. "Sorry, Ver. I know I've seen him at Dalton's, but I can't tell you whether it was that night or another." He reached out a hand to help Daphne over a rough patch of pavement. "They all start to run together after a while."

I couldn't argue with that statement. Much could be said about the nights following the war when I'd still believed Sidney to be dead, and maintaining a certain level of consciousness was no longer necessary for my work with the Secret Service.

Regardless, any hope I had that Crispin could confirm Ardmore's alibi was dashed. Which made me wonder whether he'd wanted me to be able to confirm anything at all.

We drew nearer to the club entrance, where outside several people congregated near the stairs leading down into the cellar. The low thump of drums vibrated the ground.

Crispin scoffed as a woman let loose a shrieking laugh, practically hanging on the man next to her. "But I remember them."

The trouble was, I did, too. Or at least, the woman. And one look at Sidney's face told me he recognized the man as well.

"They were here that night?" I asked.

"Oh, yes," Crispin replied in an undertone. "Made quite the scene. I'm surprised they let them back in."

As we skirted past the couple, I took the opportunity to surreptitiously observe Rockham's daughter, Lady Gertrude, with her beau, Mr. Waters. Perhaps I expected too much—and given the fact I was wed to a man as darkly attractive and fiercely courageous and honorable as Sidney that was entirely possible—but I found Mr. Waters to be decidedly lacking, with a weak chin and shifty eyes. He certainly wasn't an equal to Gertrude in good looks.

But more concerning was Gertrude. There was a wildness to the pitch of her laughter and a flat gleam to her gaze that made me worry she had been indulging in more than gin or expensive champagne. After all, these "sinks of iniquity," as some outside the smart set called them, were known not only for liquor and dancing. They also often operated hand in hand with peddlers of drugs. Members of dope gangs worked alongside many of the club owners, selling opium, heroin, cocaine, and other narcotics.

Of course, the social elite needn't attend such nightclubs to gain access to drugs. I knew women who hosted opium parties where everyone would change into their pajamas and lie around on pillows while a member of the party injected them with morphine, or sometimes even a Chinese herbalist administered the opium or heroin. But as reckless as such behavior was, at least it was done in a somewhat controlled environment. If Gertrude was indulging in drugs in such a shadowy world as this, with the approval and perhaps encouragement of a possible fortune hunter, then that spelled trouble.

One thing was clear. I would be paying another visit to Calliope. Not only to voice my concern over Gertrude, but also to express my extreme displeasure with her for lying to me. Calliope had sworn her daughter was home in her bed the night Rockham was killed, but that could not have been the case if she had been seen here. The fact that this gave both of them a more solid alibi than they'd had previously was beside the point.

Or perhaps it wasn't. After all, I'd just lost two of my best suspects. But I also had to ask myself, if Calliope had lied about this, what else was she keeping from me?

Some hours later, I sat in bed, flipping restlessly through the pages of Esther Shaw's sketchbook. I should have been exhausted, but my mind was too alert, sifting through all the information I'd learned that evening, all the questions yet unanswered. I couldn't simply lie there, not when what I really wanted to do was jump up and pace.

Sidney emerged from the washroom, smothering an enormous yawn, and then stopped to watch me as I skimmed past several mediocre drawings of London during wartime—landmarks I'd seen hundreds, if not thousands of times. He stumbled toward the bed, sliding his feet beneath the covers. "Well, seeing as you're awake . . ." he muttered wryly before he settled the covers over his lap. "Why don't you tell me what Ardmore had to say?"

"Nothing of much use," I grumbled.

Before I could turn another page, he draped a hand over my lap, halting me.

I looked up to find him watching me with a look of gentle long-suffering.

"It doesn't matter if it's useful. What did he say?"

I huffed. "He admitted he was aware of Rockham's conversion to Catholicism."

Sidney's eyebrows arched toward his hairline.

"He says Ada told him." I scowled blackly. "Even though she denied knowing about it to me." I flexed my feet beneath the covers. "Ardmore said he didn't believe it was genuine. That if Ada continued to behave badly, he would eventually divorce her. His pride would demand it."

He sat back against the headboard, removing his hand from my lap. "Yes, I suppose I can see that."

I glowered at the painting of a forest full of bluebells hanging on the wall across from our bed. I'd fallen in love with it when I first saw it in the window of a little shop in Soho. It had been during the three days following our wedding before Sidney was shipped off to the front. Needing both fresh air and sustenance, we'd gone in search of dinner and afterward had taken a stroll through the autumn twilight, stumbling upon the shop. He had snuck out to buy it for me the next morning, even though it had cost more than anything I'd ever purchased in my life. But then money had seemed an inconsequential thing when he was about to head off to war. He'd said it would make him happy to imagine me lying in our bed looking up at it and thinking of him.

After I'd received the telegram telling me of his death, I'd nearly thrown it away. I couldn't look at it without a hole of pain and darkness opening up inside me, one I'd thought for certain I would drown in. But something inside me wouldn't let me do it. Wouldn't let me take it down from the wall. Wouldn't let me even touch it, despite the hours and hours I would lie looking at it, remembering.

My gaze dropped to the sketchbook, wanting to block out such memories. The drawing on this page was, at least, of something other than London. This page and the next depicted a beach.

"Do you recall when Rockham made that rather pointed comment at the party about Ardmore having secrets to keep?"

"Yes." Sidney paused before venturing another comment. "It sounded rather like a threat to me."

"I had the same thought." I found it interesting that his impression echoed my own. "And he was rather evasive when I asked him about it. He tried to divert the subject to me, and then when I asked him more pointedly, he actually volunteered an alibi. Not that it was a very good one."

"He claimed he was at Dalton's? That's why you asked Crispin about him, and later that waitress?"

My eyes narrowed. "He assured me *someone* would remember him. And someone did." One of the barmen. "Though other employees, of course, denied knowing anything."

"So all he did was muddle the matter." He scowled. "And confirm your reservations that he's a slick piker, not to be trusted."

I flipped through several sketches of a small village, largely comprised of stone buildings. "He did tell me one more thing. Though after everything else, I'm not certain I should give it much credence."

"What's that?"

"He said I should look into Rockham's shipping concerns during the war. That there might be something suspicious about them."

Sidney seemed to contemplate the suggestion. "Rockham's estate is somewhere in Cornwall, isn't it?"

"Near Falmouth," I confirmed.

"I suppose they had a time of it dodging U-boats to deliver supplies to France."

I didn't know much about shipping, or Cornwall for that matter. But Sidney had grown up on his father's estate in northern Devon near the sea, not far from Cornwall. He knew far more about such matters than I did.

"And you say Ardmore holds some unknown position within Naval Intelligence?"

"Yes," I replied, already guessing where he was leading. "So you think he was being level with me, at least in this regard?"

"I think it's worth looking into. After all, he would be privy to such information." He tilted his head. "But then again, if there was something suspicious, why didn't Naval Intelligence do something about it?"

"Maybe they didn't have proof." And in the case of a lord, a marquess, they would certainly need more than suppositions. Even in wartime.

But who could I possibly go to for answers? No one in Naval Intelligence would share such information with me. Not even George, though it was doubtful he knew anything of pertinence. Agency cooperation being somewhat nonexistent, it was also doubtful any of my contacts with the Secret Service knew anything, either. C might have some idea, but I couldn't go to him for this. Not without proof.

My eyes fell to the page before me, and I was surprised to find the sketch was of a boat. Almost as if I'd conjured it from my own thoughts. But of course, that was ridiculous. I lifted the paper, preparing to turn the page, when something about the image caught my eye.

The drawing was of some sort of flat-bottomed schooner rigged with sails, except it appeared to have been run aground. Sand piled up around its hull, while waves lapped gently against its stern. Why such a thing had been done, I couldn't tell, for the damage to the ship must have been caused on the other side. From this angle, she looked nearly pristine, but for some tangled sails.

"I have a few friends who served in the Royal Navy, and another who served with the Coastguard provisional forces later in the war. Maybe one of them heard something."

I glanced up at Sidney. "Do you think so?"

He shrugged one shoulder. "Probably not. But now that Mr. Waters is cleared of being anything other than a bounder, I'm at a loss as to how I can assist you."

My heart warmed at the evidence he truly wished to help. Most of the men I knew, even the good ones, would only humor their wives in such a quest. But Sidney seemed to have accepted this unconventional side of me, as well as my past with the Secret Service, far faster than I'd dared hope.

I reached over to take his hand in mine. "Would you come with me tomorrow when I visit Calliope again? I'd like to question her and Rockham's son, and I have a feeling he would be more cooperative with you."

"Are you thinking he might know something about his father's shipping interests?"

"I know Rockham didn't allow Croyde to assist him much with his estates or business ventures, but surely he has some knowledge of his father's assets and concerns."

He nodded, his fingers playing with mine where they rested on the coverlet between us.

I hesitated to say what I needed to next, but I couldn't keep avoiding such a subject forever. "What of your friend Albert Rogers?" I asked evenly. "Did you wish to pay your respects to his wife?"

His hand tightened around mine, though his gaze remained trained resolutely ahead. "I suppose I should."

Those stiff words masked pain, but uncertain of how to help him and wary of his rebuttal, I focused on the practicalities first. "When would you like to go?"

"Saturday. I'll see if I can borrow Crispin's motorcar."

I nodded, swallowing the lump that had formed in my throat. "Darling," I began hesitantly, staring at our joined hands. "Darling, you know you can talk to me, don't you?"

He stiffened. "Of course." But he still did not look at me.

"I only want to help. Like you do. But I can't if you won't let me."

He didn't reply, and after several moments of silence I decided to view this as encouragement.

"So, why does Mr. Rogers's death bother you—"

Before I could even finish the sentence, Sidney abruptly turned to press me back into the mattress, his hands clasping either side of my head as his lips captured mine. As his kisses went, it wasn't the most finessed, but it was enough to make my breath come fast.

"Sidney," I gasped in protest as he eased his mouth from mine and then sealed it again. I pressed harder against his chest, and he lifted his lips from mine. "Sidney, you can't keep doing this. You have to talk to me. You . . ."

"I know. I know." His deep blue eyes were nearly swallowed by their pupils when he opened them to stare down at me. "But not now. Please, I . . ." His voice broke on a rasp. "Not now. *Please.*"

I nodded slowly, my heart surging in my chest as emotion burned behind my eyes. To see him so unnerved, so at a loss for words shook something inside me. Lately, he walked away if I tried to confront him. But as relieving as it was to have him pull me toward him instead, I wasn't certain if it wasn't also worse. For it threatened to undo me like none of his silent distance ever had.

Especially when he proceeded to kiss me like I was the air, and he was drowning. He pushed the sketchbook to the floor as his mouth inched over my skin and he peeled every layer from between us. Everything but the pain he would not give up, and my disquiet that he never would.

CHAPTER 16

I had just lifted my second cup of coffee to my lips the following morning when an insistent rapping began on the door to our flat. My eyes slid to Sidney in question, wondering who could be demanding entry at such an early hour. Granted, "early" was a relative term, given the fact we'd not risen until after ten because of how late we'd retired.

He shook his head. "Don't look at me. You're the one receiving callers at all hours of the day and night."

I rolled my eyes at his teasing, lowering my cup. "Yes, I'm sure it's all quite shocking."

"I'm sure I don't know what your mother would say if she knew," he murmured in mock outrage.

Given the fact we both knew perfectly well what my eminently proper mother would say, and it was certain to be scathing, I could only cringe. "Well, don't tell her, or I'll hold the earpiece to your head and make *you* listen."

He was as likely to tattle on me to my mother as I was to take a bath in the Thames, but he still smirked in reply. "You would try."

I smiled, enjoying our easy tête-à-tête. It reminded me of how it had been before the war, before time, and distance, and secrets had crept between us.

But all too soon it was interrupted by the arrival of Ada, who scowled furiously at me from the doorway of the breakfast parlor. Swathed in a tailored black tea dress with matching embroidery, she stood with one hand cocked on her hip and her head tilted imperiously in the air beneath a fabulous picture hat. What exactly had compelled her to emerge from her boudoir at what she would have termed an ungodly hour, I didn't know, but if it had something to do with the newspaper clutched under her other arm, I had one guess.

"Sidney, my, don't you look divine. Even at such an unspeakable hour," she proclaimed, pouring on all her charm and drama as she sashayed into the room. "Would you excuse us for a moment?" Her gaze shifted to meet mine as she removed her gloves, her eyes cutting beneath the brim of her hat. "There's something I must speak with Verity about in private."

"Of course," he replied, rising to his feet. His eyebrows arched as he turned away from her, evidently unimpressed with her display of suppressed indignation. I was finding it difficult to abide it myself, particularly as I suspected its cause.

Sadie hovered uncertainly in the doorway behind her. "Another pot of coffee, please," I told her as she moved aside to allow Sidney to pass. She nodded and hurried back to the kitchen.

"So, it seems you've been distracted from the investigation of my husband's murder," she declared, slapping the newspaper down on the crisp white tablecloth, before dropping into the chair Sidney had vacated.

I peered down at the story in the *Bystander* Sidney and I had already been sighing over not thirty minutes earlier.

> Sources say war hero Sidney Kent and his lovely wife, Verity, were spotted outside a modest rooming house in Bloomsbury yesterday afternoon. It appears the intrepid duo are looking into the murder of boarder Esther Shaw, whose death Scotland Yard has attributed to a housebreaker.

I doubted Mrs. Worley was pleased to have her rooming house described as modest, but she only had herself to blame for leaking the story to the papers.

I returned Ada's angry glare with a steely one of my own. I didn't owe her any explanation, but I offered her a brief one anyway. "A friend came to me, asking me to make inquiries about a matter that troubled her, and I agreed to oblige her." I tilted my head. "Much as I'm doing for *you*."

"But you are *supposed* to be finding out who killed my husband. Not traipsing about Bloomsbury"—she gestured toward the paper—"on a fool's errand for this Esther Nobody."

I folded my serviette and dabbed at my mouth, struggling to control my own rising temper. "I recognize you are under a great deal of strain," I replied carefully, setting the cloth on the table. "Being the primary suspect in the murder of your husband cannot be a pleasant experience, no matter the difficulties that had sprung up between you."

Her eyes narrowed as if my words held some furtive insult.

"I am doing what I can to uncover the truth, but these matters often take time and finesse. People are not always eager or willing to share what they know. Not immediately." I sat back, crossing my arms over the leaf-green bodice of my summer blouse. "Regardless, I am not answerable to you. My time is my own, and I can choose to do with it what I wish. Including assisting another friend."

"Don't you mean, including interrogating my friends about *me*." She smacked the table and leaned toward me. Her eyes were wild. "Do you think *I* did it? Is that why you've stopped searching? Level with me. Is that what you think?" Her voice ended on almost a shriek. She sank back in her chair, pressing a hand over her mouth as if to restrain herself from saying more.

"Hold on, Ada. You are putting the cart ten paces before the horse." I reached out to clasp the hand that still rested against the table. "Now, *where* is this coming from? I never said I thought you did it, nor have I stopped searching. So what, or who, has you all riled?"

She stared at me mistrustfully, before lowering her hand again to speak. "I heard you were asking questions about me last night."

"Well, of course, I was," I replied.

She gasped in outrage, her face reddening with building fury.

"How else am I to get to the bottom of all of this?" I scolded.

"All of the evidence points to someone either taking advantage of an opportunity presented or purposely committing the crime in a manner that frames you. If it's the latter, then I need to understand *why* someone would do so if I'm ever going to figure out who."

This took the wind out of her sails, and rather abruptly, for she sat blinking at me almost in bewilderment. When she did speak, it was merely to utter a tiny, "Oh."

I arched my eyebrows in chastisement. "Oh, indeed."

I released her arm, nodding to Sadie, who stood outside the door, hesitant to enter. That she—and Sidney, wherever he was—had heard everything Ada had said was obvious. The entire fourth floor probably had, and part of the third.

As Sadie scurried away, I lifted the carafe to pour myself a third cup of coffee, deciding I deserved it under the circumstances. In truth, I would rather have had something a bit stronger, but the sideboard was located in the drawing room. Though I doubtless still drank more than I should, I'd yet to develop a habit of imbibing during breakfast. It seemed best not to tempt oneself by having it near.

As if she'd finally recalled some sense of decorum, Ada waited until Sadie disappeared around the corner before timidly venturing her next question. "But . . . why didn't you just ask me?"

At this, I struggled not to snap at her, when I'd been so careful thus far to keep my words measured. I glared at her as I slowly lowered the carafe to the table, lest I thump it down and splash hot coffee. "You're right. I should be able to ask you for such pertinent details. But given the fact you *lied* to me and told me you knew nothing about Rockham's recent religious conversion, you can see why that's a problem."

"I *didn't* know," she protested, but then faced with my gimlet stare she backpedaled. "Well, all right, I did know. But you didn't expect me to admit so to that inspector, did you?"

"If I discovered you lied, don't you think he will?"

Her eyes widened. "Not if you don't tell him."

My scowl turned black.

"You won't, will you? Please. He'll think I'm guilty for sure."

"And what of your criminal record you conveniently forgot to tell me about?" I countered. "Were you ever going to inform me of that?"

She glowered. "Who told you?" she snapped, effectively answering my question. "Ugh! It was Dickie, wasn't it? The little filcher."

"I should have heard about it from *you*."

"Yes, well, I was worried it would make me look guilty."

I stared at her incredulously. "And Scotland Yard's knowing about it won't?"

She waved this off. "Oh, they don't know about it. Rockham convinced them to drop the charges. And that was over two years ago."

I shook my head, unable to comprehend how naïve she was being. "That doesn't mean the incident wasn't noted down, or that the policemen involved didn't talk. After all, it involved the Marquess of Rockham and his fiancée."

Her face paled.

"You can be certain Chief Inspector Thoreau knows about it."

"But . . . but I didn't actually hurt the woman," she stammered. Her hands clenched into fists. "I was just so mad. She was trying to ruin everything with those horrid pictures."

"Yes, I understand you were quite young in them," I murmured.

Her eyes were trained on the table, but I could tell she wasn't really seeing it. Her thoughts were somewhere in the past, somewhere that was painful. She closed her eyes, as if to banish the memory, and then shook her head. "But Rockham said he took care of it. He said I would never be bothered by that again." She grunted in anger, pounding her fists in her lap. "Men are the most unreliable creatures. They make promises and promises, and never keep them. They say they'll take care of everything, and then they leave you high and dry, forcing you to straighten up the mess they left behind. He was supposed to handle it," she muttered through gritted teeth.

I was somewhat taken aback by the breadth of this outburst. I could appreciate her frustration with her late husband, but something in her tone made me suspect she hadn't only been speaking of him.

"Do you know who the woman was who attempted to blackmail you?" I asked, choosing to focus on the problem at hand. "Do you know who she got the photographs from?"

"I never learned her name. She was just some floozy who took up with Flick Lowenstein." Her gaze met mine fleetingly before darting away. "He's the one who took the pictures."

I nodded. Then this Flick should know who she was. But she disavowed me of that notion.

"He's dead. The police found him in the river. Probably found his way there with some help. Not from me," she added at the last, as if she was worried that was what I was thinking.

Then, if not the photographer, perhaps Chief Inspector Thoreau would know her name. If he was aware of the incident—and I felt certain he must be—then it was likely he was also aware of the other players.

I reached out to touch her arm, drawing her attention back toward me. "Ada, if there's anything else I should know, now is the time to tell me. I can't help you if I don't know all."

Her eyes blinked rapidly for a moment; then she shook her head. "Nothing. That's everything."

I sent her a penetrating look, for I could swear she was still withholding something—something troubling—but she gazed back at me blankly.

However, I was learning not to trust that placid appearance, and there was one point I was determined to have an answer to.

Lifting my coffee, I took a sip. "So, who worked you into such a lather this morning? Obviously it wasn't Dickie Bennett, for you would never have allowed him into your private parlor at such an early hour." I set the cup back into its saucer before lifting my eyes to her stony face. "So a friend, then. Or . . . a lover."

She huffed. "Ardmore was concerned with the direction you appeared to be taking your inquiries. He was simply looking out for me." This ended on almost a pout.

It was obvious all was not well between them, for I could see the hurt and confusion reflected in her eyes. She must already be entertaining misgivings as to his motivations, or else she wouldn't be defending him so stridently, not only to me, but also herself. As such, the worst thing I could do was argue. She would only dig in and redouble her defense, determined not to be proven wrong.

"Well, you know him better than I do," I replied instead, setting my napkin aside.

She opened her mouth as if to say more, but my rising from the table cut her off.

"Now, if you *do* wish me to solve Rockham's murder, I really must get on with my plans for the day." I moved toward the door, waiting for her to follow me.

"What do you intend to do?" she queried uncertainly. "Maybe I can help."

I turned to face her as we reached the entry hall. "Ada, do you trust me?"

She stepped closer to touch one of my arms. "Yes, of course, I do."

"Then you must let me handle this as I see fit." I smiled gently. "And you must listen to my advice. Dashing about town, even in such stunning mourning attire as this, is not proper behavior for a grieving widow who hasn't yet buried her husband."

"It is smart, isn't it?" she murmured, brushing a hand over her skirt.

My smile slipped a notch at the evidence of where her thoughts were focused. "Yes." I turned her toward the door. "Now, off with you. I'll come to see you as soon as I have something worth reporting."

She sighed in disappointment, tossing me a wave before retreating down the corridor toward the lift.

I closed the door with a scowl and turned to find Sidney standing in the doorway to the drawing room, just as I'd expected him to be. Even better, he held up a glass of some cold libation, the ice clinking inside the glass.

"You darling man," I declared, accepting the glass from him. "Evidently, you heard."

"It was impossible not to," he remarked dryly.

"Everything?" I asked after taking a drink.

"Almost."

"Then you heard it was Lord Ardmore who helped work her into such a flap."

He slid his hands into the pockets of his pinstripe trousers. "I figured that out almost as quickly as you did."

"What I can't work out is why he would do such a thing." I tilted my glass, staring down into the clear contents. "Does he want to drive a wedge between us? Is he testing her loyalty?"

"Maybe he just enjoys stirring up trouble."

"I wouldn't be surprised if that's true. Especially if there's nothing at stake for him."

But was there? Was there something at stake? I frowned at the gin and ice in my glass. I couldn't help but feel that I was missing something. But what?

"Is it too weak?" Sidney asked, misinterpreting the reason for my glower.

I shook my head and turned toward the telephone. "I suppose I shall have to call Irene. She's certain to have seen the same newspaper article Ada and we did." I hoped she wouldn't be cross, but we could hardly be blamed for the actions of her sister's landlady.

But Irene wasn't home, and there was far too much to be done for us to go in search of her. I left instructions with Sadie on what to do if Irene paid us a call; then Sidney and I set out for Calliope's house.

We found her seated in her drawing room with her son. From the relief that flashed in her eyes at the sight of us, I suspected they'd also been enduring a trying morning, though I trusted theirs had not been at the hands of the second Lady Rockham.

Lord Croyde rose to his feet to greet me in a clipped voice just shy of rude as I settled onto the white applewood settee next to his mother.

"I'm sure you're wondering what has us so out of sorts," she murmured apologetically as the gentlemen sat in the chairs across the low tea table from us. "We've received rather a large number of angry visitors this morning, furious at Croyde's decision not to run Rockham's three-year-old filly in the St. Leger Stakes."

News of the race results and the huge crowds at Doncaster had been the front-page headlines in all the papers that morning, but I'd been distracted by the articles alluding to us.

"Why didn't you?" Sidney asked lightly.

"Because I haven't had a chance to review my father's stables," Croyde practically growled. "And I have no idea whether this filly was actually fit to run the race or father was merely bloody determined to pit her against the Earl of Derby's Keysoe. She'd contracted a respiratory infection just last month."

Obviously, Rockham's heir was not ignorant about horses or the management of them. But from the sharp glint in his eyes, I suspected the filly's recent illness was more of a convenient excuse for him to withdraw her from the race. His real reason for doing so seemed to be a determination to stick it to his father, since he was no longer here to stop him.

I studied the red-faced young man before me. He resembled nothing so much as a kettle of rage. One that was perilously close to boiling over in terrifying fashion. But I didn't think it was only rage he was struggling to maintain control of. Like his sister, he was using anger to mask his grief. The question was, how much of his fury was a result of his grief and unresolved conflict with his father, and how much was his natural temperament?

Facing him now, I had no trouble imagining him committing murder, premeditated or otherwise. But all the rumors surrounding Lord Croyde were that he was a wastrel and a profligate, not that he was violent or deliberately cruel. That didn't mean he wasn't capable of murder, but it did seem to indicate this ferocity wasn't his typical behavior.

I glanced at Sidney, curious what he was thinking. After all, he'd spent the better part of four years commanding anywhere from fifty to later three hundred men at a time, many of them as young, if not younger than Croyde. Apparently he'd also been rather notorious for flushing out the truth from them, for they'd dubbed him "the ferret."

His expression now was carefully controlled, but I could read the interest in his eyes, the concern. So I was not surprised when he suddenly pushed to his feet. "I hear you have a Buick roadster. One that will supposedly give my new Pierce-Arrow a run for her money, if Langham is to be believed. Show her to me."

The tightness around Croyde's mouth softened as he also stood. "Oh, she'll do more than that. She left Dewey's Sunbeam in the dust."

"Yes, but that was a Sunbeam," Sidney drawled in disparagement. He nodded once to Calliope and then followed her son from the room as he continued to extol the glories of his motorcar.

She turned sideways to face me with an indulgent smile. "I suppose that was a ploy to get one or both of us alone, but at this point I don't care." She exhaled a weary breath, rubbing a hand over the muscles at the back of her neck. "I'm simply happy to hear my son speak of anything other than that *bloody* horse, or the inconvenience of his father getting himself killed."

I smiled in sympathy, but that wasn't going to stop me from asking some rather pointed questions. "I know you lied to me, you know."

Her gaze turned wary.

I sank deeper into the plump pillows positioned in the corner of the couch, crossing my legs. "About Lady Gertrude. She couldn't have been in bed, because she was at Dalton's nightclub."

"How did you . . . ?" She bit back whatever else she was going to say, closing her eyes. After taking a moment to compose herself, she admitted, "Yes, you're right." She blinked her eyes open to look at me. "I didn't know that was where she was when I told you, but . . . I did know she wasn't home." She frowned at her fingers as they plucked at the cushion along the back of the settee. "She had snuck out. Again."

"With Mr. Waters," I guessed.

She nodded. "He has . . . not been a good influence." Her head lifted, grasping the implications of what I'd said. "But then, if you've confirmed they were at that club, then neither of them could have been the one to kill Rockham." She pressed a hand to her chest in relief. "Oh, thank heavens."

I allowed her a moment to gain some solace from this before playing on her guilt. "But you realize this means I now have to question everything you've told me. I have to question your motive and your son's, and whether the things you told me were meant to lead me astray."

"Oh, Verity, please," she gasped, leaning toward me. "You know that's the only lie I told. And I didn't want to, but . . . she's my daughter, my *baby*. I couldn't allow you to think she might be guilty. Not until I was certain myself. Lord knows that contrary child probably would have told you she'd done it just to spite me and her dead father." She pressed a hand to her forehead, shaking her head. "Sometimes I wonder if she has a bit of sense."

I stared directly into her eyes, giving her no quarter. "Do you know where your son was during the time of his father's murder?"

Her lips pressed together in indecision.

"And don't tell me you don't know, for I'm certain you looked into it in the day and a half since I last saw you."

"I don't know for certain, but I believe he was at a cabaret show on Regent Street and then a club on Gerrard," she murmured resignedly.

I knew the one she was talking about. It had a rather notorious reputation. One worse than Dalton's. As alibis went, it was as bad as Lord Ardmore's. But maybe as we spoke, Croyde was confiding in Sidney. Perhaps there had at least been someone honorable among his friends who could vouch for him.

"Thank you," I said. "I appreciate how trying this must be for you."

She stared up at the ceiling, giving a huff of laughter. "It's been a nightmare."

And it was about to get worse.

I reached out a hand to take hers. "Calliope, I saw Lady Gertrude at Dalton's last night."

She nodded. "She snuck out again."

My heart squeezed, not knowing how to say what I needed to without simply stating it outright. "Calliope, I strongly suspect she had taken some kind of narcotic. Likely opium or morphine."

Her expression stilled.

"I don't think liquor is the only thing she's indulging in at these nightclubs, and if she does so too often . . ."

There was no need to finish the sentence. We both knew ladies who had indulged too deeply or too frequently. During the war years, it began for many, innocently enough, as a way to escape the pain, to forget for just a little while the grief that dogged your every waking thought.

I knew, because I'd tried it. Once. Shortly after I'd learned of Sidney's reported death. Fortunately for me, it had made me violently ill, and I had never touched it again. But I recognized how easily I could have become one of the haggard morphine users populating society, no longer able to cope without their narcotic of choice, and eventually no longer even able to hide it.

Calliope's always impeccable posture seemed to slump under the weight of such a revelation as her initial shock settled into weary acceptance. "Thank you for telling me."

I squeezed her fingers and released them. There was no need to say anything more, or to counsel her on the danger of the matter. As for what was to be done to help Gertrude, that was for her to decide. Which she did with admirable swiftness.

"You know, I never gave in to the temptation to try it, but I'm sure Rockham was talked into it at least once by one or another of his string of hollow-eyed mistresses. The money to purchase such elixirs of forgetfulness always seemed to be one of the perquisites that accompanied sharing Rockham's bed. And sadly enough, it was also usually one of the reasons he grew tired of them."

Ironic that now his daughter was in danger of becoming enthralled.

She inhaled a ragged breath, gathering her strength. "Armand has been pressuring me to make a visit to his chateau near Bordeaux, and I think now would be the perfect time. Croyde will have to remain behind to handle the affairs of the Rockham estate, of course. He is the new marquess. But there's no reason Gertrude and I cannot leave." She glanced at me in query. "Unless you think Scotland Yard would object?"

I knew what she was really asking was if I would object, because as far as I was aware, the police had no reason to suspect Calliope or Gertrude. "I'll smooth it over if they do," I assured her, agreeing that the best thing she could do for her daughter was to remove her as far from the temptations of London, and the terrible influence of Mr. Waters, as possible. Her fiancé's estate in southern France would certainly do the trick. "Though I suggest you do so quickly and quietly."

She nodded in agreement. The worst thing she could do was give Gertrude time to bolt, which she was almost certain to do if she learned of her mother's plans. "I hope to sail with the morning tide."

Doing so, and keeping it from her daughter until they had boarded the train to the coast, would be quite a feat, but I trusted Calliope could accomplish it.

In any case, her words had afforded me an opening to ask something else I was curious about. "Speaking of sailing, I understand Rockham has controlling interest in a firm of shippers and exporters, and that they did a steady business during the war. It's been suggested there might be some connection between his shipping concerns and his death. Do you know anything about that? Did he ever mention any reason why someone might want to harm him because of it?"

Her brow puckered in consideration. "Rockham didn't speak to me about such things, as a rule. But . . . I do know he lost a great deal of cargo, mostly due to the German U-boats patrolling the Channel and the North Atlantic. There was always a risk."

She tilted her head. "Though, as far as I'm aware it didn't hurt him financially. He must have taken out a great deal of insurance, or the government lent their aid." She shook her head. "I honestly couldn't tell you. But I can't think of any reason someone would want to kill him over any of it."

I thanked her before allowing her to change the subject, wondering if Ardmore had sent me on a wild-goose chase. For I could not think of any reason either why someone would seek revenge over the sinking of a ship when the Germans were to blame. Unless they weren't?

But why would someone sink their own ship? For the money? I supposed it was possible Rockham had defrauded either his marine insurer or the government, but how could that have led to his death?

Perhaps Sidney would better understand the connection between the two, because I was more confused than ever, and fully prepared to move Lord Ardmore to the top of my suspect list if this proved to be another fruitless distraction.

CHAPTER 17

"What did Lord Croyde have to say?" I asked Sidney as our cab pulled away from Calliope's townhouse. I'd noticed how much calmer the young lord was when they'd returned to the drawing room. His mouth had even curled into a genuine smile, if not a large one.

"A great deal." There was a wealth of meaning beneath Sidney's words. "But the gist of it is, I don't think he did it."

"You don't think he killed his father?"

"No." He spoke with quiet certainty, turning to gaze out the window at the sun-drenched buildings of Belgravia. "He's simply an angry, directionless man. Not a killer."

That Sidney was so sure of this did not surprise me. I had anticipated he would be able to comprehend Croyde better than I. But there was something in his eyes, some shadow that wasn't there before, and I pondered what had put it there.

When I didn't reply, he must have assumed I doubted his assessment, for his voice sharpened. "He provided me with an alibi, but it will be as difficult to verify as the one Ardmore gave you. We can attempt to run it to ground, but I think that would be a waste of our time."

"Yes, and we've had enough of that for one day," I muttered.

"No, if you think he's innocent, then I trust your judgment. Nothing else points to his guilt anyway, except his position as his father's heir and their poor relationship. But many sons have poor relationships with their fathers. That doesn't mean they would kill them."

"True," he murmured, still not looking at me, and I wondered if he was thinking of his relationship with his own father. One that was so distant, it was practically nonexistent. For all that my mother was too prying and judgmental, at least I knew beneath all that criticism she cared.

"Did he know anything about his father's import/export business?" I asked.

"Very little. He claimed it was the part of his father's business assets that interested him the least, and the one his father seemed least likely to release control of, so he never asked."

"That's interesting." Why should Rockham be so determined to retain control over that aspect of his investments? It seemed an odd concern for a man who had no other interest in the sea, so far as I could tell.

Hearing the speculation in my voice, Sidney finally glanced at me. "What did Calliope have to say about the matter?"

I told him what she'd informed me about the lost shipments during the war, but he had no greater knowledge than I did about maritime insurance or government funding for lost cargo meant for British troops.

His eyes narrowed. "Although, I had a sergeant who worked for Lloyd's before the war, as some sort of insurance adjuster. He probably returned to it. Maybe he could explain how it works to us, or point us to someone who can." His mouth flattened. "That is, if he'll talk to me."

"Why wouldn't he?"

He gave me a perturbed look. "Let's just say, most returning soldiers would be none too happy to be faced with their commanding officer again asking them for information. Even Rawdon must be growing weary of it."

"That's not what I've observed. The incident at Umbersea Island aside, every time I've seen you encounter one of the men from your company, they seem pleased as punch to see you."

He scowled. "I think you're overstating the matter."

"No, I'm not," I protested, not understanding why he was so

intent on denying this. "It's evident how much they respect you. How much they wish for your good opinion."

"Well, they shouldn't!" He turned to shout in my face.

I shrank away, taken aback by his vehemence.

Seeing my expression, he tossed his hat down on the seat beside him and scraped a hand back through his hair as he exhaled a long breath. "My apologies. That was uncalled for."

I watched him struggle to regain his composure, before sending the driver, who was observing us in the rearview mirror, a reassuring smile. "Does this have something to do with your conversation with Croyde?" I asked in a lower voice.

"Yes. No." He sighed. "I suppose so."

"But he seemed calmer, lighter even. Your discussion seems to have helped him."

"Yes, but at what cost?" he muttered.

I stared at him in incomprehension, not following what he was trying to say.

He scrubbed a hand over his face. "It's nothing. Just . . . forget it. Where are we headed next? Back to the flat?"

But I could tell it wasn't nothing. Something about his encounter with Croyde had genuinely disturbed him. Something about it had dredged something to the surface that had been stewing for some time. I didn't want to just forget it. But once again, now was not the time to pursue it. Not when the cabbie was watching us warily from the front seat.

"Yes, I want to show Miss Shaw's journal to Miss Teagarden. Maybe she will know why her friend redacted her own words." Irene would be the natural person to ask first, but since I couldn't reach her, I decided Miss Teagarden might be the next best. They had lived next door to each other and shared a washroom. It meant a trip out to Wood Green, but it had to be undertaken at some point. "What about you? You mentioned your Royal Navy friends."

"Yes, I'll get in touch with them and my former sergeant at Lloyd's."

I thought he might remain in the cab as we reached our building of flats at 25 Berkeley Square, but upon seeing the phalanx of reporters outside, he climbed out to help me shoulder my way into the building. It was a good thing he did, too, for who should be emerging from our lift but Chief Inspector Thoreau. And he didn't appear in the least happy.

"Inspector, to what do we owe this unexpected pleasure?" I asked.

"Your detective work, I should say," he grumbled. "Could I have a moment of your time?"

I glanced over my shoulder at Sidney. "Of course."

We returned to the lift. The space inside felt a bit close with three men, including the lift operator, towering over me. Once we reached the fourth floor, I led the way into our flat, before excusing myself to speak with Sadie and ask her to bring some tea and sandwiches into the drawing room. I knew many of my class would never have dreamed of offering sustenance to the likes of a policeman, but Chief Inspector Thoreau was more well-mannered than some of the gentlemen of my acquaintance. Besides, I was famished, and I wasn't about to suffer a grumbling stomach simply because of some antiquated notion of etiquette.

By the time I rejoined the men, they were comfortably ensconced in the pair of armchairs positioned before our dormant hearth. A cool breeze billowed through the room from the open windows, along with the muted rumble of traffic in the street below and shrieks of children playing on the opposite side of the square. Surely the warmth must give way to autumn soon.

I sank down on the sofa across from them as Sidney finished some remark about the races at Doncaster. "The races and the weather, that seems to be all that's on everyone's mind," I quipped. "Well, except for us, I suppose."

It was a clear opening for him to share why he'd come to speak with us.

He smiled tightly. "Yes, well, I decided I should provide you with an update on the investigation, seeing as your involvement has helped us uncover several important facts. *And* you've graciously abided by my wishes not to further question the staff."

I bit back a smile, almost overcome with amusement at his stalwart determination to remain courteous, as if I would fly up into the boughs at him for daring to be frank. Experience suggested this had probably happened to him a time or two.

Sidney, on the other hand, was not above making mischief. "I believe what the good inspector means to say, darling, is that, while he would rather be wishing you to the devil for sticking your delightful nose where it shouldn't be, he can't, because you've actually sped the inquiry along." His eyes twinkled as he turned to our guest. "Is that about right, Inspector?"

Thoreau's complexion pinkened slightly and he coughed into his fist. "Er, yes. More or less."

"Don't tease him, dear," I chided. "Let's allow him to say what he needs to, in hopes it will prevent me from interfering in the future."

At this, Thoreau's face actually cracked into a genuine grin. "You two are the very devil, aren't you?"

Sidney smirked. "Only when someone is giving us a line."

He relaxed deeper into this chair. "Yes, well, I *am* grateful to you, Mrs. Kent, for your assistance." The corner of his mouth curled upward in chagrin. "Even if it is reluctantly given. You did uncover Mr. Deacon's duplicity faster than any of my subordinates likely would have."

"It helps to have a rapport with the staff," I demurred. "And I also noticed how much some of the other servants disliked Mr. Deacon. I'm not ashamed to say I played off that. Thank you," I broke off to tell Sadie as she set the tray of tea and sandwiches on the low table before me.

She nodded before hurrying away.

"How do you take your tea?" I asked the inspector, reaching out to pour.

I was glad when he didn't demur. Nothing was more tedious than trying to convince someone to accept your proffered hospitality.

"A drop of cream, please. Well, whatever the case, it worked," he continued, accepting his cup with thanks. "Deacon is now admitting he did, indeed, close the window and shoo the others out. Although I had to threaten him with obstruction charges to finally convince him to tell us all."

"But he only did so in order to preserve the scene, I'm sure." I couldn't keep sarcasm from creeping into my voice.

Thoreau's eyes crinkled in agreement. "Quite." But then his expression sobered, a crease forming between his brows. "He also admitted he never actually put the revolver back into the cabinet."

At this revelation, I nearly sloshed Sidney's tea from its cup as I stirred sugar into it.

"He claims that it disappeared from his pocket sometime during the evening, but he doesn't know how or when."

"Then anyone at the party could have slipped the gun from his pocket," I exclaimed, handing my husband his tea. "And with the window open in the study, they could have either entered or exited, or done both that way."

I frowned. Except Rockham hadn't been surprised by his killer. Which meant either the killer had not entered through the window, which could clearly be seen from his desk chair, or it was not someone who would have alarmed him at their doing so.

"Yes." Thoreau groused, unaware of my thoughts. "Deacon's decision to withhold this information from us has considerably muddied the waters. We might have been looking in a different direction all along had he made all of this known to us. Coupled with his evident loathing for Lady Rockham, it's not difficult to deduce he was intent on her taking the blame."

I blinked up at him. "So Ada is no longer your chief suspect?"

"Let's just say, she's no longer the only one."

"Because she still could have been the one to take the gun from Deacon's pocket and then opened the window to throw suspicion off her," I surmised. If so, Deacon had almost foiled such a ploy.

His lips curled into a smile as he sipped his tea. "You truly don't miss anything, do you, Mrs. Kent?"

"Well, of course, I'm sure I do," I replied. "Otherwise, I would have solved this mystery by now."

Sidney chuckled. "Verity doesn't have limitations like the rest of us."

Ignoring him, I ruminated, "But why didn't Mr. Deacon say anything at the party when he realized the revolver was missing? I mean, I suppose he decided not to admit to it later because he thought it having come from the gun cabinet made Lady Rockham appear guiltier. But why remain silent about the matter before Lord Rockham was killed?"

"Perhaps he *did* tell Lord Rockham," my husband suggested. "But of course, now we can't confirm that."

"It seems more likely he was vexed by not having realized it had been taken, and so he chose to keep the matter to himself, hoping it would turn up." Thoreau had undoubtedly taken the butler's measure.

"That, and he recognized his employers would not wish to be bothered with such a thing in the middle of their party," I admitted. "After all, they weren't about to search the house or the guests to find it, and the staff would have been too busy to undertake such a task, even surreptitiously." I sighed, sitting back to sip my own tea. "At this point, I suppose it doesn't matter. Deacon couldn't have committed the murder. Not when the other servants can vouch that he was far from the study when it happened."

Thoreau nodded. "That's true. He couldn't have murdered Lord Rockham. But his spite against Lady Rockham has seriously hindered this investigation."

Nibbling on the cucumber sandwich I'd chosen from the tray, I turned toward the window, where outside birdsong melded jarringly with the impatient blast of a motorcar horn. I should have felt relieved that Scotland Yard's suspicions were shifting from Ada. She was my friend after all, and just as when I'd begun this investigation, I still held serious doubts that she could be the culprit. But more importantly, I wanted to uncover the truth—whatever that might be—and the disquieting sensation in my gut told me that might be all but impossible now.

Although Inspector Thoreau hadn't stated it directly, I could read between the lines. If they couldn't find irrefutable proof of who the killer was, they might never attain a conviction. Not when any barrister worth his salt would be able to point to the bungling of the investigation in order to raise doubts. And while none of this was my fault, that did not make me feel better.

"You dusted for fingerprints," Sidney remarked. "Did anything of use come from that? Did they find Lady Rockham's on the gun?"

"Yes, as was expected from her handling the weapon at dinner." Thoreau frowned. "But not on the trigger. Though several of the prints were smeared, suggesting one or more people wearing gloves had also held the weapon, be it Mr. Deacon and/or the murderer. One of Lord Rockham's prints was also present on the barrel, and several of his prints were found on the gun cabinet, but no one else's. Of course, we now know that is superfluous, since the murderer didn't take the weapon from the cabinet."

"And the window?" I asked. "Was it by chance dusted for prints?"

His expression was forbidding. "It should have been."

"What of the angry visitor?" Sidney removed a cigarette from his case. "The one the servants heard Rockham arguing with in his study before the dinner party. Did Deacon continue to deny knowing who he was?"

Thoreau's heavy brow puckered with skepticism. "He swears he doesn't know the man's name, and that he couldn't possibly have anything to do with his employer's death." He leaned forward to set his cup on the table. "However, he did admit he had visited the house once before, and that he was somehow involved with his firm of shippers and exporters. We're searching for him now."

Sidney's gaze lifted to meet mine over the lighting of his fag. There it was again. Another mention of Rockham's shipping enterprise. And this one had been made quite independently of Lord Ardmore.

Thoreau glanced between us. "You know something."

"Not definitively," I hedged, deciding we couldn't very well deny knowing something when our faces had indicated we did. I shifted in my seat, uncrossing my legs to deposit my half-drunken cup of tea on the table. "But mention of Lord Rockham's shipping interests has arisen more than once, and I'm beginning to think that isn't a coincidence."

"Interesting." His eyes narrowed as he considered the possibility. "As I understand it, his firm isn't based in London, but near one of his estates. Do you happen to know which one?"

"Penjerrick Hall, near Falmouth," Sidney replied. "Apparently, he owned or maintained a majority interest in a number of businesses in the town, including an import/export business."

I drummed my fingers against the edge of the cushion beneath me, wondering at the nature of this enterprise we kept hearing about. After all, the position I purportedly held during the war was for a firm of shippers and exporters, a bogus import/export business C had created years before as a cover for the foreign section of military intelligence. Could Rockham's business be a front for something else? It seemed doubtful, but not impossible.

"Cornwall. Then the chief products would have been what? Coal and fish, and perhaps a bit of tin?" He shook his head. "Nothing that jangles an alarm for me."

I was hesitant to advance any ideas without proof, but then I realized Thoreau might have some contacts of his own. "We wondered if there was a possibility it could have something to do with his potentially defrauding maritime insurers or the government for war-wrecked goods, but that's nothing more than a theory. There's no real evidence to suggest such a thing, or that his murder has anything to do with his import/export business."

"Other than the angry mystery visitor he argued with. And these mentions of his shipping interests." His eyebrows arched in question.

I knew he was asking where I'd heard them without doing so outright, but I was reluctant to share my source. For one, Ardmore had chosen to tell me and not Scotland Yard, and regardless of my distrust of him, I couldn't help but wonder if there was a reason for this beyond a lack of faith in the police's abilities. In any case, there was a good chance that, if pressed, Ardmore might deny telling me anything of the sort. So it seemed best to keep my mouth shut, and Sidney followed my lead.

Thoreau's brow lowered when it became obvious I wouldn't share more. "Still, I suppose it could be worth looking into."

"I have another theory I also think worth mentioning," I told him, hoping it would also have the dual purpose of distracting him from my failure to confide my source. "By now, I'm sure you're aware of the incident Lord Rockham hushed up between Ada and a woman she threatened with a knife."

"Indeed? I found no charges filed against Lady Rockham," he replied, just to be contrary, I was sure.

"Come, now. I know as well as you do that simply because no charges were filed does not mean there was no incident to report. In any case, Ada confessed the entirety of it to me." To a certain degree. "And I can't help but wonder whether it has any bearing on Rockham's murder. It doesn't seem entirely implausible that the woman who was attempting to blackmail Ada might have sought revenge on them both for foiling her plans *and* bringing her efforts to the attention of Scotland Yard."

"I've encountered more bizarre motives," he conceded. "And as it happens, the moment I learned of the incident, I decided to look into the matter myself."

"You have? Then you know her name?"

"I do. And I've spoken with her."

Then she was in London, and likely had been three nights prior. But sensing his sudden reticence, I didn't blurt this out, waiting to hear what he would say next.

"She was quite forthcoming. Which is why I would say it's extremely doubtful she had anything do with Rockham's murder. Particularly given the fact she's now a prosperous physician's wife with an infant son." He shook his head. "From what I could tell, she held no grudge and even felt shame for having tried to extort Lady Rockham."

I sank back in my seat. If the woman had fallen in with a

lecher like that photographer, then she had probably been in a rather desperate position. I wondered how young she might have been. As young as Ada had been in the photographs the woman had tried to blackmail her with? Whatever the case, I was glad to hear she seemed to have found her way into much better circumstances.

"Yes, you're right. She doesn't sound like a viable suspect." I sighed, frustration bubbling up inside me to have yet another potential culprit crossed from my list. Which meant, despite exposing Deacon's lies, despite all of our discoveries and speculations, Ada still remained at the top.

Sidney and I would have to speak to the guests we hadn't quizzed, and revisit those we had. Perhaps someone had seen the revolver after Deacon removed it from the dining room table. Thoreau had said they were looking for the man Rockham had spoken with before the party. Perhaps he would prove to be a viable suspect, or able to point Scotland Yard toward someone who was.

In any case, there was much still to be done, much to be explored before it might become necessary for me to confront the possibility my friend might actually be a cold-blooded murderer.

As if aware of the bent of my thoughts, Thoreau decided to do a bit of probing himself. "I hear you're also looking into the murder of a Miss Esther Shaw over in Bloomsbury."

I fought a frown. The blasted newspaper, of course. Now anyone and everyone would know of our intentions, including Scotland Yard. That's why the newspapermen had been camped outside all day. Which also meant they'd seen Thoreau arrive.

"Yes, her half sister is a friend of mine and she's having difficulty accepting her sister's death. She asked me to look into the matter, for her peace of mind," I explained, electing to minimize our involvement.

He tilted his head, his gaze turning penetrating. "Interesting friends you have, Mrs. Kent. As I understand it, the victim worked in the postal censorship division during the war, and her half sister, another Miss Shaw, worked for some civil branch in Whitehall. I also understand you're close to a Mr. George Bentnick, whose work for Naval Intelligence during the war is rather hush-hush."

"You've done your research, Chief Inspector," I drawled, refusing to be baited, though I did wonder what point he was trying to make. If he meant to imply he knew what my role had been during the war, he would quickly discover how evasive I could be if pressed.

He turned to Sidney. "And, Mr. Kent, it has come to my attention that Sergeant Rawdon with the CID served in your company during the war. He speaks quite highly of you."

He exhaled a long stream of smoke. "Yes, well, you would speak highly of the person you'd been caught sharing investigative details with outside Scotland Yard, if nothing else but to assure the powers that be of his trustworthiness."

Thoreau's eyebrow quirked, evidently appreciating Sidney's willingness to admit when he'd been found out. "Perhaps, but I do believe he means it."

"In that case, don't take it out too hard on him. Rawdon's a sharp man. Loyal. The blame should fall on me for imposing on that loyalty. After all, it *is* difficult to disobey your superior officer, even after your duty is over."

He grimaced. "Yes, we're discovering that." He leaned forward, clasping his hands together. "All I'll say to the two of you is, mind where you step. There are some at the Yard who will not take kindly to your interference. They could cause trouble for you. Or if not you, then some of your friends. And I, for one, wouldn't want to see that happen."

Uttered from someone else's lips, this might have sounded like a threat, but Thoreau seemed only to be giving us a friendly warning.

"We'll bear that in mind," I promised, and meant it. But I'd faced more daunting opposition than this. And if those at the Yard who might disapprove thought they were going to keep me from investigating either of the crimes, they were sadly mistaken.

CHAPTER 18

Rather than travel out to Wood Green to speak with Miss Teagarden, I elected to spend the remainder of the day calling on fellow guests from the Rockhams' dinner party. I'd decided it would be more productive to speak to them and discover what they might know about the revolver and the marquess's connections than to track down one young woman who more likely than not knew nothing useful about her friend's death. Sidney, for his part, went searching for information on Rockham's shipping and exporting business, and the issues surrounding wartime salvage.

By the time I returned to the flat, I was thoroughly deflated and in no mood to attend the theater that evening, as we'd planned. Which was precisely what I told Sidney when he walked through the door but a few minutes after I did.

He scraped a hand down his face over the dark stubble that had begun to show. "I couldn't agree more."

"No luck, either?" I asked, taking in his weary appearance.

He shook his head. "I can tell you more than I ever wished to know about exports, and insurance, and wreckage, but I can't explain how any of it connects to Rockham's murder. I still need to speak with someone at his own firm, but thus far there is simply no evidence he defrauded anyone. Not even a suggestion of it."

I heaved a sigh, leaning heavily against the bureau where Sadie had laid the day's post and any messages next to the telephone. "None of the other guests were aware of anything unto-ward, either. And none of them saw anything suspicious at the party."

"Like someone slipping the revolver from Deacon's pocket?"

I met his wry gaze with one of my own. "Nothing except for Ada's *idiotic* spectacle at the dinner table," I snapped, turning to drop back on top of the neat stack of letters the missive I'd been reading when he entered.

"Who was that from?" he asked, moving to stand behind me. His hands lifted to knead my shoulders through the silken fabric of my blouse.

"Daphne. She telephoned while we were out. I asked her to help me in my search for a lady's maid, and she was apologizing because she has to travel into the country for a few days. Her mother isn't well."

Truth be told, her mother was never well. She insisted she had some sort of chronic condition, but I had met Mrs. Merrick, and I thought it was likely nothing more than a combination of nerves and a melancholy disposition. Whatever the case, she couldn't abide London, so she resided at their small country home a few hours outside the city. Daphne and her father, on the other hand, preferred London, and so spent a great deal of their time here, along with her younger brother—when he was not away at Cambridge—and her elder widowed sister, who lived sep-arately. However, from time to time, Mrs. Merrick would suffer one of her episodes, and one of her family members would have to go to be with her. That is, until she tired of them and sent them away again. More often than not, that was Daphne, purely be-cause she was the least selfish of the lot.

"It doesn't matter anyway, for I haven't the time at the mo-ment to devote to reviewing potential candidates," I declared, attempting to brush the matter aside.

However, Sidney was far too perceptive. "Then what has put this rigidity along your spine." He brushed a hand down my back in illustration, and I stiffened like a poker. "And don't tell me it's merely from interviewing the other guests. When I en-tered, I saw your face while you were reading that note."

I scowled at him in the reflection of the mirror hanging above the bureau, irritated by his ability to sometimes read me so well—often when it was most inconvenient—while at other times he was maddeningly obtuse. "She was warning me about Ardmore. Rather cryptically and unhelpfully, I might add."

"I noticed her reaction in the cab on the way to Dalton's when you were probing Crispin about him. What did she say?"

"That I should be careful of Ardmore. That she met him once, coming out of K's office." Vernon Kell, the head of the counterintelligence domestic Security Service—MI5—for which Daphne had worked during the war. "And from K's reaction, Ardmore did not seem like someone one would wish to trifle with."

What I found most interesting about this was the fact that this was proof that the two men had interacted. And that if Daphne's assessment had been correct, Kell had been on the losing end.

Who *was* Ardmore? I wished I could have a conversation with C about him, but even if my former chief would agree to meet with me, he could never share what he knew. Even if he wanted to.

"Yes, that is rather unhelpful, isn't it?" my husband remarked, though from the tone of his voice, I could tell he was still ruminating on it.

I shrugged, turning to face him. "It's no matter. Sadie has left us some cold supper in the larder if you're hungry." I was still stuffed from all the biscuits and tea plied on me at various households. "I'm going to go change out of this blouse." I lifted the offending garment away from my frame. "It reeks of Morty Calvert's Woodbine cigarettes."

Sidney's nose wrinkled in empathy. "I was going to guess you'd been visiting the Calverts. I don't understand how he can stand those stinkers. He can certainly afford better."

I was simply grateful that Sidney preferred a more aromatic Turkish blend rather than the noxious American ones. Though, in truth, I would prefer he didn't smoke them at all. But everyone did. Even a fair number of my female friends.

"Then perhaps I should go straight into the bath, for my hair is certain to reek of them as well." Not that taking a bath would be a hardship. In fact, it sounded rather divine at the moment.

I glanced up to discover a roguish glint had entered Sidney's eyes. But as he pulled me closer, opening his mouth to speak, there was a knock at the door.

His playfulness rapidly turned to aggravation. "I say, this calling at all hours is getting rather out of hand. So much so that a chap can't even properly seduce his wife in his own home."

I smiled. "It's probably Daphne come to call one last time before she departs. I'll send her on her way, and then you can resume your efforts."

However, when I pulled open the door, it wasn't Daphne who stood on the other side, but Irene. As before, she was dressed from head to toe in a shade of deep brown, but I was beginning to understand this was by choice. It might not be black, for all of us had worn too much of that shade during the war, but it was mourning attire all the same.

"I'm so sorry to call again so late, but when I heard you'd telephoned, I couldn't wait to speak with you until the morning." Her gaze took in Sidney's presence over my shoulder and my hat and gloves resting on the bureau. "Oh, but I've caught you going out again," she gasped in dismay.

I shook my head, taking hold of her arm to usher her inside. "Quite the opposite, actually."

If possible, she appeared even more drawn than two days before—worry eating away at her typically serene and composed nature. "Have you uncovered something?" she asked, clutching her handbag before her.

Linking my arm in hers, I guided her toward the drawing room. "I do have a few things to ask you," I admitted, not wanting to raise false hope. "But I telephoned mainly because I was concerned about your reaction to the article that appeared in this morning's *Bystander*."

"Oh, yes," she murmured, sinking down on the sofa. "I apologize for that. I should have mentioned Mrs. Worley's attachment to the society papers. In truth, I didn't reveal your names when I asked her to let a couple into Esther's rooms because I was worried she might inform half the block. Or worse still, have a photographer lying in wait for you."

"Then our inquiry reaching the ears of the papers was not unexpected," I murmured in relief.

"No, I suspected it might." She tilted her head. "Though I did wonder if any of them would believe Mrs. Worley's story."

I'd wondered that, too. But then again, maybe someone had confirmed her account. Maybe even the woman who helped us escape, Flossie Hawkins.

"What did you wish to ask me?" Her dark gaze flickered over my features anxiously.

I glanced at Sidney, who had taken up a position near the window. A cool breeze ruffled the tendril of hair that curled over his forehead. He normally kept it clipped short and tamed with pomade, but I could tell by the curls beginning to form throughout his locks that it was in need of a trim.

"We noticed your sister possessed some fine furnishings. Ones that appeared rather out of place in such a rooming house. Do you know how she acquired them?"

Her expression softened. "Yes, Esther always did have an eye for nice things. Some of them were pieces she purchased for a fraction of what they had once been worth and then refurbished them. Others she inherited from her grandmother." Her brow clouded. "But I recognized a few new pieces I hadn't seen before. I can't tell you how she acquired those. Perhaps she refurbished them as well, because I do know she had been saving her wages rather rigorously."

"Then she hadn't seen a decrease in her earnings?"

She blinked and then shook her head. "No, not that I'm aware of. And even if she had, she had her small inheritance from our father to rely on. I've reviewed her accounts. She hadn't touched a penny of it."

"Do you know what she was saving for?" Sidney queried, sliding his hands into his pockets as he perched at the edge of the windowsill, his long legs stretched out before him.

"She wouldn't say, but I was under the impression that perhaps she intended to purchase a small place of her own." She gazed down at her hands in her lap, where they worried the fabric along one corner of her handbag. "A few months ago, she asked whether I'd ever thought of moving to the country. Whether I was set on remaining in London. I didn't think much of it at the time, but now I wonder. Was she going to ask me to live with her?"

I couldn't answer that, or address the pain and longing in her eyes, but I did reach out to press a comforting hand to her arm.

She offered me a forlorn smile.

"What about men?" I asked. "Did your sister have any suitors or admirers?"

"No one in particular. She liked to flirt and dance as much as most girls, but if it ever went beyond that, I never knew about it."

"But do you think she would have told you?" I pressed.

A tiny furrow formed between her eyes as she considered this. "Esther and I were close, but that doesn't mean we told each other everything. What sisters do? But if she was seeing someone regular, if it was in any way lasting or serious, I know she would have informed me." She shook her head in disbelief. "There wouldn't have been any reason for her not to."

I shared a look with Sidney, half a dozen reasons already forming in my head why Esther might have wanted to keep such a relationship a secret from her sister. Perhaps the man was married. Maybe he was a colleague and such fraternization was forbidden. What if he was a German sympathizer, or a conscientious objector, or a ditch digger, or some other lowly trade? There were far too many possibilities.

"Your sister's journals. I brought them home to read, and I noticed some of the words had been blackened out, almost as if she were censoring herself."

"I noticed that as well," she gasped, sliding forward. "It didn't make any sense to me why she would do such a thing."

"Then you don't know what information she was hiding?"

"No." She lifted a hand to her temple, as if she had a headache threatening. "At first, I thought maybe they were just errors. But then I realized there were far too many of them. And no one blacks out a misspelled word or a poorly worded phrase that painstakingly." She sat taller. "Unless you could read through the slashes?"

I shook my head, and she deflated.

"There's one other thing." I crossed the room to retrieve the box of her half sister's correspondence from the cabinet where I'd stored all the things I'd taken from her rooms. Setting the box on the table, I slid it toward Irene. "Are these the only letters you found among your sister's possessions? I was under the impression she'd regularly corresponded with her cousins in France."

"Yes, the Legrands were from her mother's side, not our father's, so she was closer to them than I was." She lifted the lid to look inside, but her hands halted in midair before touching any of the envelopes. "But wait. This is all of them?"

"All the ones I found."

"No, there should have been more. Much more." Her eyes widened in alarm. "This box was bursting with them. And a second box contained even more."

I glanced at Sidney, who rose from his slouched position by the window. "Did you read them?"

"Some of them. But not all. I intended to return and do so." She flipped frantically through the sparse number of letters that were left. "But I don't understand. None of her cousins' letters from Le Rozel are here." She stared up at us in bewilderment as Sidney came to perch on the arm of the sofa next to me. "Someone took them?"

"It appears so," he replied. "And if that's the case, then this appears to be confirmation that you were correct. The thief *was* there looking for something specific. And he must have returned for it." His eyes dipped to look at me, as if I might confirm or add to this conclusion, but my mind was still locked on the name of the village Irene had just mentioned.

"I'm sorry." I turned to Irene. "Did you say her cousins were from Le Rozel?"

"Yes," she replied uncertainly.

"Le Rozel, France? Along the northern coast?"

"Yes." She looked to Sidney in confusion. "South of Cherbourg."

I pushed to my feet, pacing toward the sideboard to stare at the wall.

"What is it? Does that mean something?" my husband asked.

"Yes. No." I closed my eyes, shaking my head. "I don't know." I scraped a hand over my mouth, spinning to look at them. "It is ringing in my head as if it should mean something. I just can't remember what!"

Irene's hands clenched together in her lap. "It's hundreds of miles from where any of the fighting was in France. In fact, Esther visited them at one point during the war. Her aunt—her mother's sister—was very ill. And since her mother had passed some years ago, Esther thought she should make the trip. She even had to get special dispensation to sail into the port of Cherbourg since it had been closed to all traffic but military."

"Do you know when that was? How late in the war?"

She gazed up at the ceiling, thinking back. "Sometime in '17. Autumn, I believe. Yes, because the leaves were changing. I remember teasing her that she would miss the most glorious colors here in England. Autumn was always her favorite time of year."

"Mine, too," I murmured distractedly. The date of her trip lined up with the shift in tone in her journal, as well as the beginning of the redactions.

Something must have happened on that trip. Something she had later become anxious to keep hidden. But what?

And then it hit me like a bolt.

"Anyway, it ended up being a good thing she did make that trip," Irene murmured, unaware of my sudden inspiration. "Because her aunt did die. Not then, but a year later. From the influenza." She ran her fingers over the stack of letters she'd reorganized in the box. "And now Esther is gone, too."

"What of her cousins?" I asked, struggling to contain my eagerness. "Are they still alive? Is there a way I can contact them?"

"Yes, Marguerite and Adele survived." Her voice was somber. "I have their direction at home. I can telephone you with it."

"Yes, please. That would be helpful."

She nodded. "So, you don't think her death has anything to do with her postal censorship job?"

"We can't know anything for sure. Not yet. Not until I speak with her cousins. But, no," I said quietly. "I don't think it had anything to do with that."

Her eyes searched my face, and I suspected she'd seen more than I wished her to, but she did not press me to tell her. She didn't even accuse. Too many years of work for MI5 had inured her to the fact that there were some things she was not privy to know, some things that would never be explained to her.

Instead she simply pushed to her feet and crossed the room to take my hands between hers. Tears glistened on her long lashes. "You will telephone me the moment you can tell me something?"

I squeezed her hands in return. "Yes."

We were both silent as I showed her out of the flat. But the moment the door was shut, I dashed back into the drawing room, sinking to my knees before the cabinet.

Sidney came to stand over me. "What is it? What have you remembered?"

"Le Rozel. It was the site . . ." I halted in mid-explanation, wondering whether I should continue. Whether I was allowed to.

But then I shook my head. I'd already shared far more sensitive material with him. It was ridiculous to stop sharing information with him now, especially when what I was about to say was hardly confidential. Much of it had even been reported in the newspapers. Just not all.

I inhaled past the tightness in my chest, beginning again. "Le Rozel was the site of a shipwreck in the autumn of 1917. Well, it wasn't actually a shipwreck. The authorities couldn't find any actual damage done to her. Simply some tangled sails. But she had been beached on Rozel Point."

I rose to my feet with Esther's sketchbook. Sinking down on the edge of the nearest chair, I began to flip through the pages, searching for the drawing I wanted.

"Here," I exclaimed when I found it. "This sketch intrigued me the first time I stumbled upon it, but I didn't know why. If I'm not mistaken it's the same type of ship as the *Zebrina*—a flat-bottomed schooner. And the ship in this image also appears to be beached."

He took the book from me, examining the drawing more closely. "Yes, you're right." He handed me the sketch back. "But what is so remarkable about a beached boat? As Irene said, Le Rozel was miles from the front."

"It's remarkable because the crew of six men was missing. There were no signs of a struggle, her cargo of coal was still aboard, and nothing was mentioned as being amiss in the captain's logbooks. The table was even set for dinner, and yet the crew had vanished without a trace."

Sidney frowned. "Perhaps they were captured by a German U-boat."

"That's the theory that seems to hold the most weight. Except no U-boat ever reported their capture, and the ship wasn't sunk, as they would usually do." I shook my head. "Whatever the truth, that is not my concern at the moment." I gestured to the sketch. "But rather the fact that it appears Esther might have seen something." I glanced up at him through my lashes. "*And* the fact that, if I remember correctly, the *Zebrina* sailed from Falmouth, England."

Sidney's eyebrows shot skyward. "Falmouth. Then the *Zebrina* could have been Lord Rockham's ship."

I grabbed his hand. "Sidney, do you know what this *means?* What if these aren't two separate investigations at all? What if they're all tied up together, somehow linked to the disappearance of that crew?"

He gazed down at me in grim commiseration. "Well, then, I suggest we find some answers. And quickly. Before someone has *us* making a disappearing act."

CHAPTER 19

We both slept fitfully that night. His thoughts were, I assumed, as consumed as mine by the realization we might have stumbled onto some sort of cover-up or criminal conspiracy. One that might prove very difficult to learn about, let alone confirm. After all, the *Zebrina* had long been towed away, either put back into action or relegated to some out-of-the-way dock. Whatever evidence she might have carried had long since been destroyed. I could contact the French Coast Guard, who were the first to examine the beached ship, but I needed more information first.

The following morning, I dashed off a telegram to the Legrand sisters, Esther's cousins, asking if I could speak to them via telephone. Was it possible for them to make use of one? I knew many rural areas still did not have access to such a device, but perhaps a nearby post office or hotel allowed customers to make use of theirs.

Once the telegram had been sent off with an errand boy, I telephoned someone who *did* have such a device. One set aside for a specific purpose.

It was a risk to use the number. For one, the line might have been disconnected or redirected. For another, I might be accused of interference and interrogated for misappropriation of government assets. I thought it more likely no one would show up to the rendezvous point I relayed via code, or I would receive a stern reprimand, but I also didn't underestimate the vindictiveness of some of my former colleagues. Particularly Major Davis, who had already made known his resentment of me and his intention to see me put in my place.

I reached St. Paul's Churchyard in Covent Garden a quarter of an hour before the appointed time and with a book settled on a bench underneath the shade of a tall lime tree. During the war, I'd become quite adept at pretending to read without letting those nearby know I was observing them. I'd worn out a copy of *Les Miserables* in just such a manner. It was a skill others thought easy to master but, in truth, was all too easy to bungle.

I was by no means alone in the quiet churchyard. A handful of other people occupied the benches or strolled along the lane, stopping to admire the flowers. But none of them paid me the smallest heed. Even so, I kept my wide hat brim pulled low, lest they recognize me from the papers. I'd purchased a pair of sunglasses for just such a situation, but being so newly fashionable, I'd discovered they actually drew more attention rather than deflecting it, so I left them tucked away.

The time I'd requested for the meeting came and went. Stifling my disappointment, I was about to close my book and rise to my feet, when a woman wearing a familiar pair of staid black pumps settled onto the bench beside me. I glanced up at her with a polite smile.

"Lovely day, isn't it?" Kathleen Silvernickel commented, straightening her dark skirt.

"Yes, though a trifle too warm for my taste."

She looked up to meet my gaze. "Hullo, Ver." Her mouth quirked. "I must say, after everything that happened in Belgium, I hadn't expected to hear from you so soon."

That she had read my debriefing CX report from that unforeseen operation was not surprising. She was C's secretary, after all, and so read much of what came across his desk, at least partially. However, the fact that she'd expected to hear from me at all left me with a slightly bitter taste in my mouth. Though I'd been demobilized, my time in Belgium two months ago had left me wondering if one was ever truly let go from the Secret Service.

"Yes, well, it appears intrigue cannot leave me alone," I muttered.

"Or is it that *you* cannot leave it alone?" she retorted without missing a beat.

I nodded, conceding her point. "Perhaps a bit of both."

Her eyes lit with amusement. "Cleverness can have its drawbacks."

I gave a huff of laughter.

"What have you got for us?"

I allowed my gaze to travel over the churchyard, much as Kathleen was periodically doing. "C knows that we're meeting?"

"I wouldn't be here otherwise." She tilted her head upward, squinting into the sun. "Truthfully, he's been a bit of a curmudgeon lately. You know his moods."

I nodded.

"But your coded message had him grinning like a schoolboy. He never was much for dealing with the bureaucracy, and that's much of what his job seems to entail since the war."

News from the ongoing hearings to decide who would receive compensation for their efforts and expenses during the war, who would be awarded commendations, and what inventors would receive awards for their contributions filled the newspapers. And those reports barely touched on the tiresome arguments and debates that happened behind closed doors.

However, I suspected any giddiness he felt at receiving my message was as much to do with his innate desire to thwart those bureaucrats who sought to keep him under their thumb as a release from tedium. C had always reveled in secrecy, not inaccurately emphasizing its vital importance to an organization like the Secret Service. Bogus addresses, fictitious fronts, dual code words, even the fact that agents working for him paid no income tax in order to keep their connection to the agency out of public records was all part and parcel to C's obsession with concealment.

I also knew Kathleen was, by necessity, omitting a great number of details. I was certain the Bolsheviks in Russia and the growing unrest in Ireland were keeping C occupied, especially with such a reduced staff. However, to speak of such things to me now that I was no longer an agent, and without C's express permission, could be considered tantamount to treason.

"I need to know what information we have on the disappearance of the *Zebrina*'s crew."

Her brow furrowed as if searching her memory for the incident. Then her eyes widened as she located the information in that steel-trap of a brain of hers. "The *Zebrina*? Why?"

I explained what we'd uncovered over the course of both investigations as briefly and succinctly as possible. And then, because I knew that with such scant evidence to go on, C could easily deny supplying me with any further intelligence on the matter, I mentioned Lord Ardmore. "I'm not sure how he fits into all of this, but he's mixed up in it somehow. He's the one who first suggested I look into Rockham's shipping interests."

Kathleen's expression turned guarded. "I'll relay what you've told me to C."

I knew that was all I could ask of her, so I nodded.

She waited to speak again until a couple who had stopped to admire a flowering shrub moved on. "Can you meet in St. James's Park in three days' time? North side of the lake, across Horse Guards from the Treasury."

"Yes."

"Someone with a newspaper and wearing a sword lapel pin will meet you that morning at a quarter after ten."

"Not you?" I verified, not altogether surprised someone else would be asked to do so. However, this entire undertaking was strictly off the record, much as my investigation in Belgium had been, and the more people C involved, the less secretive my involvement became. As well as his willingness to involve a demobilized agent in matters of national security.

Kathleen adjusted a fold of her blouse, a movement that normally would not have aroused interest. But I knew her. I knew how still she sat. Any slight adjustment to her clothing was tantamount to outright fidgeting. "No, C thought it would be better if all future communications be coordinated by a different contact. That my meeting with you might appear too conspicuous."

I overlooked the fact that C had thought far enough ahead to arrange a method for future communication in favor of addressing the tension that quietly radiated from Kathleen. "I suppose I can understand that. But we are friendly. It seems reasonable that we should meet for tea or enjoy a picture at the cinema."

She turned her head suddenly to look at me. "To you and me, yes. But not everyone will see it that way."

I searched her brilliant green eyes, realizing the source of her dismay. "This is about Major Davis, isn't it?" C's second-in-command was a boorish, officious pig. One who thought women had no place in military intelligence, and despised me in particular. I scowled. "Is he making trouble again?"

She scoffed. "He's never stopped."

And she had to sit at a desk across from his office and listen to his vitriol every day. "I'm sorry."

She brushed aside my concern. "Don't worry about me. As long as C is there, Davis knows he can't touch me. But you, on the other hand . . ."

Her hesitance to speak and the wary expression that clouded her brow made my chest tighten with dismay, and that sparked my anger. "Is he still threatening to have me arrested for interference?"

She pressed her lips together as if still reluctant to speak, but my irritated glare eventually convinced her. "He's had your name added to the list of women suspected of having intimate relations with the enemy."

"What?!" I gasped, startling a bird perched on the adjoining bench and pair of older women strolling by. I forced myself to inhale a deep breath to calm myself, waiting until the ladies glowering at me in scolding had moved beyond earshot. "How?" I demanded to know in a low voice.

"He suggested it was impossible to believe that you hadn't resorted to such . . . tactics in order to gather the information you did while you were in Belgium. That you should at least be added to the list as a precaution."

I clenched my fists, struggling to contain the fury boiling inside me. I had never used my body to gain information. Had I flirted with the enemy? Yes. Had I been forced to endure their groping and insinuating comments? Yes. To not do so meant a backhand across the face, at best, or even rape or imprisonment. As a British citizen and a Secret Service agent in disguise, I could not afford to draw any more unwanted attention than necessary. So that meant enduring what I must, what every Belgian or French woman inside the occupied territories endured for more than four long years.

At one point during the war, I had been given the task of pretending to be a German officer's mistress—an officer who was actually a fellow British agent undercover. The fact that I had later slept with that man after helping him to escape from Belgium to Rotterdam, Holland, was beside the point. He had not been the enemy.

At the time, I'd already believed my husband to be dead for many long months, so I could hardly be charged with adultery, either. In any case, Sidney had already forgiven me, and such matters were not the purview of the Secret Service. They certainly weren't questioning who their male agents had chosen to "fraternize" with.

That Major Davis had suggested such a thing, that there even existed such a degrading list, was evidence of their narrow-minded, foolish belief that women were incapable of loyalty and separating the act of lovemaking from love. It also further victimized those women in the occupied territories who had already been preyed upon by their German occupiers.

But Kathleen knew all of this. We'd both faced the same demeaning looks and comments, both endured the same patronizing recommendations, both been dismissed as silly women. We'd watched as the government unfairly regulated women's activities and bodies, while it made excuses for the men. Under the Contagious Diseases Act it had become illegal for a woman to sleep with a soldier if she had a venereal disease, even if she was the soldier's wife and had contracted that disease from her husband in the first place. Never mind where the soldier had gotten the disease, and if he'd contracted it from immoral behavior.

"So I've been labeled both a loose woman and an untrustworthy one," I bit out. "Simply because Major Davis does not like me."

She offered me an empathetic smile. "If it's any consolation, C is attempting to have your name removed. It was added in the first place without his knowledge. There is a case for it." Meaning he was arguing I'd been placed on the list because of that assignment where I'd posed as our undercover agent's mistress. "But Home Office is reluctant to make changes."

Of course, they were, I thought darkly. But none of that was of the moment.

"I'll be there Monday at a quarter after ten," I told her.

We swiftly said our goodbyes, for I knew Kathleen must be anxious to return to Whitehall before Davis or one of his cronies marked her extended absence. I watched as she disappeared through the iron gates, but still I made no move to rise. Sitting quietly, I stared at the tiny birds hopping along the path, plucking seeds from the dirt.

I couldn't help but feel attacked and vilified, merely for doing my bit. No one had forced me to work at the Secret Service. I could have remained at home, assisting periodically at the canteens and knitting socks, even if the prospect of such a life now made me cringe. Instead, I'd stepped up, I'd given it my all, and I'd willingly placed myself in danger time and again. And yet, once the war had ended, all I'd received in return was a curt, "Thank you, but your services are no longer needed," and my name added to a list that might as well have been labeled "women we believe are disloyal whores."

After discovering Sidney was, in fact, still alive, I'd wrestled with my guilt over sleeping with my colleague, Alec. But when my husband had forgiven me all, and even met the fellow, my remorse had receded. I'd begun to forgive myself. This discovery threatened to dredge that all up again.

Snatching my book up from the bench beside me, I surged to my feet, making the birds before me scatter. I strode angrily through the churchyard in the direction of Bedford Street, intending either to catch a cab or, barring that, to take the tube from Covent Garden to Dover Street—the closest station to

Berkeley Square. However, before I could even round the corner, a man I'd passed, scarcely giving him notice, called out to me.

"Mrs. Kent, is that you?"

I was not new to photographers' tricks—pretending to be someone I knew, so that I would turn to look at them. But this voice sounded familiar somehow, though I couldn't quite place it. Still, I turned slowly, using the wide brim of my hat to shield my face as I glanced over my shoulder.

Startled, I turned to face him more fully. "Nimble. Why, it's good to see you."

I struggled to hide my shock, for Sidney had mentioned nothing of his former batman's injuries. Nothing of the scars that blistered the left side of his face near the hairline or his partially missing ear. It was not so bad as to require a tin mask, but still distressing nonetheless. Especially since the last time I had seen him, when he'd come to offer me his condolences on Sidney's believed passing, he'd not looked like this. I silently rebuked Sidney for not preparing me. For while I felt no disgust, only sorrow for his suffering, I was sure my astonishment had been at least momentarily evident.

"You, as well, ma'am. I'm sure you were right happy to hear Cap'n Kent survived."

"Yes, I was," I replied simply, glossing over the tangle of other emotions I'd felt. "Mr. Kent tells me you'll be coming to work for him again."

"Aye, ma'am. I told him he didn't want a shambling wreck like me for a valet, but he insisted. Said he won't take anyone else." Bemusement and wonder transformed his face. "Said he'd just go about in wrinkled clothes and soiled linens, and I can't have that. Not when the cap'n is in all the papers and the men look to him so."

"No, we can't have that," I agreed with a gentle smile.

He fidgeted, his large hands clenching and unclenching at his sides. "I'm right grateful, ma'am."

"We're glad to have you," I assured him.

There was no need to ask what had stamped the uncertainty and the heavy sadness in his eyes. All the men who had been to war struggled with such emotions to some degree. But I did wonder what he'd been doing since he recovered from the shell explosion that had obviously ended his service in the trenches. Sidney had said he'd been working at Selfridges, and given his background as a batman, that had led me to believe he was a clerk. A notion my husband had done nothing to disabuse me of, even though it was evident that with his disfigurement Nimble would never have been allowed to hold such a public position. Not in a department store. He must have worked behind the scenes, or in the basement, where the great furnaces and other such machinery were located.

Whatever the case, why hadn't Sidney said something? I knew him better than to think Nimble's injuries had made him even bat an eye. And he should know me better than to think I would object to his old batman's presence because he wasn't as attractive to look at. We'd both seen worse. Much worse.

"The cap'n asked me to start on Monday," he informed me, rocking back on his heels.

"Good. Then we shall see you then."

He nodded and tugged the brim of his hat before turning away.

I watched him for a moment, unable to suppress a smile at the sight of his familiar clumping walk. I needed to ask Sidney the reason for his nickname. My humor faded. As well as a great many other things.

The heat not being stifling for once, I elected to take the tube. Even so, I was relieved to reemerge on the street in Mayfair. The sky overhead was a cerulean blue, and bright flowers burst from window boxes and balconies. At Berkeley Square, the trees were flush and bursting with life, despite the exhaust from passing motorcars.

I was so enjoying my stroll that I decided to walk onward to Grosvenor Square. Ada would undoubtedly be pounding down my door again if I didn't provide her with some update. However, when I arrived at Rockham House, William, the footman, informed she was not at home.

I puzzled for a moment over where she might have gone, but

then shook my concern aside. Ada was a widow, not a prisoner. There were plenty of respectable destinations she may have gone. In any case, I was through being her keeper.

I retraced my steps to Berkeley Square, the sunshine and fresh air working its magic to loosen the grip of my remaining fury at Kathleen's earlier revelations. By no means did my rage dissolve—it still simmered deep in my gut, ready to flare to life— but for the time being, at least, it was banked and repressed, allowing me to breathe more deeply and for my mind to wander to other topics.

I would have to wait until Monday for answers from C about what military intelligence knew about the *Zebrina,* but in the meantime, I could make inquiries elsewhere. George sprang to mind, for he worked for Naval Intelligence, but I quickly discarded the notion. If he knew something beyond what was reported in the papers, and that seemed unlikely, then the Official Secrets Act would forbid him to share it with me.

I considered telephoning the offices of Rockham's shipping and exporting business in Falmouth under the guise of being some sort of journalist writing a follow-up piece on the disappearance of the ship, but such an approach would undoubtedly be met with suspicion. In any case, I'd promised Thoreau that I would leave the matter of finding the marquess's angry visitor from his shipping company to him, and I suspected my telephoning them to ask questions, even on a different matter, might be met with displeasure. There was always the French Coast Guard. They had been the ones to find the beached ship. But first I decided a visit to the library would be best, to refresh my memory of the facts reported in the newspapers.

Passing our flat, I intended to carry on toward St. James's Square, but for the sight of a woman lurking in the shadow of the buildings near the intersection with Bruton Place. She gnawed her lip in indecision, gazing up at the building that housed our flat. As I drew nearer, I realized I recognized her.

"Miss Hawkins," I gasped, approaching her.

Flossie's eyes widened at the sight of me, before she glanced to the left and then the right, hushing me. "Don't say my name."

CHAPTER 20

Her harsh voice startled me, but during my time with the Secret Service I'd learned how to deal with skittish witnesses and cohorts.

"I beg your pardon," I murmured in a low voice, sliding my gaze upward as if I was examining some aspect of the architecture overhead. "Shall I carry on as if I don't know who you are?"

"Nay, just . . . don't be saying me name so loudly."

I nodded, examining her strained features. She had shadows beneath her eyes, and her hat was pulled low over her dark bobbed hair. "Shall we walk?"

She shook her head. "They might see us."

I thought we would draw more attention to ourselves standing there talking while she cowered in the corner than strolling down the street, but it was clear she would not be coaxed out in the open. Something, or rather someone, had terrified her.

"You're being followed?" I asked.

"Yes. No. I-I don't know," she stammered, her Irish accent growing thicker. She glanced about her again. "M-Maybe."

I took another step closer, now able to see her pupils were wide and dilated, nearly swallowing the irises.

"I came to tell you I lied," she burst forth with.

"You lied?" I repeated.

She nodded forcefully. "About Esther. Not havin' a beau." Her eyes flickered over my features, as if searching for some reaction. "I never met 'im. She was real secretive-like. I think he might o' been married." She nibbled on her lip. "An' . . . an' I don't think he was very nice. Came home with a real shiner one time, she did. Said she got it from walkin' into a door. But my mam was married to a real piker." She scoffed at the back of her throat. "I knows a clanker like tat when I hear one."

"Why didn't you tell me this the other day?" I asked evenly. Her fidgeting made me wary of spooking her. She was like a young filly not ready for the saddle, ready to bolt.

"Because I . . . I didn't want ye to think any less o' her." Her face contorted. "She's the best girl I know . . . knew." She sniffed, swallowing hard. "But I had to come tell ye. I had to tell ye because I . . . I think he might've done it."

"You think he might have killed her?"

She nodded. "Maybe he was lookin' for some letters he wrote her or gifts he gave her, tryin' to cover up what he done. Or . . . or maybe he wasn't lookin' for anything at all, and he just roughed up her room to make it look like he was. I don't know. But I think it was him."

"But you don't know his name?"

She shook her head, glancing anxiously up the street and across to the square.

"Did you ever see him?"

"No, but . . ." She bit her lip again, hesitant to speak. "But I think he might've been some swell."

"Why do you say that?" I tried to follow her gaze as she scanned the area nearby yet again.

She shrugged one shoulder. "Just because of some of the things she said."

"What did she say?"

But before I'd even finished the sentence, she suddenly surged forward, tugging downward at her hat. "I don't know anymore. I just wanted to tell you that. I have to go."

I tried to halt her. "Wait, if you're in trouble . . ."

"I have to go," she insisted, charging past me.

I watched as she disappeared around the corner, trying to decide if I should follow her. Ultimately, I chose to let her go. She'd made it clear she didn't wish to share any more with me, and if she was being followed, my chasing after her would only serve to draw more attention.

I decided that was a big if. For there was nothing suspicious that leapt out at me about those few people who were on the street or even loitering in the motorcars nearby, and I had years of practice at perceiving such things.

In truth, the entire encounter had been decidedly bizarre. Her nervous, jumpy behavior. Her story about Esther's beau, whom she knew both too much detail about and too little. I found myself wondering which parts, if any of it, were actually true. For there was evidence she'd taken some kind of drug, most likely cocaine, and that narcotic could certainly make one nervous and jumpy. It could even make you imagine things to be true that were not.

Cocaine was yet another fashionable narcotic consumed by some members of the smart set. Although, contrary to opium, it had actually been outlawed under the Defense of the Realm Act during the war. That, along with the death of Billie Carleton, a rising musical theater star, from an overdose of the drug less than a year before had stimulated a stronger opposition to it than opium.

Cynically, I thought the reluctance to outlaw opium—which was just as much of a nuisance as cocaine—stemmed more from the two wars the British Empire had fought over it in the mid-nineteenth century. After all, heaven forbid the government should admit it was wrong about something it had gone to war over.

Whatever the veracity of her story, I decided one thing was genuine. Flossie was grieving the loss of her friend. And perhaps therein lay the reason for her odd story. She was desperate to help, and her friend's recent strange behavior had made her decide it had to be attributed to a man. But then, what of the black eye she mentioned? Was it truth or exaggeration? And if it was true, where had it come from?

In the end, I did not make it to the library. After speaking with Flossie, I returned to our flat to find out if there had been any response to the telegram I'd sent Esther's cousins in France earlier that morning. Depending on how far the Legrand sisters lived from Cherbourg, I knew it might be the end of the day or the next before I heard from them, but since I was just outside our building, I decided to check. There was no telegram, but I had received a letter from Chief Inspector Thoreau. Hand-delivered, Sadie said.

The contents were not encouraging, but for his rather cryptic indication that, if it was convenient, we could locate him at a small café just off Cockspur Street at midday. A swift glance at the clock told me that it was just now approaching midday and if I hurried, I might be able to catch him.

Of course, traffic in London rarely cooperated, and always at the most inconvenient times. By the time I turned the corner into the little side street where I knew Café Luca's was located, I'd decided I must have missed him. But, as luck would have it, Thoreau was just emerging from the building.

He halted, sliding his hands into his pockets. "Mrs. Kent, I'd given up on you."

"Yes, well, I just received your message," I panted.

He dipped his head in understanding. Then his gaze traveled over my shoulder, narrowing at something near the intersection with Cockspur. "Will you stroll with me a short distance?"

I accepted his proffered arm, allowing him to lead me at a pace slightly quicker than a stroll deeper into the little warren of side streets. Trusting he knew where he was guiding me, I waited until we'd made a series of quick turns through several narrow alleys before I spoke. "You said you managed to track down the man who argued with Rockham before the dinner party. That he had an alibi," I prompted.

"Yes, a rather solid one, too."

"Did he tell you what they'd argued over?"

He frowned at the dusty pavement below our feet. "No, refused to. And we had no recourse to make him."

"But isn't that—"

"Mrs. Kent," he murmured, surprising me by cutting me off. His brow was furrowed with deep grooves as he suddenly halted, turning toward me. "I rather like you and your husband. I believe your intentions are good. That is the only reason I'm speaking with you now. To tell you that I've been warned not to pursue this angle. That doing so would be a waste of Scotland Yard's time."

That this warning disturbed him was obvious. What wasn't was why he was telling me.

"Are you also warning me away?"

His mouth pressed into a tight line; then he swiveled, resuming our stroll as he considered his response. "I cannot tell you, or Mr. Kent, what to do. You are not one of my men," he said carefully. "But . . . I will warn you there is a hazard in pursing this further. One I want you to be wary of, lest it sneak up on you unawares." His gaze shifted to meet mine, sharp with unspoken things.

I met it squarely, letting him know I understood. "Thank you for the courtesy. I shall keep that in mind."

His eyes glinted with intelligence, realizing I was not one to take kindly to being warned away. I suspected that had been part of the reason he'd told me.

Our steps came to a halt at the junction of a larger street, and a quick glance about confirmed this was Pall Mall.

"I trust you can find your way from here."

"Yes," I assured him.

He tipped his hat. "Then I will bid you a good day. Give my regards to your husband."

"I will."

I watched him walk away, hanging back near the narrow street entrance. Several minutes later, just as I expected, a rather loutish fellow burst onto the pavement further to the east, almost colliding with a woman who swatted at him with her handbag. I bit back a grin, remaining tucked out of sight, while he surveyed the street to his left and right, and then seeming to catch sight of Thoreau, set off in pursuit again.

I was still contemplating this latest development when I returned home to find Sidney seated in one of the chairs before the hearth. His head rested against the back and his eyes were closed.

I might have believed him to be asleep, except for the clenching and unclenching of his square jaw and the tension lashing his frame.

In slumber, Sidney's entire being relaxed; his features softened and his muscles uncoiled. Having seen him in such an unguarded state only served to highlight how firmly leashed he held himself every waking hour of the day. It was as if he was always braced for whatever might come next, for whatever hatchet might fall.

I'd witnessed this persistent vigilance and guardedness in other returning soldiers. But they weren't my husband.

I stood watching him, wondering what was spooling through his mind, making his profile appear to be one carved of granite.

"I presume you've been meeting with the good inspector," Sidney muttered without opening his eyes.

It didn't surprise me that he'd known I was there. After all, I'd not taken any pains to be quiet. Or that he'd realized where I'd gone. I'd left the note lying on the bureau on top of our other correspondence.

"Did he have anything interesting to say, or was he merely cautioning you again?"

"Funny you should say that," I murmured, gliding around the sofa toward him.

He blinked open his eyes at this response to stare up at me.

I told him about the warning Thoreau had received from his superiors, and the information I thought he had been trying to relay to me without actually stating it outright.

He pushed himself farther upright as I spoke, the corners of his eyes crinkling in concern. "But you think he wants us to keep investigating?"

I sank down on the arm of his chair. "I think he wasn't pleased to be warned away from a potential suspect. That he thinks something smells just as fishy as I do. But, of course, he can't be seen to actually encourage us to do something when he's supposed to be deterring us." I swiveled to better see Sidney's face. "You do realize that Sir Basil Thomson, the head of Scotland Yard's Criminal Investigation Department, worked closely with MI5 during the war. After all, the CID was the enforcement arm for the Security Service since MI5 had no powers to actually arrest suspects. And Sir Basil has now been appointed Director of Intelligence at the Home Office, overseeing all intelligence agencies."

"Really?" I could hear the speculation in his voice as he worked out what I already had.

"Sir Basil also happens to be good friends with Lord Ardmore."

His eyes gleamed in answering skepticism. "What did your contact with the Secret Service have to say?"

I exhaled a long breath. "She agreed to take my concerns to C, but that's no guarantee they'll share anything with me. I'd hoped the facts and C's trust in me, coupled with his dislike of Ardmore, would convince him to share what they know. But now that I've discovered Sir Basil Thomson is somehow mixed up in this, and he's technically C's superior, I'm not sure he'll decide it's worth the risk."

Especially now that I'd been added to the infamous list of women suspected of fraternizing with the enemy. But I chose to omit that detail. No good could come of sharing that with Sidney, except to dredge up memories both of us would rather remain buried. Just because he'd forgiven me for sleeping with Alec while I believed him to be dead didn't mean he wished to be reminded of it. It was the same as my not wanting to relive my memories of the fifteen months following Sidney's supposed death, and the pain of knowing he'd allowed me to believe it, even though I'd accepted he had no other choice. Not without exposing me to danger and allowing the traitors to continue to walk free.

His arm snaked around me, pulling me down into his lap. "When do you expect to hear from him?"

"Monday. But that doesn't mean I intend to remain idle until then." I shifted to face him, draping an arm around his neck. "Which reminds me. We had a rather interesting visitor this morning." I told him about Flossie and her confession, as well as my own impressions.

"The whole thing sounds like rubbish to me," he stated with no compassion. "And I heard my fair share of balled-up confessions from my men at the front."

"But why would she seek me out to tell me such a lie?"

"Because she's hiding something."

I frowned at the crisp white placket of his shirt. He was right. Time and again, I'd seen those who would be better served by remaining quiet instead step forward to weave a wild tale, thinking somehow this would remove suspicion from them, when, in fact, it did the exact opposite. I'd not for a moment suspected Flossie of any wrongdoing in Esther's murder, but now I had to wonder. Was she somehow muddled up with all of this?

"Well, it seems like you've put me to shame with your productive morning," Sidney remarked idly. "Meanwhile, all I've been able to discover is that Rockham did indeed commission the *Zebrina,* on multiple occasions."

My gaze darted to his, seeing that he knew full well the import of his discovery. "Including her fateful voyage when she was abandoned?"

"Including that one."

I didn't ask how he'd discovered this, trusting he'd visited some record office and done a thorough job of it. "Then we've confirmed he definitely has ties to the incident. And that ties him to Esther, if that ship she sketched is truly the *Zebrina.*" I scowled. "But it still doesn't explain why Rockham and Esther were killed. Or whether their deaths are related."

His hand lifted to cradle the back of my neck, his fingers combing through the hairs at the nape. "Patience, my spitfire." His lips curled. "We'll get there."

I nodded, even though I wanted to argue. For there was something lodged in the middle of my chest, something that was driving me to hurry. But toward what, I didn't know. I tilted my head so that our foreheads touched, trying to still the urgent fluttering.

"You'll never guess who I also bumped into today," I said as he continued to play with my hair, sending tingles racing down my spine.

"Who?" he murmured, and I wondered if it was wrong to broach this subject while he was so content. At least, as content as he ever was while awake.

"Nimble."

His muscles grew taut beneath me. Only by a degree, but I still felt the impact his former batman's name had on him.

I lifted my head. "Why didn't you tell me he'd been injured?"

"I didn't think it mattered."

I tilted my head in scolding at this feeble attempt to fob me off. "You know it doesn't. But that still doesn't explain why you never mentioned it."

His brow formed a deep vee. "I don't inform you of every acquaintance's physical condition, now do I. Given all the lame and mutilated chaps coming back from France and elsewhere, it would grow quite tedious rather quickly," he snapped, being deliberately curt.

But I refused to be baited. "Nimble isn't just some acquaintance. And he's coming to work for you." Seeing my words had no impact, I tried a different tack. "I wasn't prepared when I met him, and I fear my shock showed. It was mortifying. I would hate for him to think I was repulsed by the sight of him. I'm sure he has to deal with enough people's horrified reactions. Mine shouldn't be one of them."

His expression softened. "You're right. I didn't think of that." His gaze slid to the side. "I don't know why I didn't tell you about it. Perhaps I just didn't want to discuss it."

I studied his rigid features, the irritation puckering his mouth. I could tell he wasn't telling the truth. At least, not all of it. But I also wondered if that might be because he was also lying to himself.

"It's not your fault that he was injured, you know," I said softly.

His grunted response indicated he thought differently. Though how he expected to have prevented his former batman from being reassigned to the infantry after he himself was shot in the chest and barely survived, and had then gone into hiding to stop the traitors, I couldn't begin to fathom.

"You were not in command of that situation," I persisted, but Sidney didn't want to hear it.

He lifted me from his lap. "We are not discussing this." He crossed the room to retrieve one of his Turkish cigarettes from the silver box on the sideboard.

"Sidney . . ." I protested.

But he shook his head, refusing to look at me as he lit his fag. "No."

He turned toward the window to gaze out at the square below and the city beyond. His back was stiff, his movements controlled, but I knew whatever emotions were swirling around inside him, whatever thoughts were flickering through his head, they were not in the least tame or well ordered. He was holding something back, something at bay, and part of me was just as afraid to know what it was as the other part of me was desperate to understand.

CHAPTER 21

Young bodies packed the dance floor of Grafton Galleries, whirling and shimmying to the ragtime rhythm, intent on forgetting their troubles. At least for a short time. At least until this song slipped into the next. And perhaps longer, if possible. If the gin poured by the bartenders was strong enough, the music played by the band loud enough, and the partner in their arms willing enough.

I sank down in the chair at the table where Sidney was leaning forward to converse with Goldy and Etta over the blare of the trumpet, though the trombone and clarinet were doing a fair job of competing with it alongside the beat of the drums and the upright piano. The strain I'd witnessed on Sidney's face earlier had not abated, and in fact, seemed to intensify under Goldy's persistent probing.

"But you said it was a good idea. You said it had merit."

"Sure I did. But I'm just one man," Sidney retorted. "Who says my opinion matters?"

Goldy's eyes gleamed with anxious uncertainty. "So you don't think I should invest the family business in passenger service?"

"I just told you, I don't know," he snapped. "Why are you asking me, anyway?" He held up his hand to stay his friend before he could say any more, just as Etta laid a restraining hand on Goldy's arm. "Leave me out of it." Pushing to his feet, he stormed into the crowd, shifting left and right to pass between bodies.

I turned back to find Etta murmuring to Goldy, who stared angrily down at the table.

"I need some air," he declared abruptly, shoving his chair back so fast it almost toppled over.

I arched my eyebrows in query as both men disappeared into the morass of bodies.

Etta sighed. "It's his family's aviation business," she explained. "He keeps dithering over what to do. Wants Sidney to make it easy for him by agreeing with him." As I'd heard him do at the Rockhams' dinner party. "He trusts him. He wants his good opinion. Which is a compliment to your husband, *ma chérie*. But that doesn't mean he should be badgering him to death."

"I don't think it's his badgering that set him off," I told her for the sake of honesty. "Not entirely, in any case."

She met my gaze with one of mutual understanding. After all, Goldy had been through the war. He'd seen the devastation firsthand, had watched friends die. He'd had his aeroplane shot down and catch fire beneath him.

I looked away before hesitantly asking, "Does Goldy ever talk about it?" There was no need to explain what "it" was.

Her dangling crystal earrings tinkled as she shook her head. "No, *bébé*. None of them talk." She turned to look at me knowingly. "And I'm not sure it's right to make them."

I didn't respond, but I felt a sharp prick of guilt inside my chest. For I had been trying to do just that, without much success. It was so difficult to know what was best. Did you leave their wounds unprodded, hoping they healed with time? Or by not forcing them to cleanse them, to bring everything out in the open, did you run the risk that they would begin to fester and rot? By thinking you spared them pain now, were you ultimately causing more later?

"I must get ready for my next set," Etta said, rising from her chair in a cloud of Tabac Blond perfume. Passing behind me, she leaned down to speak in my ear. "Don't look so gloomy, *ma pe-*

tite. It doesn't become you." She bussed my cheek and then flashed me an impish grin. "Drag that delicious husband of yours out on the dance floor. It will do you both some good."

I smiled faintly as she sauntered away, every eye within ten feet turning to watch her pass in her silver and gold fringed gown.

Her suggestion wasn't without merit. If only I could locate said delicious husband in this crush. I craned my neck, searching for him with no luck. However, through a parting of the dancers, I did spy George striding rather purposely toward me. His efforts were hindered by a girl—and a rather zozzled one, at that—throwing her arms around him as he tried to skirt past. The sight of him attempting to disentangle himself from the bird provided me with far too much amusement. Enough that when he finally reached the table where I was still seated, a wry grin stretched across his features.

"Saw that, did you?"

"Poor George. Daphne's not even here, and you still have women being thrown at you."

He glanced over his shoulder. "Yes, well. I think she thought I was someone else."

I patted the chair beside me that Etta had vacated. "Tell me. What has you aiming for me with such single-minded determination?"

"I wouldn't call it single-minded," he hedged, sliding into the chair.

I gave him an arch look.

But rather than banter back at me, his expression turned serious. He reached out to fidget with a book of matches lying on the table before him. "I received my papers today."

I blinked at him in surprise, before finally managing to reply. "You've been demobbed?"

He nodded.

"Today? After all this time."

He turned to look at me, clearly not understanding the clipped tone of my voice. "We knew it was bound to happen sooner or later. They've already cut the staff to the quick."

I shook my head. "I know you said so, but I didn't believe it. Not knowing what a bloody brilliant codebreaker you are," I hissed under my breath so only he could hear. "But that's not what has me so riled. It's the timing."

"What do you mean?" His dark eyes lit with comprehension. "You think this is Ardmore's doing?"

"You think it's not?"

"Well, no."

I turned away, crossing my arms. "That's because you don't know the rest."

He reached out a hand, stilling the leg I'd crossed over my other knee that had been swinging furiously. "Tell me."

I scoured his face. "Do you really want to know?"

He glowered. "I wouldn't have asked you if I didn't."

So, I told him about Thoreau being warned away from pursuing Rockham's shipping interests, as well as the recent developments in the Secret Service, including my name being added to that dreadful list. With each new sentence, the line of his mouth grew tighter and tighter, until his lips all but disappeared.

"Yes, I see what you mean," he conceded when I'd finished. He leaned toward me. "But then why did Ardmore suggest you look into Rockham's import/export business in the first place? Why point you in that direction at all?"

"I don't know," I admitted, having wrestled with this question myself. "Unless he's testing me somehow. Or toying with me."

George tipped his head in acknowledgment. "I would not put it past him. From what I've heard, and admittedly it isn't much, he is a rather Machiavellian figure. Always pitting people against each other for his own amusement."

Apparently, being demobilized, and in such an unceremonious, and possibly unscrupulous, manner had loosened his tongue about the goings-on in Naval Intelligence.

But he was smarting now from receiving his marching orders, and I didn't want him to regret later telling me anything. So I turned the subject.

"Whatever the case, I'm sorry you got caught up in this. You can gloss over it as much as you like, but I know you loved what you did."

He swallowed and nodded, allowing me, just for a moment, to see the hurt and unhappiness he strove to hide.

I turned away to watch the dancers, giving him a moment to compose himself. "What will you do next?"

"Back to mathematics, I suppose. I shouldn't have any trouble landing a professorship at one of the universities."

"Away from London?" I asked, alarm tightening my voice.

He shrugged. "I have to go where there are openings."

The thought of George not being nearby caused a tiny flutter of panic in my breast. After all, he had been something of bedrock for me during the war. Daphne was loyal and empathetic, but George was the friend on whom I'd known I could always rely.

I supposed in some ways he'd filled the void left by my brother, Rob, when he died in France in July 1915. Rob had always been the brother I was closest to. Two and half years older, he'd sort of taken me under his wing when our brother Tim was born just seventeen months after me and our mother and nanny were so often distracted by him. Our eldest brother, Freddy, had been the troublemaker, and far from motherly, but Rob hadn't seemed to mind my sitting close to him or holding my hand. He'd grown up to be the most chivalrous.

When he'd died, a part of me had died with him. It had certainly shattered whatever innocence I'd had left. It was also the reason I still hadn't returned to my parents' home in the Yorkshire Dales. I simply couldn't face the memories there. Not without Rob. It was cowardly, perhaps. But there it was all the same.

And now George might be leaving. The thought of him not being in the same city for me to run to if I ever needed him made my chest tight and that last gin rickey I'd downed churn in my stomach.

He draped an arm around my shoulders. "Cheer up, Ver. There's time. I won't be running off to Cambridge or Oxford, or heaven forbid, the dank cold of St. Andrews just yet."

I grinned at his jest, finding it impossible to imagine him living in Scotland. He shivered in a feeble summer breeze.

"There's time," he repeated. But I wondered whether he was reminding me or himself.

The following morning, Sidney and I took the train to Guildford to pay our respects to Mrs. Rogers. Crispin had need of his motorcar, and although Sidney had other friends he could call upon, he decided the train would be just as well.

After enduring Sidney's tense, brooding silence and anxious, lurching behavior since the moment I'd awoke, I was glad of it. Had we been in a motorcar, he might very well have driven us off the road.

As the train drew nearer and nearer to Guildford, he seemed to retreat deeper into himself, taking longer and longer to respond to my queries. It drew my own nerves taut, for I didn't understand his behavior. I didn't understand why the prospect of paying a visit to a friend's widow seemed to alarm him as much as his facing the trenches again had done two months past.

"We don't have to go, you know," I said. "We can get off at the next station and take the train back to London."

He looked up at this, though it took him another second to respond. "No, we should go."

Not "I want to go" or "I need to go," simply "we should."

"Then will you please tell me who Albert Rogers is so that I have some idea what to say to his widow?" This seemed a safer question than asking if he was well—which he was not, though I knew he would deny it to the depths of his being—or convincing him to share what had unsettled him. I knew Etta had counseled me not to pry, but witnessing Sidney in such a state, I had to do something.

He stared at me with his hollow, bruised-looking eyes, and I decided this was at least a start. Most of the trip he'd sat gazing morosely out the window.

"Was he part of the Thirtieth?" I prodded, mentioning the infamous battalion Sidney had served in for much of the war.

He shook his head. "We were up at Oxford together, though he was a year ahead." His brow furrowed, remembering. "Played on the polo team with him. He was captain his final year."

Just as Sidney had been his final year.

His gaze trailed toward the Surrey countryside, his voice lowering. "He was a dashed fine player. Dashed fine man, too."

"Infantry?"

He nodded. "Took a bullet through his napper from a sniper and then was gassed in '17."

I cringed at the fellow's rotten luck. Evidently the bullet to his face or head had not been fatal, but who knows how much damage it had done—both seen and unseen. And then to be gassed, likely by blistering, choking mustard gas, based on the date. His war had not been a pleasant one. It was no wonder if he'd struggled to recover.

"Had you seen him since the start of the war?" I asked, curious when he'd last encountered his friend.

"Once on the road to Albert. His company was headed up the line to the trenches while we were headed down it. We ordered our men to take their ease for a few moments so we could catch up."

That must have been years ago.

As if he'd heard my silent thought, he murmured, "I should have gone to see him after I returned. I meant to."

He didn't make excuses for himself, even though he'd hardly been twiddling his thumbs. There had been a great deal of paperwork involved to bring him back to life, our marriage had been fractured and in very real danger of crumbling completely, and there had also been the intrigues that perpetuated to drop in my lap.

"What of his wife? Do you know anything about her?"

"Not much. I gathered their families had been old friends, so when they became engaged it wasn't any great surprise. I met her at their wedding, and she was beautiful." He shrugged one shoulder. "In the typical English rose kind of way. I would be surprised if she wasn't still."

What exactly he meant by that, I wasn't sure. But I soon discovered.

The Rogerses lived in a lovely rambling cottage covered in trellises thick with ivy and flowering creepers at the southern edge of Guildford near the Surrey Hills. Close enough, in fact, to see the Anglo-Saxon towers of Guildford Castle and St. Mary's Church rising over the trees in the distance. A taxicab delivered us from the station to the front garden, where a woman stood in a broad-brimmed hat pruning her bushes for the cooler autumn weather, which seemed to never come.

She glanced up as we approached, providing me my first glimpse of her smooth complexion and elfin features. Beneath the hat, her rich golden locks were fashioned into a type of chignon at the back of her neck. Her figure was tidy and trim, and showed to advantage even with a gardening apron tied over her black crepe dress.

This was a woman who valued her appearance, and would never let it go to ruin, even if she had to be ruthless about it. Daphne, who sometimes struggled to maintain as small a waist as she wished, would likely accuse her of banting—following the strict diet promoted by Victorian author William Banting. For my part, I had resigned myself to being unfashionably voluptuous, though my stomach didn't run to fat and my legs were quite shapely thanks to sport. Truth be told, after enduring roasted oat chaff and pea shells as tea, sugared potato pulp in place of jam, and many other disagreeable substitutes during my time spent in the German-occupied territories during the war, I hadn't the least desire to subsist on mineral water and Fat-Free BRAND's Essence simply to achieve a slimmer figure.

Mrs. Rogers removed her gloves and strode forward to greet us. "May I help you?"

"My name is Sidney Kent," he stated haltingly. "And this is my wife. I was a friend of your husband's."

I could tell from the look in her eyes she had already recognized us, but she merely replied, "Yes, I remember you. Won't you come inside."

We followed her up the path and in through the door. She

gestured for us to proceed into a room on the left while she put away her things. Removing my gloves, I crossed toward the fireplace mantel, where a number of photographs were arranged. First a picture of Mrs. Rogers as a bright-eyed debutante, followed by a wedding portrait, and then Albert Rogers looking eager and handsome in his uniform. Though not as attractive as Sidney—and I was admittedly biased—Albert had not disappointed. He exuded confidence from every pore.

But that had been before the war. Before he'd taken a bullet to the head. How had he looked then?

The remaining photographs were of two children, a dimple-cheeked boy and a toddling girl with wispy curls. Children who could be heard even now chattering and thumping overhead.

Rather than joining me at the hearth, Sidney stood gazing out the window, as if he was already eager to escape. However, when Mrs. Rogers returned, he immediately turned and strode toward her, taking her hand. "My condolences on your loss. Albert was a good man. The best."

Her answering smile was strained. "Thank you. I know he was quite fond of you," she said as we sat on a floral chintz sofa and matching chair. "He spoke of you quite often in the last few months. He seemed to think it somewhat of a lark that you escaped the 'jaws of death,' as he called it, and tracked down those traitors."

"Yes, well, we all do what we must," he replied, tugging at the sleeves of his suitcoat.

Her gaze dipped to the floor at our feet. "Yes. Yes, indeed."

I felt Sidney stiffen beside me as he realized she might have taken a different meaning from his words, given the fact Albert was suspected of committing suicide.

"I, too, am sorry for your loss," I said, breaking the awkward silence that had fallen. "I wish I'd had the pleasure of meeting him."

"Thank you."

I glanced at the photographs. "You have two beautiful children. Is that them we hear playing?"

Just as I'd hoped, her face softened. "Yes, they are both rather fond of hobby horses, and this old house masks nothing."

I smiled. "My mother couldn't abide the sound of our clomping, so she had our nursery moved to the attics. Up there we had to keep moving in the winter or else catch our death of cold."

"Their nurse will be bringing them down soon for their morning constitutional if you'd like to meet them." She leaned forward, sharing a confidence. "They could use some practice in greeting adults properly."

"That would be delightful," I replied, hoping I didn't speak out of turn. Sidney had fallen silent since his gaff, but he didn't appear unduly strained. At least, no more than when we'd arrived. And he had always been comfortable around children.

Mrs. Rogers and I chatted a few minutes more before we heard the sounds of the children thumping and bumping down the stairs. She rose to her feet to step out and ask them to come meet us. The boy grinned broadly as she led him inside, offering us a rather grandiose, if wobbly bow, while his younger sister tried to hide behind him. She resisted all coaxing from her nanny to give us a curtsy, and I smiled, assuring her I had been the same way at the age of two. This was a lie, for my mother insisted I had never been shy or circumspect in my life, but under the circumstances, it was the right thing to say.

The little boy bounced on his heels, eying Sidney with intense interest. "Have you come to play with us? Granda gave me a new ball and I haven't gotten to try it out yet."

"Alby, dear. They haven't come to play," his mother cautioned. "They're here to pay their respects to your father."

"Oh." His face crumpled with such disappointment that I felt my heart squeeze.

And then Sidney surprised me by leaning toward the boy. "Oh, but of course, we must give this new ball of yours a toss. I can't think of anything your father would like better than for us to do so."

Alby's brow furrowed. "He couldn't throw a ball with me before he died. He said it hurt too much."

My heart clutched at the well of sadness contained in those

simple words. I'm not sure I could have spoken, but Sidney seemed to know just what to say.

"Yes, well, I'm sure he wanted to more than anything," he told him gently. "But the war took that from him. It took that from both of you, and I'm sorry for that."

The boy studied his face. "Did you fight in the war?"

"I did."

"Did you get hurt?"

"Yes, you just can't see it because it's hidden by my clothes," he said in answer to Alby's searching look. "And it won't keep me from tossing a ball."

His lips hitched into a small smile.

"Shall we?"

"Yes," he exclaimed, grabbing Sidney's hand and pulling him out the door ahead of his sister and their nanny.

I swallowed the lump that had gathered at the back of my throat, and turned toward Mrs. Rogers, who stood as still as a statue. The look on her face was an acute mixture of pain and grief, and I turned away, allowing her a measure of privacy as she struggled to master her emotions. When she was able, she rejoined me, sinking down onto the spot Sidney had vacated.

"I cannot begin to presume everything you have gone through," I murmured. "But I understand it must have been hard."

She clasped her hands tightly together in her lap. So tightly that the knuckles showed white. "There were times when I wished for death for him. His pain . . ." She broke off, inhaling a ragged breath. "It was . . . unpleasant. But I never meant it. Not really." She glanced up at me, as if to see whether I understood. "But he was also so different. And I don't mean his scars. *He* was different. I felt like I barely knew him."

"The war changed them," I answered quietly. "All of them, in one way or another."

"Yes, but . . . when you looked in Sidney's eyes after he returned, didn't you still see *him*—the man you'd sent away after his last leave?"

I nodded.

She crossed her arms over her chest, cradling the opposite

elbow in each hand. "It wasn't that way with Albert. Not after he was shot. I looked into his eyes and saw a complete stranger."

Her words left me cold. "My husband said he was shot in the head. Maybe it altered something in his brain."

"That's what the doctor said." Her voice turned bitter. "And yet he was still deemed fit enough to send back to France."

By early 1917, the British Army had been desperate for new recruits and conscription had begun. Any invalided soldier well enough to stand and fire a gun with any semblance of accuracy was shipped back as soon as possible.

"People blame me, you know," she stated almost defiantly. "For not being there. For not stopping it." But then her bravado abruptly faded. "And sometimes I wonder if they might be right. If somewhere inside I'd known what he intended. If I'd just grown too tired and weary to care." She blinked her eyes, clearing her vision as she lifted her gaze to meet mine. "I guess I'll never know."

CHAPTER 22

Sunday dawned bright and warm, just like all the days before it; however, a welcome breeze also gusted over the city, cooling the perspiration before it could gather on one's skin. Unfortunately, I had to resign myself to remaining indoors. The telegram I'd received from the Legrand sisters while we were in Guildford the day before had informed me they would telephone some time on Sunday. Words being an economy, apparently, the only other thing they had communicated was how anxious they were to speak with me.

Sidney slept late, having tossed and turned much of the night after waking from a nightmare he had refused to tell me about. His troubled slumber had disturbed mine as well, but it was Sadie's day off, and I was worried I might sleep through the ringing of the telephone. Consequently, I was not the most patient of wives when Sidney rose and proceeded to stomp about the flat in a foul mood.

I'd thought perhaps his interaction with Mrs. Rogers and her children might help Sidney through whatever painful memories he was confronting, but it seemed to have only made him worse. Not only was he uncommunicative, he was sullen and angry, and rebuffed every effort I made to comfort or reassure him.

Eventually, my temper got the better of me and I ordered him to take his sour disposition elsewhere. But even after he'd stormed out of the flat, I couldn't quell the uneasiness churning in the pit of my stomach. My conversation with Mrs. Rogers kept playing in my head. I was far from uncaring, but there were times when bitterness could describe my feelings toward the changes in Sidney. If we continued in this vein, how long would it be until that bitterness took root permanently? How long until I no longer cared?

I tried to occupy my thoughts, to focus on the facts of the case, but I mostly wandered about the flat, sunk in morose ponderings. When the telephone finally rang in the middle of the afternoon, I practically flung myself at it.

"This is Mrs. Kent," I answered.

"Verity, darling. I thought you might come to see me today."

My shoulders slumped at the sound of Ada's voice. "Yes, well, I've been busy with the inquiry. In fact, I'm expecting a rather important telephone call, so if you . . ."

"Is it about my predicament?"

"I . . . Yes, it is." If the two murders were somehow linked to the disappearance of the *Zebrina*'s crew, and I couldn't know that for sure without speaking to the Legrands, then it was true. Even if I expected the call to answer more of my questions about Esther's death than Rockham's. "So if you wouldn't mind . . ."

"I know about that angry visitor my husband received before the party," she declared, interrupting me again.

"You do?"

"Of course. And I know that inspector tracked Calloway down."

I was momentarily at a loss for words. "You know his name?"

She huffed. "Honestly, Verity. It's as if you think I don't know anything at all."

I frowned. "That's not true, Ada. But why didn't you tell me any of this before? I came to call on you Friday."

But she wasn't listening to me, determined to continue with her rant. "Rockham never trusted Calloway, you know. He thought he was a filthy piker. So I bet he had a hand in his death. I bet Rockham threatened to fire him, and Calloway snuck in through the window later and killed him."

"Hold on. Rockham told you he didn't trust Calloway?"

"Yes."

"He said those exact words?" I pressed, knowing full well from speaking with Calliope *and* Ada that the marquess never discussed such matters with his wives.

"Well, no," she admitted. "But you've seen the way he looks at people. It's easy to distinguish those he views with disdain."

Yes, but disdain did not equal mistrust.

Suspicion stirred within me. "Has Ardmore been discussing the inquest with you?"

"What a silly question. Of course, he has. He's already promised to help me hire the best barristers in the country to plead my case should the police be foolish enough to arrest me."

My hands tightened around the telephone, infuriated by the duplicitousness of Ardmore. On the one hand, I strongly suspected him of exerting influence to squash any investigation into Rockham's shipping interests, and on the other he was encouraging Ada to believe that was where the guilty party lay. And Ada, stupid Ada—who certainly should know better—was swallowing his every word.

But I hadn't time to confront that right then. Not when I needed the telephone line to be clear. "I must go," I bit out. "I'll telephone as soon as I know something."

Then before she could waylay me yet again, I rang off.

My and Ada's conversation had been brief enough. If the Legrand sisters had tried to telephone then, I trusted they would try again. But as the hours inched later and later, and darkness crept over London, I had to acknowledge they were not going to telephone that day. I stood at the window, watching the colors bleed from the sky, feeling a sinking sensation in my stomach that mirrored the setting sun.

While I acknowledged there could be a perfectly harmless, rational explanation for why they'd failed to telephone, I couldn't shake the feeling that something was very wrong. They had been anxious to speak with me. Anxious enough to spend the money to include a sentence communicating so. Why, then, would they fail to do so, unless something had prevented them?

I tried to explain as much to Sidney when he returned later that evening from wherever he'd been all day, but he suggested I was merely borrowing trouble. So I kept the rest of my worries and speculations to myself, not wanting to argue. Whether the cause was the sunshine or the enjoyment he'd derived from however he'd occupied his day, he'd returned in a calmer state of mind. He was still quiet, but at least he wasn't brooding and snippy.

I rose early the following morning and left the flat before he had even woken. After dashing off another telegram to the Legrand sisters, I turned my steps toward the library, burying myself in stacks of old newspapers to glean all I could from them about the *Zebrina* incident. At ten o'clock, with an umbrella tucked under my arm, I set off through Waterloo Place and across The Mall to St. James's Park.

The weather that day was not as auspicious as the one before. The sky was threatening rain, but for the moment the heavy, low-hanging clouds were jealously hoarding their treasures. Honeybees buzzed from flower to flower, an encouraging sign that the rain would not begin yet, for they always seemed to know when to expect such things before we humans did. One curious little chap even decided to get a closer look at my hat, and I gently shooed him away.

"He must think you're sweet. But he doesn't know you the way I do."

I glanced up in shock, startled to see Captain Alec Xavier rising from a nearby bench, a newspaper folded in his hands and a sword pin affixed to his lapel. His whiskey brown eyes laughed at my astonishment.

"What are *you* doing here?" I demanded. "I thought they had you traipsing about Europe."

He shrugged his left shoulder where he'd taken a bullet back in July. "I haven't been cleared for active duty yet."

"Yes, well, they probably would have by now if you'd stayed in Tourcoing, as Rose insisted, instead of accompanying us into the war-torn countryside with a furrow taken out of your flesh." Within twenty-four hours, fever and infection had set in. Alec was lucky the doctors had been able to treat it before it grew worse.

"You needed me," he replied unflappably.

"Did we?" I challenged, for we both knew what little use he had been during our final confrontation with a revenge-mad saboteur.

He conceded this with a nod of his head, though his smile never slipped. "Will you walk with me?"

I accepted his proffered arm, attempting to ignore the disquieting sensation of his proximity. Our history was too complicated and my marriage to Sidney still on somewhat shaky ground for me to be comfortable in Alec's presence.

Alec had infiltrated the German Army years before the conflict—proving C's brilliant forethought—and served inside Belgium as an agent for British Intelligence. I had worked with him on several fraught missions, including the one that had seen me posing as his mistress. The fateful endeavor had ultimately compromised his position, and had ended with me helping him escape into Holland, where I'd made the egregious error of sleeping with him.

Sidney was aware of the brief affair, and the three of us had even managed to foil that barbarous plot in Belgium two months past. But that didn't mean he would be best pleased to have Alec walk back into our lives. Consequently, I was also unsettled.

"C sent you, then?" I murmured quietly, wondering just how much the old dog knew about what had happened between me and Alec.

Alec's gaze flicked sideways at me. "He said he didn't trust sending anyone else."

I took that to mean C had counted on Alec's loyalty and gratitude to me for helping to spirit him out of Belgium to keep the matter quiet.

"It appears you've made some rather powerful enemies for yourself."

This statement didn't surprise me perhaps as much as it should have, but I could tell from Alec's voice it had astonished him.

"Yes, well, I needed something to keep me occupied whiling my way through peacetime," I drawled sarcastically.

A young man bustled past us, carrying a stack of papers he was risking in this weather.

I waited to speak until he was out of earshot. "I gather Major Davis has been spouting his particular brand of vitriol." I sighed. "And I suppose Sir Basil Thomson has joined the chorus?" I studied Alec out of the corner of my eye, who had neither confirmed nor denied this. "But what I'd really like to know is whether Lord Ardmore has also voiced his dissent?"

At this, Alec turned to me with interest. "You certainly waste no time in getting around, now, do you?"

"It's a gift," I quipped, assessing his reaction to mean he hadn't known about Ardmore, and wondering what that meant.

"Well, C authorized me to tell you that while Naval Intelligence holds the official files on the *Zebrina* incident, he is not without his own sources of information. I'm sure you know the basics."

"She sailed from Falmouth on September 15th, 1917, with a haul of Swansea coal bound for Saint-Brieuc, France. A run she frequently made that took about thirty hours," I supplied, having located many of the pertinent details that morning. "However, the *Zebrina* never arrived, and was found two days later by the French Coast Guard run aground at Rozel Point. The ship was undamaged, yet her captain and entire crew were missing."

Alec nodded. "The ship had suffered no damage, but for some disarranged rigging, and there were no signs she'd been boarded. Her coal was still in the hull, and the captain's logs were all present and in order. The 'official' conclusion is that the crew were taken prisoner by a German U-boat, which presumably then sighted an Allied vessel, and so fled the scene before the commander could either seize the logs, as they usually did for proof, or sink the *Zebrina*. Then the U-boat itself was presumably sunk, with the *Zebrina*'s crew still inside, unreported."

"That's a lot of presumablies," I muttered.

"And you are not the first to say so. But we unfortunately

don't have access to any other evidence. There could have been items on the ship that might indicate what happened, but C was not able to uncover what those were."

My shoulders slumped in frustration, but I should have known Alec was holding something back.

"That being said, we did have a contact in Cherbourg at the time of the incident who shared that the authorities made a search of the homes and businesses, including barns and out-buildings, all along the coast from Vauville to Portbail."

The back of my neck tingled. "Then they must have had reason to believe the crew abandoned the ship and fled into France."

He arched his eyebrows. "The entire crew, or part of it. What-ever the case, if one or some of them did, in fact, flee into France, they must have had a strong reason for doing so. Perhaps they were fearful of the repercussions from whatever went wrong on the journey."

"But what on earth could have gone wrong?"

"That is the question, isn't it?"

Learning about the search along the coast only made me more anxious than ever to speak with the Legrand sisters. They lived at Le Rozel. They would be aware of what happened at Rozel Point, and whether Esther was visiting at the time.

"It's not something that has been greatly considered. Every-one seems to assume that the *Zebrina* either drifted off course or was blown there be a rogue squall," Alec ruminated. "But if they were searching for crewmen escaping into France, I do wonder if the ship wasn't deliberately sailed there."

I glanced over at him, much struck by this idea.

"It is a rather isolated stretch of coast."

"But why?" I asked softly, not so much doubting the sugges-tion as trying to better understand it.

He tilted his head toward mine in contemplation. "Maybe they had more cargo onboard than just coal."

"Maybe," I admitted. "But the ship's manifest from Falmouth doesn't mention any. So unless all the officials in that port were part and parcel to a smuggling scheme, I don't think that's where they picked it up."

"No, but they could have stopped somewhere else along the way. Somewhere just as isolated."

I considered this notion with growing interest as we passed a nanny attempting to herd two giggling little boys down the path ahead of her. Her expression suggested it had been a trying morning.

"As I understand it, there were a great deal of wrecked goods being washed ashore along the Channel from ships being torpedoed by the German's U-boats," I said. "Such property was supposed to be turned over to the authorities, but I imagine that wasn't always the case. Particularly in the more remote areas where the Royal Coastguard and provincial authorities were less likely to patrol."

"And since they would have been written off as wrecked goods, there would be no further record of them to circumvent."

I shifted my umbrella under my arm. "But what wrecked goods could they have picked up that the discovery of their illegally exporting them would make them flee for their lives?"

It was an intriguing theory, but without further evidence it wasn't much more than that—a theory. As of now there was no evidence that any of the crew had survived. The authorities' search of the area could have been nothing more than a mere formality. And yet, why such a wide swathe of the coast? And why hadn't there been any signs of a struggle or an indication the ship had been boarded? The crew couldn't simply have vanished into thin air.

Given that, I was reluctant to dismiss any suggestion, particularly one that might explain why two murders might have been committed two years after the incident.

"I suppose there isn't a file on Esther Shaw or Lord Rockham?" I asked, hoping for even the slightest bit more information to help me find the connection between them and the *Zebrina* I was looking for.

He drew me to a stop under the shade of a plane tree next to the lake, turning to face me. "No. And before you ask if Lord Ardmore has one," he added as I opened my mouth to do just that. "I'll tell you precisely what C told me." He gazed down at me solemnly. Or at least as solemnly as Alec could manage. "It doesn't exist. It *can't* exist."

But I knew C well enough to understand what he was really saying was that an "official" file didn't exist, and he wasn't about to admit to keeping a private one. C always had been one to keep his cards close to the vest. In his position, he had to be. Though I'd long realized how much enjoyment he derived from being so enigmatic. Almost as much enjoyment as he got out of tweaking the noses of the new recruits with his antics, supposedly to test their nerves.

My lips quirked in a wry smile as I watched a trio of ducks bob in and out of the lake, wishing I could read what C had notated in that private file.

Alec's hand touched my sleeve where it linked with his, drawing my attention. My breath tightened at the sight of the concern I saw reflected in his eyes. His normally unflappable demeanor was marred by a pair of twin lines running between his two brows. "Seriously, Ver. Be careful there. Ardmore is a cypher. I don't trust him."

The seriousness of his words sent a little chill through me, for Alec was never afraid. Of anything. For goodness sake, he'd covertly waltzed through the belly of the enemy for almost the entirety of the war. If that did not require nerves of steel, I didn't know what did.

"You don't trust anyone," I countered with a light laugh, trying to brush aside the unsettling feeling his words caused.

"I trust you."

I stilled, surprised to hear him say so. Especially after our complicated history. I couldn't put a name to exactly what I saw reflected in his eyes, for Alec was good at hiding what he didn't want to be seen. But it unnerved me enough that I was the first to look away.

If he felt any sort of discomfort at this exchange, he didn't show it, for he spoke again in an even voice. "I'm also to inform you that from now on, you're to use a new code, as well as a different code name."

I turned to him in question, as he slid a tiny piece of paper into my hand. One that I knew would contain the instructions for the code.

"Memorize it and destroy the paper," he instructed.

"As usual. But why a new name?"

"Your others were crafted for your time in Belgium and France to help you pass as a citizen there. They also happen to be known by a number of people with the service. So C thought a new one was in order. Your name now when you contact the service will be Lorelei Bennett, and it, as well as your code, is only known by a chosen few."

"You must be jesting."

The twinkle in his eye told me he knew why I'd reacted so strongly. "I'm afraid not."

I narrowed my eyes. "Was Lorelei your idea?"

"Nope, the old dog thought of it all on his own."

In addition to being fluent speakers of German, Alec and I were both well versed in German culture. So we were quite familiar with the German legend of Lorelei, the beautiful siren who sat combing her hair on a rock in the Rhine River and lured sailors to their destruction.

I pondered C's choice, wondering if he was merely mocking Major Davis's accusations against me, or if perhaps his expectations of my abilities were slightly too high. If he hoped I might lure Ardmore, or any other potentially corrupt official to their destruction, he might be sadly disappointed. For one thing, I didn't think Ardmore allowed himself to be lured anywhere.

Either way, I was not best pleased by my new code name. In truth, I felt a bit unsettled by having one at all, for it was an indication that C expected me to continue to perform this unofficial role for him. Thus far it had been at my own instigation and we had both benefited, so I could hardly complain. But that did not mean in the future that C might not call on me to execute tasks I wasn't as willing or comfortable with. I supposed as an unsanctioned agent I would not be obligated to take them on, but I'd seen the way C reacted when others tried to thwart his wishes. If we were ever at odds, I was loath to discover the consequences.

"Don't look so cross," Alec remarked with an unrepentant grin. "The chief does have a sense of humor."

"That's debatable," I muttered dryly.

"I didn't say it was a good one."

I glared at him, and he touched the brim of his hat almost in salute.

"This is when I say adieu." His gaze skimmed over my features one last time. "And good luck." Then he turned to stroll away with one last wave of his fingers. "You know how to reach me."

CHAPTER 23

I reached the southern edge of Berkeley Square before the clouds decided to dump their horde. Though, perhaps more accurately, they'd decided to hurl it at us. I huddled under my umbrella as best I could, but even traveling such a short distance, my shoes and the hem of my skirt were soaked, and the rest of me glistened with damp.

In the entry hall of our flat, Sadie helped me out of my wet things.

"Thank you, Mrs. Yarrow," I said. "I'll just go change my skirt, shall I. Has Nimble arrived?"

"Yes, ma'am," she replied somewhat timidly, and I wondered if perhaps I should have been there to make the introductions. Truth be told, I'd forgotten all about my husband's former batman arriving to begin his valet duties until I passed a man wearing a tin mask when I strolled into the library.

"He took Mr. Kent his breakfast and is now settling into his room," she added with more assurance.

"Good."

"Is . . ." She pressed her lips together, as if uncertain how or even if she wanted to ask her question.

Given her expression, I expected it might be a comment about Nimble's injuries. I hadn't expected Sadie to be bothered by them, but perhaps I'd been wrong.

She gathered up my things to take them to dry before the stove in the kitchen, finding her words. "Is that what I'm really to call him? Nimble?" Her mouth seemed to almost stumble over the word.

"Is that what he asked you to call him?"

"Yes, ma'am."

"Then, yes."

She nodded and shifted to go, but I halted her.

"Oh! Have there been any messages?"

She glanced over her shoulder, shaking her head. "No, ma'am."

I exhaled in disappointment and turned to stroll down the corridor to our bedchamber, wondering if Sidney was still about or if he'd elected to take himself off somewhere like the day before. That's when I caught a glimpse through the doorway into the drawing room of his dark head bent over something. There was something in the rigid line of his back, the taut appearance of his profile that brought me up short.

Slowly, so as not to disturb him, I moved a step closer to the doorway to see what he was holding. It seemed to be a photograph of some kind, but from this angle, I couldn't tell of what.

I stood there for a moment in indecision. I wanted to know what about the photo had so arrested him, but I was also afraid that if I asked, it would be yet another thing for him to snarl at me over. Etta had counseled me not to pry, to leave his pain unprodded, but I was discovering I couldn't do that. Perhaps I couldn't force Sidney to talk to me. Perhaps I shouldn't. But I could at least keep letting him know I was there to listen if he ever wanted to.

I took a hesitant step forward, and then another, rounding the chair to see over his shoulder. It was a photograph of two boys of approximately the age of ten, standing tall and proud before a great hearth with an enormous yule log set alight. I recognized the boy on the left immediately as being Sidney. The same stubborn curl of his dark brown hair that persisted on falling over his forehead today had done the same when he was a lad. However, the taller boy on the right was a stranger to me. Though there was something in the shape of his eyes and the height of his cheekbones that suggested they were related.

"Who is that?" I asked softly, knowing he was aware of my presence. His breathing had changed the moment I approached.

"My cousin," he said without removing his gaze from the picture. "Eric." At first, I didn't think he intended to say any more, but then he quietly continued. "He died a few weeks after this photo was taken."

I held my breath, not daring to speak for fear he would stop talking.

"We were climbing the trees at the edge of his property, as we always did. Soaring elms and sycamores. We called it our kingdom in the sky," he pronounced evenly, though I could hear the pain he was trying to suppress lurking just below the surface. "But there had been a great ice storm the week before. It had weakened some of the branches. We heard the crack, never even had time to react before the branch came plummeting down on us. It thwacked Eric in the head and me in the shoulder, knocking us both out of the tree onto the ground ten feet below."

I gasped and Sidney's gaze flickered toward me before returning to the picture. "I suffered a concussion, a dislocated shoulder, and a broken leg. But Eric . . ." He swallowed. "The physician said the blow to his head killed him instantly. Or very nearly. That he never would have even felt the impact of the ground."

I didn't know what to say. It had happened almost two decades ago, but from the rawness of his voice I could tell how much it still distressed him. That, and the fact he'd never told me about being knocked from a tree by a falling limb, let alone mentioned his cousin. I reached out to touch his shoulder lightly, wary of his rejecting my offer of comfort.

He inhaled a ragged breath before remarking almost offhandedly, "But maybe it's better he died this way. He probably would have been killed in the war anyway, and in a much worse manner. It was always the best of us who clicked it."

My hand tightened unconsciously around his shoulder at hearing these words, at their glimpse into just how much pain Sidney had buried deep. Afraid I'd revealed my agitation, I strove to cover my distress with a logical question. "Was Eric your cousin from your father's or your mother's side of the family?"

"My father's. He was my uncle Oscar and aunt Louise's only son."

I hid a cringe. Sidney's father was the third and youngest son of the Marquess of Treborough. The oldest son, the current marquess, was an old bachelor, with as yet no children to his name. Which meant that upon his death the title would fall to the next oldest son, Oscar, and then consequently would have gone to his son, Eric. But since Eric had predeceased him, upon Oscar's death it would instead fall to the old marquess's third son, Oliver, and then to Sidney. Eric's death—accidental though it had been—had paved the way for Sidney, as the only living male of the next generation, to gain the title.

"Isn't that the aunt your mother was furious with for not attending our wedding?" I asked, having yet to meet many of his relatives, as most of them preferred the country to the hustle and bustle of London.

"Yes, Aunt Louise couldn't stand the sight of me after the accident. She said I reminded her too much of her son. And the unfairness of the fact that I had survived when he had not."

I felt fury bubbling up inside of me. "She told you that?"

"No, but I heard her tell my mother while I was supposed to be resting and recovering after the fall. She wanted my mother to remove me from their house as soon as I could be moved."

"And she hasn't seen you since?"

"Not when she can help it."

I was absolutely appalled by his aunt's behavior. Perhaps in her initial outpouring of grief, the pain and anger she'd felt were understandable. She had just tragically lost her son, after all, and I knew as well as anyone that one did not always respond rationally or reasonably to such heartache. But there was no excuse for her continued avoidance of her nephew, or the manner in which she seemed to blame him for her son's death. As if Sidney's surviving meant Eric had to die, when the truth was the entire incident had been a freak accident. One that could have ended in them both dying.

It did not take a great leap of logic to understand why after all these years he was sitting here staring at this photo of himself and his cousin. Albert Rogers's death had stirred up a hornet's nest of doubts and emotions over the fickleness and unfairness of fate. It had made him question again—something he'd doubtless done hundreds of times—why he had survived when so many others had not. Friends, family, acquaintances, the men from his company—for him, the list of dead he had known doubtless amounted to more than a thousand.

Unable to continue to stand over him while I grasped something of the maelstrom of pain swirling about inside him, I rounded the chair and sank down in his lap. I was relieved when he didn't resist, draping his arm over my back as I wrapped my arms around him and laid my head on his chest. I could hear the rapid beat of his heart, feel the taut constriction of his shoulders.

"You do know she's wrong, don't you?" I ventured.

But he didn't reply, and I decided talking might only make the matter worse. So instead I held him, hoping he could sense how much I loved him, how glad I was he hadn't died—as a boy or later as a soldier.

Several moments passed before the rate of his heart began to slow and the tension began to drain from him by increments. I was aware of the clock ticking away on the mantel, and the sound of the rain falling outside the windows, but everything else was attuned to him. Eventually, he stirred, reaching over to set the photograph aside; then he lowered his head to press his mouth to my forehead. His fingers combed through the hairs at the nape of my neck. "How did your meeting go?" he mumbled against my skin.

I inhaled a shaky breath, not as ready as he seemed to be to move past what just happened. Although the questions, the concerns piled up behind my lips, I was fearful of voicing them, of pushing too hard. So I allowed him to change the topic, trying to convince myself the murders we were investigating were more urgent than whatever was happening inside Sidney.

"Well, I would say the most interesting thing my contact had to tell me about the *Zebrina* incident is that the authorities searched the villages north and south of the site where the ship was beached, looking for the crew."

"They wondered if they might have escaped inland?"

I nodded.

"Then their disappearance might not be so mysterious." He frowned. "But why? What were they escaping from?"

I raised my hand in a show of bewilderment. "But we did discuss the possibility it could have something to do with the wrecked goods that washed up on the shore along the Channel from U-boat attacks."

"That would be ideal cargo for a smuggler. So long as it was undamaged and something valuable enough."

"Didn't you say you had a friend who worked for the Coastguard?" I asked, lifting my head to look at him.

"Griff Cooper. He lost an arm in '15, so they reassigned him to coordinate with the local provincial forces that took over for the Coastguard while they were away on war duties. As it happens, I believe he was stationed along the Channel somewhere. In Hampshire, I think."

"Is he in London?"

"No, but I know his direction. We could telephone him," he replied, following the train of my thoughts.

The shadows under his eyes were still deep, but the glint of curiosity I saw reflected in his pupils gave me hope that distraction might be the best for him. "Yes, let's do. But first, there's something I have to tell you."

I'd already decided I would not keep Alec's role as my new contact a secret from Sidney. I reasoned that all of this was unofficial, and he was already aware of much of my previous role with the Secret Service, even if not all, and we *had* collaborated with Alec on our last bit of intrigue. But beyond all that, I'd realized I wasn't willing to sacrifice my marriage to the whims of C.

"My new contact at the Secret Service is to be Captain Xavier." I searched his face for his reaction. "At least, temporarily. Until he's cleared to be sent abroad."

His brow furrowed in irritation. "I take it C is not aware of your entire history together."

I shook my head. "At least, I hope not. All he's aware of is that Xavier owes me his loyalty after risking life and limb to extract him from Belgium. I believe he was counting on that to keep his lips sealed about my involvement."

He scrutinized my features. What exactly for, I didn't know. Surely he didn't think I was any more pleased about this than he was? But given my and Alec's past, I allowed for his right to feel slightly mistrustful. But since it was his fault I'd ever believed him dead in the first place, and thus even considered taking another man to my bed, I was not going to allow it for long.

Whatever he saw in my eyes seemed to reassure him, for the tight lines at the corners of his mouth smoothed out. "Thank you for telling me."

"Of course."

He opened his mouth, as if he wanted to say more, but then seemed to think better of it. "Shall we telephone Cooper, then?"

I stood beside him before the bureau, waiting as he and Griff exchanged greetings and small talk—the bread-and-butter of the upper class. But once he launched into the subject we actually wanted to discuss, Sidney urged me closer, tilting the earpiece so that I could hear Griff's replies.

"Wrecked goods? Well, yes, there was a dashed lot of that during the war," he declared in a raspy, smoke-roughened voice. "What do you want to know?"

"Whenever it was found, they were required to turn it in to the authorities, correct?" Sidney asked.

"That's how it was supposed to work. But there were areas where the provincial forces were spread pretty thin. It wasn't uncommon for people to be caught keeping goods they had no right to. Many of them claimed they hadn't known they were to notify the authorities, but much of the time that was a load of rubbish. Especially when they were repeat offenders."

Sidney glanced at me out of the corner of his eye. "So, in theory, it's possible someone could have made a business of smuggling such goods out of the country?"

"I suppose so." He sounded doubtful. "If they wanted to take the bloody risk of dodging the U-boats. More often, they used it themselves, or sold it to people further inland. Or in the case of Wight, shipped it across the Solent, not the Channel."

I stiffened at the mention of the Isle of Wight, and from the look my husband cast me, he knew why.

"Wrecked goods washed up on the Isle of Wight?" he asked.

"Oh, yes," Griff exclaimed. "A great deal of it, too. Because of the currents. And the fact the great bloody island is sticking out into the Channel. The Isle of Purbeck was another point they collected. But Wight was particularly troublesome simply because we had difficulty finding locals willing to do the job of monitoring such activity in the absence of the Coastguard while they were on war duty. Caulkheads are a stubborn lot, and they don't take kindly to outsiders telling them what to do."

"What sort of things most often washed up?"

"Oh, well, anything in a cask. Brandy, tobacco, bolts of fabric, tea, sugar—you name it. Though, it wasn't always consumable. Many times contents were contaminated with salt."

"Did you ever hear of anything washing ashore of a sensitive nature?"

At this, his voice turned guarded. "What do you mean?"

"Things you might be concerned about falling into the wrong hands."

"Well, we did have an instance where a trio of boys got rather scrooched from a cask of brandy they found. And we had some incidences of opium washing ashore. There were likely more we were never notified of. But that's all I can think of that you might define as being 'sensitive.'" He paused. "What is all this about? Are you on the trail of some more traitors?"

"I can't really discuss it," Sidney replied obliquely, allowing his friend to think whatever he wished. "But you've been a great help."

I stepped back as they exchanged goodbyes, my mind brooding on what Griff had revealed. When Sidney had rung off, I spun around to exclaim, "Could it be drugs? Is that the undisclosed cargo the *Zebrina* could have been transporting along with its coal?"

"It could be profitable. After all, France began exerting a tighter control on the use of opium and other narcotics almost a decade ago, and their laws became even harsher during the war. There were some who feared the Germans were attempting to turn the French people and soldiers into addicts by smuggling the drugs into the cities and trenches."

"I remember reading reports about such debates in the French Parliament from our Paris field office. But our agents concluded that such a plot was highly unlikely, and would be nearly impossible to successfully implement." I frowned. "Of course, that doesn't mean there weren't outliers attempting such a scheme. But it seems much more probable that, *if* the crew of the *Zebrina* was smuggling drugs, their real interest lay in turning a profit."

"I agree. Trying to make this incident some treasonable offense seems a bit of a stretch. Being caught illegally exporting and importing drugs would be a serious enough crime already. One that it's conceivable they would have fled from if they were in danger of being caught." He planted his hands on his hips, glancing to the side. "Though that doesn't explain why an entire crew would run from an undamaged ship, or how it became beached in the first place."

"No, it doesn't," I agreed, returning to the drawing room. Having a sudden thought, I spun about, nearly causing Sidney to collide with me. "Unless, it was just one man. Perhaps something happened to the rest of the crew, something he witnessed, and fearful for his life, he beached the ship and ran."

His head canted to the side as he considered this explanation. "That does make more sense. But it also raises almost as many questions as it answers. And we still have no proof of any of it, nor any explanation how Rockham's and Esther's deaths connect to it."

"We might if the Legrand sisters will ever telephone." I dropped into the closest chair, trying to squash the disquiet filling me.

I couldn't explain precisely why, but I was uneasy about the fact Esther's cousins had not telephoned. Except that, if the person who killed Esther had stolen those letters, then they were aware of who her cousins were, and where they lived. And they had possessed this information for at least a week, if not longer. What if they'd decided to do something with it? What if I was too late to warn them?

"Ryde's estate is on the Isle of Wight," Sidney commented as he sank into the opposite chair, harking back to the reason why I'd reacted to its mention.

"Yes, though I can't imagine him or his late father having anything to do with this."

To call Max Westfield, the Earl of Ryde, just a friend did not do him justice, for he was much more than that. Max had been Sidney's commanding officer for part of the war, and he and I had grown rather close in the midst of a fraught murder investigation several months past. The same investigation that had resulted in Sidney revealing to me that he was still alive. Without Max's assistance, I'm not certain we would have been able to uncover and capture the traitors Sidney had feigned his death to expose.

But because I'd believed Sidney to be dead, I had allowed feelings to develop between me and Max. Feelings that did not evaporate simply because I'd chosen to forgive Sidney for his necessary duplicity and fight to make our marriage work. As such, matters were still awkward between all of us. Not that Max was in any way to blame. He had accepted my decision with grace and understanding, and even encouraged my reconciliation with Sidney. But emotions and attachments do not disappear with the mere snap of the fingers.

"One would think not," Sidney murmured. "But it is rather interesting that the late earl was a political crony of Lord Rockham's."

I glanced up in surprise, not having known this. Max's father had at one time or another been involved in almost every department of government. It was said that he could have easily pushed to become prime minister, but for the fact he preferred to work his political machinations behind the scenes.

"But remember, the Isle of Wight was only mentioned because so many wrecked goods washed ashore," my husband strove to reassure me. "As of yet, there is no connection between the *Zebrina*, Esther's death, or Rockham's murder and that island. Rockham was probably allies with dozens of politicians all over Britain."

I offered him a tight smile, appreciating his effort. But the knowledge still settled in the pit of my stomach like a cold lump.

CHAPTER 24

The Teagardens lived in a row of brick Victorian townhouses, each with its own tidy front garden. These had undoubtedly come in handy during the war when the government had encouraged citizens to use whatever bit of green space they might possess to cultivate fruits and vegetables. Indeed, I could see many of these plots were still utilized in such a way.

If Mrs. Teagarden—a spare, birdlike woman—was surprised by my visit to her daughter, she didn't show it. Nor did she attempt to intrude on the conversation. She left us in a parlor wallpapered in a faded floral print that had clearly been more vibrant in earlier days. Despite that, the rest of the room was comfortably furnished, and the rugs were newer than even the ones in my flat. I suspected it was more a matter of Mrs. Teagarden being unwilling to part with the paper than an inability to afford new.

Miss Virginia Teagarden was obviously her mother's daughter, at least in appearance. Her features were fine and sparse, her bones so tiny I would be afraid of snapping them if I applied too much pressure. But while Mrs. Teagarden had seemed to exert an iron self-control and firm resolve, Miss Teagarden appeared ready to topple over at the first sign of a stiff breeze. She sat rigidly in her chair, wringing the handkerchief she clutched between her hands, apparently already anticipating there would be tears.

Finding her in such an agitated state, I anticipated I would have to coax every little bit of information out of her. But whether because the dread and anxiety of the past few weeks had worn her down, or she'd decided to trust me, she soon began to pour out everything she knew, including much that was of little relevance. Then my most arduous task became trying to direct this spew of information.

After hearing how Esther had been an absolute darb, the most darling person she'd ever met and her best friend in the whole world, and learning how absolutely crushed and horrified she was—and shocked, oh, so frightfully shocked—I elected to speak over her to get a word in edgewise.

"You say you and Miss Shaw were close. But do you know if she had a beau? A man she was stepping out with?"

This silenced her for what was likely only a second, but after her voluble speech seemed like much longer.

"Well, she was rather hush-hush about it, but I knew she was corresponding with a man she'd met during the war. They came tucked inside the letters she received from her cousins."

I leaned forward. "He was from France?"

"Maybe. I mean, they came from France, but I think he wrote to her in English." She began to pleat the edge of her handkerchief, staring up at me through her eyelashes. "I saw one once. Just fleetingly. Quite poetic he was."

"And she kept these letters?"

"Oh, yes!"

And yet they had been missing from her rooms, along with the letters from her cousins. "Did she tell you anything about him? About how they'd met?"

"I asked, but she wouldn't say. She said she couldn't." She shrugged. "I didn't know what that meant. If he was hand-cuffed, surely word wouldn't reach his wife all the way back in France. But I promised not to tell anyone else about him." She paused. "Until now."

"But there was no one more recent? No one from London?"

She shook her head. "I mean, sure, she danced and flirted, but we all did. It didn't mean anything."

I studied Miss Teagarden, wondering who was telling me the truth—her or Flossie. I was inclined to believe Miss Teagarden purely because Flossie's behavior had been so erratic, her tale almost too detailed. But Miss Teagarden seemed to have no motive for what she was telling me, nor did she nervously venture gratuitous particulars.

There was also the fact that I wasn't actually surprised to hear there was a man in France, for I had already begun to suspect it. The changes in the tone in her journal, the redacted words, the alteration of her habits—it all seemed to fit.

Now, if only I could speak with her cousins, I might be able to confirm it. As well as my suspicion that this man was also a missing crewman from the *Zebrina*. But when I'd left for Wood Green that morning, there had still been no answering telegram or telephone call.

"Did Flossie Hawkins know about her beau in France as well?"

Esther shrank backward, shaking her head. "No, she didn't trust Flossie."

My eyebrows arched in surprise. "She didn't?"

"No, especially not after she caught Flossie reading her journal."

"When was this?"

Her gaze lifted toward the ceiling. "Hmm, a few months back. I can't remember exactly when."

If that were the case, it could explain why Esther had begun redacting the words from her own journal. But what had Flossie seen before then? And what had she done with that information?

"The night of . . . the incident," I began, electing to couch Esther's death in the most delicate terms possible for fear Miss Teagarden would put the handkerchief she still clutched to good use. "Flossie said that Esther was supposed to meet the two of you, but she never showed."

Her brow furrowed.

"Is that not true?"

"I suppose," she waffled.

"What does that mean?"

"Well, Esther didn't meet us. But neither did Flossie. Both of them stood me up."

I willed myself to remain seated, even though my heart leapt inside my chest and my muscles strained with the effort not to spring forward. "Did Flossie ever tell you why she didn't show?"

She seemed particularly struck by this question. "You know, I don't think she ever did. And *she* was the one who was so keen to go out on the town in the first place." She crossed her arms over her chest. "Ugh! That is so like her."

I didn't know whether to be glad of or dismayed by Miss Teagarden's naïveté. For it seemed obvious to me why Flossie had asked them to go out on the town that night and why she hadn't showed. She was searching Esther's rooms. And when Esther unexpectedly returned early, she'd silenced her before she was caught. The question was, had she meant to silence her temporarily or permanently? Was Esther's murder accidental or intentional?

And what had Flossie been searching for, and why? Had she stumbled across mentions of the *Zebrina* in Esther's journals and thought to somehow make money from it by selling it to a reporter or through blackmail? Or had she been searching for further information at the behest of someone else? Perhaps she'd already been beating her gums about what she'd read, and those words had fallen on fertile ears.

I was pulled from my musings as Miss Teagarden inhaled a ragged breath. "And, of course, I'll never know why Esther decided to return to her rooms instead of coming directly from Peter Robinson's after her shift ended, as planned."

I could tell her why. Esther had evidently been suspicious of her friend. Perhaps when she realized Flossie hadn't arrived at their chosen meeting place, she'd guessed where she really was and had gone home to confront her.

"It's all just so beastly awful." She sniffled. "I couldn't stay in that place. I simply couldn't. Not knowing what had happened just on the other side of the wall."

"I'm sure anyone would feel the same," I reassured her. After all, I couldn't very well tell her to try sleeping in the same room as two dead German soldiers, as I'd been forced to do one night near Pittem, Belgium. The Secret Police were rumored to be scouring the area for the two men, and there was only one secret room in the farmhouse where I was sheltering—a freezing cold cellar. Realizing my documents might not stand up to intense scrutiny, and as fearful of compromising the family living there as myself, I'd chosen to hide with the corpses.

But that had been the war, and I had known what I was signing up for. This was a woman murdered in her own home, and her innocent best friend trying to cope with that fact. There were degrees of difference.

Flossie, on the other hand, appeared to be anything but innocent. Even her tale about Esther's supposed married, abusive lover made sense now. She'd been trying desperately to throw suspicion off herself, and possibly hoping to keep me from hunting down Miss Teagarden. After all, if I was searching London for a fictitious lover, then I wouldn't have time to speak with anyone who might contradict her story.

I thanked Miss Teagarden for her help and returned to London on the train. But rather than retracing my steps to Mayfair, I took the tube to Tottenham Court Road, before finding my way back to Mrs. Worley's rooming house.

Her expression when she answered the door to my knock was one of keenness mixed with vexation. Obviously, she was not best pleased by the fact we'd slipped away from her home before she could show us off to her friends.

"Mrs. Kent, what a surprise." Her gaze shifted beyond me, as if searching for Sidney. "I can tell you, I've had no end of trouble since you and your husband were here last. Newspapermen and photographers standing outside and knocking on my door at all hours."

"Trouble that you brought upon yourself by notifying them of our presence here in the first place," I bit out past a sharp smile. They'd been a bloody nuisance, dogging my and Sidney's steps, so I felt not one iota of sympathy for the woman.

"Why, I would never," she gasped, but I was having none of it.

"Save it for the papers," I snapped, moving past her into the house. "I need to speak with Miss Flossie Hawkins. Is she here or at her place of employment?"

"I don't know," she stammered.

I frowned, recalling the hidden door and staircase leading from Flossie's rooms to the alley behind. "What do you mean? Has she not come down this morning?"

"She packed up her things and left, just like Miss Teagarden."

"When?" I knew the urgency in my voice was giving too much away, but there was no time to feign nonchalance. Not with a woman who was as voluble a talker as Mrs. Worley.

"A few days ago. Friday, I think."

The day she'd visited me to weave that ridiculous story.

"She was in a great hurry, too. Left a box behind. 'Twas filled with mostly chipped dishes and—"

"Did she tell you where she was going?" I cut her off to ask.

She blinked. "No, just said she couldn't bear to live here anymore knowing what had happened to Miss Shaw. She did seem to be shaken. Something I never thought I'd witness in Miss Hawkins. Tough as nails, that one was. And bold as brass, too."

"What about family?"

"If she had any, she never told *me* about them."

No, she wouldn't have. The only person she might have told was Esther. And she was dead. Probably at Flossie's own hand.

I glowered at the stairs leading upward, wondering at the change that had come over Flossie between the time she'd helped us escape from The Whirly's horde of friends and Friday, when she'd been waiting for me outside my flat. Something must have happened to upset her.

"Had Miss Hawkins received any visitors since I was last here? Did she receive any letters?"

She nodded. "A courier came with a message for her Thursday morning, before I'd even finished cooking breakfast. Insisted on delivering it directly into Miss Hawkins's hands, too, even though I had to drag her out of bed for him to do so. Nearly burnt the sausages. Why he was so particular, I can't imagine," she harrumphed, clearly irritated she hadn't had a chance to examine the letter first.

"So you don't know who it was from?"

She shook her head. "The lad was dressed quite proper, but he wasn't from the post office or any other telegraph office I recognized."

That's because I didn't think he'd come from a company, but a private person, and I had a good suspicion who. "How did she react when she read the message?"

Her chin arched almost in affront. "I wouldn't know. I was busy with other matters. Didn't see Miss Hawkins again until later that evening when she went straight up to her rooms, pleading a headache."

In other words, Mrs. Worley hadn't had a chance to press her for more information.

When I didn't respond, she leapt into the lull, trying to extract information from me. "Why are you asking all these questions? Surely you don't think Miss Hawkins had anything to do with Miss Shaw's death. She left earlier that evening and didn't return until well after midnight."

Except Mrs. Worley hadn't been here. She hadn't even known Esther had returned. Flossie could have done the same, either through the main door or the secret door hidden in her room, and then left again, with no one the wiser. The open window could have been a ruse. But I wasn't about to supply Mrs. Worley with any more information than I already had.

"Where did Miss Hawkins work?" I countered.

Her lips pressed together in frustration. "Well, let's see. I believe last it was some foot appliance store on Oxford Street. Frankly, the girl couldn't keep a job, and this last one was really on the verge of respectability."

I ignored her commentary, having seen the advertisements for the store I thought she was referring to in the *Tatler* and the *Bystander*. But before I turned to go, I paused to study the avid gleam in the other woman's eyes. The moment I departed she would be repeating everything I'd said to whomever would listen, along with her own flawed theories. I couldn't let that happen.

"A Chief Inspector Thoreau will be paying you a visit shortly."

Her eyes widened.

"And if he discovers you've shared anything I've discussed here with you, or anything else of a sensitive nature, he will be very cross. Very cross, indeed." I arched my eyebrows significantly. "I want you to tell him everything you've told me and show him Miss Hawkins's rooms. Including the hidden door behind that quilt."

Her mouth gaped, and I trusted I'd shocked her sufficiently to compel her to remain silent. As for Thoreau, given the warning he'd received, I knew it would be too big of a risk to contact him directly. But I trusted that if I prevailed upon George to telephone Scotland Yard, as the nephew of a lord, he would be patched through immediately. Flossie Hawkins needed to be located as soon as possible and the police had resources in that area I could not hope to summon. Not in London.

It took nearly an hour of searching, but I located the foot appliance store where Miss Hawkins had last been employed on Oxford Street near the intersection with Duke Street. It hadn't helped matters that portions of the road were torn up in order to be repaved. The noise and smells and dust were insufferable, and my quest proved to be in vain. No one at The Orthopedic Foot Appliance Company had seen or heard from Flossie in almost a week. She hadn't even collected the four days of wages owed to her.

This last part concerned me, for Flossie hadn't seemed to be in a circumstance where she could afford to overlook her earnings. Why, then, hadn't she gone to get them? It seemed to me, if she was hiding from the consequences of what she'd done, she would want to have every bit of money available to her. Unless she was hiding from something worse.

I remembered the way she kept glancing about us, as if she was worried she was being followed, as if she was frightened to be seen talking to me. Could Flossie have feared for her life?

I posed the same question to Sidney when I returned to our flat in Berkeley Square. He'd sat quietly listening as I relayed everything I'd learned that morning, and all the speculations swirling in my head while I paced up and down the drawing room.

"You're thinking of Lord Ardmore, aren't you?" he murmured, as always, moving swiftly to the heart of the matter.

"You must admit the timing of that message's delivery to Flossie is suspicious. It's the same morning Ada came storming into our flat after Ardmore stirred her up by telling her about my asking questions about her the previous night."

"Yes, but why? Why would Ardmore ask Flossie to search Esther's rooms? How would he have even known about her?"

"Maybe Flossie read something in Esther's journal, something about the *Zebrina,* and she started beating her gums about it to whoever would listen. Something along the lines of her knowing what really happened to the ship's crew. And Ardmore caught wind of it. Maybe he wanted the information Esther possessed."

"But why?"

I turned to scowl at him.

"I realize I'm repeating myself, but the question bears merit," Sidney replied steadily. "*Why* should Ardmore care what happened to the *Zebrina*'s crew? We haven't found any indication he had anything to do with it."

"No, but he does work for Naval Intelligence. If nothing else, it seems to me he would have a vested interest in discovering what became of them."

"That may be true, but that doesn't necessarily lead to Ardmore hiring Flossie to steal whatever information Esther Shaw possessed, which is what I assume you're suggesting, and then harboring or threatening her to remain silent about it. In any case, you have no proof that he had any contact with or even knowledge of either Flossie's or Esther's existence."

My hands clenched into fists at my sides. "So you're telling me you don't believe Ardmore had anything to do with this? That I've developed some . . . *vendetta* against him, and so have imagined connections where there are none?"

"What I think doesn't matter, Ver. You know that. Only the evidence."

I whirled away, frustrated by his determination to be so blasted reasonable. "I'm telling you, Sidney, Ardmore is somehow in the thick of all of this. I don't know how or if we'll ever be able to prove it. But somehow he *is* involved."

He pushed to his feet and reached out to grasp my upper arms. I almost pulled away, but for the earnest gleam in his eyes. "I don't doubt you, Ver. I don't. But we need proof."

I forced a breath into my lungs and nodded. Though he hadn't said the words, I knew I was allowing myself to get carried away when I needed to keep my head about me. If we were to uncover the truth, the full truth, it would require all our wits.

"All right, then," I murmured, dropping down onto the edge of the sofa. "Let's consider what we don't know. Rockham. We still don't know who killed him or whether his owning the *Zebrina* had anything to do with it. We don't know precisely what Esther wrote in her journals and letters that was valuable enough to steal. We don't know the identity of the man whose letters accompanied her cousins, or have confirmation that he was a member of the missing *Zebrina* crew."

I glanced at him uneasily. "We still haven't heard from the Legrands?"

"No, nothing."

I bit the corner of my lip, unsettled by their continued silence after they had been so anxious to speak with me before. "Sidney, something's not right. They should have responded to my latest telegram by now."

His eyes clouded with concern. "I agree."

"I think we need to consider traveling to Le Rozel ourselves to speak with them in person."

He nodded. "Perhaps then we can also speak with this man Miss Shaw was corresponding with ourselves."

I was relieved to hear him agree with me. The last time I'd suggested a trip to the continent, he had furiously balked. Of course, that was when we were supposed to be retreating to our cottage alone to try to repair our marriage, and instead I'd been urging him to travel back into the war-ravaged countryside of Belgium to locate a former fellow spy. Fortunately, this time the area of France where we were headed was nowhere near the trenches and devastation.

"Tomorrow morning, then," I said. "If we haven't heard from the Legrands by tonight, we'll take the first train to Portsmouth."

CHAPTER 25

I blinked hard, fighting the bleariness of too few hours' sleep and the glare of the setting sun to see the countryside before us. The priest at the church in Le Rozel had given us clearer directions to the Legrand's cottage than Irene had been able to provide the day before when I'd called to relay our intentions of visiting Esther's cousins. She'd expressed similar concerns when I explained the reasons we felt it necessary to make a visit, baffled they should have cut off communication.

However, the priest's instructions were still difficult to decipher, particularly when my eyes were so tired they seemed to play tricks on me. One directive was to turn right at the stone wall, but which one? While another told us to veer left once we'd crested a rise and could see the sea over the bluffs, but there were numerous such hills and numerous opportunities to veer left.

The grinding gears of the Renault Sidney borrowed at the port in Cherbourg did not help matters. With each grating noise, each lurch of the motorcar, the twitch above his right eye grew more pronounced, and the more thunderous his expression became. I was beginning to worry we were on a fool's errand and would never find the Legrands' house before darkness fell, making the search all but impossible.

I rubbed at the wrenching pain where my neck met my shoulder, brought on by too much strain. It had begun the evening before when George had telephoned to inform me that Thoreau had the police looking for Flossie, but that he hadn't much hope of finding her. Not after a four-day head start. Whether Thoreau had encountered any resistance from his superiors or stepped on any toes by inserting himself into another inspector's investigation, he didn't say. Regardless, I was grateful to him for taking action.

The conversation with Ada that followed only exacerbated the tension. She had been furious when I told her I was going away for a few days—no matter how short I assured her the trip would be—and had accused me of abandoning her. The worst part of it was that I could not blame her for being put out with me. Had our situations been reversed, I suspected I would have felt something similar, though I hoped I would have had more faith in my friend. If I could have shared the details of what I was searching for, perhaps she would have been more understanding, but I couldn't risk it. Not when Ardmore was her lover.

But the development that really dug in the thumbscrews to the kink in my neck had occurred when we stopped to speak to the Le Rozel priest, who told us he was worried the Legrand sisters might be unwell. That they'd failed to attend mass on Sunday morning, and they never missed. He didn't know if anyone had seen them since. He was certain he hadn't. He also confirmed that the only telephone in the village was located at the chateau we had passed on the road into town, five miles distant from the Legrands' cottage.

As we bumped and jostled our way down the narrow dirt road, I tried not to imagine what could have happened to them out here alone. Or whether the ominous noises issuing from the Renault at each jolt meant the motorcar was about to die on us. The road wound between tall hedges with occasional gaps to provide us views of the golden fields and stone buildings beyond. Then the road began to flatten and the hedges dwindled away, being replaced by scrubby windswept trees and long, waving grasses. I couldn't see the sea, or hear it over the growl of the Renault's engine, but I could smell its salty brine floating on the breeze.

We crested a rise and suddenly, almost out of nowhere, appeared the second turn. Sidney had to bear down hard on the brakes to not shoot past it. This road ran more or less parallel to the sea, giving our eyes a rest from the glaring sun as it hung low over the water. One moment we were driving through the tall beach grass, and the next the road ticked eastward, plunging us back into the leafy growth of hedges and lush fields.

There was a slight dip in the land, and there nestled between two oak trees sat a small two-story cottage. The stone of its western-facing front almost appeared golden in the light of the setting sun. Sidney pulled onto the flattened grass along the verge of the lane as we searched the building for any sign of life.

Being out here alone, so far from the village, I'd expected the sisters to have a dog to greet us. If there was, he was either shy or off with one of his owners. But over the cooling of the engine, I could hear the sound of chickens clucking. Straining to see beyond the hedgerow to the left, I noted a small barn crafted from the same stone used on most of the buildings in this corner of Normandy.

A vague sense of uneasiness permeated the place. It trickled down the back of my neck like spider's legs. "Something isn't right," I told Sidney.

His only response was to reach for his valise in the backseat. Popping it open, he revealed his Luger tucked inside among his folded clothes. This time I wasn't surprised to see it. In fact, given the circumstance, I was rather relieved.

"Stick close beside me," he told me as he reached for his door handle.

We inched slowly toward the house, the gravel crunching beneath our feet and the sun hot on the backs of our necks. But still no one came out to greet us.

I glanced downward at the pistol he clutched at his side. "Won't that alarm the Legrands?"

"Better to alarm them than to be caught unawares."

I couldn't refute that logic.

My gaze drifted over the small barn. As far as hiding places went, one could do much worse. But that didn't mean it had been used as such.

We elected to search the house first. Sidney inched up the

steps to the porch as I swiveled to scan the hedges behind us for unseen eyes. He knocked twice, and when no one answered, he turned the knob and pushed open the door. Keeping his pistol before him, he swept the room before allowing me to follow him inside.

The furnishings were much as I'd expected—shabbily genteel, but solidly constructed, and cozy. The smell of some sort of meat cooking in the oven wafted from the kitchen, mingling with the aromas of fresh-baked bread and coffee. Peeking in through the doorway, I saw a loaf cooling beneath a towel on the scarred wooden table. The Legrand sisters had certainly been here, and recently. But where had they gone? And why were they hiding from us?

Sidney climbed the creaking stairs two at a time. There was no hope of sneaking up on someone in this house. At the top stood two doors. The first opened into an airy bedchamber with two neat beds covered in crisp white counterpanes. The second room also contained a bed, but there was something about this chamber that was different. It crawled up from the pit of my stomach and prodded at dark memories.

One glance at Sidney told me he'd noticed it as well. His shoulders had stiffened and somehow the skin seemed to tighten across the bones of his face.

"Someone died here," I murmured, being the first to dare to say the words. "Not long ago."

He nodded, his gaze following mine as it trailed around the room, searching for clues as to who and why. He closed the door softly as we departed, and turned to lead us back downstairs. But something outside the window on the landing grabbed his attention.

The window looked out over the yard between the house and the barn, where a woman in a dark dress leaned around the corner, gesturing to another woman in a pale gray skirt and white blouse. She seemed to urge her to hurry behind her. Then the first woman reached behind her to clutch a hunting rifle before her chest.

The Legrand sisters, I presumed.

It was clear from their reception of our visit, they were expecting trouble. Was that because trouble had already come calling? After all, someone had died in that second bedroom, and it evidently wasn't one of them. So who had it been?

We carefully made our way down the stairs and out through the kitchen door, before following the line of the cottage around to the corner, where we knew the sisters to be concealed. Sidney peeked around it first and then drew back.

I pressed a hand to his arm, hoping we could find a way to resolve this without anyone being shot. "Let me do the talking."

He hesitated, searching my face before reluctantly backing away from the corner to allow me to step in front of him. His hand gripped my arm before I could speak. "But don't even think about stepping out into the open until I agree." The look in his eyes brooked no argument.

I dipped my head once in acknowledgment and then turned to yell in French across the yard between the two buildings. "Mademoiselles Legrand, we mean you no harm. I am Verity Kent from London, and my husband is here with me. I sent you the telegrams." When my words were met with silence, I tried again. "Please, may we speak with you? It's about your cousin Esther."

"How do we know you do not mean to harm us?" one of them challenged. "We had no trouble here until we received your telegram. We think you have brought it upon us."

This sent a jolt down my spine, confirming my suspicions. "I am sorry for your troubles, but we did not cause them. We were trying to prevent them. But it appears we were too late."

There was a short lull before the woman spoke again. "Why did you not say so in your first telegram, then?"

"Because I did not know who would see it. I did not know who could be trusted."

Tension tightened around me in bands as we waited their response. I could only hope they were swaying in our favor and not deciding how best to try to kill us.

"Please," I pleaded. "We know who killed your cousin, but

we do not know why. We do not know why they stole the letters she received from you." This was not strictly true. I had a good guess why. But I hoped this would convince them.

I turned to look into Sidney's eyes, wondering what we should do if they refused.

"We know you have a gun," the woman charged.

"We do," I admitted. "As a precaution. We could tell something was wrong."

There was another beat of silence before she spoke again. "You have been in the war."

A statement, not a question, but I answered her anyway. "Yes."

Though a truce had not been offered yet, I could feel the tension dissolving.

"I will step forward with my gun raised if you will do the same."

I glanced at Sidney, who nodded, before I responded. "We will do the same."

He slid past me, lifting the pistol high in the air so that they could see it, and the woman in the dark gown did the same with her rifle, her sister trailing after her. I followed slowly behind Sidney as we crossed the yard before halting a few feet apart. While Sidney and the older sister stood gazing warily at each other, their guns pointed in the air, I strode forward to offer the woman in the crisp white blouse my hand.

"Verity Kent," I said. "And are you Marguerite or Adele?"

She cast an uncertain glance at her sister before accepting my hand. "Adele Legrand. Welcome to our home, Madame Kent."

"From the delicious smells issuing from your kitchen, I suspect you have supper in the oven, and I would hate to see it burn because of our intrusion."

Adele's mouth curled into a hesitant, but pleased smile, proving I'd correctly inferred that the kitchen was largely her domain, with its cheery eyelet curtains and spotless flagstones. "*Oui*, madame."

"Then perhaps we should adjoin there until these two decide to stop circling each other like a pair of hedgehogs."

Sidney flicked me a look of mild annoyance.

The fine laugh lines at the corners of Adele's eyes deepened. "*Oui.*"

I followed her up the path into the kitchen, speaking of everyday things. I trusted Sidney and Marguerite would join us shortly, and so they did, just as Adele set a cup of fresh coffee before me and fresh cream. Sidney's pistol was now safely tucked away in his waistband, I noted, and Marguerite leaned her rifle in the corner closest to the door.

I pushed to my feet to offer her my hand, and found her grip to be far stronger than her sister's. As was the probing look she gave me, as if she thought her glare alone would make me confess my crimes. I allowed her to look her fill, showing her I had nothing to hide, and studied her in turn. She wished to appear competent and confident, but I could sense the fear lurking beneath. When finally she released my hand, she drew a chair back from the table in the direction where her rifle leaned, accepting the coffee her sister offered her.

I looked to Sidney, who appeared to be absorbed with his own java, though I knew he was just as watchful as the sisters, before broaching the reason for our being there. "Now, then, why don't we begin with why you did not telephone me on Sunday as your telegram said you intended?"

"Why don't we begin with why you contacted us in the first place?" Marguerite fired back, brushing back from her face a dark strand of hair that had fallen from her tight chignon.

"Fair enough," I replied evenly. "Irene Shaw asked me to look into the circumstances surrounding her half sister's death. She was unsatisfied with the police's inquiries, and she wanted us"—I nodded to my husband—"to be certain they hadn't overlooked anything."

"Why you?"

Whether she hadn't read about us in the newspapers or she was simply testing me, I didn't know, but she was certain to be frustrated by my next answer. "Because my husband and I have undertaken certain sensitive investigations in the past, and that is all I will say on that subject."

Her scowl deepened and I hastened on.

"In the process of searching your cousin Esther Shaw's rooms, we discovered that the letters she'd received from you were missing. And they were the *only* things missing."

The sisters shared a speaking glance.

"Coupled with the fact that Esther had also gone to the trouble to censor her own journal, striking out certain words and sentences beginning with her time spent here in the autumn of '17, we began to suspect that whatever had gotten her killed must have something to do with you or this place. I'd hoped you could tell me what."

Adele sank into a chair, clutching between her hands the apron she'd tied around her waist.

"You're correct." Marguerite cleared her throat, obviously not unaffected by whatever had happened, even if she was more stalwart than her sister. "Something did happen. Perhaps you've even heard of it. The *Zebrina*."

"Her missing crew? Yes, it was the only connection we could think of to Le Rozel, and it fit the known timing of Esther's visit."

She nodded, clasping her hands in her lap. "Esther watched it sail into the cape. She watched it being beached." A veil seemed to fall over her features. "She watched the young man drop over the side and stumble down the beach."

My gaze flew to Sidney's. "So a crew member did survive? *He* beached the boat. We suspected something of the sort, but of course, we couldn't *know*."

"*Oui*, and Esther, being the naïve, soft-hearted girl she was, went down to the beach to ask if he needed help."

"She was merely being kind," Adele protested. "And besides, you're one to talk. You're the one who agreed to hide him when the authorities came looking for him, and you haven't had such a harsh word to say about him all the years since." Her voice clogged with tears.

An emotion I could see Marguerite was struggling to suppress. "Yes, well, Tommy was a good man," she admitted, much subdued. "He would have made Esther a fine husband."

"Hold on. Please," I gasped, trying to catch up with all the revelations, even though many of them were merely confirmations of what we'd already suspected. "You'll have to explain. Tommy was his name, then? And he stayed here?"

"Tommy Chegwin," Marguerite confirmed. "He lived here with us. Not in this house, mind you. That would have been improper. No, there's a small squat shed at the edge of our property near the pond, and he lived there."

"And where is he now?" I glanced between the two women, both of whom seemed reluctant to speak the words Sidney and I already knew.

"Dead," Marguerite rasped. "Shot sometime in the middle of the night Saturday. Somehow he managed to drag himself to our back door, for I found him there the next morning, clinging to life. We tried to help him, but I already knew it was too late. I'd been a nurse during the early part of the war, you see. Before I'd had to return home to care for my own mother. There was nothing we could do." Her voice was flat, as if by pronouncing the facts without inflection they might hurt less somehow.

Adele wept softly into her apron.

"That's why you hid when we arrived?" Sidney said, speaking for the first time. "You thought we were the killer coming to finish the job."

Marguerite lifted her hands in a fatalist gesture. "How were we to know?"

She was right. It was the safest assumption. In her position, I would have done the same.

"They killed our dog, too. Left poisoned meat out for him. I suppose because they were worried he would alert us or Tommy."

I stiffened, not knowing why, but somehow the heartlessness of such an act made it all worse. Perhaps it was because I'd watched people living under the harsh German occupation in Belgium and northeastern France divide their meager meals to share them with their dogs. They'd decided near starvation was preferable to losing their faithful companions.

"You said Tommy would have made Esther a fine husband," I said, echoing her previous statement. "Were they engaged?" "*Oui,*" Adele sniffled. "Since the spring. They'd fallen in love, you see. While she was visiting, and then after through their letters. Which we sent enclosed with ours."

"But Tommy was still in hiding, of a sort," her sister inserted. "After the war ended, we told some of the villagers he was a distant cousin originally from Toulouse. That he'd been a victim of traumatic psychoses and needed a rest somewhere quiet and peaceful. Tommy couldn't return to England, you see. Not after what had happened. So Esther was trying to find a way to clear his name."

"Because of what happened to the rest of the crew?" I surmised, urging them to explain.

Marguerite slid forward, pressing her hands flat to the table. "You have to remember, Tommy was young. Only seventeen when he came to us. He was the youngest member of the crew. So when the ship reached the southern tip of Alderney, he said he was left aboard while the others took a dinghy around the cape to deliver their cargo."

The island of Alderney lay just northwest of here—one of Britain's Channel Islands, and apparently a previously unknown port of call on the *Zebrina*'s voyage.

"He waited for them, preparing dinner and setting the table, but the time of their anticipated return came and went, and still the crew did not come back." She continued the story, reciting it like a family legend. "Finally, after hours of waiting, he spotted two rowboats approaching through one of the portholes. At first, he thought to run up and greet them, but something about the second boat made him stop. As it drew closer, he realized why."

Her eyes widened, and I found myself on the edge of my seat eager to hear, even though I'd already guessed the answer.

"There were only three men in the boats, and none of them were from the *Zebrina*'s crew. So, he hid belowdecks, waiting to discover what the men intended to do. He listened as they lashed the *Zebrina*'s boat to the side of the deck and clomped through the cabins, fortunately making only a precursory search of the ship. When they returned topside, his insides shriveled as one of the men asked why they didn't simply set the entire ship alight. But another man told him not to be such a gormless eediot. That a fire would draw far too much attention that close to the island and bring about a search for the crew. The plan was to set it adrift and let the current take it. To let it be found unharmed anywhere but Alderney. And if a U-boat should find it first, so much the better.

"When he was certain it was safe, and the ship had drifted far from the island, he climbed back up on deck to find blood splattered on the side of the dinghy. Fearful for his life and fully aware of what the authorities would think if he was the only crew member found to be alive, he decided to sail the ship as best he could alone to an isolated stretch of coast and then run. Which, as we've already said, is when he met Esther."

"Good heavens," I exclaimed softly. He'd been right. The chance of the coast guard or the police believing such a balled-up story was minuscule. Not when a more logical explanation so readily presented itself. That he'd killed the other crewmen before dumping their bodies and the weapon he used overboard.

Sidney's expression was equally grim. "What happened when he learned of Esther's death? Was he suspicious?"

The sisters exchanged a look, Adele's somewhat challenging while Marguerite's was chagrined.

"He was," the older sister replied. "But I wasn't. I believed it was precisely what your police had said—a burglary gone wrong. But Tommy was not only devastated, he was frantic. He was certain she'd been killed because of him."

"We told him it was nonsense," Adele added, softening somewhat toward her sister, whose face was stark with regret. "That there was no way anyone could have known. But he wouldn't be convinced otherwise. And it turns out he was right."

"He stayed at his hut more than usual, grieving, but also being discreet. And still they found him."

"Then you think it was the same people who killed Esther?" I verified, curious if there were any other possibilities.

Marguerite threw up her hands. "Who else? No one here had any quarrels with him, and you said yourself they took Esther's letters. They must have been looking for information of his whereabouts."

I nodded in agreement. Nothing else made sense.

But why were they so desperate to silence Esther and Tommy? What had he known about that rendezvous in Alderney that was worth killing over?

Intuiting my thoughts, as usual, Sidney voiced the same question I was contemplating. "Did he know what the cargo was that the *Zebrina* delivered to Alderney? It certainly wasn't coal."

Marguerite's expression turned wary. "He wasn't supposed to, but he caught a glimpse of one of the labels on the casks as they were loading it. It was opium."

I slid forward in my seat. "But where did they get it? It would be doubtful they were able to smuggle it from their port of origination undetected."

She shook her head. "That, I do not know. But he did say they had stopped somewhere else to load those casks before sailing for France."

"I heard him mention it once." Adele dabbed at her red-rimmed eyes. "But I don't know if it will be of any help. The name had the word *white* in it, but there must be many such places in England."

My eyes closed in dismay, but at least we had our answer.

"You recognize it?" she remarked, correctly reading my expression.

"Yes, and the word is more helpful than you think."

CHAPTER 26

Our drive back to Cherbourg was done in silence. This was partly so that Sidney could concentrate on the dark, unfamiliar roads, as well as listen for any more ominous sounds coming from the Renault's engine than the grinding and clatters we'd heard all evening. And partly because neither of us seemed ready yet to discuss what we'd learned from the Legrands.

The crescent moon hung low in the sky over the eastern fields, and a gentle sea breeze blew through the open windows, tickling the hairs at the base of my neck below my hat. The truth was, if not for the gravity of the day's revelations—and the grating noise of the engine—I would have enjoyed myself. But no matter how lovely the moon-drenched wheat, it could not wash away the burden of these secrets.

The Legrand sisters had walked us quietly across their property to the two fresh mounds of dirt in the forest marking Tommy's grave and their faithful hound's. They said the dog had grown quite attached to the young Cornishman, and they'd known he would want to remain by his side, even in death. Staring down at the stone markers in the peaceful setting the sisters had chosen, just a few yards from a burbling brook, I'd felt the weight of the investigation, the weariness of it, dragging at my bones. Three now dead. Plus the *Zebrina*'s crew. We couldn't turn away from it. Not now.

And certainly not with Tommy's dying wish echoing in my ears as Marguerite had relayed it. He'd not had a care for himself, but he'd begged them to get justice for Esther. To find whoever was responsible. To make them pay.

But the matter of culpability was far from straightforward. For while it seemed evident that Flossie was guilty of striking Esther in the head—the act that ultimately killed her—the reason she had been there searching through her letters lay elsewhere, and that instigator held at least a portion of the blame.

The motorcar surged over a rise in the road, and then suddenly, spread out before us, were the lights of Cherbourg, cupping the darkness of its harbor and the Channel beyond. The welcome glow of civilization seemed to relieve Sidney—or perhaps it merely eased the strain on his eyes—for his shoulders dropped from where they'd hunched up around his ears and his tongue loosened.

"You didn't seem pleased when Mademoiselle Adele said Tommy had mentioned the Isle of Wight." He flicked a glance at me before returning his focus to the road. "I'm sure you made the connection, given the similar pronunciation and what we learned from Cooper."

While Adele had said "blanc," which translated to "white," I knew the word she'd really heard from Tommy in English was "Wight." And there could be no other. Not in relation to our location.

"Yes, well, I suppose I don't relish the idea of intruding on Max. After all, we've put him through enough during the course of our past two bits of intrigue." Not to mention the awkwardness of my having essentially chosen another man over him, even if the other man happened to be my husband. I knew in time that Max would move on, if he hadn't already—I wasn't so vain as to think myself irreplaceable—and our friendship could resume. But until then, it seemed cruel to keep popping in and out of his life. Cruel to him and Sidney, despite their respect for each other.

"Is that what you propose we do, then? Sail for Wight?"

"I think we must consider it. Unless Max can provide us the information we need over the telephone, but somehow I doubt that."

"I assume you're thinking the same thing I am. That those drugs were wrecked goods washed ashore on the Isle of Wight."

"At the moment, it seems the most logical explanation." I sighed heavily. "And, unfortunately, that links all of this to the late Earl of Ryde. For who else had the connections to induce a schooner from Falmouth, hundreds of miles away, to anchor off the coast of Wight, collect the opium, and then carry it across to Alderney? And a flat-bottomed coal schooner, at that. A vessel that was difficult for the U-boats to sink and also had both a reason and permission to sail into the ports in northern France."

"A ship that happened to be owned by Ryde's known political ally, Lord Rockham."

"It seems preposterous, for why on earth would an earl and a marquess conspire to smuggle drugs out of the country? But there is no other feasible explanation."

I turned to stare out the window at the passing scenery as the motorcar whooshed downward toward the town, steadily dropping toward the sea.

"So we know who likely arranged to have the drugs shipped on the *Zebrina*, but we don't know why, or where the drugs were ultimately intended to go?" He threw one arm in the air. "Or even who killed the crew?"

"I suppose there are two possible scenarios," I ruminated. "One, the crew of the *Zebrina* was met by the ship that had been arranged to meet them, and the crew of that ship killed them, either because they'd been instructed to or purely on a whim. Or two, the *Zebrina* was met by a different ship entirely, and they killed them. But then how did that second ship know about the rendezvous?"

"Whatever the case, the person responsible for arranging the rendezvous with the second ship must have been involved from the beginning, or how else could they have known?"

I scowled. "He also must be the same person who sent Flossie to steal Esther's letters and then sent some unknown assailant to kill Tommy."

"You mean, you don't think Flossie bumped off Tommy?"

His eyes glinted with cynicism in the reflection of the street-lamps.

"I briefly considered it, but no. She's no seasoned killer. I'm certain of that, even if her disappearance from London seems to fit the timeline." I exhaled in frustration. "And given the fact no one saw the shooter, and he certainly took care not be seen, we'll probably never know who it was."

If Ardmore was behind this, just as I expected he was, he could have easily recruited someone from the war who had been trained for such stealth. Someone who might even believe that such a killing was government sanctioned, given Ardmore's position with Naval Intelligence. The thought of this possibility sickened me.

"So you don't want me to ask around at the port in the morning to see if anyone remembers any Englishmen or women disembarking?" Sidney was forced to check his speed as we entered the city proper, the shale buildings closing in around us.

"They're certain to recall any number of Englishmen, but you're welcome to try. Perhaps we'll get lucky." The tone of my voice left no doubts as to my skepticism.

"What do you intend to do?"

"Telephone C. Maybe he or Xavier will know something that can help us untangle this." But I would have to wait until the morning, when Kathleen was seated at her desk, in order to do so.

"And then call Ryde?"

I turned to meet his gaze as it darted toward me for a brief moment. "Yes."

He nodded once in acknowledgment of what must be done before refocusing on the road. From the narrowing of the streets I could tell we were drawing closer to the harbor and the quaint little hotel near the quay, where we'd booked a room when we'd arrived on the ferry.

"There's one point we've yet to broach," I murmured, gripping the seat beneath me as Sidney made a tight turn at a greater speed than I would have attempted. "Or perhaps I'm the only one who noted it."

"Eediot?" he replied, quickly catching my meaning. "Yes, that struck my ears when Marguerite said it as well."

"I don't think she was mispronouncing it. I think that's how she'd heard Tommy tell the tale. And why would a Cornishman say it that way unless that's exactly how he'd heard it."

"From a Scotsman or Irishman."

They were the only dialects I'd heard articulate the word *idiot* in such a manner, grating over the *d* so hard it almost sounded like a *j*.

"It could mean nothing. Or could be the key to everything," I stated grimly. It was certainly something I was going to mention to Alec when we spoke the next day.

Sidney braked to allow two women to cross the street, and I gazed out over the waters of the harbor to our right, the light of the thin moon shimmering in its dark depths. "What do you think happened to the cargo?"

He didn't answer at first and then just shrugged. "Does it matter? Whether it was dumped in the ocean or sold in a den in Paris, it's long gone."

He was right. It had been two years since it disappeared. And yet somehow it was still wreaking havoc in the lives of those it had touched, and ricocheting outward. I could only hope it had seen its last victim.

I waited until I knew Kathleen would have been seated at her desk for a quarter of an hour before I telephoned, leaving my message in code, as arranged. Then I only had to wait—something I'd learned during the war was easier said than done.

Having nothing better to do, and being even worse at waiting than I was, Sidney decided to stroll along the harbor and see if he could, in fact, strike it lucky. He'd had a rough night, tossing and turning from nightmares, and I hoped a walk in the fresh air and sunshine might help. Or perhaps it would at least help stave off the headache I could tell was building behind his eyes.

As a consequence, I was left alone to brood in the chair by the window in our room, which overlooked the street below. Hours passed in which I discovered there were precisely thirty-two patches in the mortar of the building across the street, the publican's wife was having an affair with the young baker next door, and the old orange tomcat did not like to be challenged for his right to sleep in the sunny spot at the corner of the drapers' shop, even by passing humans. Until finally, the porter knocked on our door with the message I'd been waiting for.

I thanked him and swiftly read the note, before following him down to the lobby, where a telephone booth had been installed for the convenience of its guests. Fortunately, I'd discovered earlier that the young lady currently seated at the desk spoke no English, so she would not be able to understand anything even if she happened to overhear.

The call rang through, and I heard Alec's playful voice crackling over the wires. "What's this, Lorelei? Miss me already?"

"But, of course, darling. Like a mud lark misses his scavenge," I retorted dryly.

He chuckled. "That much, ay? All right, then. What do you have for me?"

I briefly filled him in on what we'd learned thus far, and I could hear the intrigue in his voice as he asked for clarification on a few points. "Then what you need from me is some assistance in figuring out what precisely Ryde and Rockham's scheme was, and where they intended those casks to end up?" he summarized as I finished relaying the details.

"Yes."

"Well, by that point in the war there were any number of countries with stricter laws against narcotics than Britain. France and the United States, for instance. Though I can't imagine they were bound for somewhere as far away as America. Not with U-boats patrolling the Atlantic and the difficulty sneaking them onto a larger vessel would have posed. France seems the safest bet," he ruminated. "But why would two peers indulge in such subterfuge simply to make a few extra quid smuggling opium into northern France?"

"What if it was meant for Ireland?" I suggested.

This theory was met with silence, and for a moment I thought maybe the connection had been lost.

"Are you there?"

"Yes, sorry. I was just . . ." He exhaled, gathering his thoughts.

I gripped the earpiece tighter, never having heard Alec at such a loss for words.

"I heard rumors a few months ago that at some time during the war, after the Easter Rebellion, an idea was floated about that the British should send drugs to Ireland. That if the rebels should become enamored with opium or cocaine, they might cease to fight or resist."

"That's the same nonsense that the French were accusing the Germans of doing," I murmured in a low voice, smiling at the clerk when she looked up at me.

"Yes, I'm certain that's where the notion came from. That, and Roger Casement's collaboration with the Germans to smuggle weapons into Ireland for the rebellion. Regardless, my understanding is that the idea was quashed rather quickly." He paused. "But that doesn't mean two powerful lords didn't suddenly decide they would attempt the matter themselves. Perhaps with a supply of opium that happened to wash up on one of their beaches."

The plan was worse than ridiculous. Say they managed to get the drugs into the hands of the Irish, or even the leaders of the rebellion specifically. That didn't mean they would take the drugs. Or that if they took them, they would become addicted.

But Alec was right. That didn't mean Ryde and Rockham hadn't determined to try it. If their prejudice against the Irish had been great enough, they might have convinced themselves it was a given they would take the drugs. From what I knew of the late Earl of Ryde, this sort of high-handed behavior was unsurprising. After all, he'd pulled strings to have his son promoted out of the trenches. Something Max expressly hadn't wanted.

"What of our favorite shady seaman? Could he be involved in this somehow?" I posited, referring to Ardmore in oblique terms. There were operators potentially listening, and one could never be too careful with men like him.

"It's possible. With him, it's difficult to tell where exactly his allegiances lie, or what hand he might be playing in things." His tone turned wary. "He's smart. Dashed too smart if you ask me." There was some history between Alec and Ardmore I wasn't aware of. It crept into the edges of his voice whenever he spoke of him. But it wasn't something I could ask him about now.

"Regardless, you have a difficult row to hoe if you expect the government to do anything with the information you've uncovered," he cautioned. "No one is going to want to see this aired in the light of day. Not when it's an embarrassment to the empire and could very well incite the Irish to more violence. As you stand, you have almost no proof to show for it. The boy is dead, and his testimony was gleaned from a secondary source; the girl's letters were stolen, her words redacted from her journal; her friend, who most likely took them, is missing; and both lords are dead."

Hearing the facts laid out so starkly was more than disheartening.

"Unless you can scrounge up some pretty spectacular evidence on Wight . . ." He broke off. "That is where you're going next, isn't it? I should say Alderney would be a bust if those men the boy overheard were worried about alerting the locals to their presence. Unless you find something concrete, there may be nothing that can be done."

I chewed on my thumbnail, considering his words. Though I'd briefly considered going to Alderney, I'd realized the same thing he had; that it would be a waste of time. The *Zebrina* crew's bodies had likely been left in the water off the island's deserted southern shore, where they'd rendezvoused with the other ship, but that didn't mean they were there now. Even if they were there, I didn't have the proper equipment to go looking for them. That would take a team of skilled underwater divers and a lot of specialized equipment.

"I think you're right. Wight is my next best bet."

"I'll poke around some more here. See if I can find out whether the girl was asking questions about the *Zebrina*. Ring me if you need me," he replied, then the line went silent.

I stared silently at the mouthpiece, waffling over what must be done next. Deciding it would be best to have it over and done with, I tapped the switchhook and asked the operator to connect me to Nettlestone Hall on the Isle of Wight. But the butler informed me Max was not at home, though he was due back that evening. Deflating, I asked for him to telephone me in Cherbourg when he returned.

Hanging up the receiver, I rose from my seat, offering the clerk another smile—one I was far from feeling—and returned to our room. When Sidney strolled in a short time later, he found me seated at the same window as before, lost in thought.

"Any word from London?" He held out a loaf of crispy bread, a shiny yellow pear, and a bottle of the region's apple cider. "I thought you might be hungry."

"Famished," I admitted, eagerly accepting his gifts.

Sidney perched on the edge of the bed, listening as I summarized my conversation with Alec between bites of bread. He arched a single eyebrow sardonically when I described the proposed plot of shipping drugs to Ireland in order to turn their rebels into addicts, but otherwise did not comment on its stupidity.

"If that's what the plan was," he remarked. "If that's why the drugs were on the *Zebrina,* then I suppose we can safely assume Ryde supplied the drugs from some stash of wrecked goods that washed up on his estate, and Rockham supplied the *Zebrina* from Falmouth to transport it."

"He might also have been the one who promoted the idea, having witnessed the effects prolonged cocaine and opium use had on some of his previous mistresses."

Sidney nodded. "Then what of the second ship. The one with the Irish crew. Who was responsible for that one?"

I frowned at the rug as I chewed, hesitant to admit the thought that had already occurred to me. "That could have been Rockham as well. He does have an estate in Ireland. Maybe he has shipping interests there, too, and he arranged to have one of the ships already importing or exporting cargo to France pick up the drugs from the *Zebrina.*"

"But then how did they intend to get the drugs into the hands of the rebels?"

I shrugged my shoulders. "Presumably they would have had a contact capable of doing such a thing. As harebrained as the rest of this scheme was, I'm not sure how far they thought it through."

"I wonder if Rockham's second crew was aware of his intentions for the opium. Did one of the *Zebrina*'s crewmen let the purpose of it slip, and they erupted violently?" He frowned, tapping his fingers against the counterpane. "After all, not all of the Irish are intent on rebellion, but most of them would balk at the idea of harming their fellow countrymen in such an underhanded way."

Such a scenario would mean there need not have been a third person involved, that Ryde and Rockham had concocted and arranged the entire plan themselves. The fact that any third man's involvement could be so easily omitted from the plot troubled me.

Alec had spoken the truth. The government would not want to prosecute such a case. And if it could be brushed aside because all the major players were dead, so much the better. They would readily latch on to the version of events that excluded any living participant, particularly one as highly placed and well-connected as Ardmore.

However, I felt certain there must be a third man, for a number of reasons. "The words Tommy overheard the sailors say. They didn't make it seem like it was merely a spontaneous eruption of violence. They seemed almost methodical. As if the plan had already been formed."

Sidney conceded this point.

"And what of Rockham? If there's no third man, then who killed him?" I challenged. "Or do you think a relative of one of the crewmen figured all this out before we did and killed the marquess in revenge?" My voice had grown testy, and he sent me a quelling glance.

"You're right. *If* this is all related, then there must be a third man." He tilted his head. "Though feasibly I suppose Rockham could have been the one to find out Esther was poking around, and hired Flossie to steal her letters coming from France. Maybe her sister, Irene, found out and killed Rockham."

I glared at him. "And then hired us to find her sister's killer, bringing it to our attention when otherwise we would have been none the wiser?" I shook my head.

"True. And there is the matter of who has been pulling the strings since Rockham's death? After all, someone killed Tommy Chegwin five days ago, and it wasn't Rockham."

I picked up the pear, staring down at it as a far more troubling thought pervaded my brain, one that had been nagging at me for days, but that I'd refused to give serious consideration. Now, I found I couldn't turn from it. Not knowing what destination we were bound to next.

All the other players in this scenario surrounding the *Zebrina* had met with an untimely demise. All but the late Earl of Ryde. But what if that were not true? What if Max's father had also been a victim? One whose murder had gone undetected for nearly a year.

"Would you like me to ask the hotel staff for a knife?" Sidney asked, misunderstanding my hesitation in eating the pear.

I lifted my gaze to meet his and shook my head before lifting the fruit to take a bite. Juice dripped down my chin and I swiped it away with the back of my hand, not caring how indelicate it might look. However, the pear settled like a lump in my stomach. A reminder I would have to raise the specter of his father's death with Max. I doubted he would thank me for it.

CHAPTER 27

In the end, I did not have the opportunity to speak with Max until the following evening. When he failed to telephone before we retired on our second night in Cherbourg, Sidney and I both agreed it would be best to set out for the Isle of Wight on the first morning ferry. After all, there were questions to be asked there, with or without Max's assistance. So, before dashing off to catch the ferry, I telephoned Nettlestone Hall again in the wee hours of the morning and relayed a message for the butler to pass along to Max.

Unfortunately, a crossing that should have taken eight hours stretched into more than ten on the rough seas. The weather that had been so warm and favorable all through late summer and into early autumn had suddenly decided to shift, and it did so with a vengeance. I even heard one of the old sailors predicting there would be snow on the higher elevations come nightfall. Such a forceful change seemed impossible, but the lashing wind and heaving of the sea quickly convinced me. I even became seasick, when in all my years of Channel crossings during the war, dodging U-boats, I hadn't experienced a queasy stomach once.

Happily, the seas grew calmer as we entered the Solent and docked at Portsmouth. Otherwise I'm not certain I could have convinced myself to step aboard the smaller ship that would carry us back across the Solent to the Isle of Wight.

As a consequence, it was far later in the day than we'd anticipated before we reached the island. If Max had come to meet us, it was likely he'd given up on us long ago. So Sidney spoke to some of the other passengers on the ferry and ascertained that the Pier Hotel in Seaview would be a good place for us to stay, and the establishment would even send a motorcar for us if we telephoned from the ferry office.

When the ship docked at Fishbourne, we set off toward the squat building standing next to the far more grandiose royal yacht club, only to be halted by the sound of a voice calling our names. We swiveled to find Max striding toward us with his long gait, a large grin splitting his face.

"You made it after all," he declared, offering Sidney his hand, which he shook heartily. He threw a glance upward at the low ceiling of dark clouds. "I was worried the weather might keep you." Then his soft gray eyes fell on me, and he leaned in to buss my cheek. "It's dashed good to see you. I'm sorry I didn't telephone yesterday. By the time I returned from Newport it was nearly midnight, and I didn't think you'd appreciate such a late call. But here you are now." He took in our wrinkled traveling clothes and valises. "And you undoubtedly have some spot of intrigue to tell me about. But let's see you settled into Nettlestone Manor first."

"Oh, Max, you needn't go to the trouble," I protested.

But he would hear none of it. "No trouble at all. I've already had the best guest chamber made ready for you. And I assure you my housekeeper will be quite cross if you don't accompany me. She already complains I don't entertain enough."

Our objections being brushed aside, he hefted my valise and led us toward his pale-yellow Rolls-Royce. I noticed the colorful bonnet ornament it had sported the first time I'd met him was no longer affixed in place, but perhaps his niece had re-confiscated it.

"Have you replaced your Pierce-Arrow?" he asked Sidney as we climbed inside, keeping up a lively stream of small talk as we drove east toward the villages of Ryde, Seaview, and Nettlestone. It wasn't long before we turned down a long drive bordered by beech trees, and I caught my first sight of Nettlestone Hall.

I'd once heard someone describe it as being frightfully spectacular, and they were certainly correct. The sprawling manor was built from pale limestone, which gleamed even on such an overcast day, and spread out over a leafy valley dotted with hedge-lined fields and glistening pools. Horses raced along the fences bordering the drive, almost as if they were eager to see Max return. Two hounds bounded out from a barn, yapping excitedly as we stopped before the crenellated mansion.

"Don't mind these rascals," he declared, kneeling to ruffle their heads and long ears. "Their bark is much worse than their bite."

I held out my hand so the caramel-coated dog could sniff it, smiling as she thrust her head into it, demanding I pet her.

Sidney bent over, grinning into the other hound's face. "You look like a chap who's rather fond of playing fetch. Am I right? Am I?"

The dog roofed, as if he'd understand exactly what the human had said, and we all laughed.

"I knew it," Sidney chuckled. "Perhaps later, old boy."

Max planted his hands on his hips, staring approvingly down at his dog. "You've taken his measure." His eyes flicked toward the other one now lying on my feet. "As have you. Come on," he called, rousing them to their feet to follow him through the massive oak entry doors.

In short order, we found ourselves bustled into an airy bedchamber with a cheery fire already crackling in the hearth. We changed out of our damp and travel-stained clothes and into something dry and comfortable, then adjourned to a cozy parlor, where Max stood at the window, gazing out over the rambling gardens. The rain, which had dogged us all day and had slackened just long enough for us to reach Nettlestone, was now drumming down on the terrace and bowing the heads of the flowers.

For that brief moment before Max turned, I could tell from his profile that he wasn't as sanguine as he wished us to believe. His brow was heavy with worry. But he determinedly lightened his expression as he swiveled to receive us.

Once we were all seated before the great stone hearth, where another fire licked over the logs within, and a cup of tea or something a bit stronger was clutched in our hands, I decided I owed it to him to be direct.

"Max, I'll level with you. Though I wish I could say this was purely a social visit, as you've already alluded to, it isn't." I grimaced. "But I'm afraid it's a bit difficult to explain without first telling you a rather long and winding tale."

He shifted in his seat, settling back, and then nodded. "Go on. How can I help?"

My chest tightened hearing him address me with such warmth and trust, for what I was about to tell him about his father would be difficult to hear. Sidney's deep blue eyes glinted with empathy, but I turned away, determined to squash any sentimental impulse that might impel me to keep anything but the absolute truth from Max.

I could tell my story of Rockham's and Esther's murders confused him at first, and then shocked him as I began to explain their connection to the *Zebrina*. But once I mentioned his father's presumed involvement, I was the one who was staggered to discover this was not entirely unfamiliar to him.

"You knew of your father's involvement in such a plot?" Sidney asked, displaying the same astonishment.

"No," he disputed. "Not the plot." He heaved a sigh. "But I was well aware of my father's feelings on the Irish." His mouth twisted. "He was, by no means, a great advocate of them or their independence. And he often bemoaned the blight of drink and drugs on our society. Of course, that didn't stop him from indulging in brandy or wine, but my father always did have a different standard when it came to what he and his peers were allowed to do as opposed to the rest of the world."

I nodded. I'd met a number of noblemen who were of the same ilk. It was tiresome.

"As for his friendship with Rockham, it's true. They were allies." His gaze met mine. "As he was with Ardmore."

I sat taller.

"Though, for the sake of argument, I have to ask. Why do you think he suggested you look into Rockham's shipping interests if you think he's involved? Why point you in that direction if he wanted the plot to remain concealed?"

"I've contemplated this as well," I admitted. "And the best answer I can give is that it was a double bluff of sorts. Perhaps he suspected I was already investigating Rockham's shipping connections, and so by telling me to do so, I would either allow the matter to drop, or assume exactly as you're suggesting, that he couldn't be involved. After all, if Flossie stole those letters from Esther at his behest, then she could have told him we'd been there making inquiries. Maybe he'd assumed we already knew more than we actually did."

I didn't mention the second possibility. That this was all some sort of game. That he'd wanted me to recognize that he was involved, all the while knowing he was safe from any proven connection. Why exactly he would reveal himself to me in such a manner when he could remain safely hidden, I didn't know. But perhaps there was no pleasure in such deviousness without someone being aware of it. Perhaps he needed someone to know how clever he was.

"I suppose that makes some sort of twisted sense." His finger tapped his chin. "But what of Rockham's conversion? Why would he wish to become Roman Catholic if he was so anti-Irish?"

Sidney had the answer to this. "Being pro-Catholic doesn't necessarily make one pro-Irish, or in this case, pro-independence. After all, Rockham held quite a bit of land in Ireland. Land he would lose if the rebellion succeeded. And there are those who have suggested that Rockham's conversion was all a pretty ruse. Maybe even a bid to try to keep that land by making the Irish think he's sympathetic to their cause."

His gaze met mine and I could tell he'd noticed the same thing I had. That Max seemed to be struggling to confront the real issue at stake. His hands plucked almost nervously at the arms of his chair.

"Max," I began softly.

"I know." He closed his eyes. "You want to know whether I think my father could have been part of such a plot, whether it could have been possible. And all I can say is, maybe." He sighed and then forced himself to look at me. His face was drawn with an uneasiness he hadn't exhibited a short time ago, and I'd put that burden there. "It's possible. Definitely possible. And I'll show you why I say that tomorrow. It will require a short drive to the south of the island."

"You still have a stash of wrecked goods?" Sidney guessed.

Max's gaze shifted to meet his and he nodded. "Just . . . wait and see."

The sky was already growing dark, the setting sun hidden behind the leaden clouds, and after they day we'd had, I had no desire to venture back out into it. But this delay was also for Max. He was struggling to accept everything we'd told him, and I couldn't fault him for not wanting to confront it all at once. So I chose to keep my suspicions about his father's death to myself for a little while longer. Yes, it was a reprieve for me, but also for Max. Let him sleep for one more night without entertaining the doubt.

True to the old sailor's prediction, the air had a definite bite to it the following morning. One that made me glad that, on an impulse, I'd tossed a warmer woolen dress in with the others in my valise. Still, I sat shivering in my Donegal tweed coat in the rear seat of Max's Rolls-Royce, even with a warm rug thrown over my lap. As for that snow the sailor had presaged, I could say there was none on the Isle of Wight. It wasn't cold enough here. But farther north, even over the higher elevations on Dartmoor, he might have been right.

Max and Sidney stared stalwartly ahead in the seat in front of me. It seemed neither of them had gotten much sleep. Sidney had tossed and turned as he had all the nights before, and Max's drawn face and copious consumption of coffee at the breakfast table suggested he'd done much the same.

We hadn't discussed matters over breakfast, nor had any words been spoken since we drove away from his door, except when Max had pointed out a few notable buildings or features. We seemed to be traveling south toward the Channel, and when Max turned the car down a smaller dirt track, sending us bumping down toward the beach, I knew this to be true. The water today was calmer, but still dark and sullen. We pulled up beside a large storage shed of some kind, and Max urged us to follow him. A set of keys jangled as he pulled them from his pocket and strode toward the door. That's when a lad of about ten came dashing around the shed, skidding to a halt at the sight of all of us.

"Hullo, Rex," Max greeted him. "Run and fetch Mr. Kelly and Mr. Stanton."

"Right-o!" He grinned and took off at a sprint back the way he'd come.

"He's a good lad," Max declared with approval as he searched through his keys until he found the right one. "Lost his father, like so many of the poor mites on the island. Like so many everywhere," he added more softly.

I glanced at Sidney anxiously as he made this comment, but his gaze remained trained on the door.

Max stepped aside, gesturing through the opening. "Have a look."

There wasn't an electric light inside the building, but there were gaps between the crude slats that allowed dim sunlight to seep through. It was bright enough, in any case, to illuminate the dozens and dozens of barrels and casks, and even a few crates filling the space almost to the rafters near the back.

"All of this washed ashore during the war?" I gasped.

"Yes," Max replied austerely just over my shoulder. "This and more. There are two more sheds on the island filled like this. And that's not including the casks contaminated by salt that we already disposed of, or the goods people hid or made use of before they could be confiscated."

"I think some of these may have gone bad as well," Sidney muttered as the scent of something rank assailed our nostrils.

"Yes, well. That's for the government to deal with as soon as they finally send someone to collect all of this." His tone of voice made it clear he was none too pleased with how long it had taken them to claim the goods, and I couldn't blame him. There might be foodstuffs here, long since spoiled, that someone could have consumed.

"The contents of one or two of the barrels may have made their way into the hands of some of the widows," he murmured, as if reading my thoughts. "But I figure it's merely a small portion of the compensation they rightly deserve."

I smiled back at him.

"Well done, Ryde," Sidney declared in approval.

Max reached up to rub the back of his neck. "Yes, well. It was the least that could be done."

We turned back to survey the casks again. Sidney even stepped close enough to read some of the labels.

"Then your father could have supplied the casks of opium Tommy claimed they collected from Wight," I murmured, returning to the somber reason we were there.

"Yes." He paused, and his expression turned forbidding. "And we'll soon find out if he did."

Hearing what he must have—the sound of two men's voices drawing nearer—I turned to follow him from the building.

They fell silent at the sight of me and then Sidney emerging from the shed, and removed their caps at the sight of Max's fierce scowl. I presumed the two men were Mr. Kelly and Mr. Stanton. Both were grizzled and weather-beaten, but with strong backs. These were the type of men who had been too old to serve in the army, but young and fit enough that they'd been forced to shoulder the burden of those who had gone off to fight. Alongside a few upstart, usurping women who'd stepped up to help. From the glance they cut my way, I could tell they were the type of men who didn't appreciate the interference of women, no matter how much they needed the assistance.

"I know whatever you've done, you did it at the behest of the late earl, and I will not hold that against you. But he is no longer here, so whatever bond of silence he forced on you, I'm relieving you from. I need the level truth from you men, do you hear?"

They nodded soberly. By the distressed look in their eyes, I suspected they held more than one secret, and they were furiously trying to figure out which one he was referring to.

Fortunately, Max was going to make it plain for them. "Did you load casks of wrecked goods onto a ship anchored offshore during the war?"

The two men exchanged a glance and then nodded.

"Yes, milord," the one on the left replied.

Max studied him closely. "What type of ship was it?"

"A flat-bottomed schooner. One of those coal haulers from Cornwall."

The *Zebrina*. I exhaled a shallow breath. Unless there were others.

"Did you know what you were loading onto the ship?" Max asked.

The two men looked to each other again.

"The truth!" Max barked.

Their heads snapped around, and the same one answered as before. "Yes, milord. 'Twas opium."

"Bound for?"

He shook his head. "We don't know the answer to that one. Not precisely."

Max's jaw ticked impatiently. "Then what *do* you know?"

"The earl said it was bound for the bog-trottin' rebels," the second man muttered in a gravelly voice. "That somethin' needed to be done to silence the cowardly upstarts while our boys were fightin' and dyin' for them in the trenches."

CHAPTER 28

I struggled not to react to this confirmation that our suspicions had been correct. Ryde and Rockham, and perhaps Ardmore, *had* embarked on this ridiculous scheme. And it had resulted in the entire crew's deaths, as well as Esther's, and possibly Rockham's and Ryde's themselves.

But if my struggle was great, Sidney's was too much. He whirled away with a sound of disgust, striding several paces toward the beach. I wrapped my arms tightly around me against the chill wind, tempted to go to him. However, I knew he needed a few minutes to compose himself. To master the fury bottling up in the fists he clenched at his sides.

"Who else knows about this?" Max demanded of the men.

They rattled off a few names that I suspected were islanders, but insisted they knew nothing more. This was probably true. For the late earl to have shared anything further would have been uncharacteristic. In truth, I was surprised he'd shared as much as he had. He must have presumed stirring up any resentment they felt toward the Irish would encourage their cooperation and their silence.

In the end, Max let them go. Telling them not to discuss it, even amongst themselves.

"Enough people are dead because of it," he muttered as they walked away. "I don't need islanders turning up that way, as well."

"It would serve them right if they choked on their own ignorance," Sidney snarled savagely.

Max and I turned to look at him where he still stood, hands on his hips, staring out over the Channel in the direction where, less than a year ago, the guns still thundered. Had they been able to hear them this far west? Had their nights been punctuated by the growls and rumbles like mine had been when I stayed at our cottage near the Sussex coast? His pain and anger were almost a tangible thing, permeating the salty air, raking fingernails across my heart.

"Sidney," I began gently, but he didn't want to listen.

"I served alongside a company of Irish." He turned his head so that we could see his profile. "I watched them fight just as hard as my men. Watched them bleed the same, too. And their captain—" He broke off, swearing under his breath. "Well, he was a bloody good bloke. Didn't deserve the end he got." His feet shifted toward the shore. "None of them did."

With this statement, he began walking down the beach.

"Sidney," I called out. "Sidney!"

But he didn't look back. His furious strides grew longer with each step, until I half expected him to break into a run, leaving naught but a trail behind in the compact sand. Then again, running might smack too much of cowardice to a man like Sidney.

I watched him go, uncertain what to do. I knew his outburst was less about the Irish specifically and more about all the men who'd died. All the good men who should have been here, the same as him. But what could I say? How could I possibly take away any of that pain or even make it more bearable? Every time I tried, he pushed me away.

I'd never felt so helpless. Not during all the years of the war, and all the dangerous or seemingly impossible situations I'd found myself in. There had always been something to do, something to try. But here, I was floundering. It tore a hole in my chest to realize that despite all my competence, all my love for Sidney, I might not be able to fix this. This, perhaps the most important problem I would ever confront, was beyond me.

I could feel Max watching me, probably judging me for my indecision.

But I should have known better.

"It's guilt, you know."

I turned to look at him, blinking to clear the tears that stung the backs of my eyes.

"That he survived when they didn't. It's eating at him." He turned to watch Sidney. "It eats at all of us," he added softly. "But for different reasons, it bothers some more than others."

I thought of the changes I'd witnessed in him in the last month. Before that, he'd had the traitors to pursue, and he could bury whatever he was feeling inside his anger and determination to find them and bring them to justice. And then there was me and our uncertain future to secure, and the search for my former fellow spy in Belgium. But once that was over. Once he was safely back in England, with the moniker of war hero hung around his neck, and me back in his arms, there was nothing left to distract him. Nothing left to ice over the pain—and yes, the guilt—he'd buried deep.

It had been lurking there all along. I'd seen it sometimes in his eyes when he thought I wasn't looking. I'd watched him from the hallway as he battled it sitting in the darkened drawing room in the middle of the night rather than sleeping in bed beside me. But after our time at the cottage, after learning of Albert Rogers's death, he could no longer restrain it. It was gutting him.

"You know the higher-ups used to make Kent rally the troops."

I stiffened in shock.

He nodded, his features grim. "He had a way with the men. Of reassuring them. Of bolstering them." He inhaled a deep breath, one that seemed difficult to take. "I think most of them would have walked into hell for him, or very close to it. And the upper brass knew it. They took advantage of it." His gaze flicked to meet mine. "They never would have promoted *him* out of the trenches. He was too valuable." He shrugged a shoulder. "And he had the devil's own luck."

Because he'd continued to survive when so many others didn't last beyond their first raid or battle.

"He hates himself for that. He hates that he buoyed those men up and then betrayed them by sending them to their deaths. At least, that's how he sees it."

"But he had no choice," I protested.

"A man like Kent always believes he has a choice. That he could have, and perhaps should have, refused. Even knowing he would have been court-martialed and killed by a firing squad at dawn—made an example of in front of the men to stop anyone from deciding to follow suit. But you're right. That is no choice. Not really. Not for an honorable man like Kent. And had he made it, those men he feels he betrayed would have died anyway, under someone else's command."

I stared in the direction my husband had gone, no longer able to see him around the sharp curve of the beach. I hadn't known he'd been carrying all that around inside. It was no wonder he'd begun to question the encouragement he'd given Goldy, or hesitate to offer advice where before he'd been happy to judiciously provide it. He was afraid of his words causing more grief.

I thought of him sitting in our flat, staring at the picture of himself and his long-dead cousin. The cousin whose mother still couldn't bear to look at him because he'd survived when her son had not. That had been there, too. Mixed up in all of this. Perhaps it was even the reason he'd always been a bit reckless. It wasn't because he thought himself impervious, but because he knew he was not.

The well of guilt and pain inside Sidney must be fathoms deep. How on earth was I ever to be able to reach the bottom of it? How was I ever to be able to remove even a bucketful?

I could feel my heart breaking, its little shards piercing me like shrapnel.

"What do I do?" I murmured helplessly, almost forgetting Max was there.

"Don't give up on him, Verity," he told me gently. "You have to keep trying. Keep trying to make him talk. I know you may have been told to leave it be, to ignore it and leave him to his silence. But I'm not convinced that doesn't make it worse." He turned away from the shore to look directly at me. "Be patient, but make him talk. Kent is too good a man." He glanced down the beach significantly. "Don't let him retreat."

I inhaled a ragged breath and nodded.

"I'll wait here."

The word *wait* clutched at something inside me, for Max had once said it to me in a different context. And now, like then, I felt like I'd somehow served him wrong. Especially when I'd yet to tell him my suspicions about his father's death.

"Thank you, Max," I murmured, not having the courage to look at him, and then set off down the beach.

I was glad I'd worn my walking boots, for as furious as Sidney had been, and as long as his legs were, he might have walked to the other end of the island by now. I felt a tremor in my stomach at the thought of what I would find when I finally reached him. My mind whirled, not knowing what to say. But Max was right. I had to keep trying. I'd known that before he'd even said it, but hearing it in his calm, reassuring voice had helped.

I wasn't sure he and Sidney weren't alike in more ways than they, or I, had realized.

The beach here didn't slope in a smooth curve, nor did it sport a wide strip of sand like the popular holiday destinations on the island. This strip of shore ran in jagged dips, backed by the cliffs, which seemed to circle the island in undulating waves, some lushly overgrown with foliage, while others were bare stone. The water lapped gently at the shore, leaving tendrils of seaweed mixed with the dark stones at the water's edge. Had it not been for my anxiety over Sidney, I might have enjoyed such a peaceful stroll after the tumult of the last few weeks, even with the cool breeze whipping across my cheeks.

I expected to find my husband either standing or seated on the sand, smoking a cigarette and staring out to sea, or perhaps even picking his way back to me. So when I rounded a curve to find Sidney tossing a ball with the young boy Max had called Rex earlier, I was stunned. And justifiably so, given his angry outburst. My heart lodged in my throat at the sound of the boy's happy laughter and my husband's words of gentle encouragement. He certainly seemed lighter throwing the ball to Rex.

I don't know how long I stood there watching them, or when the tears began sliding down my cheeks, for the wind seemed to dry them as fast as they fell, but I swiped the last of them away as someone called the boy's name. He dashed up some unseen trail, pausing once to wave at Sidney, before my husband turned to walk toward me. It was clear he'd known I was there, though he'd never looked in my direction. I inhaled a deep breath, attempting to pull myself together before he stood before me.

His deep blue eyes were still subdued, but the rage he'd felt earlier had drained away, and the shadows that so often lurked there had receded. He gazed down at me for a moment, perhaps studying my red-rimmed eyes and ruddy nose before speaking. "I'm sorry for my outburst."

I shook my head, and his brow furrowed in confusion. "Sidney, it's not about the outburst," I said softly. "I don't begrudge you your anger. You *should* be furious." I reached for his hand, staring down at the lines scoring his palm. "But you can't keep brushing me aside. You can't keep telling me nothing is wrong, or it's none of my concern." I looked up into his beloved face. "It *is* my concern. *All* of you is my concern."

His mouth quirked, and he reached for me. "Oh, is it?"

I pushed against his chest. "Stop that as well. Stop trying to distract me from asking questions by making love to me. It doesn't work, you know. Perhaps you don't have to hear them, but I'm still asking the questions in my head, even if I'm not speaking them aloud."

He appeared genuinely chastened, and I glanced away, lest I lose the nerve to say what I needed to say next.

"I know you're grieving for all those men you knew, all those men—good men—who died. And you *should* be. They deserve to be mourned. But I also know you feel guilty that you lived and they didn't."

He made a sound at the back of his throat, and I hastened on before he could stop me.

"You feel guilty that you survived and your cousin didn't. But that was not your fault. None of their deaths were you fault."

He opened his mouth to speak, but I cut him off.

"None." I glared up at him. "There are some things that are beyond your control. You're not omnipotent." I could tell he didn't like hearing this, but I persisted. "And, Sidney, I'm glad . . ." At this, I choked on my words and had to swallow hard to continue. "I'm glad you survived, even if they couldn't. When I thought you'd died . . ." I inhaled a ragged breath, shaking my head to try to deny the tears that pressed at the back of my eyes as he lifted his hands to rub my shoulders. "I need you. Here with me." I clutched the lapels of his coat. "Really here with me."

Gazing up into his eyes, I saw something I didn't think I'd ever seen before—a suspicious brightness. One that, once I'd blinked to clear away my own tears, I was certain indicated he was struggling not to cry. It made the tears I'd been fighting fall all the faster. For while I'd seen grown men cry, it had been extremely rare. And never my husband.

He nodded, and drew me to him, cradling my head below his chin so that my tears dampened the collar of his shirt. We stood that way for some time, giving and taking comfort, and absorbing each other's warmth as the wind whipped around us on the deserted beach. When a shiver worked through my frame, he sniffed and pulled away, sheltering me against his side away from the water as we set off back down the shore.

We were silent for a time, simply taking solace in each other's presence. However, what I'd witnessed earlier between Sidney and Rex was never far from my thoughts, or its effect on me and them.

"It bothers you that there are so many fatherless children?" I finally ventured.

At first, I worried he wouldn't answer, but it seemed he only needed to gather his words. "Yes." His brow furrowed. "It's unfair that they should suffer. That their fathers should have been taken from them."

I chose my words with care. "I know it might be a small thing. Perhaps in the grand scheme of things it's not very significant. But . . . you could make a point, from time to time, of visiting the children of those men you knew who died. Of having a toss with their sons. I saw how much it meant to Mr. Rogers's son." I nodded over my shoulder. "And to that boy on the beach." I glanced up at Sidney's profile as he stared out at the water's edge. "If you had died and left a son behind, wouldn't it mean something to you that someone had cared enough to take the time to have a catch with him because you couldn't?"

He didn't speak, but I could tell how much the notion affected him. He swallowed hard, his Adam's apple bobbing up and down. I hoped having some way he could help, no matter how small it might seem, might help him in some way in return. Maybe it would allow him to grieve and honor those men, and yet also to carry on. It would be a long road, not a short one, I knew. But perhaps this was a small step forward.

Max didn't say anything when we returned to where he was waiting for us next to his motorcar, staring out to sea in the same direction Sidney had. As if, by some compulsion, these men would always be drawn to look back at the horrors they'd witnessed, even if only to be certain they had been real and not some nightmarish figment of their imagination. I knew Max battled his own demons, but it was not my place to help him fight them. I glanced at Sidney out of the corner of my eye. Or at least, not mine solely.

The two of them shook hands, and I climbed into the rear seat of the motorcar, allowing them the space to confer quietly. For all the things I had seen as a Secret Service agent, I knew there were things I would never be privy to. Things that these two honorable officers would understand without either of them having to say a word. Whether they didn't know it, or simply wouldn't admit it, they needed each other. I was wise enough and strong enough to see that now. If I were to help either of them heal, I couldn't do it alone. But together, perhaps, we all could.

Unfortunately, as much as I would have liked to remain on the Isle of Wight indefinitely, we still had Rockham's murder to solve, as well as the pieces of the *Zebrina* mystery to finish putting together. That would require us returning to London. Our remaining answers lay there.

I said as much when we returned to Nettlestone just before midday.

"Yes, I think you're right," Sidney agreed, resting his arms along the top rail of the paddock.

Here in this sheltered spot, the wind did not blow so cold, and a handsome young filly we had been admiring had made a game of trotting toward us as Sidney coaxed her near, but never closer than fingertips reach, before darting away again. We could tell how much enjoyment she was deriving from this teasing as she tossed her dark mane, and we couldn't help but laugh at her antics.

"We need to track down Flossie Hawkins and convince her tell us what she knows," he said, offering the filly a carrot Max had retrieved from the barn.

"I can't help but be worried for her. Whoever is behind all this, Ardmore or someone else, has shown a propensity for tying up loose ends and silencing those whose knowledge could threaten him. And Flossie is most certainly a loose end."

I could only hope that Thoreau had been able to locate her and lock her up somewhere safe, because the alternative was not a welcome thought.

Max, who had been silent through this exchange, surprised me by addressing the elephant in the room I had not yet been willing to broach. "Do you think my father was a loose end, as well?"

Sidney and I both turned to look at him. I could tell what it had cost him to venture such a question in such a detached voice, and I decided there was nothing for it but to be honest. He wouldn't appreciate us holding back. Not when he was already entertaining suspicions.

"I don't know," I admitted softly. "But I confess, I wondered the same thing."

His eyes lifted to meet mine, and I could see they were stark with shadows.

"Did you have any suspicions about your father's death before we came here?" Sidney asked as the filly, who had noted his distraction, reached forward to snatch the carrot from his hand before dancing away.

"Actually . . . yes." He frowned, before adding tentatively, "I think I always have. But I kept telling myself I had no reason to be. That it was probably a normal reaction to feel when the death is so sudden and unexpected."

I stepped forward to stand next to Sidney, facing Max more fully. "How *did* he die?"

"A heart attack. At least, that's what his physician said. He *was* sixty-four. And his valet said he'd been complaining of some chest pains only a week before."

But that did not mean the event had been natural. I knew there were poisons that could mimic or even bring on a heart attack. It was possible he'd been helped along to his ultimate demise. Of course, it was also just as possible we were grasping at straws, and everything was exactly as it had seemed—a normal heart attack.

"There was no post mortem, I assume?"

He shook his head. "The war was still on, and there didn't seem to be any reason for one. There was a delay in the correspondence, and I wasn't even notified until two days later."

A tiny furrow formed between Sidney's eyes, echoing my own consternation. Max had been posted to battalion headquarters by then, which had their own telephones and telegraph capabilities. There was no reason it should have taken two days to notify *him*—the earl's son and heir—of his father's death, even if there had been a delay.

"I also received a letter from my father a few weeks before he passed." Max's thumbs rapped against the fence rail in agitation. "He said there was something important he wished to discuss with me on my next leave. That he was going to be doing everything in his power to make that happen sooner rather than later."

I shared a speaking look with Sidney. "But he didn't tell you what it was about? Not even a hint?"

"No." Max strained against the rail, his shoulders tightening beneath his gray tweed suit. "I've been racking my brain ever since, trying to figure out what it could have been." His gaze shifted to meet ours in turn. "I wonder if it could have been this."

I turned to stare out over the fields, where some of the older horses galloped in the crisp morning air. It was all decidedly odd, and also vaguely ominous. Had the late earl intended to tell his son something about the *Zebrina* affair? Had he been murdered before he could do so?

And was it too late to uncover the truth? It had been almost a year since Max's father had died.

Sidney offered Max one of the Turkish cigarettes stored in his battered silver case—the one I had given him before he left for the Western Front—and both men stood smoking, their eyes narrowed in thought.

"Perhaps there's something in my father's files. The ones at my father's office in Parliament."

I noticed he still called it his father's office, even though it was now his. His father might have been one of the most prominent figures in Parliament, but Max had little interest in politics, and had been hesitant to take up his father's seat in the House of Lords. In time, I knew that would change. Max was too conscious of the duty he owed his country not to take some part in government, no matter how small.

"I've gone through all his papers here and at the London townhouse. And there were many." His expression turned longsuffering. "My father had a tendency to keep meticulous notes, about everything. So I'd hoped there might be some mention of what he wished to tell me. But I haven't found it, or any mention of this smuggling business. Though maybe that last part isn't so strange. After all, my father was far from stupid, and they evidently wanted no trail." He inhaled a long drag from his fag and stared down at the glowing tip.

"But it bothers you nonetheless," I guessed.

He nodded. "It's simply not like him. He was nothing if not a creature of habit, and that included recording everything." He grimaced. "Even his conversations with the men he'd essentially bribed and extorted to have me transferred out of the trenches after my shoulder injury."

It was evident how much this move by his father still bothered him.

"I'd thought he would wish to keep anything of a sensitive nature at one of his homes, but perhaps it's in the boxes of things from Parliament. I've been hesitant to dive into those, but now that there's a reason, I'll have to make it a priority."

"Who else had access to your father's papers?" Sidney leaned against the fence, and now that he was paying no attention to her, the coquettish little filly had decided to creep up and nuzzle the back of his neck with her nose. "Oh, now you'll let me touch you, you little minx," he crooned, stubbing his cigarette out on the ground and reaching out a hand to run it down her neck.

Max's lips curled in a brief smile at his horse's ploy. "There was a few months' delay before I was demobbed and able to return to deal with them and other matters. But the steward here and my solicitor in London quite properly locked the desks and file cabinets, and even the study doors, in order to keep everything secure until I could contend with it. They're both good men. I have no reason to doubt their assertions."

"Anyone else?"

"My sister, I suppose. But I trust her implicitly."

In other words, if someone had removed or tampered with some of the late earl's papers, it had either been done before the doors were locked, or someone Max trusted had done so later. But once again, we were merely speculating.

"I'm sorry I don't have anything more definitive to offer you," Max murmured, misunderstanding the source of the look of frustration that had flashed across my face.

"Oh, no, Max," I hastened to reassure him, stepping forward

to touch his arm. "It's not that. And I'm terribly sorry that we should be adding to your worries over your father. I know this can't have been easy for you."

He shook his head. "Don't worry about that. Truthfully . . ." He exhaled a heavy breath. "I'm rather relieved to have someone to share this with. I considered contacting you about it half a dozen times, but then I decided I was being foolish." His gaze shifted between me and Sidney. "And then, of course, I didn't want to interfere."

My lips compressed into a tight smile, understanding what he meant. "Well, we will see this through, wherever it leads." I glanced at Sidney, pleased to see him nodding so decisively. "But it will take conclusive proof in order to convince anyone to do anything about it. As my contact with the Secret Service has already pointed out, no one in the government will want word of this hackneyed plot of your father's and Rockham's leaking out. And that means anything surrounding it will also be hushed up. Unless we can prove, beyond a shadow of a doubt, that someone"—and by someone, I was speaking of Ardmore—"contrived to murder two peers of the realm, a crew of English sailors, and, at the very least, was responsible for enabling the situation where an honorable Englishwoman was killed."

Both men looked as daunted as I felt by the entire situation, but hopefully deep in their guts they felt the same burning anger I did that Ardmore should have been able to get away with all this, and no one had been the wiser. I also admitted to feeling a slice of fear that he might have done so before, and would do so again in the future, if he was allowed to go unchecked. That could not happen.

Max was the first to speak. "Well, then, I suppose we should roll up our sleeves and set to work. Did you wish to catch the next ferry back to Portsmouth?"

"I think that would be best," I admitted, feeling a pressing urge to return to London.

He pushed away from the fence. "The sooner the better. There's murmurs that there may be a railroad workers' strike brewing."

"Heavens!" If the railroads stopped, then so would food and coal distribution, and just as cooler temperatures had set in.

He nodded grimly. "And if that happens, some of the other industries' unions might revolt, and we could have a full-scale general strike on our hands."

Hearing this, I started to realize Max wasn't as unaware or disinterested in the running of the country's welfare as he might seem, or as out of touch as his residing on the Isle of Wight might make him appear.

"I'll follow you to London as swiftly as I may," he added at last.

But before he could lead us toward the house, I halted him with a hand on his arm. "Take care, Max. If Lord Ardmore is behind all of this, if he's managed to do all that he's done thus far without anyone noticing, then he's certainly being kept apprised of my movements. Sooner or later he's going to realize you're helping us. If he should fear what you might know . . ." My fingers tightened around his sleeve in alarm.

"Have no fear, Verity," he assured me. "I'll take precautions."

By this, I suspected he meant the same thing as my husband— carrying a pistol. I could only pray that would be enough, for them both.

CHAPTER 29

Due to a number of delays, we did not reach our flat in Berkeley Square until after ten o'clock. On many days, that was about the time we actually set out for our evening on the town, but days of travel and early mornings had exhausted us. The very thought of sliding my feet into a pair of dancing shoes made me want to crumple to the floor.

Fortunately, there was nothing that couldn't wait for the morning, and Nimble was there ready to greet us at the door, since Sidney had telephoned from the Isle of Wight to let him know we were returning. The marvelous young man swept my things from my arms and soon had both Sidney and I settled before a crackling fire with a warm cup of tea and a plate of sandwiches Sadie had prepared for us before she left for the evening. At that moment, I think we were both exceedingly pleased to have a live-in servant again, no matter the loss of some of our privacy. I truly did need to find myself a maid at the first opportunity.

I thumbed through the stack of messages and correspondence Nimble brought in to me. Ignoring much of it for the moment, I scanned the notes from George and Ada, both of whom I'd telephoned before departing the island. George relayed a message from Chief Inspector Thoreau, stating he would call upon us the next morning. Given the fact he'd been cautioned not to interact with us, this surprised me, but I suspected there would be a reason.

The message from Ada was far more vexing. She thanked me for finally remembering her, and remarked that it was evident where my priorities lay. Then she told me I could call on her tomorrow, but no earlier than noon for she would undoubtedly be out late. I would have rolled my eyes at her childish behavior had I not been so furious at her obstinacy. Here, I had been trying to aid her, and nearly at every turn she had become determined to thwart me.

I knew Ardmore was partly to blame for this, whispering in her ear like a forked serpent, but he could not be blamed for all. Ada was a grown woman. If she wanted to play the fool, that was on her.

Seeing my furious expression, Sidney asked what had so irritated me. I passed him the message, staring into the flames in the hearth as he read.

He sighed and shook his head. "Why are you attempting to help this woman? Why are you even her friend?"

The arguments I would have made a week ago did not spring so readily to my lips; however, I did make a token attempt to explain her behavior. "I realize she's under a great amount of strain. And who knows what nonsense Ardmore has told her about me."

"Cut line, Ver! What rubbish. Strain or no strain, she's treated you terribly." He wadded the missive into a tight ball and hurled it into the fire. "Truth be told, I'm not certain she *isn't* guilty of the crime."

I watched the paper as it crumpled and slowly turned to ash. "Truth be told, I'm not certain either," I admitted softly, finally putting into words the worry I'd been carrying with me ever since Thoreau had told us they might never be able to successfully prosecute the case.

His head reared back in shock. "You're not?"

I shook my head.

"Then why do you keep investigating?"

I turned to look at him. "Because I don't want it to be her. I don't want to have to admit a woman I called my friend is capable of such a thing." I closed my eyes tightly. "Because I don't want to accept that she duped me, and lied to me, and used me for her own ends."

Sidney's hand stole into mine where it rested on the sofa between us.

I inhaled a ragged breath, blinking open my eyes. "And because if she did do it, I don't think it was initially her idea. I think Ardmore instigated it. Becoming her lover, sowing the seeds of discontent, suggesting she might be better off without Rockham, and the only way to be truly rid of him was death." I narrowed my eyes. "She said something once: 'He was supposed to handle it.' And although she tried to brush it off as something else, I couldn't help but think maybe Ardmore was supposed to arrange the murder, but when he didn't, she took matters into her own hands."

"So you've been hoping connecting Ardmore to the *Zebrina* incident would connect him to Rockham's death?"

"Yes, but I've also been hoping it would present us with another possible triggerman, another possible way Rockham was shot. So I wouldn't have to face the fact that my investigating for her might have enabled her to get away with it."

He squeezed my hand. "That's not your fault. Deacon is the one who tampered with the evidence and lied to the police."

I turned to him jadedly. "Yes, but his tampering and lies might not have come to light, at least not in the same manner, had I not interfered. It isn't a comforting thought to think that I was used in such a way."

He fell silent, contemplating the truth of those words, an unintended echo of the guilt he also carried. His thumb brushed over the back of my hand in soothing strokes. "What are you going to do?" he asked a few minutes later.

I inhaled a deep breath, firming my resolve. "Find out the truth." I narrowed my eyes. "Even if I have to trick her into giving it to me."

"Dead?" I repeated rather stupidly as I blinked at Chief Inspector Thoreau in astonishment.

"I'm afraid so." His sympathetic expression communicated he understood how much I wished this to be otherwise. "Miss

Flossie Hawkins was found in the doorway of St. Anne's Church two nights past, apparently dead of an overdose of cocaine."

I pressed a hand to my forehead and rose from my seat to cross toward the window. Below, I could see the spot where I had spoken with Flossie just a little over a week ago. I'd noted then that she might have indulged in the drug, but an overdose? It all seemed rather too convenient.

"There was a suicide note tucked into the pocket of her dress confessing to the murder of Esther Shaw. She claimed she was searching through her things for something to steal when Miss Shaw came home suddenly. She knocked her over the head so that she could escape, but swears she never meant to kill her. That it was an accident. She tossed the room and opened the window, hoping to throw suspicion off her. And it worked. At first."

Until Esther's half sister, Irene, had asked me to look into the matter.

"How nice and neat," I drawled sarcastically, before swiveling to face the inspector where he perched across from my husband on one of our emeraldine sofas. "But then why didn't she take anything from Miss Shaw's room?" Except the letters, which Sidney and I knew had been her real target. "And why did she run? Why not take her life in her own rooms rather than flee?"

And what had been in that note the messenger delivered to her the day before she ran? A threat?

No, it was all too coincidental.

"People often panic in such situations. Maybe she feared you were on to her," Thoreau suggested. "And it wasn't until later that her guilt got to her." But I could tell from the reserved tone of his voice that he held just as many doubts as I did.

"Is that why you dared to come to us with this after being warned away?" Sidney said, speaking up for the first time. "Because Miss Hawkins is dead?"

"That will be my excuse should someone learn of this conversation." His eyes were sharp with unspoken things. "The investigation will be closed in another day or two. Sooner if we can verify Miss Hawkins's handwriting, but it appears all other examples of it have disappeared."

"All?" Sidney asked doubtfully.

Thoreau nodded grimly.

Yet another happenstance to add to the file. I shook my head in disgust. I didn't believe for one minute that Flossie had committed suicide. And if I was reading Thoreau's tight-lipped countenance correctly, he didn't either. But without proof there was nothing we could do. Not when the alternative explanation wrapped everything up so neatly in a bow.

The inspector pushed to his feet.

"Thank you for telling us," I told him earnestly, though my tight stance might have said otherwise. I trusted he understood my frustration.

He turned to go, but then paused in the doorway. "Oh, and because you've been involved with both inquiries, I'll also take leave to tell you we had one anonymous person come forward to claim Miss Hawkins had been a mistress of Lord Rockham's at one time. *But* we haven't been able to corroborate that with anyone else." He arched his eyebrows significantly and then strode from the room.

I narrowed my eyes at this suggestion, not trusting it one iota. How very devious of Ardmore. So that if the *Zebrina* incident should ever come to light, there would be a record—no matter how paltry—of Rockham's connection to Flossie, and therefore a plausible excuse for why she took Esther's letters.

I heard the door to our flat shut with a click and, emitting an infuriated little screech, rounded to face the window. If it wouldn't have been the height of uncivilized behavior, I would have thrown something, such was my rage. Ardmore had been one step, if not ten, ahead of us at every turn.

"I know, darling," Sidney murmured, placing his hands on my shoulders. "But let's remember, with Ardmore we must play a long game. He might have outwitted us at this turn, but we'll catch him in the end." He turned me to face him. "I would lay my odds on you over anyone else any day."

I inhaled past the tightness that seemed to have taken up permanent residence in my chest. "Thank you." I realized he was trying to cheer me, but at the moment it was small consolation. He squeezed my shoulders. "I mean it, Ver." His deep blue eyes stared into mine intently. "Don't let him gum the game. Not when you're about to confront Ada. That's exactly what he wants. To rattle you."

I forced myself to take an even deeper breath, realizing he was right. If I was to have any chance of outsmarting Ardmore, I would need to keep my head about me, to make note of every detail, no matter how small. For if he was to make an error, it would be a tiny one. One so minuscule that it might go unnoticed. Perhaps to all but me. It would be the strike that I would use to finally catch him out.

"Better?" he asked me.

I nodded.

But then he surprised me by leaning down and capturing my mouth in a rather searing kiss. One I felt clear down to my toes.

"What was that for?" I gasped into his mouth when he pulled back.

His lips quirked. "Just because you're so bloody gorgeous when you're angry." He pressed another swift kiss to my mouth before stepping back, forcing me to stand on my own two feet. "Come on. Let's get you to your appointment with Lady Rockham."

I felt somewhat disgruntled that he didn't appear to be nearly as affected by that kiss as I was, but I allowed him to pull me toward the door and help me into my Prussian blue velvet coat with its roll collar.

Despite the nip in the air, we chose to walk to Grosvenor Square—Sidney correctly assuming this would help me subdue whatever remained of my temper. By the time we reached Rockham House, I was as cool as the autumn breeze, and ready for battle.

Ada had asked me not to call on her until midday, but we had deliberately timed our arrival to be about thirty minutes earlier. Not so early that she could fob me off by claiming to still be in bed, but early enough to make her cross. Ada was more likely to let something slip when she was in the heat of anger, as evidenced by her pulling a knife on that woman who had attempted to blackmail her.

Of course, Sidney saw this quite differently. Which is why, in concern for my safety, he'd insisted on accompanying me. Though he agreed to remain downstairs while I spoke to Ada privately. I did not fear Ada turning violent on me, but I promised to be vigilant nonetheless. After all, when working in intelligence, one swiftly learned that the situations that most often turned deadly were the ones no one had ever anticipated.

I was almost surprised to find Deacon still answering the door. Part of me had expected him to give notice, or for Ada to insist her stepson sack him, but it appeared either Deacon was holding his ground or Croyde had proved intractable. Perhaps both.

However, when he opened his mouth to attempt to deny me entrance, I swept past him. "Lady Rockham will see me now, whether she wishes it or not," I declared, passing him my gloves and hat.

I met his martial gaze with a firm one of my own as I unbuttoned my coat, and I realized perhaps I had been a bit unfair to the man. He was undoubtedly pompous and meddling, but he had recognized something before I had—how false Ada was playing all of us.

Given that fact, and that he could prove a valuable ally if necessary, I softened the gleam in my eye by a fraction—one I trusted he would notice—as I handed him my coat. "You shall want to remain at hand."

He blinked. It was only one startled flicker of the eyelashes, but for a man of Deacon's stalwart nature it was every bit as indicative of his astonishment as a loud gasp would be from others.

I climbed the stairs swiftly, not failing to note the sight of Ada's maid above as she made a quick reversal to hurry back down the hall toward her mistress's room. Given this, I fully anticipated the stage to be set when I entered her private parlor. I paused just outside, lifting my right foot to untie my shoe, before rapping sharply on the door.

Ada lay draped languidly in one corner of the same green velvet chaise where she'd sat when she last received me. Though attired in naught but a negligee and her vermillion silk dressing gown, I could tell that her hair had been artfully tousled and her face lightly rouged and powdered. Her mask was in place.

"What now?" she scoffed, tucking her leg up underneath her, as McTavy slipped past me into the hall. "Have you come to scold me? While the cat's away the mice will play?"

I found it interesting that she considered me the cat of this scenario, but chose not to rise to her bait. "No, I'm done with that," I declared breezily as I settled into the chair across from her, taking a moment longer than normal to arrange my skirts. When I glanced up it was to find a look of mild consternation furrowing her brow.

"I mean it, Verity. I'll not hear it from you."

"Of course not." I laughed in the face of her frown of confusion. "You are a grown woman, are you not? You may do as you please. I've no say in the matter."

"Yes, but aren't you concerned I shall be implicated for having the audacity to venture out on the town and enjoy myself after such an unspeakable tragedy?" she jeered.

That this had been quoted almost verbatim from someone else, I had no doubt. Just as I had no doubt who that someone was. But I kept my blithe smile firmly affixed. "I rather think you're already implicated, darling."

"What's that supposed to mean?" she demanded.

I allowed my brow to pucker. "Well, you've known you were the main suspect from the very beginning. I don't think that has changed despite my best efforts to the contrary."

Her eyes flashed. "Your best efforts, hmm? Gallivanting off to France. I don't think you've really tried at all. Perhaps you're no better than the rest of 'em." She tossed her hand out, presumably at the ubiquitous *them*. "Perhaps you'd *like* to see me charged with murder."

"I'm sorry you feel that way," I replied calmly. "But I cannot conjure suspects out of thin air. Perhaps if you know something . . . ?" I trailed away in question.

Her gaze searched mine, evidently trying to decipher what I meant, what I knew, but I continued to gaze back at her with what I hoped appeared to be artless candor.

"Ardmore told me suspicion has shifted away from me," she asserted, twining the belt of her dressing gown around her finger.

"Has it? Toward where?"

"Perhaps that Calloway chap from Rockham's shipping business. I told you he can't be trusted."

I tapped my chin. "Yes, you suggested he must have snuck in the window later and shot him."

"Precisely!" She nearly leapt from her chair in her vehemence. "You should have been searching for him. Not flapping off to the continent."

"Except the police had already told me he had a rather incontrovertible alibi."

Her lashes fluttered. "He does?"

I nodded, watching some of the glibness fade from her face. "And what made you think the window in Rockham's study was open?"

"I . . . well . . ." she stammered, her eyes flaring wide. "I mean, it was, wasn't it?" She recovered, arching her chin. "I must have just assumed . . ."

"But why would you assume such a thing? The police implied the suspect came from inside."

"Yes, well, if it wasn't a servant, and the house was locked up, then they must have come in through the window," she insisted, growing angry.

"Not if it was shut and locked as well," I countered.

"It couldn't have been."

"Deacon said it was."

"Well, he's lying," she snarled. "The window wasn't locked. It was open. I know! I know because I . . ." She broke off before she could finish the thought, but the damage was already done, and the look in her eyes told me she realized it.

I stared at her in shock, almost unable to believe what she'd just admitted. The small part of me that had still not wanted to think her capable of such a thing, capable of such duplicity, shrank from it. But the greater part of me leaned into it, knowing I could not let her slink away from what she'd done.

Meanwhile, her eyes narrowed to slits. "Clever Verity. Too smart for her own good. Ardmore warned me about you."

"Why should Ardmore need to warn you?" I tilted my head. "Unless he put you up to it?"

She sat taller. "No one put me up to it. It was all me."

I scowled. "Don't be a fool, Ada. He used you for his own ends."

"You're the fool. Everyone saw how zozzled I was that night, how unbalanced." Her contemptuous glare let me know how cunning she thought she was that she'd duped everyone. "*If* the police can find enough evidence against me, it will never stand up against my barristers' arguments."

The barristers she'd already told me Ardmore would secure for her. Anonymously, of course.

"They will once I tell them what you've told me," I declared, rising to my feet.

"Now, you see, that's where your cleverness wears out." She lifted her hand, wielding a pistol she'd tucked into the cushions of the chaise.

My heart surged in my chest, but I refused to react. After all, it wasn't the first time I'd had a gun pointed at me. Though it was certainly the most personal.

I arched a single disdainful eyebrow. "So *you* were the one who tucked that revolver in your chair before dinner. Or perhaps you *did* take it in with you."

She shrugged.

"You planned to make that distasteful quip at dinner all along," I accused. "To provide a reason for your fingerprints to be on the weapon, and as sort of a double bluff."

"Well, you fell for it, didn't you?" She gestured with the gun. "As for the fingerprints, I could have simply worn gloves, but that just made me look even more suspicious."

I slid my right foot slowly from its Derby pump, the tea table blocking my movement. "So, you took the revolver from Deacon's pocket and waited until all the guests left and the servants retired, and then you crept down to his study and shot him."

She tipped her head carelessly. "Just as I intend to shoot you."

"With my husband below and a whole houseful of servants?"

"I'll do what I must."

Despite her blasé attitude, I could see the fear reflected in her eyes, the knowledge that she was cornered. Because of this, I knew there was no talking her down. She would do it. In her mind, the coin had been flipped, and she thought she had no choice.

Given that fact, I felt no compunction about what I would have to do next.

"That's sad to hear. . . ." I broke off, glancing toward the door as if I'd heard something. Then in the same movement, I flipped my shoe at the far wall. With the table in the way, I could not flick it directly at Ada, but nonetheless, I trusted her reflexes to work against her. She jerked the gun at the offending projectile and fired, while I hurled the not inconsiderable weight of my handbag at her head. It struck true. Not that I doubted it would, having played enough rounders and tennis with my brothers to know my aim was accurate.

Before she could recover, I darted around the table, leaping on top of her to grab the pistol. We grappled for only a second before a strategically placed knee in her abdomen forced her to drop it. I pushed off her, backing away as she clutched her head and midsection, cursing foully at me.

Sidney burst through the door a moment later, his pistol drawn, while a rather winded Deacon straggled along behind him, as well as half a dozen other servants. Sidney's eyes scoured me from head to toe, as if to ascertain I was all in one piece, his gaze pausing for a moment on my shoeless foot.

"My apologies. We seemed to be having a difference of opinion," I explained airily. "Lady Rockham thought she would shoot me before I could tell the police she'd confessed to Lord Rockham's murder, while I preferred that she not."

Sidney's shoulders dropped. "Dash it all, Verity," he gasped in relief.

"Well, don't blame *me*. It wasn't my idea."

At this comment, I caught sight of William's cheeky grin beyond my husband's shoulder. Much as I would have liked to issue my next directive to him, I knew to whom the honor must be given. "Send for Chief Inspector Thoreau," I told Deacon.

His eyes glinted with unholy glee, and I realized he would be even more insufferable than ever. No matter. After today, he would no longer be my problem.

Tucking his own pistol in his pocket, Sidney moved forward to wrap one protective arm around my waist, while he reached for Ada's pistol with his other hand. I gladly relinquished it to him, taking comfort from his solid presence. As unaffected as I wished to appear, my insides were quaking.

At the sound of sniffling, I glanced up to find Ada's face turned toward the wall, her shoulders shaking as she wept. Given the fact that she'd just tried to kill me, I had little sympathy to spare her, and serious doubts whether her outpouring of emotion was even genuine. Nonetheless, I wasn't without mercy. Especially if she was willing to testify against Ardmore, little good that her words alone would do.

"It's not too late," I told her. "You can still mitigate your sentence."

She didn't turn to look at me, but the sound of her sobs softened, so I knew she was listening.

"Tell us what you know about Ardmore, and I won't tell the inspector you attempted to shoot me."

For a moment, I thought she was considering it. That is, until she snarled, "You can go to the devil."

What power Ardmore had over her, I didn't know, but he must have held something more, something I'd missed. Ada was nothing if not an opportunist. Which meant that whatever Ardmore was using to guarantee her silence was more than a fickle promise to provide her barristers. Barristers who would be hard-pressed now to get her out of a murder charge she had confessed to.

No, there had to be more. And if it wasn't some greater leverage keeping her quiet, then it must be fear. But fear of what? Ada did not scare easily. And simply the idea that he had silenced a women like her with such terror made ice slide down my spine.

CHAPTER 30

By the time Thoreau had finished with us and Ada had been hauled off to Scotland Yard, the afternoon was well advanced, and my stomach was protesting my failure to eat luncheon. Sidney led me out the door of Rockham House toward the cab a footman had hailed for us, the late-September sun beating down on its roof.

"Spiro's, then?" he asked.

"Heavens, yes." It wouldn't be a celebration exactly, but at least we would be assured a good meal.

He grinned at my enthusiasm, but my answering smile died on my lips at the sight of the man standing beneath the shade of a plane tree in the square across the street. Sidney's gaze followed mine over the roof of the motorcar to where Ardmore watched us.

I couldn't decide if he was here merely to gloat, or if he wished to speak with me, but before I could reconsider, I found my footsteps rounding the boot. Sidney must have tipped the cabbie something for his trouble, for he had to hurry to catch up with me when I was already halfway across the street. A passing motorcar blared its horn, but I ignored it. Whatever Ardmore's reasons behind this encounter, I was not going to let him think I was afraid or intimidated by him. Nor was I going to be goaded into revealing more than he already knew.

Inhaling deeply, I summoned up my steeliest nerves. The same ones I had tapped into when faced with the probing questions and wandering hands of a suspicious officer of the German Secret Police at the entrance to a town west of Ghent. One wrong word or false flicker of an eyelash and he could have imprisoned me without recourse.

In comparison, this confrontation was hardly life-or-death. But somehow in the pit of my stomach I felt it was just as important. And from the gleam in Ardmore's mossy-green eyes, I could tell that he knew I realized this, too.

I came to a stop a short distance from him, but did not speak as the leaves rustled around our feet, crunching under the wheels of a passing perambulator pushed by a nanny.

"Mr. and Mrs. Kent," he declared, dipping his head to me. "I understand Lady Rockham has just been arrested for the murder of her husband."

"Yes, Scotland Yard took her into custody a short time ago," I replied evenly.

He clicked his tongue. "How terrible. Now, whether the charges will stick"—he shrugged—"we shall see."

I remained silent, deciding to leave the unhappy discovery of Ada's confession for him to discover later. Preferably when it would make him look the most foolish.

"But such a discovery could not have been easy for you. And here I thought you were off chasing another lead. Something to do with Rockham's shipping interests."

That he was toying with me, there was no doubt, and enjoying himself while doing so, if the way his eyes crinkled at the corners was any indication. He knew very well he had been the one to first suggest the motive for Rockham's murder lay within his import/export business.

He glanced casually toward a passing bus. "If not for such a distraction, you might have realized Lady Rockham was the culprit sooner."

I struggled not to react when his gaze returned to mine, sparkling with malicious glee. Fury raced through my muscles, demanding an outlet. One I refused to give it.

"Yes, well, no avenue of inquiry is ever truly wasted," I said. "Everything builds upon itself, and one never knows when the information one has gathered will prove to be some sap's undoing."

"I should hardly think 'some sap' would be difficult to outwit." I shrugged one shoulder noncommittally. "You would think so, but some are so full of themselves that they're remarkably oblivious to their own pitfalls."

If I hadn't been staring directly into his eyes, I would have missed the way his pupils flared ever so slightly, before returning to their normal size.

"Yes, well, I should say the same goes for overly keen investigators. Who knows what compromises they must have been willing to make to their morals during war. Particularly a woman who might have found herself in a dangerous place."

This was both a threat and an implication. One that Sidney did not take kindly to, for he strained forward against my arm where ours were linked, ready to leap to my defense. But I tightened my grip, holding him in check.

"Oh, dear me. Have I caused offense? For certain, I never meant to," he assured my husband in a voice that was wholly disingenuous.

"Of course, you did," I retorted, unwilling to make a mockery of courtesy when we could speak plainly. "But while my husband might be unused to such accusations, you are not the first close-minded, unimaginative man I have heard make such insinuations about females." I sighed. "In fact, it grows rather tiresome."

He chuckled, as if I'd just said something humorous. "I'm sure it does." His gaze cut to Sidney. "Though I'm certain the same can't be said of your husband."

Sidney glowered at him.

Ardmore hefted his walking stick and straightened his coat. "Well, then. I must be off. Oh, but didn't I hear you recently paid a visit to Lord Ryde. I never did get the chance to express my condolences on his father's passing."

These words were spoken lightly, but they sent a jolt down my spine. One that I was not certain I'd successfully hidden.

"*Please* convey them to him for me."

I did not reply, being too preoccupied with resisting the urge to slap him across the face.

His lips curled. "I do so look forward to seeing you again, Mrs. Kent. I trust you won't keep me waiting long." He arched his eyebrows and then set off across the square at a stately pace.

I forced myself to look away, though I wanted nothing more than to glare daggers at his back. Knowing him, he would probably sense it, and bask in the enjoyment of infuriating me. Clearly he derived some pleasure in matching wits with others, and much as I was determined to best him, that did not mean I had to offer him the satisfaction of my company to do so. I would be well advised to remember that in the future. Unless there was something distinct I wished to gain from our interaction, I would be better off depriving him of my charms.

Sidney, on the other hand, seemed more than ready to confront him. "That man has just made a grave miscalculation by threatening you," he bit out. "I had been hesitant to believe someone could be so devious, so underhanded, and so calculating to not only manipulate such a plot, but also see it carried out. But now I see it. Now I have no doubts. He bloody well brought about the murder of all the people you believe he did, including Lord Ryde. And likely more. For a man like that doesn't stop until someone forces him to."

That was what I very much feared, and that it was up to us to somehow do so.

I lifted my face toward the blue sky, allowing the cool wind to sting my cheeks. Anything to blunt the emotions tumbling about inside me.

"What I don't understand is to what end all of his efforts are for?" he muttered. "Is he supporting the Irish rebels?"

"I don't know," I admitted. "But the situation in Ireland is only growing worse, and if I'm certain of one thing, it's that we have agents posted there. Agents that, as a director in Naval Intelligence and a friend of the Director of Intelligence, he may know about. If he is an undeclared rebel, he would be poised to deal Britain some critical blows."

In truth, I was conflicted about the Irish issue, feeling a great deal of empathy for the Irish and their desire for independence. But I was not conflicted about the fact I didn't want to see Secret Service agents harmed. I had toiled too long and too hard for the agency, and I undoubtedly called some of those agents friends.

"But I'm not certain that's what all this is about," I hedged, urging Sidney to stroll with me around the perimeter of Grosvenor Square's garden. "Or not entirely."

He tucked my arm more firmly into his side. "Whatever the case is, we'll figure it out. And we've got Ryde helping us out."

"Yes, and C and Xavier are alert as well." My gaze scanned the park. "Honestly, I shouldn't be surprised if C has Ardmore under surveillance." There had been a man seated on a bench under the shade of an evergreen earlier who was now gone. But whether he'd been following Ardmore at C's behest or us at Ardmore's, I didn't know. For Ardmore had unquestionably been monitoring us. I'd suspected it before, but now I knew it.

It was then that I caught sight of one of the more persistent reporters who sometimes dogged our steps. He must have caught wind of Ada's arrest. And if he had, then other reporters and photographers would not be far behind.

"Blast!" I exclaimed, hurrying Sidney along the path.

"What?"

"Unless you wish to be descended upon by the horde, I suggest we find a cab. And fast," I added, as I glanced back to find the reporter had caught sight of us.

Sidney lengthened his stride, practically dragging me in his wake, and raised his hand to signal to a passing cab on the other side of the square. Fortunately, his height and sense of command compelled the cabbie to stop. He helped me inside and then climbed in after me, slamming the door just as the reporter ran forward shouting a question about the Rockham murder.

I glanced out the rear window as we sped away, just as a photographer snapped a picture of us departing. I huffed in exasperation, wondering if we would find more men camped out in Berkeley Square. Truth be told, all Ardmore had to do was read the newspapers to discover what we'd been up to much of the time.

We remained silent on the short drive to our flat, conscious of the cabbie's eyes watching us in the mirror, and the fact that at least one of the reporters was certain to track him down and ask him what we'd said. At our building, the doorman, Sal, was waiting for us. He hustled us inside past the half dozen reporters lying in wait—a number that was certain to grow—and across the lobby to the lift.

Once in our flat, Sidney headed straight for the sideboard while Sadie and Nimble went to prepare tea and sandwiches. I crossed toward the window, staring down at the crowd gathering on the pavement below. There would be no Spiro's today. Not unless we could contrive a way to make our way there without being seen.

I sighed, wishing I felt some sort of accomplishment at having solved the murders of Esther Shaw and Lord Rockham. Instead weariness and disillusionment filled me, along with a healthy dose of anger and frustration.

Sidney joined me in my contemplation, passing me a gin rickey. "You seemed like you could use one."

I didn't respond, but I tipped the glass back, draining it of half its contents before turning to slump down on the deep window ledge.

"What's eating you?" he asked lightly as he sank down beside me. "The fact that Ardmore got away?"

"Of course," I replied, turning the cool glass between my fingertips.

"But that's not all," he prodded.

"He was right, you know. He did distract us with that shipping business. If I hadn't been so keen on pursuing that, and finding anyone more culpable than Ada, I might have seen the truth sooner. The same goes with Flossie. And she might still be alive."

"That's not your fault, Verity, and you know it. And Ardmore's suggestion that Rockham's shipping interests were to blame was not the only reason we pursued that angle. There were other indicators." He nudged me, making me lift my gaze to meet his. "Had we not followed up on it, we might never have realized the depths of Ardmore's duplicity, nor solved the mystery of the *Zebrina*'s missing crew. *He's* the one who made an error, you know. He dangled that carrot before you simply to divert you, never thinking you would uncover the entire truth. He underestimated you. And now we know more than he ever intended us to."

I hadn't thought about it that way. It gave me a little surge of hope. Though I still couldn't wash the bitter taste of Ada's betrayal or Flossie's death from my mouth. Not even with another sip of gin.

Sidney reached up to loosen his tie as he stared into his drink. "You can believe you're doing the right thing, the only thing you can do, and still discover that what you thought was the right choice also has consequences."

My heart constricted, already guessing what he was referring to.

His brow furrowed. "Take me, for instance. I allowed my reported death to go uncontested. I hid from my own countrymen and set out to find the traitors in my battalion alone because I saw no other way to do so. No other way to keep you safe and to bring the men responsible for so many deaths to justice. But my decision still hurt people terribly. Nimble and the other men in my company." He glanced up at me, his eyes stark with regret. "And you."

I reached out a hand to touch his face.

"In some situations, there is no winning. No right way. You can only make the best choices you can, and hope the people your decision might have harmed will forgive you in the end."

I leaned forward, pressing my forehead to his cheek as I fought back my own answering emotion. "I do forgive you," I told him, letting go of the last remnants of resentment I'd been holding on to. "I do, Sidney."

His arm wrapped around me, pulling me close, and he turned his face to press a kiss to my forehead. But I wasn't content with that and lifted my mouth to meet his instead.

We might have remained that way for some time, if not for the clearing of a throat in the doorway. Sidney released me reluctantly, before turning to address Nimble, who had politely averted his eyes. "You can set the tray on the table."

"Yes, sir," he replied, a smile tugging at the corners of his mouth.

Once he'd departed, I couldn't help but give a little laugh. "I suppose we shall have to accustom ourselves to living with servants again."

"Yes, well, the day I allow the presence of servants to dictate when and where I kiss my wife will be the day I become a monk," he declared. His gaze flitted over every inch of my face. "I endured almost four and half years away from you. I'm not about to sit at a discreet distance simply to preserve my staff's modesty."

"Then I suppose I'd best add 'not easily shocked' to my list of qualifications for a lady's maid."

A roguish twinkle lit his eyes as he pulled me close again, speaking a hairsbreadth from my lips. "Yes, dear wife, you'd best."